THE
BEACHHEAD

ALSO BY CHRISTOPHER MARI

Ocean of Storms (with Jeremy K. Brown)

THE BEACHHEAD

CHRISTOPHER MARI

Text copyright © 2017 by Christopher Mari

Published by 47North, Seattle

www.apub.com

Amazon, the Amazon logo, and 47North are trademarks of Amazon.com, Inc., or its affiliates.

ISBN-13: 9781503942622
ISBN-10: 1503942627

Cover design by M. S. Corley

Printed in the United States of America

For Juliana, Olivia & Luke
Gutta cavat lapidem.

Angels have no need of an assumed body for themselves, but on our account; that by conversing familiarly with men they may give evidence of that intellectual companionship which men expect to have with them in the life to come.

—*Thomas Aquinas*

There are many statues of men slaying lions, but if only the lions were sculptors there might be quite a different set of statues.

—*Aesop*

CHAPTER 1

On a sharp and clear night like this one, John Giordano could glance down from his lookout post in the hills and see all that remained of the human race. The lights across the city flickered soft and yellow in grid-like patterns, so regular that no one observing them from any point above could doubt that an intelligence of some magnitude lived on this coast. If such observers were in no hurry and had watched for a long-enough time, they would have seen the lights' warm fingers stretching ever outward, north and south, east and west, filling the dark spaces at the edges of town—and even upward. The most recent buildings in the city were now three stories high—significant, though still two stories lower than the ramparts of the city's walls. Births, good crops, fair weather, and luck had added considerably to the initial population of 144,000. Two generations had joined those remnants of mankind and helped them build this city.

John turned the collar of his worn brown leather jacket to the autumn wind and adjusted the strap of the carbine slung over his right shoulder. The air was ripe with the scent of the sea. After scanning the ridgeline, he glanced down again at the nighttime city and tried to imagine the early days when the Remnants lived separately from one another, in caves and mud huts, in anything that would protect them from the elements and prying eyes but could be abandoned easily if need be. It had taken years before the adult Remnants were comfortable enough with the idea of building that it didn't feel entirely crazy.

Few Remnants ever talked much about the end of the world or the days just after the Arrival. The still-living Remnants were just children when they came to this planet, so their memories of life before the Arrival were as impressionistic as anyone's childhood memories. Whenever they did speak of Earth-of-old, they tended not to talk of the last days, but of things from their youths: books they read, toys they played with, or items that mankind once had but no longer did—electric lighting, motorized transportation, cures for infectious diseases.

John ran a hand through his short-cropped blond hair and smiled as he walked his perimeter and thought of his grandfather's stories. A young man in his thirties when he was brought to this shore, his grandfather loved to speak of his childhood far from this place. Because John was able to recount so many of his grandfather's stories, his friends joked that he must be a Remnant himself, flash-frozen and thawed out two generations later. But he had never found it hard to recount stories that were told well and set in memorable places.

He once found his grandfather lying on the beach in a chair of his own design. Made of a stretchy fabric he could sink into, it folded into three parts, and by setting its pegs into notches carved in its wooden frame, one could adjust it to raise the head or lower the feet. Grandpa had been in a mostly upright position, facing away from the sea toward a rock wall covered in a greenish-red vegetation. The air was thick with salt and wet earth. John, fourteen at the time and on weekend leave from his first year in the Defense Forces, had walked down to the beach to tell his grandfather to come home for supper. Cold as he was on watch this night in the hills, he could still remember the way that warm sand had felt on his bare feet.

When he'd found his grandfather, he feared for a moment that the old man might be dead. The book splayed open on his hairy gray chest hardly moved. After several steps John could see him smiling through his thick beard. It was a perfect smile, serene. Years later when he learned what the word "beatific" meant, he would describe his grandfather's smile that way whenever he recalled it—the beatific smile of a perfectly content old man.

"Hey Johnny," he said, sitting up a little, "you caught me at my daydreaming."

John, who had always been more comfortable with his namesake grandfather than with his own parents, asked what he had been thinking about. A bemused light passed through his grandfather's hazel eyes before they settled on his grandson.

The old man sighed and nodded toward the mossy rock wall. "My mother's backyard. A lot of great days spent out there. She had quite a garden behind that brownstone in Brooklyn, the whole place lined with all kinds of plants and flowers. I wish I remembered all their names, but I do remember she had rosebushes, pink and red and intertwined, beautiful things. Ivy grew up the back wall, sort of like this. My favorite thing to do was sit out there on warm nights after my summer job and read in a chair not unlike this one until the sunlight gave out. Then I'd watch fireflies flickering in the twilight."

"Fireflies?"

"Bugs with illuminated butts." He shrugged. "One year my mother and I discovered a birds' nest in the ivy. We didn't want to disturb the birds, but we were curious to see if there were eggs in it. I took a ladder out, and sure enough there they were, three of them. But that wasn't the surprising part. You know what else we found in that ivy?"

John shook his head.

"A flowerpot my grandfather—my mother's father—had nailed to the wall, probably decades earlier. I never knew it was there. And my mother had completely forgotten about it." He passed a hand across his head. "But evidently the birds hadn't. They had made their nest in it."

John laughed. "And this is what you were grinning about?"

His grandfather shrugged again and turned back to the rock face. "Among other things."

That summer John had often found his grandfather near that mossy rock face on the beach. Sometimes the old man would be there doing research, trying to piece together bits of the medical knowledge humanity possessed in the years before the Arrival. Other times John would find him nose deep in a book they knew to be a classic or—usually but not always—the Bible. Then there were times when he would find his grandfather just staring at that rock wall, watching the sea breeze lift its reddish-green foliage. Toward the end that's the way he found him most.

After his grandfather died near what most of his fellow Remnants guessed was his seventieth birthday, John suggested that they bury him not with the other dead in the cemetery to the west beyond the city's walls but out on the beach beside that rock face. The Council met and decided it would be permissible since the tomb was far enough from their water supply. John had helped to carve his grandfather's name in the rock, the only difference between his name and the dead man's being his grandfather's MD.

A whump, more felt than heard, pulled John from his memories. His eyes shifted back to the ridgeline nearest the beach, and yes: a slight flash of light came from behind those hills.

They're here.

If they stayed on the ground, it would take them about twenty minutes to travel through the underbrush to the party of Remnants waiting at the designated spot on the beach. Now more alert, John kept a keen watch on his surroundings, aware that if something were to happen, it would probably happen very soon. Yet it all still seemed normal, same as it ever was.

He raised his collapsible spyglass to his right eye and made a quick scan of his immediate area and then another of the perimeter around the city. Outside the city no noises, no lights, nothing. He resisted the urge to recheck his carbine. He gave it another few minutes, then lit his torch with a match palmed from his watertight pouch. He raised his flaming brand to signal all clear to the nearby perimeter guards, who would then relay the message on. All clear—at least as far as they could see. The guards would remain at the ready just in case.

John imagined that all of them—mostly Seconds like himself, but a few Firsts in command positions—were simultaneously trying to picture the biennial ritual about to take place. They knew that a party of Remnants, twelve in all, waited on the beach, unarmed and bareheaded in white robes, for the Friendlies. The Friendlies would come unarmed and wearing only loincloths, as had been agreed upon since their first official visit a half century ago. None of the Seconds—and probably only a few of the Firsts—knew how or why these rules had been established. Twenty-six visits, if you counted the Arrival, and nothing had ever deviated from ritual.

"Hiya."

John spun on his heel, surprised by the closeness of the voice behind him but not by whose it was. No one but Kendra McQueen could sneak up on him like that. Kendra, just turned twenty, was by far the stealthiest soldier he had ever met. He'd like to think it was simply a matter of training, that her being two years past the mandatory four-year term of service in the Defense Forces had honed her covert-ops skills. But he had *twelve* years of additional service and not a tenth of her ability. Kendra had already possessed such skills when she entered the service at fourteen and had only improved since then. Some suggested, only half jokingly, that angels held her under her arms to lighten her tread. Others believed she had found the lost crate of Eastern books and had gleaned her skills from them. Of course, there were some who believed that her encounter with that Orangeman had to be the explanation—but the only people who thought that were the ones who didn't know the true story. John didn't know or care how she did the things she did. He was just glad to see her moonlit face and know she was on his side.

"You're out of position, Lieutenant."

"So rat me out to the superior officer, Captain. Oh wait—right." Her wide mouth drew up into a mischievous smirk.

He couldn't help but chuckle. "So they're down."

She unscrewed the cap of her canteen and shook her head before taking a swig. "I swear that landing gets softer each time."

"They've had enough practice."

"So we're assuming this is the same as always."

He shrugged. "Why shouldn't it be? It's a checkup, one the whole human race gets every two years."

"You're starting to sound like one of the crankier Remnants, John."

"Let's say I appreciate such a healthy level of suspicion."

"Let's say I agree with you."

"Figured you might."

Kendra raised her sniper rifle and peered through the scope in the direction of the beach. "I just wish the Remnants would bring a few of us with them. They're not getting any younger."

"Don't worry about them. I think they've gotten sneakier and smarter with the years."

"Still. What's General Weiss? Fifty-five? Sixty? They're going to have to trust us at some point."

"They do—it's just, well, you know the problem."

"Nobody's saying they have to trust just the Firsters."

"But the Firsts are their children, despite everything. And our own goddamn generation—"

Kendra flashed him a look. "Lord's name."

He ignored her admonishment. "And our goddamn generation is too indifferent. You know that."

She shook her head and smirked again. "Not all of us, friend. But I see two members of our illustrious generation have just drifted from position." She snapped a half-serious salute. "Semper fidelis, Captain."

"What?" John turned to see what she'd spotted, but she was already disappearing into the woods, probably to ream out a couple of Novices. "Semper fidelis, Kendra," he muttered to the wind.

If history were any guide, the meeting with the Orangemen would end a few moments before dawn, just as the sun began to light the coastal horizon in the east. A signal would flash down the perimeter line to indicate that the twelve Remnants had been spotted walking along the beach toward the outskirts of the city, where other members of their generation would be waiting for them. A week later a brief report would describe the meeting in slight and almost meaningless detail. No Firsts or Seconds believed that the reports included everything that had taken place on the beach, but until any of them were in positions of authority, they would never know for sure.

His grandfather had been chosen three times as a representative for these meetings with the Orangemen Friendlies. The first two meetings occurred when the elder Giordano had been a member of the government, the last when John was a boy and had just recovered from a particularly bad fever. The illness had infected much of the city, killing several dozen and incapacitating hundreds for weeks. What disturbed his grandfather most about the outbreak was the way it had slain far more young than old.

His grandfather had volunteered for that final meeting, although John didn't find out that he had done so until after the old man had gone down to the beach. While he was in his room recovering from his illness, he overheard his parents insisting that his grandfather beg the Orangemen for a cure. The conversation had surprised him; there were few things his parents ever agreed on. Then his mother grunted. "Of course, he won't do that. None of them will. How can we expect love and mercy from the Orangemen if we're so unwilling to give it?"

About two weeks after his grandfather returned from the beach, John found him in the Archives. He liked to visit his grandfather there. Part of the appeal was the location: the only fortified bunker in the whole city, filled with all that remained of human knowledge. There, deep in a dry underground cavern, were the original books brought with the Remnants when they arrived here. Every piece of their fragmentary knowledge of human existence was contained in those dusty yellowing pages. As a child, it had been hard for John to imagine that *millions* of books had once existed. He couldn't picture a single volume more than the 4,453 that had survived. He'd once asked his parents if they knew exactly how much was missing. His mother answered, "A civilization."

The vast majority of the books were in English, their spoken language. The next largest group was Latin, then Greek. A few were in the dead Spanish language—mostly Bibles and religious writings—but they also had several works of Russian literature. References in the books to things that they knew *nothing* about made them sharply aware of how much of mankind's rich diversity had disappeared. Worse still was what they had lost themselves—a crate of Eastern writings, mostly in Chinese and Japanese, many about religions like Buddhism and Hinduism, that had been in the initial inventory but went missing sometime after the Arrival.

At first they copied everything by hand or memorized it, as had been suggested in a book by an author named Ray Bradbury, so that it would never get lost or forgotten. Eventually they redeveloped movable type and built their first printing presses. With them, they were able to make as many copies of the original works as they needed. They had even written and printed a few hundred original books since the Arrival, but none, not even his grandfather's medical books, were consumed with the same zeal as the most recent printings of *Paradise Lost* or *Anna Karenina*.

On that visit he found his grandfather where he usually did—sitting at a desk surrounded by papers and open volumes, his long Roman nose so close to the printed page that it looked as if he hoped to absorb the words through his eyeballs. John pulled an English translation of Ovid's *Metamorphoses* from his grandfather's desk and sat in the chair next to him. It was open to a passage that described the ancient pagans' idea of creation:

> *There still was lacking a being more venerable than animals such as these, one with greater powers of thought and reasoning who might be master over all other living creatures. Thus man was created, and although the other animals look down upon the earth, the creator of all things gave man an uplifted countenance and caused him to look to the sky and raise his upturned face toward the stars.*

He looked up and found the top of his grandfather's gray head facing him. "Grandpa, you understand everything in these books, right?"

The old man stopped reading, blinking clear hazel eyes. "No."

"Think you ever will?"

"Not likely, Johnny." He twirled his pencil at the stacks surrounding him. "Even these precious few that remain are too many for a lifetime."

"Then why keep reading them over and over? You seem smart enough."

The old man snorted. "I'm smart enough to know that I know nothing—and dumb enough to believe I'll someday learn enough."

John was quiet for a moment. "Why'd you go with the other Remnants to see them?"

His grandfather smiled again, but this time some of the light had gone from his eyes. "I think that question has pretty much the same answer as my last."

No one seemed to have his grandfather's sort of patience anymore, that strange blend of self-determination and faith that so many Remnants who had gone to their rest had possessed in life. All the Remnants he had ever known had it, whether they had been eighty or eight on the day of the Arrival. Maybe it came from being among the few to have survived the destruction of the human race. It made sense they were determined to keep what was left of it alive and believed that they could. But they were also smart enough to know that nothing lasted forever and that someday their knowledge—even the most closely held parts of it—must be shared with the Firsts and Seconds. Could his generation really be so complacent—and his parents' so dangerously naïve—that the Remnants thought they were all still unready?

A flash of torchlight, a pause, then two more quick flashes along the perimeter. A warning signal. He took another scan of the perimeter with his binoculars but saw and heard nothing—no lights, no sound. He glanced at the sky. About two hours until dawn. So what could be wrong? He slipped his carbine from his shoulder and flashed the stand-ready signal. Then he took his position and waited. Even the steady nighttime hum of the native insects seemed muted. Ten minutes later Kendra emerged from the woods, her coal-black hair flecked with bits of brush. She was slightly out of breath, likely because she had gotten it into her head to scout all the way to the beach and double-time it back up the foothills.

He handed her a canteen. "Just had to hoof it down there, huh?"

"What does the book of Revelation say?" She grinned as she gulped in cold mountain air. "'He that overcometh shall inherit all things.' Right?"

"Trouble?"

She shrugged as she swigged some water. "Depends. They're back early."

"Why would anyone flash a warning signal for that?"

She handed the canteen back, eyebrows arched. "Because there's more than twelve of them coming back."

CHAPTER 2

And I John saw the holy city, new Jerusalem, coming down from God out of heaven, prepared as a bride adorned for her husband.

—The Book of Revelation 21:2

Jacob Weiss had awoken three hours before dawn. Being awake didn't surprise him; he never really slept well on the nights of the Orangemen's visits. That said, this really was a godforsaken hour: too early to begin a new day and too far past the one just ended to add anything to it. It had always been to him a lonely and anxious hour that had gotten only more so with the years, filled as it was with so many memories of prayers said and so few answered. And still, one above all. He could hear Amelia now, a ripple of sound from decades earlier. And then, always, the voice of Dr. Giordano—"I'm so damn sorry, Jake"—telling him his wife had died in childbirth.

Weiss stretched thick old muscles and slapped cold water on his face from the basin on his bureau. Then he dressed in his tan-and-brown uniform and strapped his sidearm on his belt and debated about going up to the perimeter to check on things. For a while he stood in his kitchen rolling cigarettes, smoking one and then a second before pocketing the other three. His commanders were all capable and well trained. Showing up now would only make them think he didn't trust them. He brushed his bristly gray hair in the small mirror with the plain metal frame hanging in the hallway. Each family had received one soon after old Sammy Langhorne had first perfected laying a thin layer of metallic silver onto glass by chemically reducing silver nitrate. A small gift from an exuberant time, when, in relearning how to do things, what was old became new again.

He opened his front door and went out into the empty street with no direction in mind. It felt good to be out of doors. The cold air rushed into his lungs and made his broad chest less tight.

Lonely as he felt, he was also somewhat surprised to be glad to be alone. Sometimes living in the city among so many people, with so many voices around him all day and long into the evening, made him yearn for his boyhood. His family had lived in a cabin he and his father and his brother, Andrew, had built in the hills. The walls had been fastened together with metal taken from the cargo containers that had deposited them on the beach during the Arrival. But much of it, including the furniture, had been built from the wood of native vegetation. Unlike many Remnants who had been adults during the Arrival, his mother had believed they should build something that could survive more than a single season. She wanted to take a chance on permanence.

Weiss wondered how much remained of that old cabin in the hills. He hadn't been in that area for decades, not since his early years in the Defense Forces. He passed it all the time then on routine patrols or on perimeter-duty nights like this one. Had the roof caved in? Had the doors and shutters fallen off?

Maybe I should go up there and see. Hike up with Andy sometime.

Perhaps they had left some token of their stay there, something half-buried in the overgrowth that they had forgotten. He doubted it. His mother had been very thorough about cleaning out the place once the Remnants had agreed to abandon their isolation and build the city.

As he approached Central Square, he thought of his parents and so many others long gone. Their descendants were now asleep in their beds behind the darkened windows he passed. Each of them—asleep or awake, talking or praying—knew what night it was: possibly, as every night, their last night as living beings.

Whatever the whims of providence, Weiss and his Defense Forces were still responsible for their lives and their continuing existence as a race. It was something he never thought about during the day, only on cheerless nights like this. Was the anxiety of the hour less about the pair of lives he'd lost at three in the morning all those years ago than about the thousands of lives that could be snuffed out unawares because they were foolish enough to believe in this city, in their supposed strength in numbers? Wasn't that exactly the kind of arrogance that had doomed the human race to begin with?

The surrounding gaslights brought nearly the luster of late afternoon to the square and diminished the density of stars in the sky above. Such lights now ran down most of the main streets except for the outermost blocks. Having recently tapped some new natural gas pockets, there was talk among the engineers of adding gaslights to private homes soon, as they had already begun to do in public buildings.

Weiss stood under a lamp, arms folded across his barrel chest as he fingered his mustache. Progress.

"'And there shall be no night there; and they need no candle,'" a voice said brightly from not far behind him. He turned and saw Gordon Lee flipping his long black hair out of his eyes as he came up along the square, a leather workbag slung across his slim shoulder. "Revelation 22:5. Good thing we decided to name the city New Philadelphia and not that other one, eh?"

"Good to see you, Gordon." Weiss extended his hand. "Working late?"

Lee shrugged as their hands joined. "The kids in Sector Seven had a gas leak and were worried, so they called in a professional." He jerked his chin at the lamp Jake had been studying. "Please don't tell me there's something wrong with that one too."

"What? No—I was just thinking."

"Thinking about how dangerous all these lights are, I bet," Lee said with a laugh. "That's the problem with you military types. You all think we should still be living in mud shacks in the hills and hunting with the rifles dumped here with us during the Arrival."

Weiss grunted. "I don't mind the newer rifles." He looked down the road in the direction of the beach. "You're telling me it never worries you, Gordon? Even on these nights?"

"*Especially* not on these nights. Why should they attack us on the nights we're expecting them? And for that matter, why pop in for a visit every other year for the last fifty-two years? Seems to me if someone wanted to get us—Friendlies, Hostiles, both—they had plenty of opportunities before we turned the lights on."

"Seems to me you don't worry all that much."

"Such is the critique hurled at my generation by members of yours. No offense, of course."

"None taken."

"Actually, I worry about plenty of things. For the last three hours I've been worried about a gas leak. Now that the lights are back on, I'm worried about how I'm going to wake up my wife so I can get laid. I'm thinking 'Be fruitful and multiply'—a cliché, I know—should do the trick."

"How's Sofie anyway?"

"Good. Very good. Thanks. I'll tell her you were asking for her."

"Do that. I miss her a lot. As a drill sergeant she was one of my best."

Lee smirked. "And as a niece?"

The rapid pace of boots tearing at the fieldstone road snatched their attention. They turned to find a pink-faced Novice of no more than fourteen, his rifle shouldered, his hand clutched around a scrap of paper. The young soldier almost forgot to salute, then snapped a quick one at Weiss while panting heavily.

"General. I'm glad I found you, sir. Captain Giordano asked me to double-time it over to your house to give you this."

Weiss unfolded the damp and crumpled note and read its penciled contents. "'The twelve are returning early from the beach.'" He read the next line silently and glanced up at the Novice. "And they're not alone?"

"No, sir."

His jaw set. "How many?"

"Just four others, sir. All unarmed. No signs of a kidnap situation or hostility of any kind. They should be reaching Gate Six at any moment."

Weiss glanced at Lee and found him surprisingly silent. Then he turned his attention back to the boy. "Where's Captain Giordano now?"

"With the other perimeter guards, sir. They're on alert, in case of an attack. The captain's sent an armed escort to the beach to accompany our people and the, uh, guests into the city."

"Let's go. I want to meet them at the gate. Gordon, you're a civilian militia commander. Sound a general alert, but make sure not to start a panic."

"Me? Really, don't you think that someone else might—"

Weiss glared at him. "I want this city awake and ready for anything. Now let's move."

When New Philadelphia was laid out, there were many who believed there was no point in encircling it with a wall to keep out an enemy who could simply launch an attack from the airspace above or from an even more comfortable distance in orbit. Others pointed out that there were practical reasons for building a wall—not the least of which was to keep out the carnivorous predators that had thinned their numbers considerably during the years in the hills. Weiss's father, who had lost a younger sister to such a beast a year after the Arrival, was one of the first to advocate building a wall as well as having a patrolled outer-defense perimeter. "I'm not so worried about protecting ourselves from Hostiles who might or might not find us," Dave Weiss said at the time, "as much as I'm worried about defending ourselves from the enemies here and now. If we're the smartest beasts on this rock, at least, we better start acting like it."

Once they agreed to build their walled metropolis, the Remnants looked to the celestial city of New Jerusalem in the book of Revelation to aid them in its construction. They even built the wall with twelve gates, oriented to the major points on the compass. If only they, like the people in Revelation, also had guardian angels manning the gatehouses.

New Philadelphia was without question a beautiful city. Not just in its stonework and gently curving streets, but also in its overall design. The Archives held some photos of cities on Earth-of-old but far more descriptions, so they built with the best precedents in mind: maximum concentration of people with easy access to open lands and common spaces. Half of the acreage inside the walls was dedicated to farmlands, orchards, public greens; the other half to row houses with deep front and back gardens. This design made the homes easier to heat in the winters, yet open enough to provide ventilation in the summers. A fringe benefit of the design hadn't eluded the builders: ample escape routes in case of emergencies.

For people who had lived isolated in the wilderness for some time, the city's walls had to provide freedom within, not the feeling of a penitentiary. No one ever grumbled about being so close to growing flora or having enough light and fresh air. And having foodstuffs inside the city when the crops outside the walls could not be accessed for whatever reason brought peace of mind against the possibility of a long siege.

Weiss and the Novice moved quickly through the streets toward Gate Six. By the time they reached it, armed militia members were out of their homes and making their way to their appointed positions, though many seemed as if they wanted to join the growing civilian crowd. Weiss found Kendra McQueen and the armed escort she had led to meet the twelve and their guests. The Novice seemed only too glad to be dismissed.

"Lieutenant," Weiss said, "what's our sitrep?"

"They arrived at the entrance to the gatehouse a few minutes before we showed up, sir. I don't know how they got here before us, but they've been holed up in there ever since."

Weiss squinted. "You mean you haven't seen them?"

"No, sir. None of us in the escort have. And the captain of the guard on duty said all she could make out were our twelve people flanked around four robed figures of varying sizes."

"Varying sizes? As tall as Orangemen?"

"The guard wouldn't know, sir," she said. "Not having ever seen an Orangeman."

Weiss raised an eyebrow. "Why didn't you go in and find out?"

Kendra bit her lip. "The twelve won't let us, sir."

"'Won't let'?"

"They've barred the door, told us they were all right but needed some time."

"*Who* specifically told you, Lieutenant? Whose voice did you hear?"

A pause. "Grace Davison."

"Grace?" Weiss looked down and chuckled. "Figures."

Kendra shrugged. "No one wants to have it out with the last of the real old-timers."

"Of course."

"And she specifically said that you and I couldn't go in."

"Really?" Weiss asked. "Did she say why?"

"I'm not sure, sir. I assume it's because we're the only ones outside of official delegations who've seen an Orangeman in recent years."

Weiss put his hand on her shoulder and squeezed it. "That was a long time ago, Kendra. And I can't imagine that—"

"Jake?"

The voice that spoke his name was thin and wheezy but still somehow strong and firm. Weiss turned to see a familiar caramel-colored face crowned by short white hair that he could recall being salt and pepper for the longest time and—if he thought back far enough—jet black. Grace had been as much a mother to him as his own, with all of the emotions that accompanied such a relationship. Behind her wrinkles were still the eyes of the youngish woman who had educated him and so many others. From her lips in their first one-room schoolhouse he had learned of the beauty of biology, the glory of Walt Whitman, the bittersweet history of human achievement, the miracle of the Scriptures. As she stepped through the darkened doorway of the gatehouse, Weiss realized that despite his being commander of the Defense Forces and an authority second only to the Council's, he would have a hard time denying any request Grace made.

Weiss gave her a courteous nod. "Grace. Good to see you. Mind telling me what's going on?"

She walked in short but steady steps toward a low stone railing. She leaned against it, then tilted her head back a bit to look him in the eye. The soldiers gathered to listen. "I speak with the unanimous authority of the twelve relating to matters that we will put before the Council in our biennial report."

Formality. Not good.

"Grace, while I understand and respect your ambassadorial authority, as commander of the Defense Forces, I have to insist that—"

She held up a vein-ridden hand. "I need three representatives, one from each of our people's generations, to enter this gatehouse with me to verify who is inside and spread this truth to all members of their generations. Jake, you'll represent the Remnants."

Weiss leaned in. "Now wait just a damn minute—"

Grace ignored him and set her eyes on Kendra. "My dear, I helped your mother deliver you. You will represent the Seconds." Grace now looked past both of them into the crowd, hoping to find her final representative among the armed escort and guards.

"If you need a Firster, how about me?"

All eyes turned to see a woman, tall and slim, coming toward them. Though her mane of red hair was now slit with gray, it was hard to mistake the striking and indomitable Petra Giordano for anyone else.

"Petra." Grace's voice was quiet and filled by a growing smile. "I couldn't have asked for a better Firster."

"No," Weiss said flatly, without turning, as Petra joined them.

"I'm not under your command, Jake," Petra said happily enough.

"Which is exactly why you're not going in. This is a defense issue, Petra. I can't have a civilian in there."

"At least not one who believes your macho defense posturing is a lot of bollocks."

"Enough, please." Grace straightened, ready to climb the stairs back up to the gatehouse. She looked from Petra to Weiss and back again. "This isn't a defense matter. It might make it simpler if it were. Now come with me."

"What are you going to show us?" Kendra asked, one hand on her rifle.

Grace touched her arm. "Nothing you'll need that for, dear. But something that will shake your expectations as much as the Jews' were when the Messiah came as a lamb."

Weiss stepped between them. "Grace, you're asking a hell of a lot."

"Jake, you trusted me when you were a boy. I'm asking you, just one more time, be that faithful little boy again."

"Four unknowns have entered the city gates. And you're—"

"Please, Jake. I'm not senile. I'm not crazy. I'm not being forced to say this. The only reason I came out and not one of the others is because most of you still trust me. Now please."

With a stiff, short nod from Weiss, the selected representatives followed Grace inside and up the steps. Kendra led the way with her rifle's safety off. The passage into the gatehouse had been made purposely narrow and dark so city defenders inside would have a fighting chance against infiltrators. Now they knew the fear they had hoped to inflict on any enemies entering these fortifications.

The interior of the gatehouse was round like the tower itself. As they turned the corner and entered the tower's main room, they found the twelve had lit torches. Emerging into the torchlight, Weiss could see shadows flickering across every wall and object in the room. The twelve—old faces one and all but none older than Grace's—looked calm but determined as they surrounded the four guests who sat on the ground.

"General Jacob Weiss is the head of our armed forces," Grace began. "He will guarantee your safety."

The tallest of the four stood. He was taller than the average man but not nearly as tall as the shortest Orangeman. Lit from behind, his head appeared only as a hooded void, blacker than a moonless night. It reminded Weiss of a picture of Death he had seen in a book in the Archives.

"General Weiss," the stranger said. He removed his hood to reveal a ruddy face with thinning fair hair and a rust-colored beard. "I can't believe we've finally found you."

The other three stood and pulled off their hoods as well—a woman, darker and shorter than the man, and two children, both with features similar enough to peg them as brother and sister and likely the offspring of the adults. Weiss found himself shaking hands with the man and then the woman, who clasped his hard hand in both of hers.

"I'm William Tyler. This is my family. It's been so long since we hoped, since we even imagined—"

Weiss eyed the man. "You're . . . human."

Kendra was shaking her head. "This isn't possible," she said. "No one else survived. No one—just the Remnants."

"It's a miracle. A miracle." Petra pressed her hands against her lips, tears flowing freely as she rushed to touch these newcomers. "It's a gift from God. We must tell everyone!"

"I don't understand," Kendra muttered, then turned to Grace. "New people brought by the Orangemen? What does it mean?"

Grace's hand found Kendra's forearm and gave it a squeeze. "A change is coming, child. A great change."

Weiss, turning from the tumultuous exchange of greetings between Petra, the twelve, and the newcomers, looked at Grace. "That much is certain."

CHAPTER 3

And I looked, and, lo, a Lamb stood on the mount Sion, and with him an hundred forty and four thousand, having his Father's name written in their foreheads . . . These were redeemed from among men, being the firstfruits unto God and to the Lamb.

—The Book of Revelation 14:1,4

The sun rose out of the ocean, warming the streets and turning the hazy-yellow moon into a ghostly specter. People hustled out of their homes, casting long shadows on the ground in the early-morning light. Some were off to their rotating monthly work assignments in town or out in the fields. Older children ran through the streets, enjoying their last few weeks of freedom before reporting for Defense Forces training, their younger siblings either lagging behind in bunches or within their parents' arm reach. Other than a low-level pulse of excitement in the air—not dissimilar to the way a child felt the night before a birthday or Christmas—it was hard to tell from the surface just how much their lives had changed overnight.

John wandered down to Central Square, feeling this pulse. He didn't have anywhere to be. Having been on duty all night in the hills, he had been given a day of R & R. He could have caught up on sleep or spent the day with friends, just talking about the Newcomers' arrival. But there wasn't anyone he wanted to discuss it with other than Kendra. He had only glimpsed her for a minute after she and the others had left the gatehouse.

The Newcomers' existence seemed to prove one thing: more than the original Remnants had survived mankind's destruction. All his life he had been told this was impossible. John of Patmos, writing in the book of Revelation, had foretold that only 144,000 would initially survive the end times. And the first census, taken right after the Arrival, proved that *exactly* that number had survived. But if these additional four had lived, could other humans be out there somewhere? Yet for that to be true, it would mean that the book of Revelation—or at least the way they'd been interpreting it—wasn't accurate.

A terrifying idea. If the Remnants hadn't survived to repopulate the human race and bring about the New Jerusalem, as foretold, then why were they here? Through every loss and pain, with each misery in the repetitive chore that living could sometimes be, John had never fallen into a pit of grief, because he more often than not believed it would all make sense in the end—the struggling, the trials, the messy road to survival. His grandparents and others of their generation had been spared to make the world anew. He would be a part of the creation of paradise.

He watched the men and women in the square and the children running across the grass. In their excited murmurs and laughter, he felt anticipation building for the report the twelve would make to the Council tonight. Surely some of the people around him were feeling similar confusion and conflict. They couldn't all be like his mother.

His mother. She never wavered, never questioned. He couldn't talk to her about his confusion. And talking to his grandfather's headstone wouldn't help much.

Which left Kendra. He took a step or two in the direction of the barracks, wondering if she'd be in her dormitory this time of day. He didn't know what he'd say to her or how he'd say it. He didn't have anything that would help either of them make sense of it all. Yet he knew whatever would come next, he would be with her. They were fellow travelers and had been since the day they met.

His mother was another matter. The joy she felt, the miracle she believed she'd witnessed in the gatehouse last night—he couldn't understand how she felt so certain considering all the uncertainty before them. And her quoting the book of Sirach to him—"What is too sublime for you, do not seek; do not reach into things that are hidden from you. What is committed to you, pay heed to; what is hidden is not your concern"—was just too much. Didn't she think secrets should ever be revealed? Shouldn't faith someday be rewarded with confirmed fact?

Still, wasn't what she felt about the Newcomers' appearance the very definition of faith, that everything was going according to plan? And what he felt the exact opposite?

He wanted to believe. Just not on the simple terms of the contract his mother had signed with her conscience.

Maybe that's why they had never really seen eye to eye since his father and Christian disappeared. His mother didn't want to consider anything that couldn't fit into the patterns she'd woven in her head long ago. Her idea of free will was drifting with the current and accepting where you wound up. And Ecclesiastes seemed to back her up: "Whatsoever thy hand findeth to do, do it with thy might." Her passivity was all over that one.

But she's wrong. Free will isn't passive. It's an active choice. Faith is accepting that you have no control over events but only how you choose to deal with those events—and that's where free will comes in.

A thought stopped John in his tracks as the wind filled his ears. *If free will isn't passive, then what is it? Maybe free will is an extension of the evolutionary process, an organic trial-and-error method to make us all the more enlightened, more evolved beings. Maybe it's actually the fulfillment of evolution—a point where we take charge of random actions and reactions and give moral weight to them.*

His head spun. He needed sleep. He needed to see his friend Kendra. And he also needed more hours than he had before tonight's meeting to make sense of things, more than just the howl of the sea breeze to answer his questions.

Maybe New Jerusalem won't come as we expect it, fully formed from heaven. Maybe the Remnants, in building this city, were right all along. We have to make it and earn it piece by piece.

Just as he was about to leave, he saw Sofie Lee crossing the lawn of the square with her three daughters. Irene, the eldest, was probably close to the age he'd been when he and Sofie, two years older, had shared their first kiss. Seeing her with Gordon Lee's children, that voice in his head that was not his own asked: *Don't you know all this is a dream? When we die is when we wake up. Ain't that something?*

Sofie held a hand aloft as the girls raced ahead of her. He waved in response and watched her as she approached him, her hands in her pants pockets, her figure still slim and girlish despite her years in the Defense Forces and three childbirths. It was strange to think of her as thirty-two. She still had those freckles on that upturned nose. She still smiled that smile. Ever and always she'd be Sofie Weiss, the ruddy fifteen-year-old he'd had the guts to kiss on her roof the night of the lunar eclipse, the one he sipped unblessed wine from a canteen with in the pouring rain the next summer, the girl so full of terrifying brains and energy. She couldn't be a mother. And he couldn't be so different from what he was all those summers ago. It all had to be a dream.

The girls yelled "Hi John" at him as they ran past. Sofie barked out orders to the eldest, something about keeping an eye on the younger ones. The girl, freckled and pointy chinned, a mirror image of Sofie at the same age despite the black hair she had inherited from her father, grumbled something juvenile in response. Communication delivered, Sofie turned to him, her face warm and bright and friendly.

"Hello John. Long time no see."

"It is at that." He leaned against the tree behind him. "Funny we don't run into each other more."

"Yeah, funny that. Almost think you were trying to avoid me."

"What I mean is, it's not like we live in a big city of old, like New York or something, where most people didn't even know the neighbors who lived on their block."

"True enough. What do you think about the news?"

"What news?"

Sofie laughed as she slipped a renegade strawberry-blond lock back into its bun. "Where have you been, fella? The Council's agreed to have three representatives from each generation at the meeting tonight when the twelve give their report."

"Really?"

"That's all you've got to say? It's unprecedented! They've never done that before. And what's more, the Newcomers are going to be there too. So we'll get reports of what happened on the beach right from our *own* people, none of the usual Council filter."

"It's good—I guess. A lot to process, you know?"

"Tell me about it. What do you know about them?"

"I wasn't in the gatehouse. But they're human, four of them, a family. I think."

"I wish we knew more. Well, we'll find out soon enough. And with Gordon being there—"

"Gordon's one of the reps?"

"They wanted his scientific and engineering knowledge to help them evaluate the Newcomers' testimony. Hopefully whatever he can glean from them will help us convince the Remnants not to be so scared of technology. The more our generation gets from the Newcomers, the more leverage we'll have."

"I guess. Yeah. Hopefully."

She leaned in conspiratorially. "You think he'll be safe there, John? You on security?"

Now we come to the point of things. "I haven't seen the roster, but at a Council meeting, Sofie? I can't think of a safer place."

"I mean, with them there."

"I'm a hundred percent certain they're not a threat to Gordon Lee."

"That'll be a load off his mind."

He grinned. "Don't you mean your mind?"

She laughed and shook her head. "Better run, Johnny. Don't be a stranger. You're always welcome."

Good old Sofie, he thought. Always knew the right ways to motivate people into giving her what she wanted. *Well, almost always.*

Grace couldn't recall how many Council meetings she had offered testimony to or how many times she had sat on the Council of Twelve to hear it. She couldn't even remember the more personal parts of these meetings—for example, which of her fellow Remnants she had reported to. It had nothing to do with senility. Procedural matters always tended to blur together in her mind. But she knew she would remember this meeting and this report for the time she had left. Even if fate took all memory from her before her physical life was claimed, it would never be able to erase this.

Grace was ninety-six years old, as they measured years on this planet. She might well be older in Earth years, but much had been lost before the Arrival and forgotten since, including the way time had been measured on the home world. It had been a long time since she or anyone else had thought in old-style time increments.

She didn't find it so great a loss, even for such personal matters as determining her exact age. She had been forty-four Earth years old when she and the others walked out of the cargo containers on the beach; since that time this planet had moved around its sun fifty-two times. So she was ninety-six and would tell anyone that number with a straight face should they dare ask.

Of course, when the Orangemen deposited them on this planet, there were others who were older than she and a few her age. But all of them had now crossed over to await New Jerusalem's appearance in the sky, when all would live with the Lord. Only she, of the adults who arrived here, still lived. Why, she had no idea. Perhaps to guide the descendants of those who'd struggled alongside her in those early days. But she tended to doubt that.

People like Jake and Andy Weiss were just boys then. But neither they nor any of these children who call themselves Remnants really remember how it was, either in the last days or right after the Arrival.

The murmuring and muttering of the other eleven representatives sitting with her in the anteroom outside the Council chamber drew her out of her memories. In a few minutes, she would testify before the Council—and this select number of representatives of their children and grandchildren—that she believed a miracle had come with the four foundlings from the beach. And that, together, they would bring about the New Heavens and the New Earth—praise God.

Grace closed her eyes to the chatter. The room was warm and dry with the heat from the fireplace. She opened her eyes and looked around once more before shutting them again. Let them believe the old woman had gone to sleep. She wanted to think in peace. Against the speckled darkness of her closed eyelids, she never saw anything other than what she had been that first morning on the beach: an angry woman searching frantically. Scattered across the sand were the twelve massive cargo containers they had just emerged from. Her son and daughter were missing. Ernest had been fourteen then, stocky with baby fat and awkward with adolescence. Nancy was just twelve, hanging on to childhood with long arms and coltish legs. Her children had been in the White Place with her, but somehow—she couldn't remember how it happened now—they'd been brought to the planet on different transports. Her husband was dead, killed in the last days. Everyone she ever knew was dead except for her children. She had to find them. The terror she'd known then still made her wince, still wanted to squeeze her heart silent.

What must they have looked like on the beach that morning, all 144,000 of them, flailing around like ants in fear that a heedless child's heel would return to crush them even now?

She remembered it all. Their squinting faces as they shielded their eyes and emerged from the artificial light onto that sun-bright beach. The air shimmering with heat. The ocean waves flashing with glaring sunlight, more heard than seen in those first few chaotic minutes. The pure smell of the salty sea air. Wherever they were, the light was real and the air was fresh. After all that time—how long was it?—cooped up in the antiseptic artificial environment of the White Place, it was almost overwhelming to be in a living world again. From what she could tell just by the accents around her, the Remnants had been scooped up from every human colony across the Sol system, but she couldn't imagine any of them—even the ones like her who had come from Earth—had ever experienced an environment so pure as that beach.

The sensations—warm and inviting as they were—almost made her want to give up the search for her children. She was alive and in a living place. Was it wrong to want to feel like a human being for just a single moment after what they had endured for so long? But then she heard the hysterical screams of other parents calling for other children, other spouses calling for their mates, and wondered if they were calling for people still alive, like she hoped she was doing, or for the dead. She had to find Ernest and Nancy. They had come too far together to be separated or to die alone. Even as angry as she was then, she couldn't imagine a universe that cruel.

Hands pushing and shoving, voices buried by other voices, the thudding of rocks and sticks on unfamiliar metals, clothes tearing, random scents of food, a human smell of sweat and fear turning animal—all of this and more was the last of humanity herded together onto a single beach on a planet who knew where. A moment more and these people, hungry for their loved ones, wearied by a journey from death and destruction, eager for some understanding of what was happening, these remnants would become a mob, animals. And that moment was upon them. If it came, it would show that they didn't deserve to live as individuals or to continue as a race. She felt the moment coming, building and building, ready to burst its hot death upon them all. She didn't want to die like that, so alone, so seemingly undeserving of life. And then—

Silence.

Silence as exactly 144,000 pairs of eyes looked to the sky. Silence as these bitter dregs of mankind beheld a pair of humanoid beings—orange skinned and about seven feet tall, with heads slightly larger than the human variety and big iris-less eyes as slate gray as a chalkboard—hovering about twenty feet off the ground. Both were naked except for their grayish loincloths and gold metallic belts and sword scabbards, their bare chests revealing that one was seemingly male and the other female. No hair covered their bodies, not arms or chests or eyebrows, except their heads, which were closely shorn. Flapping translucent wings arching from their backs held them aloft.

It was the first time that any still-living member of the human race had seen the beings they would come to call the Orangemen. Whether those forms were their true ones, no one had ever yet proven, even these long years after they had come to consider them both their greatest enemies and their truest protectors.

The female one began to speak in words that somehow could be understood by everyone. "We have brought you here so that your race may enter into a new life. We do not wish to see you harmed any further. We assure you that you will be left in peace to do as you will."

"Peace?" a voice, hollow with loss and longing for death, cried out from somewhere to Grace's right. "You bastards leave us in peace? You destroyed us! Destroyed our worlds! Our whole fucking civilization!"

The male Orangeman gestured. "In these containers you will find food, animals, supplies—all basic tools taken from your old world. You will also find some of your weapons, so that you may hunt and protect yourselves from the indigenous wildlife. We have salvaged as much as we could find of your literature and history. Learn from it and build anew. Repopulate your race."

"Fuck you!"

"You burned our world!"

"You killed us all! My whole family!"

"Everyone's dead! You goddamn bastards!"

The Orangemen waited for a lull in the commotion. The female continued: "Nothing can be done to change the past. The past is fixed, the future unwritten. Turn to the future with virtue. The last days are gone, the suffering gone. And the world can be made anew."

"Are you sorry? Do you feel any remorse, you inhuman monsters? Answer me!"

Both of those impassive orange faces turned to face their accuser below them. A pulse seemed to pass through the male's jaw. The female turned to him, but after a moment she faced the crowd again.

"We will visit every two years from this day to check on your progress. We will not interfere with you or harm you—but we will protect you from those who would harm you. Leaders of your tribes should visit us here on this beach. We will come unarmed and ask you to do the same. We will walk together, speak together—perhaps someday we will even share a meal. Until then, love one another."

With a great flap of their translucent wings, they were gone, riding farther and farther into the blue sky until blotted out by the sun. No human being would set eyes on an Orangeman for the next two years. And by then, things would be much different.

All eyes had been on the sky. Grace didn't see her children approach, didn't hear Ernest's voice until he was nearly on top of her, couldn't believe he was there clutching Nancy's hand as if they were still young children. As she swallowed them in her embrace, she saw over their heads other parents finding their children, everywhere, all around them, at the very same moment.

Cries of joy and reunion at exactly the same instant.

A miracle.

Then a flash far up in the sky caught her eye and was gone.

"Grace? Grace?"

She opened her eyes. Hard to see, but it looked like someone was calling her into the Council's chambers to give her testimony.

Weak old eyes. She shook her head and stood up, feeling strangely more peaceful and assured than she had in the last fifty-two years. *Weak old eyes but God willing a stout heart.*

"Anytime you're ready, Grace," Andrew Weiss, the chairman of the Council, said once she had taken her seat at the witness table.

"The twelve met the Orangemen on the beach as usual," Grace began, looking at the Council on the raised dais and at the representatives of the First and Second generations seated at a table perpendicular to it. "None of us expected that it would be anything other than the usual sort of meeting: the Orangemen there to check our progress and offer encouragement and advice, not to render aid or services, and to assure us that the Hostiles were still unaware of the human race's continuing existence."

She took a sip of water from a cup that had been set before her. "We described how many people had been sickened during the last warm season by that diphtheria outbreak. Told the Orangemen how hundreds had suffered for weeks and dozens had died before the season passed. We explained we didn't want intervention, only answers to some questions that we were sure people had solved in the years before the holocaust. We said we were fairly certain that humanity had discovered a diphtheria vaccine, since none of the old medical textbooks told us how to treat it."

The two Orangemen—a pair of males she did not recognize—had been typically impassive about the request. Grace noted how as the twelve had walked along the moonlit beach with their guests, airing grievances, seeking assurances, none were prepared for what came next.

The shorter of the two Orangemen—more than a foot taller than Grace had been at her zenith—turned to her. His grayish eyes reflected the flames of the signal fire they had lit to mark their location. "What if we were to tell you that there might be someone who can help you with your medical needs, someone who would not disturb our pact of noninterference?"

Grace looked at the one who spoke, then the other, and snorted. "I'd say, with respect, that I already ask God for help every day."

"It is said," the Orangeman replied, with an almost-smile on his statue-like features, "that God does his work in mysterious ways. Please follow us to that rock outcropping ahead."

He gestured with long, expressive fingers. The group followed toward a narrow cove. Grace could feel the youngest Remnants—Felix Collins and Enrique Cordova in particular—tense up. But as they approached the outcropping, they could discern no force of Hostiles hiding there, no clusters of winged soldiers ready to slaughter them. They saw nothing except four robed figures waiting silently between the rocks and sea, framed by a night sky thick with stars.

"It is my belief, Council members," Grace said now, "having spoken to these four Newcomers, that we are witnessing the age of the Millennium, the end of our thousand years of peace, as foretold in the book of Revelation. These Newcomers—the Tylers—are the beginning of the pagans being raised for judgment."

Petra Giordano gasped at Grace's pronouncement. The old woman glanced in Petra's direction and nodded, her mouth a confident line.

Each pair of eyes in the room turned to the chairman, looking for guidance. Leaning on his elbows, Andrew gave his heavy jowls a rough rub and looked at Grace with wary and hooded eyes. "Are you certain, Grace? Did the Orangemen tell you this specifically?"

She held his gaze. "If I'm right that Revelation is reaching its fulfillment, then the birth of the New Nations is at hand and the New Jerusalem will soon descend like a bride from the sky. But first we are going to go through a great trial—and we need to be ready for it."

"A trial?" Gordon Lee wondered aloud from his seat. "Would you please elaborate?"

"A war, Gordon," she answered with a quiet sadness. "The last great rebellion against God. What we do with these Newcomers will decide our fates in this coming life. I ask you to now judge. Judge wisely." Then she stood up and left, with the other eleven members of the beach party following in her wake.

The six representatives of the First and Second generations began to murmur among themselves, none more so than Lee, who was shaking his head and sputtering in disgust.

Sitting on their raised dais, the Council of Twelve watched the commotion in the chamber for several moments before Andrew Weiss used his pumice-stone gavel to bring the room to order. Long considered the more genial of the two Weiss brothers, Andrew imagined many in the room were surprised to find him so red-faced with annoyance. Then again, all of the current Council members had served numerous times and no such outburst had ever occurred in chambers.

"Order, order! I remind the representatives that you are all here at Grace's request. Please show some respect for this institution by controlling yourselves. You're not children, any of you, so don't act like it."

Lee snorted at the last remark. "I'm sorry, Mr. Chairman, but the Millennium? Really? Has a thousand years passed since the end of the world? I'm not going to just sit here and have anyone, even someone as respected as Grace, make such absolutely baseless pronouncements without—"

"Gordon, believe me, I sympathize with you," Andrew interrupted. "Now if you are all done, I'd like to ask one of you to go into the anteroom and ask the guards to bring in the Newcomers. Tell them the children don't have to come in unless they wish to be with their parents."

He watched as Petra rose from her chair and opened the door to the main entrance. Her son and his handpicked guard detail were waiting with the Newcomers on the other side. Kendra could clearly be seen trying not to speak with the children, who were fidgeting and asking lots of loud questions: Are there a lot of kids in the city? Do they like to play baseball? How many people were pilots before they got here? Have you ever had ice cream? Do Orangemen ever laugh? Kendra, wincing a grin, averted her eyes.

"Go on." John put a hand on the man's shoulder. "We'll take good care of your kids. They seem to want to tell us all about this baseball thing."

Andrew watched as William and Eva Tyler stood in unison and entered the Council's chambers and heard the heavy wooden door shut smoothly behind them. The simply built candlelit room of wood and stone could have been any kind of common meeting place, from a court of law to a Lutheran church.

"Please." Andrew gestured to them to approach the witness table. "Come forward."

"I want your assurances as leaders of this community that no harm will come to our children," Eva called out.

Andrew climbed down the dais's three steps and met them in the center of the main aisle, arms open. "My dear lady, I promise your children are in safe hands. I swear this to you as a father and a grandfather. Here we consider every child a blessing, each a gift and a hope for the future." He waved them forward. "Now please."

As they approached, Andrew returned to his seat and Hector Phillips, the most junior member of the Council, came down the steps to swear them in. The Tylers placed their hands on a very heavy Bible so they could promise to tell the truth, the whole truth, and nothing but the truth. Even Andrew thought the ritual both serious and absurd, yet he hoped the Tylers were comforted by the idea that they could testify together. He glanced around. One member of the Council was taking handwritten notes, as were most representatives of the First and Second generations.

"We'll tell you what we know," William said. "But you have to tell us how you got here, how this—it's all so unbelievable—"

"In time. Now if you please—"

The bearded man glanced at his wife and sighed. "All right, here goes. My name is William Tyler. This is my wife, Eva. We have two children, Peter and Tess. I'm an engineer—was an engineer—at the Mars colony. My wife is a doctor. She did research in the colony on the long-term effects of low-gravity environments on human physiology." He looked at Andrew. "Do you know a lot about the Mars colony?"

Andrew almost shrugged. "We'd like to know about it from your perspective."

"Okay. Well, the colony was composed of about a hundred or so families like ours, who rotated in and out every Martian year—roughly every two Earth years. We were all normal, everyday people doing work we thought would one day hold the key to human survival." He laughed.

Eva gave him a knowing glance before she took up the story. "I guess each of us thought it possible that humanity could easily be wiped out. A meteor could destroy all life on Earth—or a plague. We believed it was important to spread humanity out so the race could survive. A lot of colonists thought as we did. We went to bed at night dreaming of a terraformed Mars, with a breathable atmosphere and a warmer climate, and spent our days trying to make that happen. It all seemed so possible—and we were willing to do the work."

"Then the attack came," William said. "We didn't know about it right away on account of the lag time. And at that point in the year, the delay was about twenty minutes because Earth and Mars were at their farthest distance from each other. Not that it would've mattered if we had been closer. We couldn't have helped. All we could've done was hear civilization being murdered a little quicker."

Eva squeezed her husband's hand. "We did not know who had attacked Earth or what was happening. No one had heard of any intelligent extraterrestrial life-forms—and certainly none of us would have believed that they would wipe out humanity like some silly old science-fiction movie."

"Is that what you thought?" Petra asked. "That the Earth was destroyed by *aliens*?"

"Petra—"

She shot Andrew a look. "Mr. Chairman, why are we here if we're not allowed to question the witnesses?"

"You'll be able to, Petra. Just let them have their say first." He turned to the Newcomers. "Please."

Eva frowned. "In any event, we did not know what had happened. We tried to raise Mission Control in Houston, then Star City, then Jiuquan—all nothing but static. Then we tried the other outposts. The lunar colony first, then the mining colonies in the asteroid belt. We even tried to hail the Chinese-manned mission that was heading out to the Saturnian system. Nothing. We did not know if anyone could respond, if anyone anywhere was still alive. But we knew one thing: we were probably going to be next."

"We always thought the attacks were simultaneous," Lee said, scratching his ear. "We didn't realize there was a delay in the attack on Mars."

"Gordon, please," Andrew said. "They're still giving testimony."

"From our point of view, every outpost was attacked simultaneously except ours," William continued. "If there was a delay between the other attacks, we can't tell you. I can tell you that on the Mars colony it was utter chaos over the next few days. No one knew what to do, not one of us. There were just over four hundred of us, lots of kids. We had no weapons, no way to defend ourselves other than blowing up our own nuclear power plant and likely killing ourselves in the process."

"We did not have to wait long," Eva added, then turned to her husband. "Was it even a week? Long enough to worry about what might happen, but not enough time to prepare for it. Our nuclear power plant was the first thing hit, from orbit it seemed, then the laboratories and dormitories a few minutes later. Not nuclear attacks, more like flashes of lightning, electromagnetic pulses knocking out everything. The power, it was almost biblical."

"Indeed," Petra said quietly.

"William thought we would be safest underground, in the lower levels, which were the most heavily shielded from radiation. He brought us all down there, myself, the children. He pleaded with the other colonists to come along, but . . . it was all just too crazy. He had been working on something in the lower laboratories in his spare time—something that could function on the planet's geothermal energy in case of a system-wide failure of the nuclear plant."

"It was a cryo-chamber," he continued, clearing his throat. "I'm not sure how familiar you are with cryogenics—"

"Mr. Tyler," Andrew said, "I ask that you please just assume our ignorance."

"Okay." He looked sheepish. "Cryogenics studies the behavior of materials at very low temperatures. In this case, we had been experimenting with cryobiology. Should our station suffer some sort of catastrophic failure, it would be necessary to freeze the inhabitants in suspended animation while a rescue team traveled from Earth. As my wife mentioned, these chambers would be powered by the planet's own geothermal heat. We knew it worked on lab animals, even on the colony's dog, but we had no idea if it would work on people or for how long."

"You can't imagine the screams," Eva added. "It was—"

"It was a chance for survival," William said flatly, "and we took it."

"And it worked," Eva continued, "until the day the Orangemen—as you call them—woke us from our sleep and brought us here. Wherever this is." Her gaze traveled across the men and women on the dais. "Were they the ones who destroyed the Earth?"

Andrew looked back at her for a long minute, chin resting on his outstretched thumb. "Not the same ones. But fallen ones—a faction of Orangemen we call the Hostiles—did wipe out most of mankind."

Eva's eyes held no recognition. "'Fallen ones'?"

"Fallen angels," Petra answered. "Demons."

"Fallen angels?" William rubbed his beard. "Well, anyway, we're still not sure how long we slept. We're hoping you might be able to help us with that too."

"The children think it's only been a few weeks," Eva explained. "We have let them think that. They were terrified when the Orangemen took us from the cryo-chamber. And then there was that—whatever it was that brought us here."

"I know it's difficult," Andrew said. "But would you tell us about it? Where were you *just* before you got here?"

Andrew could sense as he posed this question that every member of the Council awaited the answer with tensed interest.

William looked at his wife and nodded. "A white place—comfortable enough but completely barren. It's hard to remember for some reason. I think we were well treated by the few, er, Orangemen we saw—but everything was so sterile, so cold. Food without flavor. Water—water as if it was purified to perfection."

"You say a white place?" Lee spoke up.

"Not a heavenly sort of white," Eva added.

"More like a limbo," Andrew suggested without emotion.

"Yes," Eva responded. "No sense of time passing, no sense of movement."

"Or place or destination." Andrew tapped his chin. "And then you arrived here, not knowing how you even came to be here."

"Sir," William began, "you act as if you—"

"Speak from experience?" Andrew asked in a flat voice. "Yes, we've all had that experience. All of us sitting here on this dais arrived here the same way as children, some of us with our parents, others with the last dregs of humanity."

"Arrived here as children?" William blinked several times and stared at them. "I don't understand. But that would mean Earth was destroyed—"

"More than fifty years ago by our calculations, at least as we measure time here," Andrew added.

"Here?" Eva asked. "Where are we?"

"We don't rightly know. Other than to say that this is the last human civilization still in existence. What you see here in this city is all we believed was left of mankind."

Petra smiled without showing teeth. "Until you arrived."

Andrew glanced sidelong at her, said nothing, then spoke to the Newcomers. "Your appearance here has presented us with something of a dilemma, I'm afraid. It's something we can explain to you far better in more informal settings. I would suggest we adjourn for the time being. You and your family need a bit more time to recover from your journey privately."

"Sir!" William stood up, pushing off the table. "I don't know what to say, I don't know what I'm allowed to say, but permit me to ask one thing of you before we leave."

"Of course."

"Can we . . . stay?"

"Stay?"

"Permanently, here, with all of you. With other human beings. We can't—we can't go back with the Orangemen."

"I seriously doubt they'd let you," Lee muttered, just loud enough to be heard.

"The Orangemen won't be back for another two years," Hector Phillips explained. "We only ever see their representatives every other year."

"As I said earlier, my wife is a doctor and I'm an engineer," William continued. "Surely there's something we can contribute to your city."

Eva stood with her husband now. "We could not help but notice how primitive things seem to be here. You obviously were not left with much. We could help improve your medicine, your technology—"

Andrew nodded. "Yes, we can always use medical know-how. Tell me, Dr. Tyler, I could not help but notice your accent. Do you speak—I believe the language was called Spanish?"

"Yes," she replied, a wrinkle in her brow. "It was my first language. I was born in Argentina."

"I thought so. The lilt of your letters reminds me of someone I knew long ago, a woman, but she was one of the early settlers who died. She was planning to translate our Spanish books for us before she passed. You see, when we were deposited here, the Orangemen left us with a number of books, a few of which were in languages none of us could read. So we don't know Spanish as a living thing. All we've been able to figure out is what words translate the one Spanish Bible we have into our Latin and English ones. But we don't know pronunciation, all that. It's one of the many things we lost."

Eva smiled. "I would be happy to teach you. And to translate whatever books you have that I can."

"Wonderful, that would be—"

"Mr. Chairman," Lee began, "this is too much. Now really I must ask—"

"Gordon?"

"Technology?" he asked, wide-eyed. "What *technology* can they give us?"

"Gordon," Andrew said. "I believe we're getting ahead of ourselves."

Petra turned on him. "Gordon, come on now—"

Lee held up his hands. "I know technology may not fit into your worldview, Petra, but *really*—don't you think that particular view could stand a bit of—"

Andrew's sharp clack of the gavel, banging now for several seconds, grew louder and more furious. "Gordon, that's the end of it. Let's discuss this later."

Lee gave a mocking bow. "Of course." Then to the Tylers: "Bad manners."

William turned to Andrew. "We'll gladly share with you any knowledge we have and will help in any way we can."

Andrew smiled and nodded. "Of course you will. But let's discuss all of this later, when you're a bit more informed as to the lay of the land here and"—he turned to the generations' table—"emotions are a bit more under control."

He rang a bell to summon the guards to bring the Tylers back to the anteroom, where everyone inside could see the children still waiting.

"Please shut the door on your way out, Lieutenant McQueen," Andrew said.

As the door closed behind the Tylers, a heated silence filled the room. Andrew watched Lee stand up and stretch dramatically. Lee then leaned against the hearth-warmed stone wall with his arms folded and said, "One hundred and forty-four thousand—plus four? And showing up fifty years apart? Now that doesn't quite work, does it?"

CHAPTER 4

"Hey Jake, how's about we take a walk down the beach tomorrow?"

Jacob Weiss had no illusions about why they were going or what they would be talking about. Although technically it was against civil law for serving Council members to speak with friends or relatives about issues before the Council, Andrew, as chairman, also had the right to consult with the military leadership, who happened to be his brother, on matters of defense. So while the brothers were not doing anything technically illegal, that technicality didn't prevent either of them from thinking it might be a wise idea to have their conversation in as isolated a place as possible.

Knowing they would be outside the city walls for most of the day, they both took along light packs with provisions and their carbines. Andrew, the heavier of the brothers and the elder by two years, would want to rest three or so miles into their walk and make camp to eat. Jake, in better physical condition, planned his day around his brother's desires—eat when they decided to rest, walk on for another couple of miles, rest again, then turn back and repeat the rest stops. Jake didn't see such gestures as a burden, having had to consider his older brother's wants since childhood.

Andrew was already on the beach, his pack in the sand at his feet, his rifle lying against it. "Let's walk south."

"Sure," Jake said with a curt nod as he adjusted the straps on his pack and set off.

The brothers said nothing at all for the first mile or so. They walked side by side on the brightening beach. Their shadows, thin and long, stretched out alongside them. They listened to the waves breaking against the shore and smelled the salt air, each seemingly lost in his thoughts and comfortable leaving the other to his. Jake couldn't recall anyone else in his life with whom he could be silent for so long. Certainly not his wife. Amelia and he had filled their time together with endless conversation, even about the most trivial matters. Sometimes they even bickered just to fill the silence.

It's said that you can't be silent for long in the company of someone you're uncomfortable with. Despite their silence, Jake was not always perfectly comfortable with Andy. As much as he loved him, he had never quite come to understand him. He wondered if it was always like that between brothers.

"How's about a break?"

Right on schedule. Andrew laid his rifle in the sand and pulled his pack from his shoulders. With a sigh and a scratch at his shaggy gray hair, he leaned against the pack as he sat in the sand.

Jake stood over his brother, watching him down the edge of his nose, then set his own rifle and pack down. Andrew was obliviously pulling at his bootlaces to free his hot and tired feet.

"Think I'm going to cool my dogs in the surf a bit," Andrew said. "Might still be a bit chilly."

"Sounds good. Be right with you."

A few minutes later the brothers were standing barefoot in the frosty surf, their pants rolled up to just below their knees, feeling the sand under their heels get sucked back into the undertow. The first time they swam in this ocean they had been just kids. A clear memory, despite all the years, one they often recalled together. It was around the time the adults had agreed to begin living together as a community. The proposed city was already being called New Philadelphia, despite the protests of some who wanted to name it New Jerusalem. The brothers, dark haired and strong and lanky, knew the work would require a lot from their developing muscles, but they were eager to help because it would also allow them to come to this beach, someplace they had not been since just after the Arrival. The beach still felt like a reward. A day in the sun and surf—though neither had ever admitted it to anyone but each other, they couldn't imagine the promise of heaven being any better.

Jake smoothed his trim mustache with the L of his thumb and forefinger. "You know, we're going to have to talk at some point, Andy."

Andrew kept his gaze on the horizon, where the blue sky met a slightly darker blue ocean in a clear line. "I don't trust them."

"The Newcomers or the Orangemen?"

He snorted. "Neither."

Jake grunted a laugh.

"I know I don't have any real reason to distrust *our* Orangemen," Andrew added quickly. "They've left us alone and watched over us and have kept us hidden from the Hostiles—but they haven't exactly helped us either."

Jake wiped ocean spray from his wire-frame eyeglasses with his handkerchief. "So why'd they bring us these four? To help us?"

"Or to test us?" Jake added impassively.

Andrew turned back to the horizon. "I think that's the problem here. The Newcomers are *clearly* a test for us. Do we trust them and accept what help they can provide? Or do we spurn their help because we're being offered some of the same vanities and comforts that led to our destruction?"

Jake shook his head. "'Vanities and comforts'—"

"What else would you have me call them?"

"Necessities for our survival."

"Now you sound like my Sofie. Or maybe she's just sounded like her favorite uncle all these years."

"Let's cut to the chase, Andy. What're you asking me?"

"I'm asking you what you think, Jake."

Jake shifted out of the holes his feet had sunk into and milled around his brother in the surf, hands in his pants pockets, head down. "I think none of this makes any damn sense."

"Go on."

"Four Remnant humans *alive* after all this time, Orangemen deciding to drop them off here and now—even trying to understand who and what the Newcomers are is setting our people at odds."

"And how. You should've seen that meeting."

"It seems like a test. But who's testing us?"

"Jake—"

"I'm not trying to be blasphemous. I'm just saying we can't be sure. And not to be paranoid, but how do we know these Orangemen are 'our' Orangemen anyway? Sure, this pair came on the appointed date, but the Hostiles have found us before."

"One rogue Orangeman, that one time—"

"One who did enough damage."

"So that girl says."

Jake looked at his brother, jaw set. "Let's just skip that."

"Skip what? That what happened six years ago up in that clearing has made you a doubting Thomas?"

"The point is that the Newcomers' presence is stirring up debate among our people, getting us to distrust ourselves, our beliefs."

Andrew chuckled. "You've never feared—what'd you call it?— 'healthy debate' before."

"This is more than debate. Or about *our* differences of opinion about what the Orangemen are."

"Opinion, you say—"

"This is the beginning of factionalism, the kind that causes lines to be drawn and wars to be fought, just like the ones we've read about and feared all our lives. Some, like Grace, are going to take the appearance of the Tylers as the fulfillment of Revelation. Others are going to say it can't be—that the foretold thousand years haven't yet passed."

"Go on."

"Look, we haven't had any strife in all the years we've been here. No wars. No crime. Despite all our initial differences in backgrounds and faiths, we've all developed a single set of beliefs: that what happened to us, both here and on Earth, sure as hell looked like it was Revelation fulfilled. If God really gave us anything through the Orangemen, he gave us peace and unity on this rock. And now we're at risk of losing it."

Andrew was quiet for a moment. "Point taken. Anything else?"

"Just one more piece of paranoia I'd like you to indulge."

"Shoot."

"We know the power of the Orangemen. We know that prophecy foretold that only a certain number of people were supposed to survive—the exact number that in fact did. So here are my questions: How do we know that these four really are the risen pagans of Revelation? Hell, how do we know if they're even human?"

Andrew's eyes took on a stung look, as if he had just been smacked in the mouth. "God in heaven. What do we do?"

"If they're Hostiles?" Jake mused on this for a few moments. "Drive them out. Or kill them if we can."

"And if they are human?"

Jake threw up his hands. "Then Grace may be right."

"How can she be?" Andrew growled. "As you rightly note, the prophesized thousand years haven't passed."

"I'm not sure. But on the off chance she is right, then I don't know what to do. But we better find out what they are for certain before we do a damn thing."

Gordon Lee stirred himself out of his twisted sheets to face his day. He would later admit in his journal that nothing about the day seemed like it would be one filled with epiphanies. Half-awake, he had overheard Sofie rushing the girls off to school about an hour earlier—so much intense shushing whenever one of the young loud-mouths came near his bedroom door—but all of that frantic energy had dispersed, leaving their house abnormally quiet. It was in that quiet hour that he tried to twist himself back to oblivion again, only to find thoughts of his dreary existence keeping him on the less pleas-ant side of dreaming.

For several minutes he stared at the exposed beams of the ceiling, thinking about the amount of heat lost on any given cold night in this house. He came up with a rough (but fairly accurate, he thought) estimate and then multiplied it by the number of homes in the city, shaving off percentages here and points there. After another minute he decided to discount the oldest buildings, which were fully exposed on all four sides to the elements (if he had had his druthers, they would have been pulled down a decade ago), and concentrate on ones like his own, built in rows and better protected. Ten minutes after he had begun he had a number in his head, representing the total amount of energy wasted across the city each night the temperature dipped below freezing. The actual number didn't matter. What did matter was that he knew he could do nothing about it. Or about much else in this backward world.

Stumbling out of bed, he scratched his trim chest and shambled over to his dresser, where he poured cool water from the pitcher into the basin and splashed some on his face. Then he wandered into the kitchen to see if Sofie had left him a fresh pot of coffee. He closed his eyes in bliss when he saw that she had—just needed some warming. Sofie was very considerate and very good-looking—a wonderful combination if one must be married to only one woman. He stirred the coals in the fireplace, set the pot on the grate, and ate a torn-off chunk of bread while he waited for the coffee to perk.

She really was a fine wife—strong and smart and *determined*. The walls between theirs and the houses next door were thin enough to make him realize he could've married a god-awful shrew. She knew that his work—primitive as it was—was important and mentally challenging. Yes, it required him to work odd hours, but she always gave him enough space in which to do it and kept their three little loudmouths at bay. She even tolerated his occasional frustrated rants because she knew he was right and agreed with him. More than agreed with him. Encouraged him to do as much as he could, almost as if she could see the future he wanted as much as he did.

His greatest frustration—his lifelong bafflement really—was the Remnants' blind acceptance of their lot. They *tolerated* so much of what happened to them. And tried to block out what they knew they had lost. They made do with the primitive weapons and tools the Orangemen had left them with. They revered the scant number of books they'd found in the containers and shrugged off what was missing—the vast, unimaginable treasure trove only hinted at in their surviving volumes.

Yet nothing—bar none—frustrated him more than the infamous missing collection of Eastern books listed among the initial inventory. The religious books on Buddhism and Hinduism and the like, he could not care less about. But there had been so much more there, books on science and mathematics. Perhaps some moron had left the box too close to the tide or had decided to use the books for kindling. It didn't matter. Their loss was a personal irritation to Lee, who had been told all his life that his ancestors hailed from a place called China, one of the most ancient and revered civilizations on Earth-of-old. So much of its knowledge only glimpsed now, so many questions left unanswered. Who was Confucius? What was the I Ching? What was in Chairman Mao's *Little Red Book* that had stirred a generation?

And why did the Bible not mention China at all? Every time he read it, Lee tried to find China in it—perhaps by another name—but could find nothing that seemed to fit with the pieces of information he had on it. He couldn't imagine any reason for God wanting to hide an entire civilization. And for that reason among others he found it hard to believe God was behind any of this at all.

Not knowing about China was one thing. Knowing just a bit about the old world's technical advancements and not always having the tools to recreate them was an entirely other matter. Cures to so many diseases. Long-distance wireless communications. Nuclear power. Spaceflight. All things human beings had once achieved but could not recreate with their level of technical know-how and lack of raw materials. Instead he found himself puttering around trying to perfect gas-lighting for people who often feared it and lived in a city with wooden water pipes and compost piles in their backyards. Pathetic.

He glanced at the mantel above the fireplace and spotted the bottle of homemade whiskey given to him by one of his colleagues on his last birthday, then heard the spattering hiss of the coffee. Irish coffee. At least they hadn't lost knowledge of every creature comfort.

CHAPTER 5

In matters that are so obscure and far beyond our vision, we find in Holy Scripture passages which can be interpreted in very different ways without prejudice to the faith we have received. In such cases, we should not rush in headlong and so firmly take our stand on one side that, if further progress in the search for truth justly undermines this position, we too fall with it.

—Augustine of Hippo

Petra rapped three times on Grace's front door. The old woman met her at the threshold after a few moments. She'd been visiting her mentor each morning since the Newcomers' entrance into the city. The Newcomers' sudden appearance meant a great change was coming—one that she and Grace, as fellow teachers and spiritual leaders of the community, agreed they must help prepare the people for.

Grace greeted her wearing a brown shawl over her bony shoulders. She was shivering despite having a good fire already blazing in her fieldstone hearth. Set atop the grill on the fire was Grace's teakettle, a hand-forged Christmas gift Petra had given her some fifteen years earlier when their relationship was one of teacher and student. The kettle began to whistle at almost the same moment Petra crossed the threshold. Securing her long red hair in a ponytail to keep it from the fire, she lifted the

---

kettle as Grace brought out handmade teacups and a plain breakfast of freshly baked bread, fruit jams, nuts, and cheese. Once places were set at the table nearest the fireplace, the two women bent their heads and folded their hands.

"Bless us, O Lord," Grace prayed, "and these thy gifts, which we are about to receive from thy bounty, through Christ our Lord. Amen."

"Amen," Petra repeated, then pulled off her gray cotton turtleneck sweater.

She knew whenever she visited Grace that she needed to do two things: dress in layers and pack her patience. In addition to Grace keeping her home almost stiflingly warm, she liked to "jaw"—as she called it—for a while before getting to the important matters at hand. It was a pretty common avoidance mechanism used by many Remnants.

Grace talked about the birth of the twin Abu girls two doors down a week earlier and how their parents, Rotimi and Frances, had invited everyone to the baptism scheduled for that afternoon. She talked about how her houseplants needed so much water because of the heat inside the house. She talked about the Shakespeare sonnets she had read when she woke up at five and the Psalms she had read before going to sleep last night at midnight—then suggested almost as an aside that Petra might want to consider getting her seventh graders started on both. Petra made a mental note of that as Grace picked up a blanket she had been knitting, a beautiful thing composed of rich intricate swirls of warm earth tones, and joked that it was something no one at her age should ever contemplate beginning unless she had a written guarantee from the Big Man Upstairs that she'd live at least another year.

Jokes about her imminent yet never arriving demise always elicited a wheezy laugh from Grace. Petra just fixed a grin back at her, never comfortable enough with such easy talk of death. While she believed in the afterlife, she had experienced enough death in her forty-nine years of life not to make light of it. Death—the existence of it, the reverence for it, the guilt associated with it among the Remnants who had lived to old age—had clung to her childhood home like a musk. Patrick and Carolyn Rogers had been broken by the death they had witnessed on Earth in the last days. Her parents could never really talk about what had happened, not even with the other adult Remnants. She knew her parents had been married on Earth some years before the Apocalypse, but to this day she had no idea if they had had other children there. Her father had been nearly forty when she was born three years after the Arrival. Those blank years had haunted her, even as a child. Petra was convinced that whenever her parents had looked at her they never saw anything but dead faces that resembled her own.

Yet her parents' losses had helped to form and strengthen Petra's own faith. Whenever they had talked of good things from Earth-of-old, she could see the hand of a loving God at work. And she saw that hand even at the worst times in her own life: when her husband, Sam, and her older son, Christian, long gone, had been lost at sea. She knew the grief should have destroyed her. Yet it hadn't. God had carried her in her time of grief just as he had her parents. She saw God's hand now, helping to purify and ready humanity for the new world coming in the days ahead. If her parents could have her and still find purpose, despite witnessing the end of human civilization—maybe even the deaths of their own children—who was she to have doubts?

"The people aren't ready," Grace said, stirring Petra out of her memories. "There is uncertainty in the air. And fear. People who are unsure of what will come next will fight because in changing times they cling to what they already know." She set her nearly empty teacup on the table. "You need to make them understand, Petra. You need to help us keep the peace."

"Me? Wait. Don't you mean us, Grace?"

Grace laughed. Her arms were folded across the sunken breasts of her reed-thin chest, the palm of her right hand pressed to her face. "Child, how long do you think I'm going to live? I'm blessed that I've lived this long and seen so much. I've seen this city built and generations born. And now I've seen the Newcomers. But when New Jerusalem descends from heaven like a bride, I'll already be on the other side. *You* have to prepare the people, you and those who follow you. All I can do is help you as much as I can for as long as I can."

"What's coming, Grace? We've talked about so many things. I see that things are changing—and I feel that they are—but I don't understand everything. And the timeline in Revelation is, well—"

Grace laughed again. "Muddled?"

"Well, yeah."

"Think so, huh?" Grace nodded once, twice, as if she had been simply waiting for a question to be asked and now knew it was the time to answer it. "Fair enough. And so it is muddled. That's why it had so many interpretations before we got here. But I still see prophecy being fulfilled, as many did in the end days. As we all did that first day on the beach when, out of that chaos, all of our children were miraculously returned to us—*every single one of them*—at the very same instant."

Petra took her thick-veined hand, as knotty and as fragile as a dry tree branch, and gave it a gentle squeeze. "Tell me what you see and how you see it."

"You Firsters never believe us old-timers when we talk like this."

"We do. We've never lost faith or had doubts. We just believe in peace more than in walls and standing armies."

"Peace will come, in God's own time. But not without strife."

"Tell me. Please."

"The one hundred and forty-four thousand survived. And in the years since, we've begun to rebuild humanity. We've been rewarded with peace among ourselves—and with others," she said, bumping her chin skyward. "Now a new time is coming. These four—they're the beginning of what Revelation describes as the pagan resurrection. You heard the Tylers. They're good people. But they don't know God. They love knowledge without wisdom and they survived like animals, instinctually—by burying themselves in holes. But they, like all of us, will be raised for judgment. And more will come. Whether this will happen before, during, or after the last great rebellion, I don't know. But all things will be made new. It has been foretold. And now we're witnessing it."

"How do we—how do I—get the people to understand what's to come?"

Grace put the younger woman's hand between her old ones. "Follow the Apostles. Go out and preach the good news. Gather the believers, and get them to preach as well."

Petra thought of her students, her duties. She pictured her desk at home piled with papers. She then thought of John and was glad he was grown. It made it easier to walk away from everything else.

"When should I start?"

Grace looked at the light shining through her window. Outside were the first stirrings of the morning—footsteps, greetings, conversations, laughter. "No time like the present."

Right on time. Hard not to spot that ramrod-straight posture in this crowd. Always the good soldier. Always on schedule. Always doing what he's supposed to do, even with his doubts.

"Uncle Jake?"

"Sofie." She held up her cheek for him to kiss. "Good to see you. What're you doing out this way?"

"Off to my shift in equipment repair." She looked at her uncle for a long moment. "Were you just out to the cemetery?"

He grinned. "Getting pretty regular in my habits, eh?"

"Yeah."

"You ever go out there to see your mom?"

"Not really. I don't see much of a point." She tucked a lock of strawberry-blond hair behind her ear. "So, you've heard about what

Grace and Petra have been doing lately? Going out and preaching about the Newcomers?"

"Sure. Why?"

"Did you know they're planning on having a big meeting in Central Square tonight?"

"I've heard mention."

"And it doesn't . . . worry you?"

"Why should it?"

"Uncle Jake."

"They've a right to free speech. I think they're just trying to ease people's fears. No harm in that."

"How's talking about a possible last rebellion against God easing people's fears?"

"Sofie, you know it's not as simple as that. They're talking about something that leads to everlasting peace—"

"Come on, Uncle Jake."

"Listen, I have to run. I'll be by soon to see your girls, and maybe we can talk then, okay?"

Sofie watched her uncle walk down into the crowded street, his posture back to full attention as he acknowledged hellos from acquaintances with that confident nod of his. A moment later she felt a familiar arm slip around her waist and a pair of lips kiss her cheek. She didn't turn to face her husband.

"Got the supplies," Lee said as he rubbed her back. "Was that your uncle I saw you talking to?"

"Yes."

"Does he know about the glorious revival meeting tonight?"

"Yup. And, like Dad, he's doing *nothing* about it." Sofie turned to him. "So the question is, what're you going to do about it, Gordon?"

58

That evening, Central Square was filled with hundreds upon hundreds of Remnants and Firsters and Seconds, all standing in various attitudes. Grace and Petra were on a canopied platform that occupied the center of the square. Grace had spoken for much of the time and was now eating and resting at the back of the platform as Petra preached and answered questions shouted out by members of the crowd.

"You must not give in to doubt or fear," Petra continued. "Don't consult such emotions. Push them out. We have all endured great hardships, lost many loved ones. But we have been purified and made stronger by our trials and struggles. A new breed of humanity lives here, divorced from hatred and petty jealousies. We can worship God with clear hearts, knowing we are loved and ready for judgment along with our pagan brothers and sisters who—yes, as we have seen, praise God—have begun to rise from the dead."

"Oh really, this is too much!" a voice, not from the platform, said quite loudly. The crowd turned almost in unison to discover Gordon Lee standing against a nearby tree.

Petra, stunned into silence, stared at him until Grace appeared by her side. Grace leaned over the platform's edge, balancing herself on her cane, and said in a quiet but firm voice: "If you're drunk, go home and sober up, my son. We can talk later. There's no use in your being here now."

Smirking and putting a finger aside of his nose, he then wagged it at her. "You'd like it if I were drunk, wouldn't you? It'd make these people doubt what I have to say. But apart from a glass of wine with dinner, I can assure you I'm quite sober. So I won't let a little drinking get in the way of my logic—though I do hope my logic will get in the way of these people's belief in the complete accuracy of your prophecy."

Lee then mounted the three steps and stood on the platform just to the left of Petra and Grace. He smiled at them, then turned to the assembly. "My friends, I think it is important—especially among the faithful like ourselves—to question interpretations made by a select few of a specific, shall we say, generational demographic."

"No one has ever said you couldn't," Grace said clearly enough so that the audience could know a debate was on.

Lee smiled thinly at her. "True enough. But our own thoughts in such matters are often disregarded unless they agree fully with the ruling generation. But I digress." He turned back to the crowd. "The point is we just simply don't have all of the information. And we haven't *ever* had all of the information. We have but a handful of books from Earth-of-old. A mere handful. Why this selection, I don't know. Perhaps this was God's way of letting us know the true path. Fair enough. I won't debate the larger point. But we can all agree that all our lives we've been told to look back to the Bible for proof that the prophecies about the end times had come, just as it was foretold in Revelation. I'm here to tell you that we've been getting only one interpretation of events, just one—*their* interpretation." Here he pointed at Grace and Petra. "The Bible, as you all well know, does not present exact dates or clear facts. It also, it must be said, does not spell out destiny through prophecy alone. So let me be clear: no destiny, no clear historical record."

He held up pleading hands. "So what's my point? Friends, some of our other books tell us that dinosaurs once walked the Earth, that all life evolved from lower life-forms. These truths are not in the Bible. They were discovered because men like us devoted their lives to uncovering them one fact at a time. Let us take a cue from them. Let us devote this time to truly understanding humanity's end and its new beginning here on this planet. Let us decide for ourselves how Revelation speaks to us as individuals—not simply as adherents to an orthodoxy. Let us, in the end, think for ourselves, decide for ourselves what the Newcomers mean."

The heat of the crowd, not that long ago fueled by devotion to the prophecies being revealed by Grace and Petra, dissipated, leaving behind a sudden absence of noise. A moment had come and passed. A click. A connection. A change.

Grace took a step forward and looked at Lee, intently studying him in full view of the audience.

"Gordon, you talk about evolution as if this is some sort of new revelation." Her play on words brought up chuckles from the crowd. "We know the Bible cannot be taken literally in that sense. But the Bible is inspired and inerrant, and what it teaches *is* the truth. Saint Augustine, as you may recall, did not believe that the six days in the creation story were *literal* days, since it was absurd to imagine mornings and evenings could exist with no sun to have them."

"Which just proves my point—that Scripture has more to offer than just your interpretation."

"Let me finish. Genesis is the way the creation of life was explained to our ancestors. It says the Lord created the Earth in six days. But who can say how long a day is in God's eye? And who says that the seventh day of rest isn't the time between the Lord's first and second comings? We can't—we mustn't—read everything literally. But the guideposts are still there, markers we must recognize. And I'm telling you that we're seeing such a marker today!"

"Because of what Revelation says?"

"Yes. Because of Revelation," Grace responded, her puckered chin held high in defiance.

"Let's go over what Revelation says exactly, shall we?" He smirked. "The world was destroyed?"

"Burned out to a pulp," she said with a lost look in her eyes. "We all saw it. Endless days of suffering. Those not destroyed in the initial attack, which, as Revelation says, burned a third of the Earth, died from the lack of food, plague, the poisoned water, or under the heels of the invading armies. The Orangemen coming down—you can't imagine it." She looked at him from under weary eyebrows. "Do we have to go through this?"

A genuine sense of sorrow passed over Lee's face. "This must be unpleasant for you. I apologize and will refrain from additional questions in this area. So yes—the Earth was destroyed and the Remnants survived."

"Yes, we did. Only later, after we conducted the first census, did we begin to believe we were truly the firstfruits, sealed by God."

"Sealed how? On the forehead, according to Revelation?"

"Again you're being too literal."

"Please bear with me. Weren't the survivors supposed to be *Jewish* people?"

"We are of the twelve *spiritual* tribes of Israel. We even came down in twelve cargo containers, each holding twelve thousand people. Are some of us Jewish ethnically? Yes. These days it's likely all of us have some Jewish blood in us somewhere."

He wagged his finger at Grace again. "Seems you're getting off here on a technicality."

"And you are using technicalities to undermine inherent truths of our faith. If you had been alive in the last days and during the days after the Arrival, you would not be filled with such—"

"What, reservation?"

She made a face, as if she had tasted something bitter. "Mischief."

"Don't go back to that old chestnut about not being here during the Arrival. We who were born later really can't help that!"

"If only you had been," Grace continued. "Maybe then you'd understand how much we've gained. You'd know all that has passed from us, the ways of war and division, that you'd better appreciate what our faith has accomplished here. True peace for the first time in human history."

"Peace through conformity. Peace through reverential awe and fear of the unknown."

"'Unknown.' We saw them!" Grace said, her voice filling with emotion. "We saw them, all of us. Angels they were, perfect in face and form and bearing. At first we feared they were the ones who destroyed us—but they brought us here from the White Place, they gave us redemption, they gave us and our children a peace unlike man had ever known—"

John had been watching the exchange for some time before he saw Kendra's short-cropped dark hair in the crowd and forced his way through to her. She was standing with several soldiers, all from his company. Her bright-blue eyes flashed a look of relief at him. "Where have you been during all this fun, Captain?"

He laughed. "Where's Weiss?"

"Dunno. Nobody seems to be in charge of security here."

"I don't like where this is going."

"Just give the word."

He nodded. "Much as I'd like to, I think you better take the lead."

"A little awkward with your mom up there, huh?"

"Uh-huh. And not to mention Gordon."

Kendra gave a couple of nods, and a half dozen soldiers followed her onstage, John a step behind her. She barked a "Pipe down!" at Lee before heading over to Grace and Petra to tell them in a kind but firm way to go home. Lee griped behind her back, "Oh now Weiss has got his favorite pet doing his dirty work for him, eh?"

"Gordon," John said gently, a hand on Lee's arm. "Time to go home."

Lee turned on him. "And you, John? They must think it awfully funny to send my wife's old boyfriend here to shut me up."

"Come on, Gordon. Enough. Please."

"Johnny," Petra said, "we're not afraid of what he has to say. Let him speak. Daylight is the best antiseptic."

"Mom, please. Look at the crowd. This is getting out of control, and you know it. Grace, tell her."

Before Grace could answer, Lee shoved John's hand from his arm. "I'm not going anywhere. These people want to hear what I have to say." He turned to them. "Don't you want to hear what I've got to say?"

A roar of approval rose from the crowd, mingled with a fair amount of boos. Kendra stepped in and said through gritted teeth, "Move or I will carry your skinny ass out of here in front of your adoring fans."

But the crowd was still murmuring, which only egged Lee on. "Their interpretation is bollocks. We were brought to this world! Where does it say that in Revelation? Humanity was supposed to rebuild the Earth, not this backward planet. And the New Jerusalem is supposed to come from heaven, *not* be this poor imitation built from the sweat of our brows. My God, think for yourselves—"

"Lieutenant," John said as he and Kendra grabbed Lee under his arms. A quick glance over his shoulder brought the other soldiers forward to take his mother and Grace from the stage.

No one made any effort to interfere. Coming down the steps, John challenged the grumbling crowd with a steely gaze as he had been trained to do. The eyes of hundreds of men and women and children peeled away from his. Long after he had left the scene he carried those looks with him. Their faces were like ones he had seen in photos in the Archives. They had been the faces of terrified citizens living in a police state.

CHAPTER 6

John had been meaning to talk to Kendra since that night at the gate-house with the Newcomers. He had seen her several times in the weeks since, always while on duty. And when he had tried to find her in the off-hours, she was nowhere to be seen. He didn't ask her bunkmates where she was, nor anyone else she was friendly with—not that Kendra had many close friends. He wanted to see her, sure. But he didn't want anyone to get the wrong idea. He wanted to help if he could and was ready to accept any help she could offer in return.

But it wasn't just bad timing that had prevented him from seeing her. General Weiss had asked him and a handful of trusted officers to guard the Newcomers. The Tylers weren't prisoners, officially, but they hadn't been allowed to mix with the general population either. The doctors had recommended a general quarantine of at least two months. *No one knows what germs they carry* was the official justification. But John—as well as anyone else with half a brain—knew that he and his fellow officers were the Tylers' jailers in everything but name. What he hadn't realized was that he was also becoming their friend.

The Newcomers had been living in a house in an isolated section of the city, an area that was home to much of New Philadelphia's textile and furniture manufacturing—what little of it there was. It was a noisy neighborhood by day but very quiet at night. John had read about such neighborhoods on Earth-of-old and tried to imagine what those streets must've felt like at night, long after the quitting-time whistles had blown.

The house itself, built long before that section became a commercial area, was a fine one. It had been constructed early in the city's history by a long-dead Remnant, an architect on Earth-of-old. He had designed it in the style of an Italian villa, with a columned interior courtyard garden still bursting with lush cultivated greenery. If it were a prison, it was certainly a very comfortable one, despite the daytime noise from the surrounding streets. Often when John assumed his post, he found the whole Tyler family in the sun-dappled courtyard, the parents watching the children race between shrubs and columns before sitting down to eat a meal.

No one had ordered John not to talk to them. And in spite of the quarantine, he hadn't even been asked to adhere to basic protocols— something he knew his grandfather would have insisted upon if a true quarantine situation existed. Maybe it was because he felt comfortable talking with the Tylers. Maybe it was just because he was naturally curious about them. Or maybe the Weiss brothers figured the best way to get intelligence was to have trusted men like him strike up easy conversations with these mysterious strangers. Whatever the reasoning, it didn't matter. Here he was.

His conversation with William Tyler that morning was the main reason he'd spent the day looking for Kendra. The two men had been in the courtyard enjoying the comfortable morning air in lightweight jackets. The noise from the street was little more than a dull background rumble from where they were sitting.

William had looked out across the courtyard from a bench in the garden, his elbows on his knees and his hands folded between them. "So you all think the Orangemen are the angels and demons described in the Bible?" His broad face, recently freed of its beard, was bright pink and clean-looking.

"Can't speak for all of us."

"But most, right?"

"The Remnants witnessed the events, so they can speak to them better than I can," John said, sitting next to William. The children were playing nearby. Eva was somewhere inside. "Many of them were nonbelievers before the last days on Earth, so the realization didn't come easily for them. Grace Davison, if you can imagine it, was what she likes to call an 'evangelical atheist,' a psychology professor who had built her career 'dismantling' religions."

William shrugged. His thin shoulders swam in a white shirt a size or two too big for him. "It's not so unbelievable. Alcoholics often become the greatest teetotalers."

"I know you're skeptical about this."

"Not skeptical, just a bit surprised that everyone accepted the attacks as prophecy fulfilled."

"Is it really that surprising? The world *was* destroyed, just as predicted in Revelation. And exactly the number predicted in Revelation was saved. And since that time we've built a new kind of human race here—also predicted. Our society doesn't have any of the troubles of Earth-of-old. No one goes hungry. No one steals. No one has ever been seriously assaulted by another citizen. No one has ever been murdered."

"But it's not a Utopia. You're all forced to serve in the military, aren't you?"

"It's not a military; it's a defense force. And we're not forced. If we're healthy enough for it, we're asked. Everyone understands the need to protect the little bit of the human race that's still alive."

"And what if someone did refuse? Would they be ostracized?"

John shook his head. "No one has ever refused, because we all understand why it's so important to serve."

"You're describing a kind of group society collaborating in a way I find hard to imagine."

"Isn't that the point? People here aren't like the ones you remember."

"Come on!" William said with a laugh, deep and rich. "No grudges at all? Rivalries? People who just don't like each other's faces?"

"We know there were once all kinds of divisions in the world. The books we have tell us that much. But we don't see any divisions between us. We only see the human race—and we'll protect that with our lives."

"Please don't think—"

"I don't think anything. You're just asking questions."

"I think I'm dancing around the big one, though." William cracked his neck, as if to prep himself. "Okay, so I'm asking, Captain. Are you certain about what the Orangemen are?"

John kept his voice flat, his face expressionless. "You mean certain that they're angels? They're winged creatures with perfect forms. Some protect us. Others hunt us, looking to do us harm just as the fallen angels did in the Bible."

William held up his hands. "I'm sorry. I'm not trying to question your beliefs as much as understand them better. But let me ask this: among the Remnants, were there any scientists or doctors? I mean, not just psychologists like Grace Davison."

"Sure. Quite a few."

"Did any of them think the Orangemen might be something else? I mean, you're all not even certain that the Orangemen were the ones who destroyed the Earth, right?"

"The Friendlies told the Remnants very early on what had happened, that fallen members of their race had destroyed humanity. And to answer your first question, my paternal grandfather was a doctor. He always had a lot of theories. But he and the others, after seeing what they saw and reading Scripture, accepted that the Orangemen were the angels and demons of the end times. At least, that's what they told us."

Tyler rubbed his clean-shaven face and looked straight at John. "Did anyone ever think the Orangemen might simply be aliens?"

"Aliens?"

"Yeah. Not angels. Not demons. Just intelligent beings from other worlds."

"I remember my grandfather once saying there was a lot of discussion in that direction early on. But the ones who had been scientists couldn't safely *prove* they were aliens. I think what they felt and saw in the last days convinced them that these weren't just another kind of mortal being."

"Understandable."

"I mean, think about it," John continued. "Think about all the years humanity had searched the nearby stars and had never discovered even the slightest *hint* of intelligent life."

"You know about the searches for extraterrestrial life?"

"Whatever I could find in the Archives, though there's not much. In fact, we don't have any books on astronomy, though we do have one or two about searches for aliens."

William smiled at that. "Of course, just because we didn't find them doesn't mean aliens don't exist."

"You've got a funny way of thinking about things, Will. No offense. The authority of a hundred and forty-four thousand *eyewitnesses*—far more eyewitnesses than the original Apostles—saw this and believed. Yet you'd toss out all that testimony in support of a theory that aliens must exist simply because the galaxy is so big and somebody has to be filling up some of that space. I mean, that's the crux of the argument, right?"

"But what if?" William urged. "What if the Orangemen *are* aliens? And what if them looking like the angels from Scripture is just a simple twist of fate?"

When he finally saw Kendra, she was sauntering down the street toward the barracks from the direction of Central Square, her hands in her front hip pockets, lost in thought. He stood directly in her path until she looked up, blinking as she recognized him. She whistled low and long and pushed her olive-brown cap back on her head with her thumb under its bill.

"Wanna go grab a beer?" she asked. "You look like you need it."

"Sure. That is, if you're buying."

"Be glad to, once they ditch this impeccable bartering system of ours. But let's not hit the usual places."

"Lead on, Lieutenant."

While most people bottled their own liquor, there were about five bars in the whole city that served beer of decent quality. Kendra and John knew most of them very well and almost everyone in them. So he had little idea where she planned on going to avoid the usuals until she ducked into a corner shop—really no more than a stand that traded staples from an old couple's front room—and emerged a minute later with two bottles and a grin spreading across her wide mouth.

"No beer. Red and white wine, though. One of each. Probably bottled ten minutes ago and not worth the two hours of cleaning I promised the owners to get them."

"Fine. Where we going to go? The square?"

"Nah. I know a place."

"Oh you *know* a place."

"Yeah." Her smile was cocked higher on one side than the other. "Interested?"

A few minutes later he found himself being led back into the industrial part of town where the Tylers were being sequestered. For a second he was sure Kendra was leading him to their house. Could she have figured out where they were being kept? But then she turned down the next street and made her way to the city wall. The section she seemed to be looking for was about halfway between the two closest gatehouses. They could see the guards in both towers in the middle distance, their silhouettes a hard black against the starlit night sky.

John had little idea what was going on as he watched Kendra glance from one guard tower to the other.

She handed him both bottles. "Watch the streets, okay?"

He nodded and kept a lookout but wasn't surprised to find the streets empty on all sides at this hour. People were staying home for a lot of reasons—to talk, to speculate, to sleep. Familiar surroundings were always a comfort if one feared the future.

When he turned back, Kendra was nowhere to be seen. He could see straight down the wall for blocks and had a clear view of the street heading out perpendicularly before him. Gone. Completely vanished. But she couldn't have just disappeared. Stealthy as she was, he was sure he would've heard the crunching of the gravel all around them. He looked back and forth, squinting into the night.

"Hey!"

The call came from just to his right, near to the ground. He looked down. There was a hole in the wall that hadn't been there a second ago. Kendra's dark head was sticking out of it, her eyes bright blue and bemused.

"Hiya."

"What the hell—"

"Just make sure the coast's clear before you follow," she said, and was gone. Then her head popped out again. "And don't break the bottles."

A quick glance around and he was in the hole, bottles tucked into his leather jacket and buttoned tight against his chest. What he had ducked into wasn't a hole as much as a tunnel that—if Kendra's lantern light in front of him was any indication—led clear through the thick city wall and out into the countryside behind it.

The light he had followed was gone when he got to the outer opening. The rich smell of dewy vegetation all around him was overwhelming, a living perfume. Ten paces from the wall he could see Kendra's pale face in the moonlight, partly hidden by shrubs. He waited for her to give him an all-clear sign and then joined her. Lying

71

next to her, their faces obscured from each other by leaves of grass, he heard her say, "Watch this." Then she tugged on a half-buried rope of serious vintage.

The rope pulled up a stone that perfectly sealed the tunnel. Even from their close proximity, he couldn't tell that there was a void behind it.

"The rope also replaced the slab at the other end at the same time."

"Did you build this?"

"Nah. Found it. A long time ago. Me and Alex used to sneak out this way as kids. Come on."

Alex. The offhand reference to her dead boyfriend didn't hit him as hard as the fact that a six-year-old mystery had suddenly been solved. He followed her through an overgrown path into the hills. The bottles clinked dry and safe in his jacket.

The first time he had met Kendra McQueen she was fourteen years old and had been missing for three days. He was a young lieutenant then, twenty-four years old, years past his relationship with Sofie Weiss. Was she already married to Gordon then? God yes, and for a long time too. It didn't matter. All that mattered was his career, moving up the ranks, doing what was asked of him. With his father and Christian gone, with his mother growing ever more connected to her faith to better understand their deaths, finding purpose in orders and rigors made sense to him then.

He was part of the search-and-rescue effort for Kendra. No one wanted to call it a recovery yet, although many feared that she had been killed by one of the animals in the hills. How she had gotten outside was a mystery, but after three days of searching inside the walls it was clear she was no longer in the city. And Alexander Raymond, her boyfriend, didn't seem to know anything about her disappearance.

No one suspected malice. There had never been a crime committed in all of their history. But many of the old-timers began to wonder if something was amiss. When it was suggested they search outside the city, the Council agreed to it readily. There was comfort in that. If they found Kendra's bones picked clean beyond the walls, the civilization they had built was still safe.

When he first spotted Kendra in the woods, the moon was high and out over the tops of the trees in a cloudless sky. He remembered following it with his eyes for a long time, looking at its ever-present hazy dust cloud and wondering once again how and when that V-shaped crack had marred its face. After searching the surrounding hills for several hours, he found himself in a clearing. At its southern edge, just as it sloped off to a rugged lower valley near a stream, was a young girl, bluish pale in that moonlight, wrapped in a colonel's olive-brown field jacket. He remembered her hair was dark and ratty. It looked unwashed. Only later did he learn that it was caked with blood. But her eyes he had never forgotten. Not because of their color, a somewhat eerie sky blue, but because of their lack of fear. Not the eyes of a scared young girl, lost for more than three days. Tired eyes, worried eyes, yes, but there was something steady there too—maybe something new. He couldn't make sense of those eyes or of her. As he stepped nearer, he heard a sound just over his left shoulder and turned to find Colonel Weiss leveling a carbine at him, a discarded pile of dry wood in the grass at his feet.

"Thank God." Weiss shouldered his weapon. "I was just going to build a fire and wait for help to come in the morning. But now that you're here—" A glance at the girl told her not to worry. "Are you tired, son?"

"No, sir."

"Good. Drop your pack."

John did as he was told. The girl watched them from inside the colonel's jacket a few feet away. Weiss approached her and gestured for his lieutenant to follow.

"Kendra." He crouched by her. "I'm going to ask Lieutenant Giordano to take you home. Remember what we talked about. You don't have to tell anyone what happened without me there, not even your folks. No one. Understand?"

She nodded once, twice. Her oval face was calm, her wide mouth almost serene. Her eyes left the older man's face only for a second to glance at John. "Colonel, where are you—"

"I'm going to stay and take care of things, just like I promised. And John here is going to help me once he brings you home." Weiss looked over the rims of his glasses at John, who nodded. "That okay, Kendra?"

"Yes, sir. Thank you."

He didn't smile, just rubbed his thick-fingered hand on her shoulder. Then he stood and thumbed to John to follow. As they stood at the end of the clearing away from Kendra, Weiss gave his orders without taking his weary eyes off the girl.

"The girl has blood all over her. Most of it is not hers. Her only serious wound is on the heel of her foot. Might be infected. So you'll have to carry her. But she's probably all of ninety pounds. Think you can handle that?"

"Yes, sir."

"Once you get her home, get her a doctor your grandfather would've trusted, not one of the resident quacks. *Don't* talk to her parents. *Don't* ask her anything at all. She may want to talk to you on the way down. Try to keep her quiet, but don't force her to shut up. And whatever she does say to you, even if it's to tell you she's got to pee, it's a military secret, understood?"

"Yes, sir."

"Once she's home and you've got a doctor, haul ass back here. Tell no one—and I mean no one—where you're going. You and I have a job to do."

Weiss was right. Kendra probably hadn't been more than ninety pounds then. The colonel's jacket, wide enough to fit across his burly back, hung off her in a shapeless heap and was too big for her everywhere except in the sleeves, where her bare wrists stuck out from them by at least three inches. Mostly reed-thin arms and legs she was then, gangly and awkward. A child growing a woman's body in hiccuping fits and starts. She said nothing as Weiss lifted her onto John's back and gave her shoulder a final squeeze. She spoke only after they had left the clearing. "Don't worry if you've gotta put me down or something."

"I won't for a while," he said. "But you'll be the first to know."

John wondered as he walked what he might say to his soldiers if they found him in the field carrying the girl they were all searching for—and avoiding all contact with any of them. Sofie used to always say he was never a very good liar. Whenever she said something he completely disagreed with, he'd give her a noncommittal grunt and she'd laugh and call him on it. To try to become a good liar when he didn't even know what the hell was going on . . .

"It doesn't make any sense."

He hadn't been sure if Kendra was talking to him or herself, so he said nothing.

"I mean, that's what you're thinking, right?" she asked. "That it doesn't make sense."

"Wasn't thinking anything."

"Liar." She rolled the word out long. It was a kid's taunt, with a bit of flirtation to it. "It doesn't make sense to me, and I know more than you do. So I'm thinking you're thinking that it makes *no* sense."

"I'm just glad we found you. I'm glad to be the one who takes you home to your parents."

"You're just saying that because he told you not to talk to me. Not to ask questions."

"Okay," he said with a grin in his voice. "You got me."

"Doesn't mean I can't talk to you, though."

"Suppose not."

She didn't say anything for a few minutes. He couldn't read her. Was she putting up a brave front, or just plain loopy? There was a hole in the conversation they were dancing around that held a lot more than where she'd been for the last few days or why Weiss was being so damn secretive.

"Your name's John, right? John Giordano?"

"Yup. Like my grandfather."

"You ever think nothing makes any sense, John?"

"Everybody thinks that at fourteen. I did."

"That's not what I mean."

She went quiet again. The absence of conversation made him more conscious of his footing as he hiked downhill, of the girl's weight, of the sweat pooling under his arms and in the small of his back.

"So what do you mean, Kendra?"

"You ever think the stories they've told us since we were kids are as much to help them make sense of things as they are for us?"

That quieted him. "Depends on what you mean by stories."

She scooted herself farther up on his back. "Like what the Orangemen are. What they *really* are."

"Whatever they are, God must've put them here for a reason."

"Of that I have no doubt." Arms tighter around his neck, she leaned her cheek against his back. "I just wonder about the stories. Toughest thing in the world to believe is that things have a purpose even when so much of life makes no sense. Like all those people who died on Earth just for us to survive, you know?"

He said nothing as he dodged a few stray eye-level tree branches reaching out into his path.

"Nothing?"

After another minute, he said, "I think you mean more than that."

He could feel her smiling against his back. "Yeah, I do. But I promised Colonel Weiss."

John laughed. "Okay. Care to tell me how you managed to get out of the city?"

A trilling laugh rolled out of her and buried itself between his shoulder blades as she shifted her grip around his neck. Three hours later she would be home in bed, both she and her parents crying relieved tears, and he would be out in the hills still feeling that sly sound, half woman and half child, in his bones. And he could still feel it now six years later as he followed Kendra deeper into the same hills.

They hiked for two miles, more or less straight uphill from the point where they left the wall to a level plateau that overlooked the city and the beach and the sea beyond. Kendra appeared to know exactly where she was going and how quickly they could get there, despite the darkness. She had always been good in rugged terrain as long as she had been in the Defense Forces, but now her steps looked to fall in familiar places; her hands found grips she knew would be there. On the plateau she turned and grinned at John, her chest heaving, her face probably flushed from exertion in the darkness. She took a swig from her canteen with a slightly trembling arm and passed it to him.

"Ready? Come on."

He paused for only a moment to take in the view. He didn't hike into the hills often and rarely at night, except of course on perimeter duty or when the Orangemen came for their visits. This particular area he had never been in. The plateau had been purposely cleared long ago, although vegetation was ratting the edges like flames consuming a piece of paper. Plant life on this planet was slow growing but tenacious. Once it got hold of something, it was hard to uproot it. His grandfather had called it unkillable.

It took him several seconds to guess where Kendra was headed. For a moment it looked as if the plateau was just a stopping point before marching on to the next part of the hill to continue their climb. Then a glint of moonlight cracking through the trees around them revealed her destination: a cabin, long abandoned and being consumed by the brush around it. One of the homes the Remnants had thrown together in the early years before they agreed to build New Philadelphia.

Following her inside, John wondered if the people who had built the tunnel through the city wall had built this cabin too. Maybe some Remnant wanted a quick escape to higher and more familiar ground if city living didn't quite work out as planned. A long-forgotten escape hatch. He turned to ask her about it, then thought better of it. Some things were worth the questions; some just weren't.

"The fireplace still works," she said once they were past the ivy-covered doorframe. "And there are some candles here somewhere. Let's see if there's some decent wood around."

After a few moments' work, the candles were found and lit and the fire was warming the snug single room. He went back outside to get another armful of wood, enough to last the night if necessary, and then settled on the floor near the fireplace opposite Kendra. They could see the stars whirling across the nearly cloudless night sky through patches in the thatched roof. Like other Remnant hill homes, it was made from native wood and pieces of the odd metal taken from the cargo containers they had arrived in. This one had used the metal pieces as doors and shutters, all now fallen off. Whatever furniture had filled this room had long been wrecked or burned, so they reclined against a pair of logs someone had dragged inside and set perpendicular to the hearth. For all he knew, it might've been Kendra herself, along with Alex. He could almost imagine them here, teenagers then, hungry for each other. It was easy to imagine. He had been in similar moments with Sofie.

The cabin was warm enough for them to pull off their jackets despite the lack of a door and missing patches of roof. As John unbuttoned his and pulled out the wine bottles, he motioned to Kendra to give him the corkscrew.

"Um, I thought you had one."

He laughed and thought for a second. "Wait, I've got it." He pulled out his father's thin-bladed clasp knife and used it to force the corks down into both bottles. He held them up, grinning at her as the corks bobbed at the bottom of the bottlenecks. Kendra took the white one. He sipped the red and was glad that they could be here together on this quiet night sheltered from the city below.

"So." She wiped her mouth with the back of her hand after a long drink. "What's on your mind, John?"

"A lot." He laughed, then took out some rolling paper and some leaves and made a pair of cigarettes and handed her one. "Where do you want me to start?"

She gathered her knees in her arms, clasped one hand over the other wrist, the bottle dangling from her free hand. "Maybe start with the craziest thing bothering you. Should get easier from there."

She was serious, despite the lightheartedness. Fine by him. "Are the dead really better off than we are?"

"Are you asking this because I mentioned Alex before?"

"Yeah. But also because of my father and brother. My grandfather, of course."

That stopped her for a moment. Her eyes grew wide and glassy. Then she tilted her head to one side and pointed with the bottle out the front door. "The dead won't see the morning light come dappling through the leaves of that tree. They won't feel that warmth on their faces."

"But do you think they're at peace?"

She shrugged. "Maybe they know peace. But life isn't about peace. We have to be grateful if we'll be fortunate enough to experience both."

"So you think we'll experience both?"

"All of us?"

"Let's keep it simple. You and me."

She smiled now, teeth showing. "Now *that's* the craziest thing bothering you. You went out of order, Johnny."

"Suppose so. Sorry. I don't understand much anymore."

"Join the club." A knowing laugh. "Any food?"

John reached for his knapsack and tossed it to Kendra, who found a loaf of french bread and some dried fruit and nuts inside, all wrapped in rough brown paper. She tore off a hunk of bread and handed it to him, then munched on some of it and a piece of fruit.

"Since the Newcomers showed up, they threw off all these warm ideas and neat little plans people had. Everything fit and now it doesn't.

And then there are people like my mother. They've found a way to make the Newcomers fit every last tenet of our faith."

"And here you are, having to be the contrarian to all comers."

"And here I am." He slapped his thighs. "But you think like me, which is why I'm here talking to you and not to somebody who's just going to give me some line."

She took another mouthful of wine. "Or Grace."

"Grace talked to you? When?"

"Not long after the Council meeting." She dragged on her cigarette from near the dead center of her mouth, about where her upper lip curved up to its highest point. "She meant well. She's always meant well by me. I think she wants me to believe that all this is happening for a reason—even what happened just before you and I met."

John flicked his cigarette butt into the fireplace. "That's part of what I wanted to talk to you about."

No response. Just a sidelong look through her eyelashes.

"Weiss has asked me to guard the Newcomers. The man Tyler's been kind of talkative. They're interesting people. They're not like us. They're not believers. At least that's my impression. They—at least he—seems to doubt that the Apocalypse happened the way we've been told it happened."

She glared at him. "So what, all those Remnants just made up what they saw on Earth, what they saw here that first day on the beach?"

"I don't think that's what he thinks."

Another drag, then her cigarette butt followed his into the fireplace. She looked down at the bottle in her hand. "And what do you think?"

"I don't know what to think, Kendra. We know what the Remnants have told us about them, and we know what *we* know of them."

She clucked her tongue. "'And never the twain shall meet.'"

"Shakespeare?"

"Kipling." She took a long pull from her bottle. "Have you been up to that clearing since the night we met?"

"Not even on patrol. And even if we went looking, I'm not sure we could find the spot. Weiss and I were pretty thorough."

"Who're we to say what instrument God chooses for mankind's destruction and rebirth?" she asked suddenly. "Angels, demons, other men—it doesn't matter. That's what the frigging Remnants never get straight. It doesn't matter if everything that happened in the last days matches up perfectly to what was written in Revelation. It all still *happened*. And we're here now and we're alive and we need to prepare ourselves for what's to come."

"But do we know what's to come?" John felt courage from the wine flowing from his belly. "Christ almighty, do we even know if there's a plan?"

"Don't ever say that." She set the bottle down and leaned in close to his face. "You were just talking about the dead? All those people we loved who died, all those people who died so the human race could get a new birth here. If those deaths were just a function of biology, why do we still grieve? Why do we feel loss here so awfully"—she gripped her shirt atop her heart—"that we'd prefer death than to keep on living in such grief? Don't talk to me about wondering if there's a plan, just because a bunch of idiots down there are a little mixed up about what the Newcomers mean. We have to have faith, or we can't do a damn thing."

"'No great deed is done by falterers who ask for certainty.'"

Kendra cocked her head to the side and wagged her finger. "Now that's Shakespeare."

"George Eliot."

"Well, at least you learned something in all that time you spent in the Archives with your grandfather."

"Something, sure. Enough to know I know almost nothing. So what do we do?"

She laughed in a relieved way. He wasn't holding her lecturing him against her. "What do we do? Live as best we can and try to make sure no one gets hurt in the process."

"Oh sure. And how do we start?"

She shook her head, wide-eyed and grinning. "You can start by kissing me."

Later, as they huddled under their pack blankets and leather jackets near the dwindling fire, he ran his hand against the hollow of her bare hip bone—the first time he had ever felt it—and thought about how far she was from the rangy girl he had met six years ago. Yet her eyes were the same as the ones that had challenged him then. They still held within them all those voids where neither he nor anyone else living would ever be allowed to go.

Kendra sat up, shoulders rolled, with the blanket tucked under her arms, and tipped the dregs of the white wine to her mouth, then passed him the empty bottle before settling back down again. She leaned her head back, inches from his face. "We ought to try that again before the wine wears off."

He laughed, swallowing the last of the red wine. "Okay by me."

She caught his gaze. "Who knows what we might cook up, eh?"

He propped himself on an elbow to face her. "Really?"

Her grin was almost shy. "Who knows?"

"The idea of it doesn't make you nervous?"

"We're well past the common age of betrothal, Johnny."

"Be serious."

She reached up and touched his face. "Not with you. The idea never has with you."

"Since when?"

"Since when?" She shook her head. "Probably since we met. Does that seem weird?"

"Maybe not on your end. But on my end it might've been."

"The Remnants made the age of consent low for a reason. Lots of couples are years apart."

"It's not just the age difference. I've always been afraid to tell you, Kendra. I could hardly admit it to myself. I've been afraid to tell you as long as I was sure there was something to be afraid of because—"

"Because?"

"Because what I feel for you—" he began, then closed his mouth and started again. "I would've rather not had you than have had the possibility of losing you."

"You won't lose me, Johnny boy."

"No, I'm serious, Ken."

She rubbed his cheek. "You won't lose me. You're only allowed so much loss for one lifetime. I think I read that in a manual somewhere."

He shook his head. "I've lost enough to know that losing you would be the loss I couldn't take. That's all."

"I love you too." Her lips brushed his, her words in his mouth. "God, I love you so much."

They slept nestled warm against each other until the next morning. He woke long before Kendra and watched the sunlight shoot bright and new through the leaves on the tree she had pointed out the night before. It was a good and beautiful sight and made something old and sentimental catch in his throat. He didn't look at trees in this way very often.

Had he seen sunlight brighten a tree like this the morning after he first met her?

He couldn't remember that morning six years ago at all. But that night—there was little about it that he had forgotten. That night he had followed orders to the letter. He had gotten Kendra home, brought a doctor to her house, kept his mouth shut in front of her parents. All that was needed for him to do then was to follow the colonel's last order—to double-time it back up to that clearing in the hills.

He had found Weiss at the far edge of the clearing, almost where he and Kendra had left him. It had grown overcast since he had been gone but the moonlight was still bright enough to see across the field. A carbine lay across the older man's lap. Between two thick fingers was the smoldering butt of his last cigarette. The scattered butts of several others had been snuffed cold in the dirt around his feet. Weiss had the attitude of a man on guard duty, casual but ready to respond if needed.

"Glad you could make it back." He stood up and mashed out the cigarette with his heel. "Anyone ask where you were going?"

"No, sir." John took a sip from a proffered canteen.

"Anyone follow you or hear you coming this way?"

"No, sir. I made sure of that."

"You made sure." Weiss huffed out a laugh. "Giordano, remind me to tell you later how long that little girl eluded me." He shook his head. "If she hadn't stepped on that branch—"

"Sir?"

"Never mind." He jerked his thumb over his shoulder. "It's this way. And remember, this is your blood oath, son. No one can ever know." Then he lit his collapsible field lantern.

They entered a part of the forest where the brush was dense and thick. John kept both hands high to block unseen stray branches from hitting his face and fixed his eyes on the colonel's lantern a few paces before him. Every once in a while he looked up at the heavy green canopy high above their heads, hoping that some of the moonlight that had been present earlier would shine through. The terrain was level and free enough of obstacles. They were on a path of sorts—a dried-up streambed maybe—that cut through the brush. Half a klick into the brush, they emerged in another clearing that was almost identical to the one where he had first stumbled upon Kendra and Weiss. In this one, however, a single tree stood off-center as a lonely guard over a nearby rock outcropping.

A step behind Weiss, John could feel the older man tense up. After a moment's pause, Weiss headed straight for that tree standing apart from its surroundings. Something was lying beneath it that wasn't stone.

Weiss set his lantern down atop the outcropping of rock, high enough to throw its light on the object on the ground. The colonel stood back. Stepping lightly and slowly, John made a complete circle around what he had been brought there to see, not realizing that his carbine had slipped from his shoulder and into his hands, safety off.

The moon he had been looking for during their trek through the forest emerged from behind the clouds and set the whole clearing into sharp relief. He wasn't sure if it was a blessing. There, lying on the ground before his feet, was an Orangeman.

John had never seen one. To his knowledge, no one other than the Remnants had. It was all they had described the Orangemen to be and more—a perfectly formed male figure, human-looking except for the fact that he was massive, about seven feet tall, orange in color, with a head slightly larger than a human's and a pair of translucent wings on his back. His slate-gray eyes seemed to be open and unseeing, but without irises it was hard for John to be certain.

"Is he dead?" he asked without looking at his superior officer.

"Yes."

John lit his field lantern and crouched down to examine the Orangeman, who was slumped in a heap on his right shoulder. His broad wings were lying cocked and awkward, like a dead bird that had crashed into a tree. He seemed to be less orange in color than John imagined they would be, and his perfectly chiseled face was not quite the platonic form his grandfather had described—but both of these things could be explained by the fact that he was dead. Wait. Dead? An Orangeman dead? Was such a thing possible?

John shook his head. "Is it a Hostile, or a Friendly?"

"A Hostile, I'm pretty sure."

"How can—what happened?"

"I found him—it—here. With Kendra. I killed it."

"Killed it? How the hell can you kill an Orangeman?"

John looked again at the corpse and ran his light along its length. Then again, slowly, until he found what he was looking for: a bullet hole just under the left armpit. The tiniest trickle of something—he imagined it to be blood but wasn't sure—ran from the wound, down the barrel-shaped chest, and across the flat belly before winding its way down to a growing pool on the ground beneath its right hip. He—it—was as dead as any living creature could be dead. It didn't make any sense. It was like waking up one morning to discover you were breathing out of your eyes. An Orangeman dead. And killed by a man, to boot.

He turned to Weiss. "Why? Sir, I don't understand."

"It was attacking her, Giordano."

"Attacking?"

"It was raping her, son." His thick bulldog features pulled into a deep grimace. "I stumbled upon them, and it was raping her. So I killed it, and now you're going to help me get rid of the damned thing. If people found out what happened here—" The older man shook his head. "The people have to be protected from this."

"Protected, sir?"

"Yes. Protected."

"Even from the truth, sir?"

Weiss looked at him, his face a half-moon in the lamplight. He hardly opened his mouth to speak or to raise his voice. "*This* isn't the truth. Whatever it is, it isn't true to any one of us."

Weiss didn't need to explain any further. John knew and understood. The Orangemen were both humanity's mortal enemies and constant protectors. The Hostiles had destroyed mankind. The Friendlies had been trying to keep the survivors safe and secure as mankind forged a new path. From this planet, men would defend themselves until their race was reinforced enough to begin anew and they no longer needed to fear the fallen beasts who brought them to their end. That was what they knew and understood. Not this.

Yet whatever this was, it was still a higher form of life than they were. And still one of God's creatures. As John broke out his field shovel from his pack and helped Weiss find a suitable spot for an unmarked grave, he felt like Adam in the garden hiding his nudity among the trees. When they finished their grisly work as the rising sun's rays lit the peaks of the mountains around them, he still felt like Adam, even though God had not yet asked him where he was or what he was doing. John almost wished he would. At least then he would know what the result would be.

CHAPTER 7

Jake Weiss had stood in the street outside the Council chambers for twenty minutes, smoking cigarettes and flicking their butts to the curbstone.

He shook his head with disgust. Fifteen fistfights in the last week. And these on top of a dozen reported the week before. Obscene.

Typically, there were never more than two or three a season. And then only because somebody drank a little too much. He was sure he couldn't name insobriety as the cause of any of these recent ones.

He didn't want to go inside. He wasn't sure anything he'd hear in there would make his thoughts any clearer. In his more gullible moments, he thought his whole life had been a clear narrative. But deep down he knew that wasn't entirely true. A narrative wasn't a whole truth, just a story told. It was a construct. It needed an author and readers who believed what they were being told.

They didn't often talk about it—except among themselves and then only on rare occasions—but most Remnants recalled with remarkable clarity all the hushed conversations they had overheard their parents having with other adults about what the Orangemen might be. Jake was no different. It was hard not to remember anything having to do with the Orangemen. Seeing them that day above the beach after that endless time in the White Place—it was something all of them still felt in their chests like the surging warmth of a glass of wine. So it went without saying that any conversation about the Orangemen could easily stir a young Jake Weiss from a warm bed and a dreamless sleep, even after another long day of helping the adults build the city.

On that comfortable breezy night, his parents had left ajar the window shutter to the room he shared with his brother while they sat with a pair of friends on the front steps. Mostly they spoke in drowsy tones about work that needed to be done or that so-and-so needed to be reminded of the importance of some all-consuming project. That night, however, they were speculating about the Orangemen. The kind of speculating people had done for thousands of years under starlit skies as vast and as wondrous as this one. Jake didn't recognize the other two voices, but the way they spoke with his parents was easy and familiar. He glanced at Andy. Sound asleep. Jake crept out of their bed to stand next to the window.

"None of us here saw them up close on Earth," the woman was saying, "so we can't be sure."

"But they *were* there. We saw them in battle," the man said. "A war between humans and the creatures who destroyed us. So who's to say they aren't the beings described in the book of Revelation?"

His father chuckled. The old man had a way of releasing tension in even the most heated of debates. "We're Jews—and secular ones at that—so I can't say I'm that familiar with it. But as I understand it there's a lot of contradictory information in there—just as there is in the Old Testament."

"I'm not so sure about that," his mother said.

"Hmm?"

"It's really not easy to fit what actually happened at the end of the world into what Revelation predicts will happen—the earthquakes, the attacks, the war. There's too many parts. But yet it fits, if looked at the right way. And there's the fact that we were left with so many

Bibles. That alone is a very potent fact. It's not surprising if people are starting to believe that what's in there was clearly foretold."

"Any number of reasons could explain the Bibles," his father answered. "Maybe the Orangemen raided a bunch of motels. Now don't laugh. I'm only half joking. It might explain how lacking we are in the major scientific fields and how we're overstocked with Western literature. They might've collected these books as haphazardly as they collected the last survivors."

"Haphazard?" the man asked in bewilderment. "We came from only twelve points. And what about the census we took right after we got here?"

"He's got a point, honey. I mean, exactly one hundred and forty-four thousand? The exact number that had been predicted? A number confirmed by the head count taken again and again in the weeks that followed?"

"Okay, Louise. Here's an alternate theory," his father said. "What if these things are just—I dunno—aliens and left the Bibles here to *force* us into thinking of them as near-omnipotent beings? What if that's the simple reason?"

"Simple?" the man asked. "Sounds more complicated than what I've been saying."

His father laughed again. "Man, you take too much stock in the supernatural, Frank."

"And you too little, Dave."

"And what if," his mother asked, "what if that kind of thinking is what caused Armageddon in the first place? What if we've been too arrogant and not reverent enough?"

"But reverent to what?" his father demanded in a raised but still playful voice. "The power of God? Superadvanced beings? What?"

"Maybe," the woman said, "just respectful of the fact that as a race we've thought for so long we were the top of the heap. And we're not. One way or another, we never have been."

Jake crept back to the bed. Andy was awake but quiet, likely woken by his father's voice. Jake tried looking for a comfortable spot but couldn't seem to find it.

After a while, Andy spoke. "They're wrong, Jake. Don't you think otherwise."

"Wrong about what?"

Andy snorted. "Everything. They think too much, talk too much."

"How so?"

"They all talk about the Bible like they *know* it. I've been reading the Bible. It says in there all we have to do is love God and love our neighbors as ourselves. Seems to me to be easy enough to do."

"But what about the Orangemen?"

Andy turned to him, his deep-set eyes disappearing into the shadows on his face. Jake could feel his brother's breath on his cheek. "I know what they are. I knew it when I saw them hovering over the beach. And you did too. You knew it in your bones."

Jake thought about it for a second. "Yeah, I did."

"They're trying to think their way out of that feeling, but they can't. That's why they're making us build this city, instead of having us wait for New Jerusalem to come out of the sky. Because despite all their doubts, they know we've got to get ready to build a new race—a more decent kind of human being—right here for when the time comes."

"And when will the time come?"

"Dunno. That's not up to human beings. But you and me better make sure to be ready."

"Will we?"

"Yeah, we will. Because we're brothers and we love each other and we'll always have each other's backs."

Almost a half century later, the Weiss brothers stood side by side before the dais in the Council chambers waiting for their invited guests to arrive. Andrew was certain it wouldn't be a very long or very pleasant meeting.

"Still not sure this is a good idea, Andy."

"You got a better one? If we don't do something now to get them to cool things down, we're going to have a lot more than fistfights on our hands. This rabble-rousing has to stop. Fistfights are bad enough. What if somebody, God forbid, decides to pull a gun on someone else?"

"And your solution is to—what?—scold them like misbehaving students? Yeah. That'll work."

"Dammit, Jake—"

Petra and Grace entered the Council's chambers first, but only as fast as old Grace could walk aided by her cane and Petra's arm. They were as early by as many minutes as Gordon and Sofie Lee were late. Andrew wasn't surprised. In fact, he was pretty sure his daughter had told her husband to show up late. A little spiteful—almost teenage—willfulness on her part was not atypical behavior.

The two pairs sat at the tables in front of the platform. A trick of the light coming through the shutters made it seem as if they were balancing on ends of a scale. To Andrew, it was more than a bit funny and pretty much appropriate.

"We've asked you all to come here to impress upon you the seriousness of just what you've done to our city with that little stunt you pulled. You've sown dissention, confusion, and discord into a community that has long been at peace with themselves and with their neighbors. And now look what's happened with all—"

"Where's the rest of the Council, Mr. Chairman?" Petra asked, ignoring Andrew's opening statement. She had allies there.

"This isn't a formal Council meeting. If it were, we might have to consider bringing you all up on charges." He snorted. "Charges we've never needed to use in the half century since we began to build New Philadelphia."

"So what's all this about?" Petra asked.

"The old carrot and stick," Lee muttered, shaking his head. "I wasn't expecting that. Really."

Jake had been leaning against a nearby wall, arms crossed, listening to this exchange. "We're worried about people getting hurt, Gordon. Fights are already breaking out over what the Tylers really mean. Sofie, you were in the Defense Forces a long time. We've got enough trouble worrying about whether the Hostiles will find us. We don't want to have to worry about policing ourselves too. We've never had to, and we don't intend to now just because you've decided to make your private spat as public as possible."

Lee shook his head. "This isn't just about the Tylers themselves. What the Tylers are—what they represent—is vastly important to our future as a society. Their knowledge alone could significantly improve—"

"No one is disputing their significance," Andrew cut in. "But we just can't—"

"When are you going to let them go?" Sofie spoke up. "Uncle Jake, why are they being held prisoner?"

Ah, this is your part to play. Andrew looked at his youngest daughter, her pointy chin thrust forward, arms folded across her chest, all armor and defiance.

"No one is imprisoned, Sofie," her father answered in his public voice, soft and level.

"But they're not *free*, Dad. Do you really think they'll gladly give us whatever knowledge they have after being locked up for so long? How is keeping them isolated going to get them to trust us?"

"I understand your concerns. But we have no experience with any newcomers, so it's better to be cautious. What would you do in our place? Think about it now. Should they come into our midst without their knowing anything about us or us about them? Just because they're human doesn't mean they can be trusted."

When Jake cleared his throat, Andrew glanced at his brother. "Might as well tell them, Andy."

Andrew nodded. "And consider this: What if they aren't in fact human but are Hostiles in disguise? We know from the Bible that the beasts of old took on different forms—"

"But you have no proof of any of this!" Lee said. "You're just feeding into their interpretation of what the Newcomers are."

Jake looked at Lee over the rims of his glasses. "We have proof of *nothing*, Gordon. That's the point."

Lee looked from one brother to the other. "If they're allowed to be questioned by the whole community, then maybe we, *as a community*, can dismiss some concerns more readily. This is too big an issue to be decided solely on our leadership's say-so."

"That's how a representative democracy works, Gordon."

"You set yourselves up like Pharisees," Petra said, condemnation in her voice. "You judge for all of us."

"Not our intent," Jake replied. "We're just trying to protect what's left of the human race as best we can."

"Sounds noble," Petra said, "but you both know that throughout human history many miscarriages of justice have been carried out with the best of intentions."

Andrew groaned. "Petra—"

Grace, who'd been sitting quietly, her rootlike hands folded over the head of her cane, spoke. "When you two were just boys, I remember the whole community used to decide all matters of great importance—such as agreeing to build this city."

"Things, as you know, are a bit different now, Grace. Our population, thankfully, is much bigger, we have a formal government—"

"I'm well aware of the differences, Mr. Chairman. I helped create this representative democracy."

"So what do you suggest we do?"

She leveled her gaze at him. "Let the Tylers into our community. If they are what you fear they are—Hostiles in disguise—they will make their true natures known soon enough. But if they're not, if they are what the faithful believe them to be, then we have no fear of them, for despite the crisis they may herald, through that final trial leads the way to everlasting peace."

"Or through them leads to a further advancement of our civilization, the likes of which we have never known," Lee added.

Grace nodded in Lee's direction. "Let our people judge them as individuals and among themselves and as a whole. This is a decision to be made by everyone, not just the Council. Or the two of you."

"Strange as this may sound," Sofie said, "we're in total agreement with Grace."

"At least on this," Lee said, smiling at the old woman.

"Of course," Andrew said. "They will be released once the threat assessment has been deemed to be nil."

Grace let out a soft chuckle, dry with experience. "You sound so much like the politicians of old, Mr. Chairman. So I will play politics with you. Refuse to release the Tylers in short order for evaluation by the community, and you'll see rallies among our people that will make the one in the square seem like a family gathering for Sunday dinner. I'll live long enough to do that, and Petra will carry on for me if I don't. The choice is yours." She stood and, with one hand on Petra's arm, hobbled out the door.

When the Weiss brothers were alone in the chamber, Andrew turned, a look of disgust on his face. "This is all your damn fault."

"My fault, Andy?"

Andrew groaned and got up from his chair. "'If you want to keep the human race going, never allow an argument to go unsettled.' That's what the old-timers told us. That's the advice they gave us that you've always so cavalierly disregarded."

Jake slipped his hand into his uniform's inside jacket pocket and took out his rolling papers and tobacco pouch. "No one ever said that particular piece of advice was Bible truth."

"Don't get cute, Jake."

"I'm not." Jake finished rolling a neat cigarette, licked the paper closed, and lit it with a match from the wooden box next to the metal candelabra on the table. "I'm here to keep the peace and protect our people. I do that. But I'm not about to force anyone not to think for themselves." He grunted. "Then we really would be Pharisees. Or worse." He took another drag, then looked at his brother through the blue-gray smoke. "This is about Sofie again."

"It's not about Sofie."

"Cut the crap, Andy. It's always about Sofie. You have five living children who revere you. And yes, your youngest daughter has always questioned you, questioned our beliefs, questioned everything. She's always wanted more."

"What's that old expression, Jake? 'Curiosity killed the cat.' Augustine wrote that before creating heaven and Earth, the Lord 'fashioned hell for the inquisitive.'"

"Yet he still questioned things. We *revere* him for his questioning. And if I remember right, Augustine believed that the Bible should not always be interpreted literally, but metaphorically—especially if it goes against what we know from science and our God-given reason."

"*You* ask questions about every damn thing. She had to get that from somewhere."

"So it's my fault, huh? Okay, let's say it is."

"Or let's say it's in the blood."

"Right." Jake smirked as he fingered his mustache. "Dad was never sure about everything that had happened to all of us. You always took that as weakness on his part."

Andrew leaned the better part of his bulk on his knuckles against the edge of the table. "When I see her—God almighty—I see you, I see Dad, I see the doubts and the skeptical eye." He looked at his brother with love and weariness. "I see everything that brought the human race to its end."

Jake smoked his cigarette and did not say anything for a long time. "We're still nowhere on what to recommend to the Council about the Tylers."

A derisive laugh bubbled up from Andrew's throat. "Well, I'm sure glad you haven't come to a decision about that all on your own."

"Now what's that supposed to mean?"

He waved the comment away. "Forget it."

"No, say it."

"You know what I'm talking about, Jake. When you came down the mountain with that girl."

"Kendra? What's this with you, old-grudge night?"

Andrew said nothing.

"Andy, we were right not to tell anyone about that. Think about what would've happened if—"

"If people found out that a fourteen-year-old girl and her boyfriend had fled the city to have sex in the woods?"

"Dammit, Andy, that's not what happened, and you know it."

"We know that she and the boyfriend were having sexual relations before they were legally betrothed."

"I was there. I saw that Orangeman. I killed him, as I could've killed any man. You gonna call me a liar?"

Andrew again said nothing, just nodded a couple of times without looking at his brother.

"Clear your damn head, Andy. You're taking this too personally. What has any of that to do with the Tylers and the decisions we have to make right here, right now?"

"I just need to know I can trust you, Jake, whatever happens."

"I've always had your back. You *know* that."

"But will you follow my lead here?"

"What're you suggesting?"

"We don't know what the Tylers are—just as we don't know what that Orangeman was that you killed."

"At the next meeting our Orangemen said that he was a Hostile, probably rogue."

"Right." Andrew smiled. "But if that were the case, why didn't anyone ever come looking for him?"

"I'm not following."

"What if these Tylers *are* the search party in disguise?"

"Seems six years too late for a search party. But again, we're going in circles. We don't know."

"But we have reason to fear it as a possibility. So we kill them quietly before either side can question them. Everybody's left with a mystery but not a menace that will tear the city apart."

Jake weighed his brother's words. The soldier in him thought it made sense—sacrifice four to save a race. Had he done anything very different when he saved Kendra and kept quiet what that Orangeman did to her? If he had to do it all over again, he would. He knew that. But this? Was this the kind of decision a new race of man should make?

"Supposing we could even get away with it—and that's a really big if. What if we're wrong? What if they're not Hostiles, not demons in human forms, whatever? What if they are human and *exactly* what Grace believes them to be?"

Andrew nodded his resignation. "We need to know one way or the other. We need more evidence."

Jake tossed his cigarette on the wood-plank floor and tamped it out with his heel. "Let me see what I can do. But until then, get the Council to stall this release."

CHAPTER 8

No one except Kendra McQueen had ever ventured more than six miles beyond the hill perimeter of New Philadelphia. Even back in the lawless days of living in the hills, the Remnants had not gone much beyond it. Whether this was an agreed-upon decision or just a matter of subconscious groupthink, neither Kendra nor John—nor anyone in their generation—ever really knew.

The city had been built close to the beach, not far from where the Remnants had landed all those years ago, on a rising plain surrounded by high hills that spooned much of the shoreline. While people had traveled many miles up and down the beach, north and south, the lands past the hills that encircled New Philadelphia on three sides were a mystery. Along the tops of those hills was the perimeter—not a fortification or a demarcation in any way, just a worn-down path where generations of humans had stood watch day and night to ensure that none of them would ever be caught off guard again. Inside the perimeter was the last of human civilization. Outside of it? None of them knew. Forest from the look of it. Mountain streams. The realm of predatory animals. Beyond the perimeter was the world beyond—whatever world it was that the Orangemen had stuck them on.

As John hiked toward the perimeter with Kendra, he remembered a story his grandfather told him of an ancestor who, having come into his father's fortune as a young man, sold all of the father's property in Italy and traveled the world for years before going broke and coming to America, where at fifty he married a young widow, had children, and painted merchant ships in Brooklyn until his seventy-fifth birthday. "And that's where we all stayed, generation after generation," his grandfather said, "until we wound up here."

To most, rebuilding the human race, protecting and nurturing every child, took precedence over exploration. Whether such thinking was progress was still a matter of debate. "Mankind was exploratory, had been since the earliest days in Africa," John could hear his father saying. "We needed to see what was over in the next valley and where the source of that freshwater spring came from. It was normal and natural to think like this, to seek out the new. This paranoid fear of the unknown, that takes away the best part of being human. It sets us back on our instinctive heels instead of allowing us to step forward using our reason." Good old Samuel Giordano could talk when he wanted to.

Yet John had felt that kind of fear. It was an old thing and made him wince when he thought about it long enough. The fear came along with him every time he went on perimeter patrol. Alone up there on moonless nights, that paranoia crept out from under his skin. Some soldiers claimed fear kept Novices sharp until they learned how to conquer it. John was never sure he had ever conquered it. He suppressed it because he was an officer and people were relying on him. But he never mastered it, because he knew he could never account for the infinite variables of the unknown.

At the top of the hill, they stopped and swigged from their canteens and looked at the beaten-down dusty path before them that meant they were about to leave civilization. He stared into the woods beyond. Nothing. He tried to breathe the fear out of his nostrils.

Kendra—his Kendra at long last—looked at him, nodded a couple of times, whistled, adjusted her short dark hair under her cap, and sighed. "Okay, so here goes, eh?"

"Nervous?"

"Um, yeah."

"Me too. So we gonna do this?"

She touched his arm. "Don't think about your dad and your brother."

He glanced back at the city in the valley below them. "I'm just thinking of better ways we could've spent this morning."

She kissed him once on the mouth and let her lower lip hang between his for a second. "Me too, pal." Then she slipped her carbine from her shoulder and crossed into the world beyond, following the gushing stream that provided their city with its fresh water back to its unseen source. A second later and another glance back and he was right behind her.

He and Kendra could have said no. It hadn't been an order. Still, it had all the bells and whistles connected with one. A message had come for them—urgent—that General Weiss wanted to see them in his office in the barracks ASAP. The messenger, a very baby-faced Novice, had found them walking together a few minutes after they'd traversed the tunnel back into the city after spending another night at the cabin. They'd sent the clueless kid packing with a return message that they would see Weiss in a half hour. Just enough time to clean up.

They found Weiss sitting behind his rough-hewn desk, the one that they both knew had been made by his parents. Books and papers were scattered about the desktop. Several pencils lay by his writing hand along with a small manual sharpener. Between his elbows was a leather-bound Bible, open to the well-thumbed pages of the book of Revelation. In a half circle around it were a number of open and unopened volumes, including an English translation of Augustine's *Confessions*, several maps, several files, and three memoirs by Remnants.

The names on those spines were unfamiliar except one: John Giordano, MD.

The younger John had of course read his grandfather's only book years ago, more out of respect than because of any intellectual curiosity. The bits he recalled from it were mostly funny anecdotes from his grandfather's youth on Earth. Why the general had the old man's book among these others, he had no idea.

"Thanks for coming," Weiss said after answering their sharp salutes with a tired one of his own. John looked at him and felt he seemed more than a bit old. John had never thought of him as old. But now in the morning light the general's face was cut with reminders that he had more years behind him than there were ahead.

"I'm setting up a recon mission," he began, lighting a cigarette. "And I need volunteers. I need soldiers I can trust, reliable people I trust as much as members of my own generation but young enough to handle the rigors of this mission. I need people who can think for themselves no matter what they may face and still feel an obligation to their community. And two names immediately spring to mind."

"Sir," John began after glancing at Kendra.

"Now, Captain, before you snap to attention and agree to it out of some silly sense of duty, it won't be held against you if you don't want to go."

Kendra nodded. "May we ask what the mission is?"

"Simply put, the mission is to find where the Newcomers came from. We know their story, but we'd like to know how they got here. We've long suspected that our Orangemen maintain some kind of . . . presence on this planet, to watch over us and make sure we're protected from the Hostiles."

"General," Kendra said. "But that would mean there was no point in building a walled city."

"This surprises you?" Weiss drummed his fingers on his desk. "None of us who lived through the last days ever imagined that something as simple as a walled city would keep out invaders who could strike from the air. Although the wall protects us from native predators, it was built for psychological and spiritual reasons. We were left basically bare-assed in the open with a few guns and fewer hopes." He shrugged. "It made sense then."

"I'm sorry, sir," John said, "but do you and the other Remnants know exactly where this Orangemen presence is?"

Weiss pointed at one of his maps. The cigarette now smoldered between his thick fingers. "They always come from the northwest *over* the hills. We've all seen the flashes of light coming from that direction. Time and again it's been recorded that they arrive somewhere out there and are found by our people around two miles to the north on the beach."

Kendra gave him an incredulous look. "But they could be using that direction just to throw us off. Maybe they're looping around from the south. Maybe they come across the sea. They *do* fly."

Weiss rubbed his eyes under his glasses. "All true."

"You have to admit it's not a lot to go on, General."

"It's not, Captain. But you've seen what the Newcomers have done to our peace in the short time they've been here. We need to know if they're a threat, if they've actually come from our Orangemen or from Hostiles posing as our Orangemen." Weiss gathered two of the books in front of him and a folder filled with handwritten sheets of paper. "These two books are collections of first-person accounts of every single encounter we've ever had with the Orangemen, starting with the Arrival. And this is the report of the most recent visit, when the Newcomers showed up. Study them. Maybe you can see something in them that we never have."

John and Kendra glanced at the materials. "How long do you expect us to be out there, sir?"

"No more than forty days."

"Sorta biblical, don't you think, sir?" Kendra asked with a cockeyed grin.

"Not intentionally," Weiss replied, taking another drag. "It just happens to be the end of the Tylers' official 'quarantine.' So forty days—no more—and you get your asses back here to report what you've found."

John took the books and report from the general. "When should we give you our answer, sir?"

"Twenty-four hours. Once you've read everything."

"Or we can just give you our answers now," Kendra piped up. "I'm in."

John nodded toward the pile of reading in his hands. "Well, I guess I'm in too."

"Strictly volunteer," Weiss said. "You've still got your twenty-four hours. Semper fidelis. Dismissed."

In the overcast morning light outside, Kendra adjusted her cap and wrinkled her nose. "Think he noticed?"

"About us? Hell yeah."

"Think of it as his gift to us. A sort of honeymoon. But with carnivores."

"Honeymoon, eh?" he asked with a grin.

"Okay, it's a little ass-backwards. But you've gotta admit, it's about the kind of honeymoon we'd have."

They hiked until shortly before nightfall, watching their breath become ever more visible as the sun pitched down toward the tree line. Just as John was about to suggest that they set up camp instead of continuing on to the stream's source, they heard a low, roaring rush of water nearby. Using their machetes to clear through the brush, they came upon it— the source of their city's fresh water bursting through an ivy-covered rock face about forty feet high. They pitched camp away from the spray in a clearing on one side of the rock wall.

Twenty minutes later, Kendra had sparked a roaring fire. She kept her back to it as the temperature dipped. John had finished pitching their tent and was digging through their packs for the worst of their field rations. Before leaving they had agreed to eat their rations in worst-to-first order, while mixing in whatever fish or game they could find. Looking at the hardtack and canned beans in his hand, he imagined waking tomorrow morning to find Kendra and her rifle long gone.

John opened the can and set it on the grate over the fire next to the coffeepot. Kendra spoke without turning. "Coffee will be ready in a few minutes."

"So will the beans, for better or worse." John's gaze moved from the beans on the grate toward the sound of the falls nearby. "Glad you decided to pack some coffee."

"Just because we're leaving civilization doesn't mean we can't be civilized."

"Speaking of civilization." He handed her one of the two cigarettes he just rolled. "There's not much of this, so we'll have to go easy." The falls were now more heard than seen as night fell, at least until the moon rose to fill its white foam with yellow light. "Funny to think we're the first people ever to see this, even though we've been using its water all this time."

She gave him an almost imperceptible shrug as she smoked in the backlight of the campfire. "We're not the first."

"You're probably right. We haven't gone *that* far from the city. It's likely a few Remnants went beyond the perimeter in the early days."

She smoked some more, then turned to him. "Not what I'm talking about. I mean we're not the first ones here *today*."

"What?"

"Not here," she said, jerking her chin at the ground by her feet, "or here or, um, there."

John immediately noticed two things: first, that Kendra was sitting with her hand on her sidearm's holster, and second, that from the bank of the stream to the clearing where they had made camp were several footprints, partly obscured by his own blundering ones. And in each spot near a mostly clear print was one of Kendra's.

"Son of a—" He shook his head. "How old?"

"This morning."

"Direction?"

"Not from the city."

"*Not* from the city?"

"Nope. So no one's following us."

He crouched next to the clearest print and examined it by torchlight. "Can't tell one way or the other. It could be some son of a bitch with big feet or some Orangeman with tiny feet."

She gestured at the tracks. "Our friend here was wearing boots. Know any Orangeman cobblers?"

"So what're you thinking?"

"So much for cuddling up tonight." She picked up her carbine. "Rock-Paper-Scissors for first watch?"

I'm fifteen, I'm always fifteen, and I'm shaving my face in our house mirror, but after a minute it doesn't look like my face really. The mirror image, not mine, sort of twisted like a film over my eyes. I rub it away. My father stares right back at me, and it's clearly my father, nose a bit thicker and more Roman than mine, hair a shade or two closer to brown. And he's telling me not to worry. He's read all these things, and it's not like they're going that far anyway.

We're on the pier. How? My older brother's loading things onto the boat—what? Boxes? Satchels? Christian's two years give him that much more comfort in his own skin, his hair a bright reddish from Mom but toned down somehow, sun bleached against his seaside tan, his skin more olive now than I could ever get.

Anger. At both of them. It's in my shoulders and right down to my bare feet on the hot dock. Christian's going to be married soon, but I have Sofie already, Sofie still and always and forever? That's not it. I've brought them a net full of oranges that we grew together from seeds in the city's greenhouse, the bundle weighing almost as much as I do, but I don't dare let them drop, because Dad and Christian will need them even though they'll be gone only a week. Grandpa used to read about scurvy and sailing in the Archives and explained it to me. The oranges are beautiful things, bright with life in my white hand. I pass each of them one from the net, and we stand together before the boat, sucking our oranges bone-dry and spitting the seeds between the wooden slats of the pier. We make a game of it. Then my father and brother drop their pulps on the sunbaked slats; the last vestiges of moisture in them land on my bare feet. Then they're gone and the boat's gone, so I slip under the pier and find all the teenagers there pawing at one another to the edge of sin, trying not to go over it, everyone including Kendra and Alex, even though they weren't teenagers then, just babies really, and I ask them how these wild orange trees got under the pier, and Kendra says to me, as Alex nibbles her neck, "You brought them here, Johnny. That's the reason why they're here."

The olive-green roof of the tent shimmered slightly, and the flap, slightly open, let in the first traces of morning light, cold and sharp and good. John stumbled out of his bedroll and toward the tree line at the edge of the clearing to relieve himself. Kendra was nowhere to be seen.

That dream. No surprise. He had been thinking of his brother and father ever since they left the city. It was making him stupid. First the tracks he didn't see, and now he was out here barefoot and without even a knife on him. He doubled back to the tent to retrieve his sidearm and toiletries and wandered over to the falls to clean up. A little cold water would do him good. At the falls he found Kendra's clothes lying in a messy heap on the grass.

"Good morning there, sleepyhead."

Kendra was swimming in the middle of the pool around the falls, the morning smoke on the water still thick and rising. The temperature couldn't be more than just above freezing. But her lips didn't look blue. In fact, her cheeks were an almost-cartoonish rosy pink.

"You're *clearly* nuts."

"Nuts would be thinking I could spend another fricking minute as stinking and as filthy as I was from that hike yesterday. Come in. It's not nearly as cold as you think. Must be a hot spring around here somewhere."

"Or you pissed in the water."

She stuck out her tongue and rolled her eyes. "Har har."

John looked around. "What about our friend?"

She kicked off a nearby rocky overhang that stood out from the shore like a diving board and whirled around in the center of the pool, her dark-haired head as black and slick as a seal's. "Recon for the last hour. Nobody's been anywhere near this whole area since before we arrived yesterday."

John stood at the water's edge, brushing his teeth and looking around him. The air did seem cooler than the water. He looked around again as he scooped up a handful of water and rinsed.

"Would I lie to you, pal?"

He shook his head and stripped and waded into the water but left his pistol as close to the edge as he dared. Kendra slipped her head under before emerging again, blinking water from her eyelashes.

"So, Captain," she asked through her grin, "where to next?"

"I dunno. I guess it depends on where that trail you found leads to. But we did come—"

"That's not what I meant. I meant about us."

"Shouldn't have called me Captain, then. Mixed signals."

She swam closer. "Yeah, probably shouldn't have called you that and been naked at the same time."

"And wanting a serious conversation. Really confused at that."

"So what do you want to do about us?"

"You're serious about this serious conversation?"

"That's kind of why it's called that."

"Do?" He laughed. "What do I want to do? I want to marry you the minute we get back. What brought this up?"

She swam around in a lazy semicircle. "Last time I was out beyond the perimeter was when you found me with—"

"I don't care about that, Kendra. I never have."

"But what you don't know was that I was with Alex before that. Often. We started right when I turned fourteen." She laughed through her teeth. "All *those* rumors at least were true."

"Still not caring here, Ken."

"Come on—"

"Come on what? Okay, you were with Alex before you were betrothed. So what? Would everyone peg it as a sin of the flesh? Sure. Was it? Sure. But again, so what? It would've been a hell of a lot worse if you lied to me about it."

That quieted her for a minute. "Since we're playing honest, Johnny—"

"Shoot."

"Were you ever with Sofie?"

"With Sofie? No. Came close enough a couple of times. There was someone else, though. A little older than me. My first times were with her. I'd go to her often and did so for many years, but that's a long time done with now."

"Oh."

"She doesn't matter. And Sofie's married to Gordon now. And Alex is dead. Forgive me for being so blunt, but it's true. We're clean, Kendra. No ties."

"And you really don't care." Her blue eyes, filled with the reflection of the morning sun in the water, searched his face for doubt, hesitation, dishonesty.

"I swear to Christ I don't."

"That's quite a vow."

"And it's meant. Just like all my vows to you will be."

She blinked. "Well, okay, then."

"Are we done with this seriousness now?"

"The personal serious. We've still got that public-trust stuff to deal with."

John floated on his back and found himself surprised to be so relaxed. "So the question is, where do we go?"

"My recon suggests our friend came up this way and then made his way down to the valley beyond here. He didn't much care to hide where he was going—footprints all over, broken branches, he even stopped to pee—all of which either suggests he doesn't suspect anyone would ever bother to follow him or he doesn't think anyone else is around to follow him."

"Doesn't give much of a clue to his identity. Other than the fact that he's probably human, since he pees."

"Again, wouldn't necessarily take that for a sure sign."

"Fair enough."

"So do we follow him?"

He dunked himself and swam up, then wiped water from his eyes. "We're out here to find something about where these Newcomers might have come from. It only makes sense to me to follow a trail, any trail."

"And how far do we take this? How long do we go on?"

"I don't know. Until we get some answers."

"Glad I fell for an honest man." She paddled closer to him. "So should we start now?"

"Not necessarily."

"A very honest man."

CHAPTER 9

For the first two days after leaving the falls they had good weather. The daytime skies were knife sharp and filled of the kind of high white clouds that painters on Earth-of-old often showed behind saints to suggest their clear and direct connection with heaven. They hiked in a roughly northwestern direction, always away from everything they had ever known. It had been cold both nights and all the way through each morning afterward and didn't warm up to shirtsleeve weather until well past midday. On the third night the air coming down from the mountains to their north brought the first real cold with it. Despite the chill, they enjoyed the nights as they sat huddled around a fire in thick sweaters and leather jackets.

Such was their pattern those first days as they walked through the open, unknown valley. They found themselves feeling fortunate that the trail they followed was so clear and the valley itself so full of wonders. It was rich and lush land, abundant with wild fruit trees and herbs. The whole place could probably be ready for cultivation in a generation or less, depending on how many hands would be doing the work. And that was only the little they saw as they hewed close to the trail they were following. At night, lying in each other's warmth, they heard the scratching and cawing and scurrying of wildlife. They smiled at each other's faces in the dark tent. Game and plenty of it.

If ever human beings were going to live outside New Philadelphia, this seemed a fine place to begin.

Beginnings. John had thought a lot about beginnings while hiking those first two days through the valley. What they meant, how people defined them. In school—but more so in late-night conversations with friends—it had been suggested to him that God is unbound by the concept of beginnings and endings. God never needs or desires a do-over. He knows what will happen but always allows us the power to do what we will and start over as we need to. Each day since the first day men used their intelligence for the first time, humanity had been given a chance to begin anew, make a choice, the right choice. And now here on this planet all that was left of the entire race had tried to do that.

Beginnings. A related thought crossed John's mind, sparked brightly and maintained a long afterglow as they took a break one night at dusk. He thought they should abandon this lunatic trek and make their separate peace here in this valley. Long after they had settled in for the night, he would lie awake, seeing the house they would build, the fields they would plant and till, the game they would cook over the fire. He could see his wavy blond hair thinning, his skin slackening over sinewy muscles, Kendra's bright eyes lining, her breasts drooping. Several times he had come so close to suggesting it aloud that he knew he was serious about it.

Then the rains came.

They came at night during the deepest part of their sleep but were not hard enough at first to penetrate the depths of their dreams. A little before dawn the skies finally burst open. Lightning illuminated their tent for moments at a time as the storm drew nearer. In those moments they could see each other's faces—blue white and flash-frozen in the instant—as they sat facing each other and feeling the sides of the tent suck and buckle in the wind. They waited and waited for something—daybreak or a lull in the downpour—but the storm's increasing intensity masked the dawn and kept them wondering about sunup until at least an hour after the sun had already risen.

"We're not going to pick up the trail again in this, are we?" John asked Kendra's silhouette after a while.

She shook her head slowly. "Nope."

"There's a question that should've been rhetorical." He whistled. "Okay. We'll worry about what to do next later. Let's eat breakfast until this stops."

Kendra unbuckled the tent flap's opening and looked up at the hard-angled rain. She glanced at John and shook her head again. "We'll be eating for a while."

It didn't take much longer for water to begin seeping in. Even their breath turned to moisture right outside their mouths and soon beaded the tent's walls before running down them in rivulets. The water seeped through the floor of their tent, then through their sleeping bags, then through their socks and pants. At that point there was no choice but to abandon the tent, which they did just after making a best effort to secure everything inside—especially their food stores—in dry containers, in tarps, in whatever they could find.

They stood outside their tent, their hair matted to their foreheads, and watched the canvas slowly give way under its sheer soaked-through weight. As the tent caved, they looked around for shelter. Nothing nearby. They had seen little of the kind as they crossed this open valley.

"We can't stay under one of these few trees," Kendra called over the downpour. "We'll be electrocuted."

"If we don't freeze to death first. Suggestions?"

"No shelter back that way for miles. We should scout ahead for a bit. This camp—or what's left of it—isn't going anywhere."

John slapped his wet thighs and then shouldered his pack. "Can't say I disagree. Lead on."

They walked for an hour or two in what they thought was a mostly straight line, but drifting always as the rain twisted around and against them. John shivered as he and Kendra pulled each other along. Soon he began to seriously wonder about the possibility of hypothermia. If they didn't find someplace dry—and soon—he couldn't see how they would survive.

Heat was lost more quickly in water. He knew that from the time he spent swimming at the beach. Even though they weren't swimming now, they were drenched to the skin, their clothes so saturated that their jackets felt as if they were weighing them down. He could feel Kendra's teeth chattering against his chest as he held her. She tried to hold him steady as best she could against the shivers that convulsed through him. Something soon—someplace dry—someplace—

There, suddenly, off on the horizon: a grassy knoll, a rock glistening against the rain. They pulled each other forward, feeling no cold or pain, just the awful hunger of hoping against hope.

A cave. Small, yes, no more than four feet high and only about eight feet deep and wide. Large enough to crawl into. And inside, amazingly dry, its mouth turned from the storm's onslaught. They tore off their wet clothes and tossed them in a heap after finding some dry blankets deep inside their packs. Wrapping themselves tightly inside them, anchored to each other, they slept.

He did not dream that night. She did. Her dreams usually came out in a jumble, never linear. But this dream was a memory replayed, just as if it was one of those films they described in that book she liked. What was it called? *Great Cinema of the 20th Century*. What was harder to believe: that such a miraculous, perfect record of existence like film had once been real, or that so many beautiful people had all been alive at the same time? Harder still to believe—that their generation was descended from people who had looked like that.

She had been looking at that book when Alex came in to see her. She was home alone. Her parents were out, weren't they? Where? It didn't matter. None of it mattered, because Alex was there and had come in as he always did now, sulky and shuffling and without knocking, and talking before she even had a chance to look up.

"You better say something, Kendra," he said, almost wheedling. "Everybody's starting to think it's me."

She peeked at him and thought for the first time that he looked a bit freakish. His face was at that awkward midpoint between boyhood and manhood, a shadow of beard cropping up across his pudgy cheeks just underneath the finest reddish mountain range of pimples. His black hair lumped up in thick curls, probably because he had come right from bed to talk to her. She pictured him tossing in his bed, imagining her face on his ceiling, rushing out to find her. How romantic. It was the middle of the night, and she hadn't been sleeping much. She remembered that very well.

"Since when do you care what people think?" she asked without lowering the book. "Oh—I'm sorry. I had you confused with a vertebrate. You *only* care what people think. That's why you've told everyone about us going up to the woods."

His indignant face popped over the edge of all the pretty ones in her book. "I never, not once—"

"Don't you shit me, Alex."

"Kendra—"

"So just go off and tell your little friends about this." She shooed him with a brush of her fingers. "I'm sure they'll believe you."

"Kendra, why are you doing this?"

She lowered the book. "I'm not 'doing' anything."

"That's the point!"

"So you do it." She shooed him again. "You're good at getting people to believe anything. Get them to believe this."

"Kendra, they think it's me. They think I'm the one. You've gotta tell them the truth."

"I don't have to tell anyone anything. And I don't care what people think. The people who matter know everything anyway."

"Jesus Christ, Kendra!"

"Lord's name, Alex. Careful."

"They—I mean, my parents—they want us to—"

"And to that I'm saying no. Because you're a useless little loud-mouth prick of ten-second endurance."

"I swear I didn't tell them about the cabin. I didn't tell them anything."

"Save it. What, were you afraid they thought you killed me or something? Like I couldn't snap your skinny ass in two."

He suddenly and unexpectedly dropped to his knees before her. "Please, Kendra. I'm begging you."

She laughed. "You're pathetic. You're sixteen and act like you're five."

"For God's sake, Kendra."

"Get. Out. Now."

"I swear I'll do something if you don't tell them. I swear I will."

She sat up and looked at him nose to nose. "You don't have the guts."

Half crying, half moaning, he ran from the house. She went to the door to close it on him and the empty night. Then she sat back down on the couch and read about old movie stars to try to stifle the waves of nausea flickering through her. She knew she'd have to talk to her mother—and most likely Grace. One thing at a time. Get through the night first. She gave the small curve of her belly another

116

careful touch and looked at photos of a beautiful man named Cary Grant.

She thought he looked like an angel.

Kendra muttered to herself when she awoke, then wondered how she hadn't woken John. Still half inside her dream, it took a while to recognize him, but she was glad to see that it was him and not anyone else. Before they had fallen asleep in the cave, Kendra suggested that they sleep with their heads facing the opening. Any other way seemed like sleeping in a tomb. She was glad she had. The sun was on her face.

John was sleeping so soundly. She slipped out of the blankets, stretched once outside the cave, then ducked back in to gather their filthy, wet clothes and spread them on warm rocks in the sun. Even if the clothes didn't get completely dry, they would probably feel more comfortable walking back to camp in them instead of being stark naked. It was a warm morning, warmer than any so far since they'd been out here, the air still humid from the night's storm. Her flesh goose-bumped a bit, but she was comfortable.

She remembered the first time she'd been naked in the woods. She stretched again, this time examining herself as she did. So different from what she'd been then, still long and lean, but not nearly as awkward, toned from all her years in the Defense Forces. Had she left when her four years were up, as her mother suggested, she might've developed the larger breasts—her one admitted physical disappointment—common in her family. She milled around, considering what to do. She frisked her underwear but realized it was still too wet to wear. Instead she ducked back into the cave and took both of their sidearms to make sure the rain hadn't damaged them. She grinned as she neatly snatched John's from beside his head. Then she found a warm place to sit in the dewy grass and began to dismantle them on an oilcloth she had taken from her pack and tried to keep the dream from her mind.

The tattoo on the inside of her left forearm, close to the wrist, caught her eye. The ink was starting to become greenish and a bit blurry already, but it was still clearly an ichthys, the only tattoo she had and the only one she'd thought she'd ever need. She'd gotten it after finishing her Novice year. Most kids got some sort of tattoo after that hellish first year. She traced its two intersecting arcs with the tips of her fingers until she completed its entire profile. She hated when people called it a Jesus fish. It always seemed to cheapen its historic importance to the early Christians as an identifying mark in hostile times. Alex called it that, stupid idiot spiteful Alex, who still came to her in dreams.

She'd finished dismantling her pistol when she saw something—a dull, reddish glint—at one corner just inside the cave's mouth. She decided to dig it up.

It took a while. She crouched in the corner and slowly worked the object out of the hard-packed earth. As she exposed more and more of it, she could see it was curved and smooth, though pitted from having lain in the ground for however long. After wedging her nails, then her fingers, under an edge, she yanked it free.

It was a bowl. It wasn't any bowl that she recognized. Not a fruit bowl or a soup bowl or some piece of crockery. And stranger, it wasn't made of ceramic, definitely not clay. Nor was it carved from wood. And it wasn't metal. She couldn't understand how it had been forged.

"What've you got there?" John asked as he poked his head from the cave. Like her, he was still naked. He sat cross-legged next to her and kissed her on the cheek.

"A bowl, I think." She handed it to him. "I mean, I know it's a bowl, but I can't figure out what the heck it's made of." She ran her fingertips across its curvature.

John ran his own fingers across its pockmarked but still smooth edge. "This looks like it had some kind of a cover to it. See that ridge all around? Like something fit into it."

"Yeah. Looks like. But what is it?"

He shook his head as if remembering something and laughed. "You know what I think this is?" He pointed at it, grinning. "Plastic."

She gave him an incredulous look. "What's plastic?"

"I read about it. On Earth-of-old, they made everything out of this stuff, from bottles to spaceships. It was cheap, easily made by their advanced technology, and very durable. Dad used to say he wished he could get ahold of some of it. Let's see, there was polystyrene, PVC, nylon, synthetic rubber—"

"Listen to you," she said with a snorting laugh. Then she ran her hand against the curve. "You're telling me you think this thing is made of that stuff?"

"Gotta be. It sure isn't any material we use."

"Okay, Johnny. So humor someone who's spent more of her life outside the Archives than you have. How'd it get all the way out here?"

His hand slid along its muddy interior and cleaned it out as best he could. "Good question. Best guess is that it's probably been here since the Arrival."

"I thought they didn't have anything like this in the cargo containers— just basic tools, weapons, crop seeds—"

"That's what I thought too." He looked off into the distance. "But we also thought that everyone had stayed together to build the city. That no one lived beyond the perimeter. If this guy we're following isn't a mirage on both our parts, then that's clearly not the case."

"Now you think this guy's a Remnant? Just because of this?"

"I don't know, Ken. I think he's connected to this bowl somehow, whoever he is."

She took the bowl from his hands and rubbed its weather-beaten edge. "Doesn't look like he's eaten out of it anytime recently."

John laughed. "Maybe he left it in a storm along with the rest of his supplies . . . like some other people we know."

"Cute. So what's the plan here?"

"Salvage what we can from the campsite and then keep following this general direction."

She looked at the soaked ground all around her. "It's a pretty remote shot we'll find our friend."

"I'm open to suggestions, babe."

The campsite had not held out as well as they had hoped. Although they had done their best to secure their gear, the storm had exacted a serious toll. A full two-thirds of their food stores were ruined and a third of their ammunition. Their tent was too waterlogged and torn to salvage. Their spare uniforms and many of their clothes were infested with aphids. They set them apart from the clean ones and burned them as soon as they were dry enough.

They then strung up what they hoped could be dried and saved—their boots and their leather jackets, sleeping bags, some sweaters, underwear—but it was clear they would be living off the land much earlier than they had anticipated.

They warmed themselves in the sun, wearing mostly-dry underwear and watching their clothes flap in the afternoon breeze. Lying there, Kendra told John she was reminded of doing something similar as a kid after falling down exhausted from playing hide-and-seek through her mother's clotheslines. They passed a flask between them and a canteen of clean water and grumbled about their losses—especially their tobacco. But they also tried to look at the bright side. Their cooking supplies were still in good shape. They still had their knives and carbines and sidearms. And they both seemed none the worse after the freezing storm. The only odd thing seemed to be a faraway look that had grown up in Kendra's eyes. John wondered if it had been the bowl. It couldn't be the supplies. Knowing her, she probably had already planned a way to maximize their reserves.

He tossed a twig at her. "Penny for your thoughts, kiddo."

"Hmm?" Her bright eyes were still on the clothes snapping in the breeze. "What's that?"

"Nothing. Just something my mother used to say when we were daydreaming. So what're you thinking about?"

"The Nephilim."

"The what?"

CHAPTER 10

It wasn't the first time he had ever heard the Nephilim connected with Kendra. But it was the first time she had ever mentioned them to him—and very likely, to anyone else.

After John had carried Kendra down from the mountain six years earlier, something in their society had changed. In a ritualistic city of routine rhythms and limited expectations of surprise, everyone in New Philadelphia suddenly had something novel to talk about. What had happened to Kendra? Had she run away? How had she gotten way up there in the mountains? And more troubling to the rumormongers, no one—not Jacob Weiss, not her parents, not Kendra herself—would say a word to anyone about exactly what had happened or how it had been possible for a young girl to survive more than three days and nights in the woods. The generalities that came out of the Council—that she had gotten lost and that apart from a few minor injuries she was fine—did not sate a public looking for a feast of facts. And because gossip filled a vacuum about as well as anything else human beings had yet to devise, people began to speculate—and speculations became facts. The fine citizens of New Philadelphia—God's chosen people—became prisoners of the iron bars of gossip and found relief in the hint of scandal.

Then six weeks later the news hit. Kendra was pregnant. Just fourteen years old. Unmarried. Hadn't even spent time in the service yet. A minor in all of the ways that counted. On Earth-of-old, maybe it might not have been much of a scandal. The Remnants always said the last days had been decadent. But in New Philadelphia it was a shock beyond imagining. On occasion people married while still in the service, at sixteen or seventeen, with their parents' permission, and began having children soon enough, but no one had ever been pregnant that young and unmarried to boot. Once Kendra's condition became known, the city would talk about nothing else, despite all the admonishments from many Remnants to "judge not."

And the questions kept coming. If Kendra had been going up to the mountains to lie with Alexander Raymond Jr. in half-ruined Remnant huts, why didn't she marry him now in the sight of God? Why the delay? Why not give that blessing of a child the gift of married parents? That talk stopped as a new word began being bandied about: Nephilim.

About seven or eight weeks after Kendra had been found, Gordon Lee sidled over to John in the mess hall at the barracks. Whenever Lee saw him, usually without Sofie, he'd hang on John, an arm around his shoulder or a hand gripping the crook of his elbow, as if they were somehow bonded because they had both been romantically involved with the same girl.

"So, rumor has it that you were the one who brought Miss McQueen down from the mountain."

"Not much of a rumor," John replied through a chunk of roll dipped in gravy, "if I filed a report with the Council saying just that."

"Then you're the man who can settle a bet between me and a few of the other engineers."

"Doubt it."

"Here's what we're thinking. One, this story about her and the Nephilim is just her looking for attention—as if she hasn't had enough already. Two, it's actually true—but none of us buys that one. Three—and don't tell Sofie this—she was knocking boots with old man Weiss and they cooked up this cover story. She does seem like a minxy little thing."

For his curiosity, Lee got a punch in the mouth and two knocked-out molars. John's right hook earned him a month of KP duty. He had never enjoyed a punch more.

Six years later, Kendra and John marched side by side as they came upon another wooded area. An abrupt transition separated the prairie land they had been hiking through from the very dense forest they were about to enter. Kendra joked how it almost seemed as if somebody had decided to drop a fully mature wilderness right here, just for giggles. As they located a point of entry, John wondered if he should've pressed her harder about mentioning the Nephilim earlier.

He knew what she must've thought: that the creature that had kept her prisoner in the mountains for three days was not a rogue Hostile as their Orangemen had suggested at the next beachside meeting. A man couldn't kill an angel, fallen or otherwise, even if that man was Jake Weiss. But you *could* kill a Nephilim, the beings described in Genesis and Numbers. Many biblical scholars believed that the Nephilim were simply ancient warriors, the giant-sized children of Seth who had rebelled against God. But others, including a number of the more creative gossips around New Philadelphia, looked at the line from Genesis—"the sons of heaven had intercourse with the daughters of man, who bore them sons"—and other religious texts to conclude that the Nephilim were in fact the hybrid offspring of fallen angels and human women. Somehow Kendra had come to believe that the gossips had been right.

"John, look at this," Kendra called from just up ahead, stirring him from his thoughts. He wanted to hold her face between his hands and kiss her. As he climbed the ridge of the small hill she had hiked a moment before, he planned to do just that. But what the sunlight dappling through the tree branches revealed stopped him cold. Kendra was already running down toward it. He chased after her. When he got to the bottom of the hill, he followed her over the little stream she had just crossed, then stood with her under the tree that had drawn her attention, each of them grinning like mad at each other.

She gave him a cockeyed salute. "So I figure I'm on the right track, Captain, sir."

He threw an arm around her and kissed her cheek. "Never doubted your instincts for a second. Let's ditch our packs and go up."

They climbed the twelve sturdy wooden slats that had been nailed to the trunk of the tree and poked their heads through the opening of a platform of well-hewn wood. Kendra decided to test it first with a bit of her weight before scampering all the way up. She nodded to John to follow. Then they stood there laughing as they looked down on the small hill they had just passed over and even part of the valley they had been wandering through for the last day or so.

"A tree house. A freaking tree house!" Kendra bounded across its width and length, grinning the whole while. "This is too much."

"I don't think they built it to play in." John leaned over the railing and popped a small bit of metal from a thick tree branch with the point of his bowie knife. "Look at this. I'd bet a week of guard duty this is an arrowhead."

"An arrowhead?" Kendra examined the bit of metal, running her thumb pad along its sharp curved edge. "Ah, a hunting platform."

"We did hear a lot of animals at night."

She reached out her hand for his. "Let's keep going while we have the light."

Under the tree house again, Kendra crouched to search the nearby brush for the faintest hints of a trail. After a few minutes she tossed her chin in an easterly direction. They shouldered their packs and took off. For a long while they were following a trail of some sort, albeit a very old and rutted one. Neither the tree house and arrowhead nor this primordial path appeared to have seen any use in a long time. John wondered if they were coming to the point where they would have to turn back. They were no closer to finding this rumored presence of

Orangemen on this planet, no closer to finding out who or what the Tylers were or represented. Without adequate protection from the elements or a full stock of supplies, they'd have to discuss returning soon. Besides. They had Weiss to consider, all the tensions they left behind in the city. He looked at Kendra alongside him, the line of her jaw set firm. Would she agree to it when the time came? Shrugging and returning home would not be easy for her.

They had clicked off at least another two miles after a half hour or so of brisk hiking. Kendra stopped to crouch again in the brush. "Animal tracks here—fairly fresh. No sign of our old friend, though. Jesus, help me! If only it hadn't rained."

"Kendra, do you think that we should consider—"

Before he could finish his thought, she had stood up and elbowed him in the ribs. He glanced in the direction she indicated. When he turned back to her, she was already smirking at him.

There, in a clearing in front of them, was a rough lean-to built of logs and sealed with hard-packed mud. Its open side was turned away from the prevailing winds. As they approached and circled it, they saw its three walls and sloping roof were in fine shape. It was definitely old, its top and part of its interior furry with wildflowers and weeds and other plants whose seeds had found its mud habitable. Never had anything looked so inviting.

"Son of a bitch," he muttered. "And here I was just wondering where we were going to find shelter for the night."

"I wouldn't curse it." She nudged him. "Someone's looking out for us. Anyway, it'll give us someplace comfortable to talk."

He looked at her, tugging at his earlobe.

She grinned in a blink-blink, mock-innocent way. "About what's been bugging you since we left the old site."

"Oh that. I thought you meant something important—like who's been going nuts with a saw out here where no people are supposed to live."

"So sure it's people?"

"Orangemen don't build hunting platforms or lean-tos."

"How about plastic bowls?"

He scratched his neck. "None of this makes sense."

"Ah," she said quietly. "Then this is all part of the same conversation."

"Okay. You've *officially* lost me."

Kendra shook her head and sighed. "I'll get the campfire going. See if you can break out something edible."

They tore most of the vegetation out of the lean-to and had made camp within an hour. Their supplies and bedrolls were tucked in the lean-to, and a can of beans was heating on the fire Kendra had made. As night fell, they poked at the fire to keep it hot while they discussed inconsequential things: drinking their remaining coffee only in the mornings, setting traps for small game if they were going to stay here for at least another night—the sort of mundane talk people filled the empty air with when they had awkward things to say but didn't know how to say them. They passed the remnants of their flask—the whiskey warm and good on their insides—to each other, hoping that would help.

Then the ground shook hard, a slight but very clear tremor. They waited for it to subside—a fault line nearby?—but it kept growing stronger and closer. A few seconds later John yanked Kendra up by the arm from her seat on the log and shoved her into the lean-to. Even as they covered their heads and lay on their bellies inside, they were convinced it was an earthquake, though neither of them had ever really felt one.

Rising dust blurred the air between the lean-to and the fire as the tremors intensified. And with the dust came the creaking and breaking of branches and something else—animal noises. Trumpeting and fearful animal noises, growing closer with every second.

They lifted their heads from their arms. Through the dust John could see something coming toward them, something very large. He squinted and saw legs—or what he thought were legs—flashing through the flickering campfire's glow, dozens of them, maybe even a hundred. They came and came and came. He couldn't shake the feeling that they *were* legs despite their size, hairy ones the width of tree trunks carrying on them animals (or beings) he could not see through the darkness and the dust.

Kendra covered her mouth with her shirt to protect herself from the choking dust as the creatures pounded through the camp, veering away from both the fire and, thankfully, their lean-to. The clamor and the mad dash went on for many long minutes. Then the tremor diminished into a dull thud almost indistinguishable from their hearts beating against the floor.

Kendra was up in an instant and dashed to the fire to pull out a flaming torch. A second later she dove into the brush, running like mad after whatever had come through the camp. Another second and John was in pursuit, carbine in hand as he chased the bouncing glow before him into the starlit, moonless night. Then the light ahead was gone and silence engulfed him as he was left alone with his own rhythmic heavy breathing. He ran faster, holding the rifle before him to keep the branches from lashing his face.

He nearly bounded into Kendra when he came upon her in an acre-wide clearing about a half mile from the lean-to. Not far away he could hear running water—a stream, or more likely a river from the sound of it. Kendra was still wielding her brand like a club.

"They went over the water," she said, half out of breath. "I could hear them crossing, splashing through. I couldn't catch them. So huge, so fast."

John put a hand on her shoulder as he gulped in the night air, colder here near the water and away from the fire. "Take it easy, Kendra. It's okay."

She shoved his hand away and glared at him. "It's *not* okay, John. None of this is okay. What were those things? Did you see? Were they Nephilim?"

"I couldn't see them clearly," he said in a quiet voice. "I don't think they were Nephilim."

"Well, how would you know? You don't know shit about them."

"And neither do you."

"You're so sure, aren't you?"

"What're you talking about, Ken? How the hell is this stampede connected to what happened to you back then? We don't know what that creature—*he*—was, other than the fact that he seemed like an Orangeman."

"I know what *he* was," she spat through her teeth, "a whole lot better than any of you."

She marched toward camp. He let her go and knew when he got back he would probably find her already asleep—or pretending to be—in her roll. He stood in the clearing, his breath finally coming in even beats again. He listened to the rushing water in the distance and looked up at the stars. With the morning light might come some answers, but until then all he could ask of the stars was the same question man had always asked them on his most contemplative nights.

Then he turned back toward the water and knew where they would be going, even if both of them no longer understood why.

CHAPTER 11

"Well, if the size didn't prove it, these tracks do," Kendra said, looking up at John from her crouch. "Nothing human—or humanoid—made them."

"Never seen anything like them," John muttered. "You?"

"Nope."

He squatted down next to her and fingered the clearest set found at their campsite. Right near the fire pit, where they had spilled some water just before the stampede, were four very clear prints now drying in the mud, only two of which overlapped each other. It seemed that they were made by almost perfectly circular hoofs, very unlike any animal tracks he had ever seen. They made him think of some illustrations of demons he had seen in some of their Bibles, man-beasts standing erect on hoofed hind legs and sporting leathery bat wings.

"Whatever they were," Kendra began, "I'm not inclined to stick around here to see if there's more of them headed our way. How about you?"

John could hear a bit of embarrassment in her voice over her outburst last night. He let it go without comment. Kendra had never apologized in her life for anything. "Agreed. We should leave."

Her eyes widened. "You don't mean go back to the city?"

He walked toward the lean-to with his hands in his pants pockets. "I've got a better plan."

It took Kendra less convincing than he had imagined to dismantle the lean-to—what they had called their "starter house." And it took longer—almost two days instead of one—than he'd imagined to cart the logs they needed down to the river and to reassemble them there as a raft. As a seafaring ship it was far from ideal, but the raft floated and was large enough to carry them and the remainder of their supplies. After a couple of test runs across the width of the river, they took up their makeshift paddles and set off with the current.

Days passed without much notice. On the river the air was colder than on the banks, but both the air and the sense of easy movement was refreshing and invigorating. The country they traveled through was mostly prairie lands, varied only by the occasional clumps of trees and brush and framed by mountains in the deep distance—places they could always keep in view but would likely never touch. When they tired or needed to sleep for the night, they sought out little coves to settle into, although sometimes they had to travel longer than they liked because the shoreline was too marshy. Because the land was flat and low, they often had little protection from the elements, and they snuggled together in their bedrolls wearing all of their clothes. They were never more tender with each other than they were on those nights. Without protection or trees or even the sound of animals in the night, it seemed as if they were the only two people left in the world. That was how they felt when they'd started this trip. What they had shared since had only added to their closeness.

In the mornings they waited for the smoke to rise off the water and the temperature to warm just enough so they could risk it and jump in for a quick bath. After all their squealing and yelping in the water, they didn't talk much when they were on the raft. Sometimes whole mornings would pass without their saying a word to each other. They would fish but caught little. They would watch the gentle current as they paddled and searched for any glimmer of life along the river's banks. The sky was clear and the air soft. They did not need to paddle often. John felt their silence was proof of their comfort with each other. It gave credence to his belief that true intimates were the only ones comfortable enough with one another to allow long silences. But when he mentioned this idea to Kendra, she laughed. "Being dead tired every day helps."

Her cap pulled low over her eyes, she squinted through the sunlight, wrinkled her nose at him across the raft. "You ever think you'd be a sailor?"

John raised his eyebrows and glanced back at her. "You mean in general? Or because of what happened to my father and brother?"

"Being on water can't be easy for you."

"I swim at the beach all the time."

"That's different—and you know it."

"Suppose it is."

He watched some reeds near the eastern bank blow in the wind, all curved down smooth like a combed head of hair. When it died down for a moment, everything was completely still. Then the silence gave way to the whoosh of that breeze again and the lackadaisical dipping of their paddles in the water. He hadn't realized what it would be like being away from the unrelenting noises of New Philadelphia. Out here, so many thoughts rushed to fill the silence his ears heard but his city-bred mind couldn't fathom.

"It wasn't easy for me, especially at first. My grandfather hadn't died long before. You might not remember. I expected Dad and Christian to come back from the first seafaring expedition with so many stories. I figured they'd be heroes. It was such a huge adventure to me, something that kept me from getting in too much of a funk about Grandpa. I never expected them to just . . . disappear. To not have closure like that—"

Something between them had shifted. John found himself still talking. "My mother has always seemed to take it better than me. She said,

'The Almighty has his own purposes.' I think she read that somewhere. Maybe it gave her comfort, the idea."

"I think I'm with your mom on that one."

"Oh man. You're gonna go all Petra Giordano certain on me?"

"No." She smiled. "In the long view, these things may make sense. To us who are so finite, so limited in scope and understanding, so close to tragedies, they just don't."

"That's what they tell us in school about the Apocalypse whenever someone asks why God would let the world get so bad that he'd need to destroy it." He glanced at her. "But do you really think tragedies happen for a reason?"

She was quiet for a while and focused on the bending reeds. "Enough has happened to me—and I guess enough time has passed—for me to believe that they do. That invisible forces work on us at every moment of our lives, even though we might not see them or feel them or understand why."

He smiled at her. Never had honesty and fortitude looked so good in a Defense Forces cap. "I didn't have your faith, Kendra. Not after I lost my father and brother. I shut down, unsure of anything, unwilling to get close to anyone else."

"That explains Sofie Weiss," she said flatly and almost with a smirk.

He dipped in his paddle to correct their course.

"When she was my drill sergeant, everyone heard how she supposedly threw you over to marry Gordon Lee. But I never bought that story. I'd catch her now and then looking at you whenever you'd pass. She was crazy about you. Still is."

He said nothing.

"You broke it off with her—right?"

He looked at her.

"I'll take that as a yes."

"Sofie always . . . questioned things. Not the way you or I might. She questioned everything, everything except her own certainty. She was so sure she was right about everything. Hard being around someone like her. And it got a lot worse after the ship was lost. Her endless questioning—it made everything worse."

They had long since stopped paddling and kept only an occasional eye on their direction. "So what restored your faith?"

He snorted a laugh. "You."

"Me?"

"You. On that mountain. I never understood the certitude of saints until then."

"I'm no saint," she muttered with distaste through her teeth.

"No. You're not even sort of close."

"Oh thanks."

"Wait. What I mean is, despite what happened, you were still whole. You still made jokes. The part of you that made you who you were was untouched and remained untouched, even after we got back home and all those people said all that shit about you. You took the worst life had to offer and were still fully alive. Lots of people deal with a lot less and wind up far more broken."

She shook her head, an incredulous look on her face. "I think you're laboring under a delusion about what I am, Johnny."

"Nope," he answered. "You're just laboring under a delusion that you need to keep this mask still."

"Mask?" She let out a throaty laugh. "Why, Captain Giordano, in another life you might've been a poet."

"In another life, a bad one. No, what I mean is—" Something out of the corner of his eye silenced him. "What's that?"

Kendra turned in the direction he was facing, shielding the sun's glare from her eyes with the edge of her hand. In the mid-distance of the flatlands off the eastern bank, an undulating black mass was spreading across the green-brown ridge of the plain. At first it seemed to spread like a wildfire, but then the mass tipped up the ridge and rotated left, then right, before pulling back over the ridge out of sight, leaving the plain as verdant as it was before.

Kendra glanced at John. "Was that what came through our camp?"

"Dunno." He plunged his paddle into the water and turned toward the riverbank. "Let's find out."

After five minutes of hard paddling, they had landed on the eastern shore not far from where they had seen the black mass disappear over the ridge. They tied their raft to some brush, then, as a further precaution, tossed their gear ashore far from the edge of the river's high watermark.

"If we travel light," Kendra said as she checked her rifle, "we'll be at that ridge in three, maybe five minutes." She grinned. "Ready?"

"Just go slow as we approach," he cautioned. "We don't know what we'll find on the other side."

They crossed the expanse freed of their packs and with their carbines held high. The ground was flat and even and apart from some high grass offered an unobstructed view of the ridge as they approached it. John motioned to Kendra to ease up at the bottom of the embankment, and she did. They crept toward the ridge to slow their pace and calm their breathing. Halfway up, they dropped to their bellies to peer over the edge.

There had been no way for them to prepare for what they were now seeing—or even to know if what they'd glimpsed would still be on the other side of the ridge, as fast as it had been moving. What had seemed like a single black mass moving across the landscape was in fact thousands and thousands of individual animals.

"Buffalo," John muttered. "My God, it's a herd of buffalo."

Kendra's voice caught in her throat. "It can't be. Weren't they hunted to extinction? I think I read that in a book in the Archives."

"They almost were." He felt his eyes watering. "My mother once said it was one of mankind's greatest sins—and greatest achievements that they were brought back from the edge of extinction."

"But what—what are they doing *here*?" Kendra said as she peered at the great beasts with their shaggy brown coats. They were more than six feet tall and around ten feet long. Every supple undulating movement of their slow-motion grazing was hypnotic.

"I don't know," he said. "I just can't understand it."

"I want to take a closer look."

She stood up and slowly began to work her way down the other side of the ridge. John said nothing, just watched her hips find the most careful steps in the grass until she disappeared from sight. Then he got up and followed her. She approached the outer edge of the herd and came within about two feet of the snout of the nearest one, who looked at her as if she were as interesting as a tree.

John came down toward her, still fearing that she could get trampled at any second. She shook her head at him.

"They've never seen people, John. They couldn't have."

He moved to stand beside her, trying not to make any sudden shifts as he progressed but keeping his carbine at the ready. He watched the herd lazily milling around as they chewed the high grass.

Her face burst with joy and mischief. "I bet you could even pet one."

"Kendra. Don't."

"I didn't say I would try it."

"Good."

He looked at her, then at the animals all around him, each alive, each so beautiful, each a survivor of a near extinction. He looked at them and thought of all the ones who hadn't lived, human and buffalo, whose lines had ended on a planet dead for generations. And he thought: *And this one lived and this one lived and this one lived*—the same thought he often had while walking down warm nighttime streets in the city and seeing old couples walking hand in hand or laughing crowds of tipsy Novices or young parents out on an evening stroll with their children. Why had all these lived and others had not? Billions of lives cut short. A million billion children unborn. An infinite number of useful existences extinguished, prevented, smothered, silenced, deleted. And this made sense? And this was justice? He looked at these magnificent beasts, the ones that had lived, and his face broke as he caught Kendra's eye.

"We haven't had any meat in days, Kendra."

"Oh Johnny." She looked all around. "John."

"And it's getting pretty cold at night and we could use their skins."

"You son of a bitch."

She looked into the eye of the one nearest her hand. He was a bit smaller than the others, perhaps not fully grown. She could see her reflection in his eye if she stood at the right angle.

"I'll do it," he said. "From the ridge."

"No," she said with finality. "I'm the better shot, and I'll put him down clean."

He said nothing. She made her way back up the embankment as he followed in her wake. He was to her left and slightly below her as she leveled her rifle at the one she had been tempted to pet. It was a clean shot that brought down its victim and cleared the plain of survivors, leaving man alone again in the world with his works.

CHAPTER 12

The buffalo were running over a cliff. He watched as they dropped one by one and almost too slowly over the side and somehow wound up in his mouth. But no, that didn't make sense. They had cooked the one they shot. So why did he taste blood?

John awoke and coughed and spit out blood and sand, then felt inside his mouth to see if he had done more that bite the inside of his cheek. All the teeth were still there, somehow still tight. He spat a couple more times with his head on the sand. The spittle went from bright red to pink and dissipated very quickly when it hit the water nearby. He soon realized he wasn't just spitting into the water but was sitting mostly *in* water, soaked to the skin and having no idea how he had gotten that way.

He looked up. His head spun as he tried to clear his vision. Splintered fragments of logs surrounded him, the hemp ropes that had bound them together drifting limply around in the surf.

They had smashed up in rapids. A painful ache sprinted down his left shoulder into his wrist as he sat up. He tested each joint in slow deliberate motions until he realized they moved on their own. Nothing broken, just badly bruised. Lucky, lucky. He turned to Kendra to tell her that he was okay. Not there. She couldn't have run off. He stood up to get a better look at his surroundings. A small waterfall, a pool at the end of this point of the river, gentle, calm. Bits of their raft and pieces of their supplies drifted around. The smashed wooden stock of one of their carbines spun in a gentle circle.

No no no no no. No God no. Please not this. No please. Anything else. No not anything else. Don't let her be badly injured or even hurt. Don't let there be injuries I can't see, something that will—God no. How did we miss the rapids? Shit shit shit. Nowhere in sight. Retrace the river, Giordano, she might've been tossed off earlier. Go go go.

The rapids had come on suddenly. They had been coasting downstream with ease—a whole morning like that it seemed: bellies full of buffalo, their raft riding low in the water because they had salted and stored as much meat as they could.

They had felt guilty about all the meat they had left on the carcass. They were still thinking of that and of the Orangemen and Kendra's pregnancy and John's dead father and brother and not really at all about the job at hand, so they never noticed the river's gradient increasing bit by bit, never saw the turbulence starting to stir up until the current started to really foam, and by then it was too late because they were in the thick of the rapids and trying to steer a raft that handled as well as a pig might— and then, what? A rock? No—a tree, half-submerged and leaning out at an angle over the foaming river. No way to turn and then—

Here. Now. And no Kendra.

Please. Please let her be perfectly fine. Protect us from all anxiety—

"Kendra!" His voice was raw and hoarse as his teeth chattered. "Ken! Ken!"

He stopped and turned away from the wind rustling through the tree branches surrounding him, away from the cascade of the waterfall in the distance, even from the lilting rattle of the nearby reeds. He clenched his chattering teeth together and wanted to stop the pounding of his own blood so he could listen better. A faint sound across the pond. He looked. A large piece of raft wreckage was wedged upright and half-embedded in the sand. He stripped off his sopping jacket and boots and swam across. The cold water snapped his dull head back into sharp consciousness.

A minute later he was tearing through the debris on the other side, pushing logs and shredded strips into the water. A groan, down below all this, made his world rational again.

"Thank you, Lord, thank you." He sat down next to her and pulled her into his lap as gently as he could. "Kendra?"

"My fault," she muttered through cracked lips as he wiped sand from her face and hair. Apart from a nasty gash about three inches long in her hairline, she looked okay all over. "I did it."

"Kendra—no. I'm here. I'm okay. Open your eyes."

A roar ripped through the air and unhinged their world. John lifted his head and looked all around, searching the horizon. From a grove of dense evergreens behind them came another roar, louder and closer this time, and then almost on top of it, the snapping and crashing of heavy tree limbs.

"Kendra." He shook her. "Kendra, wake up."

Her now-open eyes were sharp in their blueness but unfocused. She struggled to recognize him. He shook her harder.

"Kendra, we have to run." The snapping and crashing were closer still, the animal roars now sounding inside his skull. "We have to run—now."

He pulled her up by the wrists. She stood on her own, seemed to see him more clearly, then flinched at some sound—something close. He put his good arm around her waist and dragged her along as he tried to take off in a sprint. Another crack behind them and the clarity of the roar told him that whatever had been in the woods was now in the clearing and no more than a hundred yards behind them. He didn't stop to look. He hitched his thumb into a belt loop of Kendra's uniform pants and practically lifted her one-armed into the air as he ran.

Her head half bobbing on her shoulders, Kendra turned to look behind them. John saw her eyes grow wide.

"Run, John."

John glanced back long enough to see something thick and dark and very large entering the clearing.

Kendra tried to get her legs under control so she could run with him. He felt her steadying and slipped his hand from her waist to take her hand in his to help pull her along. He kept running without looking back often. Slowing his pace even for a second would give whatever was barreling toward them that much more of a chance of overtaking them. They stumbled across uneven ground, hand in hand, looking for any cover that might give them protection from whatever was chasing them.

A moment later they were in midair. The ground had fallen out from beneath them as they ran off an embankment that had been obscured by the high prairie grass covering it. They tumbled several feet before rolling to a spot near a tree trunk in a small clot of woodland. Their heads low, they crawled back up to the edge of the embankment to see if they could recognize whatever it was that was about to kill them.

On the plain between the far evergreens and their ditch were a half dozen woolly mammoths.

John found it hard to believe what he was seeing was not part of a delusion or a dream. Their curving tusks, most more than a dozen feet long, were held high as they ran, their dark eyes peering out in terror from their shaggy coats. The cold air steamed with their warm breath as their nearly ten-foot-high bodies cleared the embankment as if it were the slightest bump in a road—but then they found themselves blocked in by the same thick trees Kendra and John had come to rest against.

The beasts scampered in a panicked semicircle for a minute, then screeched in absolute terror as a saber-tooth tiger leapt onto the back of the closest mammoth.

Now hidden in some brush at the top of the embankment, John reached for his sidearm but found the holster empty. He went for his bowie knife instead, found it on his belt, and held it in front of them until Kendra nudged him and handed him her sidearm.

John took the pistol but had no idea if it would be any more effective against these monsters than the knife. Either way he wouldn't surrender their lives without a fight.

The mammoth bucked and reared. The saber-tooth dug its claws in deeper. As the other mammoths ran in terror up the embankment and back into the woods they had come from, the tiger opened its massive jaws and sunk its teeth deep into the neck of its prey. The mammoth flung its trunk back and forth over its head and shoulders, trying to reach its killer, but it had neither the strength nor the reach to pull the tiger off. John could see its legs beginning to buckle even as it hopped around like mad.

Two shots rang out from the tree line behind them. The mammoth reared again, and in rearing so suddenly it managed to toss the saber-tooth off its back. As the mammoth ran up the embankment after its herd, the tiger hit the ground in an embarrassed heap and righted himself as if looking for someone to blame. Then it raced after its prey, practically leaping over Kendra and John as it did.

From their ditch neither of them had any line of sight—no idea where either the saber-tooth or the shooter was lurking. As Kendra started to get up, he pushed her down gently.

"You stay here while I go topside."

Her eyes were more focused now, though bloodshot and wearied. By pain or confusion, he didn't know. "Leave me your knife, John. Just in case."

He slid the bowie knife back out of its sheath and presented it to her handle first. She took it with her right hand, steadied it with her left, and sat back in the brush, trying to be as inconspicuous as possible.

"Five minutes."

She gave him a lopsided grin. "I'll take that as a promise."

John paused at the top of the embankment before climbing over. He had no idea what he'd find on the other side and even less of a clue about whether Kendra's drenched and ancient M1911, the one she had gotten from her grandmother, would even come close to stopping a saber-tooth tiger. He didn't have to crouch very low to stay hidden in the tall prairie grass. After the tumult of the last few minutes, the silence was strange and unnerving. Any rustle in the wind was that saber-tooth stalking him; any twig snapped underfoot was the shooter cocking his rifle. Sweat dripped down his nose. He felt nothing but his own wheezy breath rattling through his chest. The cold air and his drenched clothes felt disconnected from him. After a few minutes of fruitless crouched searching, he took a deep breath and risked poking his head just above the high grass.

The saber-tooth was gone. He was sure of that. No creature that large, that fierce, that *hungry* could keep still for so long with such easy prey like himself nearby.

He took another breath and stood up to get a better look, making a 360-degree turn with Kendra's pistol cocked as he did. And there on the horizon, coming from the edge of the far woods, was a man, framed by the setting sun. A man with a heavy shotgun leaning in the crook of his elbow, making his way toward John. On horseback.

At least John was pretty sure it was a horse. As with the mammoth and the tiger, he had never seen a live one. Yet it looked very much like the poetic creature described in books from the Archives. He was so transfixed by the fluid grace of its head and neck and haunches as it approached that it took him several moments to level his pistol at it. Neither the horse nor the man reacted until John called out when they were about twenty yards away.

"I swear by the Lord God I will put a bullet through you if you do not halt."

The burly man, whose face was obscured by a wide-brimmed hat, tugged gently on the reins. His horse stopped. He lifted his free hand and held it up while keeping the other cradled around the shotgun.

"I assure you, sir, I mean you no harm."

"And I assure you, sir, that I will kill you if you make a move."

"I saw you and your companion running. Are you both safe?"

John took a few careful steps forward without lowering his gun. "How did you get so far out here?"

"'Out here?'"

"Away from New Philadelphia."

"Ah." The man smiled. John could see that much of his face. "I imagine I could ask you the same thing. But you see, I've never lived in your city. My parents were Irish country folk, and they didn't want any of that."

John blinked. "Are you a Remnant?"

"A what?"

"A Remnant. One of the survivors of the Apocalypse."

"I'm afraid I don't know your term, sir," the man replied in an even tone. "But I am one of the survivors you speak of—though I was a boy of only four at the time."

John shook his head. "That's not possible. All of the Remnants went to live in the city. That's what they agreed to. All of them."

"Perhaps if you put your weapon down and I returned my own to my saddle holster, we might discuss this. What do you say, ay?"

John nodded. "Okay. On three. One. Two. Three."

John slid Kendra's gun into his holster as the man returned his to his saddle. He then proceeded to climb off his horse and lead it toward John. On the ground the man was far less imposing than he had appeared in the saddle. He was of average height and trending toward the portly side. His fair face was open and held an amused and inquisitive look. If he was an Orangeman in disguise—like some people claimed the Tylers were—he could not have picked a less threatening figure to inhabit.

He removed his hat to reveal a shiny bald pate that was framed by a narrow fringe of close-cropped brown-gray hair. He was easily the age he claimed he was. Only his eyes seemed younger. The man smiled again as he held out a work-worn hand and John took it.

"How do you do?" His voice was crisp and bright and betrayed an accent that probably derived from those Irish parents he mentioned.

"My name is Captain John Giordano of the New Philadelphia Defense Forces."

"Giordano?" The man cocked his head. "Giordano, did you say?"

"Yes. Why?"

"Nothing." He paused. "John baptizing Jesus in the River Jordan and all that, you know." He cleared his throat. "I'm quite pleased to meet you, Captain. I'm Jack, Jack Lewis. I should say my friends call me Jack. I've such a silly given name."

"You have friends? Out here?"

"Oh yes. Old friends. They don't live near us, but we do see them from time to time."

"Us?"

"Yes. My youngest daughter, her husband, and I. Prisha's circled 'round while we've been talking to check on your friend. Don't worry, Captain. She's a good girl, studying to be our region's doctor."

John glanced at the embankment behind him. His training had taught him to take this man down and make sure Kendra was safe. Yet he somehow knew she was and that he was hearing true things. He looked around, thinking of the animals that had chased him down here, the strange unseen creatures that had run through their camp—and now human beings, living human beings. He wondered if all he had seen was making him feel so flushed and warm, despite his wet clothes.

"What is this place?"

Lewis smiled and looked off in the distance. "Well, that depends on what you believe."

CHAPTER 13

The fever came on as John rode on the back of Jack Lewis's horse. It crept into him, as his fevers usually had, starting in the middle of his back and working its way outward to his limbs. He didn't notice it much at first. He was too transfixed by the lolling rhythm of the horse beneath him, the grade of the well-worn path they followed through the woods, the scuttling and rustling of small and unseen creatures, the sharp clip-clop of Prisha's lead horse, and the weary look on Kendra's face when she would toss back a grin at him as she held on to Prisha's waist.

Before they agreed to leave together, Prisha told them that Kendra had only a mild concussion and assured John she would make a complete recovery with a bit of rest. John knew he should believe her—no one had sought to do them harm when they could've easily done so—and at first couldn't understand why he didn't. That distrust was his initial hint that he was feverish. How often had he seen feverish people become paranoid? And he well knew what fevers did to him. He still found it odd that he had survived so many, even that bout of scarlet fever when he was twelve. Now so far from home, he had little expectation of surviving this one if it turned out bad.

Once out of the woods, they found themselves in a neat clearing of sharp and definite borders. They passed through a gate in a wood-rail fence built to contain the horses and an extensive and well-maintained vegetable garden, now lying fallow. On the opposite side of their path was what looked like an autumnal grove of fruit-bearing trees at least several decades old. The thick old trees partly obscured their final destination: a wide and well-built one-story log cabin with two fieldstone chimneys rising into the setting sun. The cabin, not new by any means, had portions that looked newer than others. A family lived here and had lived here for a long time, perhaps generations.

When next John looked around, he was in a bed. He didn't know how he had gotten off the horse or through the front door, but when he opened his eyes he had been stripped of his wet clothes and was shivering under several heavy woolen blankets. The blankets were soft, and their cool earth tones made him feel as if they could break his fever. Prisha was stirring coals in the fireplace as her father sat on the edge of the bed. She was so young and pretty, this girl, with her dark skin and beautiful straight black hair and high cheekbones. She looked nothing like her father except in the eyes. Her eyes were the same shape and color green and seemed just as intelligent and as mischievous.

John tried to lift his head to find Kendra but couldn't see her. The old man patted his shoulder as a father might. His soothing voice was already growing warm and familiar.

"Easy, Captain," Lewis said gently. "You're not well. You fainted right off my horse. I don't think that dip in those freezing-cold rapids did you much good." He opened a small clay vial and shook something into his hand, then cradled John's head in the crook of his arm. "These are called aspirin. It's an old medicine known to cut fevers."

"My grandfather—a doctor—never used them."

"I assure you they are quite reliable. Saved my life and those of my children more than once. Now don't chew them. Just swallow them with some of this water."

John did as he was told and then sat back on the bed and let sleep start to take him. As it did his ears fixed on the Lewises' hushed conversation.

"Once they're both on the mend," Lewis told Prisha, "we'll let the others know. No reason to rouse everyone when these two can barely talk."

"Do you think they're really from the city?"

"It appears so. A genuine miracle they found us."

Prisha touched her father's shoulder and squeezed it. "Or fate."

The next morning Kendra winced as she tried to roll away from the sunlight coming through the crack between the shutters on the far side of the room. They'd been recently painted green, a nice green. The color brought a cheer to the small, warm room. She tried to sit up, winced again, then decided to wait and conserve her strength. She slipped her hand under the pillow and found the bowie knife. If she could rely on her good aim, she could put all her strength into a single thrust. That is, if only her head would stop pounding. She went to touch the cut in her hairline and found it covered by some kind of bandage.

She turned her head a bit more and saw her clothes and underwear draped over the hearth and wondered if she had the strength to get across the room and put them on.

"I thought I heard you stirring," a voice said from near the foot of her bed. Kendra glanced in that direction and saw Prisha standing in the doorway, holding a two-inch-thick slab of wood in her hands. As she approached, Kendra could see that the wood was in fact a tray and on the tray was an earthen bowl of soup and what looked like a matching, perspiring mug of very cold, very clear water.

"John?"

"Resting." Prisha set the tray on a nearby table, made of the same rough-hewn wood the walls were made of. "I'm afraid you've had a mild concussion. You'll need to rest a while here, but you should be fine."

"Can't rest—we have to get back, report in . . ."

"There's little chance you could get back now in your condition. Any pain right now?"

Kendra snorted. "That's an understatement."

Prisha smiled as she helped Kendra into a semi-sitting position and repositioned the covers over her naked body. "We have an analgesic that may help with the headache. I'll bring you some. But you should eat."

"I want to see John first."

Prisha touched her arm. "Eat first; then I'll help bring you to him. He has a fever, but he's young and strong. Both Father and I feel he'll mend quickly."

"You need to tell me everything," Kendra whispered as she gripped Prisha's sleeve. "I need to know."

"Need to know what?"

"None of this makes sense." A tear ran from one of Kendra's bloodshot eyes in a long streak down her cheek and onto her pillow. "I need to know. You have to tell me. Are you—are you the resurrected pagans? Is the Last Judgment upon us?"

Prisha took Kendra's hands in hers. "I am your friend. You have nothing to fear among us."

"But I—I have so much to confess."

Prisha smiled, her white teeth flashing in the semidarkness. "Eat. Get strong. Then we'll go see your John."

Within an hour Kendra was back in her uniform and pleasantly surprised to find that it had been both cleaned and mended. With a proffered crooked elbow and a tender pat on her hand, Lewis led her into the adjoining bedroom. John—her John, as Prisha called him—was lying on the bed, looking pale and clammy beneath the blankets. Even though Kendra had seen him only yesterday, he looked thinner somehow, diminished. The sudden smallness made her stomach spin almost as much as her head. From the day he'd carried her down that mountain, John Giordano had never seemed small to her.

"He's been in and out of consciousness this morning," Lewis said as he helped her into a chair Prisha had moved toward the bed.

"Is he getting better?"

He sighed. "The fever seems a bit weaker today, and there's no sign that pneumonia's developed, which is very good."

Prisha squeezed her shoulder. "We'll leave you with him for a while. But then you should get some rest yourself."

Kendra didn't look at John until the bedroom door clacked shut behind her. After she did, she found it hard to keep tears from welling up in her eyes. She had heard concussions made you more emotional. If he saw her crying, she would blame that.

"Hey," she said, leaning forward to take his hand. "Hey there, buddy."

What was it about a sickbed that made you think the worst things and say the stupidest ones?

She watched him snort and stir. He seemed to hear her breathing, if only for a second. She knew what this was. It was a moment among moments. She would always recall this scene in the clearest details down the whole vista of her life, because she knew that whatever came after this sickbed, her memory would shape it sharp and clear and permanent. His profile. The awkward angle at which she sat so she could bend forward to touch him. The low-burning flame of the candle swimming in its soup in its clay holder. The way her wrist with the tattoo on it looked as she held his limp hand. The sickly hot feel of John's skin. The way the fever seemed to shimmer the air between them like an uninvited ghost. The prickly feeling on her neck that told her the Lewises were waiting just outside. All this, all of this moment, would never leave her. There would be no do-overs after this moment. Her life would be only one way or the other.

"You better get well soon, okay? I've been thinking about how I've got a lot of apologizing to do. You know this is big time, Johnny—me apologizing. So if you want to hear it, you better get well soon, or I might change my mind, okay?"

His eyes flickered for a moment, then closed again. She wet his lips with a damp cloth that had been left by a bowl on a nearby table. Another detail.

"Don't think you can get out of loving me like this, pal," she said with a half grin as she leaned close to his ear. "You don't get to check out just because you're afraid of losing me first. You don't get to quit. You never ever get to quit."

She kissed his hot forehead with pressed-tight lips once, then again. "Semper fidelis."

She squeezed his hand, then stood up and left the room without calling for help. When she reached her own bed, her head throbbed so much that she was sure she would cry or throw up. But she refused to do either. So she held on to the bed, felt the coolness of the pillow against her cheek, and got back enough strength to minister to John four hours later and then four hours after that. And she kept up that routine—four hours on, four off—despite admonitions from the Lewises, until John's fever broke two days later. Then she slept the entire next day with nothing in her mind except the unclouded vista of what her life would now be.

"You're really quite a remarkable young woman," Jack Lewis said as he stepped out onto the porch to find Kendra sitting on the front step lacing up her boots.

"John's on the mend and Prisha's with him now," Kendra said, swinging her leather jacket around her back and tucking her arms into its sleeves. "Prisha was the one who suggested I go out for a short walk."

"I can't imagine my budding young doctor said that without *some* prompting."

"You've got me," she said with a grin, then stood up and looked at him.

"Might I see the cut on your head?"

She leaned forward a bit and let him lift the bandage—what he called "the plaster"—and inspect the wound.

"Nice small neat stitches," he said with obvious pride. "My girl took her lessons well. You shouldn't have much of a scar, and most of it should be covered by your hair."

She placed the bandage back on her head herself. "I suppose I've never thanked you for saving us."

Lewis shook his head as he pulled a pipe from his jacket pocket and began to fill it with what looked like tobacco. "Couldn't have you out there being eaten by the saber-tooths, now could we?"

Kendra looked out toward the woods in the distance. The tree branches had been shedding steadily, leaving the arching treetops looking ever more like the heads of balding men. It was hard for her to imagine all the life that existed out there. How stupid she had been! Apart from her people and a few predatory animals outside the city walls, she'd imagined this world to be a big green emptiness. The sea—that she knew teemed with life. But all this rugged land, these woods and streams—she had thought it nothing more than an oversized garden. What idiocy.

"Are they really saber-tooths? And woolly mammoths? And buffalo?"

"I'm fairly sure they are."

"How did they get here?"

"A good question. But one I have only speculative answers for, I'm afraid."

"Best guess?"

"They were brought here with us," he said.

152

"Even the extinct ones?"

His eyes twinkled. "I never said that it was an entirely good theory."

"There's so much I want to ask you."

Lewis stuck his pipe between his teeth, lit it, and puffed away for a time, then gestured toward the fields. "I think I'll join you on that walk. You can ask me what you like—and you can tell me all about my fellow survivors. It's been a long time since I've had any word of them."

Kendra talked first. She told him nothing she felt would compromise the city's defenses, but she did describe their journey over the last weeks and the basics of their mission. Lewis listened to every word without comment, nodding now and then, as they walked among the fruit trees in his grove. The colors of the autumn leaves were a rich tossed salad of reds and browns and oranges, with a few defiant greens hunkered down in spots. He plucked at a few clinging dry leaves while leaning against an apple tree and puffing on his pipe.

"And you think if you should find out where these Tylers came from, you might discover their true purpose, if they are in fact in league with the Hostiles or are with the ones who brought the survivors here and visit your people every other year?"

"That's it in a nutshell," Kendra answered. "We don't know anything. But we do need to be ready to defend what's left of the human race."

"But you don't know that's all there is of the human race," Lewis said. "After all, we're here too."

Kendra folded her arms across her chest as she leaned against a tree. "You know, you never told us. How many's 'we' exactly?"

"I don't have an exact number. All of those who chose not to stay and build the city," he answered. "Those survivors and their descendants."

"All I've seen so far is you and Prisha," Kendra answered. "That proves nothing."

"I'm telling you this on my authority."

"I'm not much for authority."

He laughed. "Everything we believe—from evolution to religious revelation—we believe on authority. You believe the world ended—and you weren't born until decades later."

"Many people witnessed it. My family. John's. People we've known for years."

"In other words—"

"Authority. Cute."

A playful look danced across his face. "Not very trusting, are you?"

She shrugged. "Force of habit when you've been defending a beach-head all your life."

He chortled. "You mean your city? That captive farm community? That defensive alliance? That's no beachhead. You can't fight from there, hemmed in by hills and the sea."

"You've got a better plan, living out here?"

"No, I can't say we have."

"So what do you have?"

"Just faith. Faith in the future. I suppose it's our battle plan. Mine, anyways. Faith has always been a beachhead into a hostile land. True belief, I mean, not just the hope one grasps for when following ritual-istic rules and regulations or building walls or conducting drills. This kind of faith may not bring you the comfort that comes with those things, but it can bring you truth. Tell me, do you have such faith in New Philadelphia?"

Kendra took a step back. "What are you?"

He shrugged. "Merely someone who perhaps sees things a bit differently than you do, Kendra."

"How so?"

He tapped the bowl of his pipe against the trunk of the tree he was leaning against and scattered the dead ashes at the base with the tip of his boot. "The people who live out here are not unlike the ones you know in the city who lived through the end of the world, who saw the Earth burn, who saw the waters of our world fill with blood, who saw the armies descend from the skies, who lived through the Armageddon. We know what happened, just as those in the city do. We just chose to respond to it in a different way."

Kendra cocked her head. "I'm still waiting for the how."

"How? Each in his own way."

"I don't understand."

"Look," he said with a bemused sigh. "You can't expect a hand to react the way an ear might, now can you? Yet both are part of the same body. In the same way, we're all part of the same body—all of us Remnants, as you call us, all of us humans, in fact—different organs and cells working sometimes together and sometimes separately to keep the whole alive."

"So you're human?"

He laughed again. "What else could we possibly be?"

"Orangemen," she said quietly. "Or Nephilim."

"Now I don't understand."

"Skip it. So, just to be clear. You have no contact with any Orangemen out here? They don't maintain some sort of a base in the vicinity?"

"No to both questions, I'm afraid."

Kendra wrinkled her nose. "Do you have any rolling tobacco? I'm not much for pipes."

Jack took out another pouch and some rolling papers and handed them to her. Kendra put together a neat cigarette in a few expert moves. As the smoke hit her system, she felt a bit light-headed but not in a bad way. She took two more drags before going on.

"Some of our people fear the Tylers are Hostiles in disguise—demons sent to infiltrate us by appearing human and sowing dissent among us. Demons did such things in the Bible. As did the Antichrist on Earth."

"You mean—" he began, then closed his eyes for a moment before sporting a pained grin. "I try not to discuss him, my dear."

"Suit yourself. But the book of Revelation warns us that the devil will be 'loosed a little season' to stir mischief among the people."

"So it does. Not that I've read Revelation very recently."

"It's not an implausible theory."

Lewis nodded. "I understand it all too well. Living in semi-isolation out here, one tends to develop a healthy fear of the unknown. And I understand the protective instinct of your city's leaders, just as any parent might. You'd do anything to protect your children, suspect all strangers. Just imagine being mother to what you thought were the last dregs of humanity." He shook his head. "But you're too young to understand those kinds of worries."

"I was a mother once." She wasn't sure why she said it at all until long after it left her mouth.

"I'm sorry. I didn't—"

"I had a miscarriage. After it happened, I couldn't understand why I couldn't save the baby. I was supposed to protect it. So I know that feeling. I feel it even now for John in kind of the same way. I would do anything to protect him . . . even if it meant damning my soul." She looked at the ground. "I don't know why I'm telling you this."

"Because you trust me a bit, perhaps?"

"I probably said it for a lot of reasons, but that sure ain't one of them."

"Forgive me, Kendra," he said after a long period of concentration, "but you do seem to think of things in black and white. Someone or something is either all good or all bad. As I understand it, isn't the whole point of Christianity the idea that all men must be regenerated in order to truly become the immortal creatures they're intended to be?" Receiving no response, he asked directly: "Come now, do you really think you're going to be damned?"

"That's none of your business."

"Quite right. But let me illustrate my point in a different way." He gestured at the trees around them with the stem of his pipe. "No one knows when one will get a perfect piece of fruit. Sometimes we discard fruit because it's sour or tiny or even just a bit bruised. But perhaps that piece we carelessly toss over our shoulder has seeds that, once they become mature trees, may ultimately produce the perfect piece of fruit."

"So you're saying what? That my child will redeem me?"

"What I'm saying is that life is trial and error. It's about how we face our trials and overcome our errors that matters most. We must keep trying, and we shouldn't think of ourselves or others as simply bad fruit. We might just need a bit more love and careful tending. And then, with that tending, our seed—what we do—might produce something truly wonderful. And then we would find ourselves awake inside our greatest dreams."

"That's a pretty story." Kendra finished her cigarette and extinguished it with her heel. "Belabored but pretty."

"You've not seen me on my best day," he said with a grin. "Give me time; I may yet convince you. In the meanwhile, would you mind telling me what you mean by the—Nephilim, was it?"

She shuddered. "You know, I'd like to go back now. I'm getting a little cold and tired."

CHAPTER 14

And there appeared a great wonder in heaven; a woman clothed with the sun, and the moon under her feet, and upon her head a crown of twelve stars: And she being with child cried, travailing in birth, and pained to be delivered.

—The Book of Revelation 12:1–2

It would be winter soon. The cold rains of late autumn had swept almost all of the leaves from the fruit trees in the grove and turned the rich fallow soil of the fields a deep reddish brown. Since Lewis and Kendra had walked the fields around the cabin, neither had spoken about what passed between them. The Lewises remained considerate hosts and Kendra a helpful, although still-recovering, guest. Much of their time was now spent indoors. They concentrated on prepping the home for the winter—stocking up on firewood, canning and preserving food, salting meat, finding and sealing cracks in the log walls where tingling fingers of cold air might try to poke in. By the end of that same week, John felt well enough to walk around the fields with his arm about Kendra. She supported him as much as he was willing to let her. As they walked, he told her about the time he'd been ill with scarlet fever and how Christian had carried him over his shoulder back and forth to the privy several times a day because he was too weak to walk on his own. At the barn he joked about their building a cabin next door to the Lewises. She wrinkled her nose and said she'd think about it only after the last frost. Neither of them said what they were really thinking: that they had to go home. And soon. People back home—people they loved—were depending on them. But they also needed to get well in order to survive the journey. In the meanwhile, they would find out as much as they could.

They had learned a great deal from both Lewises since John's recovery. Childhood stories bubbled out of Jack Lewis all the time but often during or after a meal. He told them all he could remember about the early days in this wilderness with his parents, being reminded here and there by Prisha about something he had once told her and her two brothers and two sisters about their grandparents. Often he smiled while recalling a story. A childhood like his didn't seem to lack smiles, despite the hardships.

He hadn't been more than nine when his parents decided to leave the camp the Remnants had established on the beach, just before the building of New Philadelphia. This was not long after the elders had agreed—John and Kendra had always been told unanimously—to build a city. Even though he had been just four during the Arrival, the impression the Orangemen had made had never left him. He recalled how they had hovered in the sky and asked the humans to love one another, so they had always tried to. They had said to rebuild the race, so he had had five children with his now-deceased wife, Prisha being his youngest. He talked little of his late wife. Her loss seemed too painful a subject.

The Orangemen had also said to begin anew. But they had never told them how. Lewis's parents—independent thinkers both of them—decided to do that in their own way, as did many others who did not agree with the decision to build New Philadelphia.

Lewis had no explanation for why the other Remnants had never told them about the people who didn't come to live in the city. By his count, at least fifty couples and families had trickled away from the beach to find their own paths in this new world. While to them they seemed like a good-sized group, it was hard to imagine they'd been missed on the beach.

These fellow iconoclasts who'd chosen to live in isolation even from one another had one thing in common: a willingness to try to build a different kind of humanity in the days ahead. They all hoped that separation might help people to love one another more and thereby prevent another near extinction. So they would make their stands apart from one another and live as best they could.

Pioneers. That's how they thought of themselves—not unlike the Puritans who found a new life in the American wilderness but even more so because they didn't have a single religious mind-set to guide and unite them. They believed they would have to pioneer an entirely new society, a whole new way of being that might someday incorporate itself into the prevailing thinking in New Philadelphia—or then again perhaps not. Their loose confederation had not gotten that far yet. Such isolation allowed for much reflection and a very slow decision-making process. It was hard to make quick decisions when one rarely saw one's neighbors apart from a general meeting every ninety days.

Lewis told them all of this as they sat on his porch on what John's grandfather would have called an Indian-summer evening. With his pipe clenched in his teeth as he rocked, Lewis might as well have been one of the nineteenth-century pioneers of the American West who sought to find their own purpose in a still-virgin country.

"So have you come to *any* decisions in all this time?" Kendra wondered aloud from her place next to John on the first step, a mug of Prisha's delicious tea warming her hands.

"Not really," Jack said with a sigh. "But we have come up with a number of working theories."

John perked up. "Such as?"

The older man glanced at his daughter. She sat near him on a hand-carved wooden bench. "Well," she began, "a number of us at least have a theory about what we're all doing here."

"Go on," Kendra said.

"Our books tell us that a lot of the creatures around here are native to Earth—"

"Wait," Kendra said, holding up a hand. "You have books here?"

"Our people procured a number of books from the campsite on the beach," Lewis explained. "Books on building and agriculture and biology, Bibles, quite a number of Eastern texts—"

"Back up a sec," John asked. "When you say Eastern texts, do you mean books about Eastern religions like Buddhism and Hinduism?"

"Yes," Lewis answered. "And Shinto and Taoism. All the religions born in the Asian nations of China, India, Japan, and the like."

John shook his head. "I'm sorry. You've got to forgive me. You see, we only know *of* these religions, that they once existed. But we know nothing about them. The only books the Remnants had about these religions disappeared long ago." He sighed. "Some of our people even believe they were spirited away by Orangemen who didn't want the human race to go, well, astray again."

"I see," Lewis said. "No, as far as I know, we have them only because our parents took them and never returned them, like bad library patrons."

"A weak explanation," John suggested.

"I was quite young when they packed their supplies. I'm not entirely sure why they took the specific books they did take," Lewis said with a shrug. "Let me turn the question 'round: If you were going off to rebuild civilization, what handful of books would you take with you?"

John laughed. "Fair enough."

"Won't Gordon Lee be pissed when he finds out?" Kendra asked, wrinkling her nose.

John shook his head again. "Sorry. Private joke. Please go on. You were talking about your theories."

Prisha gestured around. "Have you ever thought that it's entirely possible that the only reason we're here is because this is the Orangemen's, well, menagerie?"

John squinted at her. "Menagerie?"

"The books tell us that many of the birds and fish here are native to Earth. Unless there's some remarkable parallel evolutionary development going on, these creatures came here with the people you call the Remnants."

"Including me," Lewis said, waving his pipe above his head.

John raised an eyebrow. "So the Orangemen—the ones who saved us—snatched up creatures great and small from Earth in some kind of cosmic Noah's ark?"

"It has the beauty of having precedent." Lewis pulled the pipe from his mouth and stopped rocking. "And it would explain a great many things."

"Yeah, everything except those mammoths and saber-tooth cats," Kendra said over the rim of her mug. "Maybe they're native to Earth, but it's not like they were walking around when anybody got into any cosmic ark."

Thoughtful puffs of smoke encircled Lewis's head for a few minutes before he pulled the pipe from his mouth. "Those here who believe in God feel that God, through the Orangemen, sought to populate this world by taking creatures from *all* periods of Earth's history—that the reason the saber-tooths are here is because God chose them and other 'extinct' creatures to build a new world that was more suitable to his original design, before the *original* fall of man."

"How is that possible?" John wondered aloud. "Those animals were long dead."

Kendra's pale face was suddenly bright with understanding. "From *our* perspective. God is above time."

Lewis leaned forward, his thick elbows on his thicker knees. "Think of it this way, Captain. We perceive time as a line going from left to right. Birth is left, death right. Start of the world left, end of the world right. But God is a part of all of that and above it at the same time. Having always existed, he knows what has happened, what *will* happen. He sees, if you will, the entire page upon which the lines of our individual lives are drawn. Indeed, the lines of all existence, all reality."

"As well as different *planes* of reality," Prisha added. "The Eastern religions, particularly Hinduism, had no problem believing in an infinite universe—or even a multiverse—unlike their Western counterparts."

"You're being far too ungenerous, Prish," her father said. "The Westerners came 'round—or back around—to the Semitic idea of infinity and nothingness once they gave Aristotle the heave-ho."

"Aristotle?" Kendra asked. "Sorry, I haven't spent as much time in the Archives as John. Who's Aristotle?"

"A significant and ancient Greek thinker, who lived long before the early Christians," Lewis explained. "He was very influential on the thinking of early Christian scholars, so much so that they chose to agree with him that the universe had always existed in some form, even though *their own Bible* taught them that it had been created out of nothing."

"Wait, go back," John said. "There's more than one time period? An infinite number of universes? How is that possible?"

Lewis looked at his guests. "Forgive me. We're getting ahead of ourselves. Let's use mathematics. You accept the idea that you cannot subtract five from zero, that you still have zero? And that you cannot add any number to infinity and get more than infinity?"

"Sure. Of course."

Lewis grinned. "That's the same with God, Captain. He's always the same, because he's infinite. The very definition of the infinite, like its counterpart zero, is that it stays the same no matter what you subtract from it. So whatever is taken from whatever time period matters little. It is all part of the infinite."

"So what are you saying?" Kendra asked. "That what happened to the human race is only one of an infinite number of possible outcomes?"

"Possibly." Lewis shrugged. "Or that the human race itself is only one possible outcome."

"But why?" Kendra shook her head. "If God knows everything that would ever happen, why did he let humanity die? All that destruction, all those dead children—"

Lewis gave an almost imperceptible shrug. "Free will, my dear. It all comes back to that. God loves us enough to not have made us automatons or machines. He gives us the choice to love him back and love one another and improve the world. Or he allows us to destroy ourselves— even while giving us this final hope of redemption in this new world."

"Wait." John held up a hand. "What about that other theory your people have as to why the saber-tooth cats and mammoths are here with us?"

The wind rustled through the deserted tree branches around them. It was still warm but growing colder.

"Some of our people are not at all inclined to find spiritual meaning in what happened to us," Prisha added. "So they look elsewhere."

John arched his eyebrows. "Where exactly?"

"I suppose it comes from the fact that it's hard to ascribe specific intents to the Orangemen's actions. Many of us believe it is pointless to try," she added. "The Orangemen saved a handful of people and abandoned billions they did not kill outright to die in brutal and indescribably horrifying ways. And they left us only primitive tools to work with—no real knowledge. Did they want the survivors to live or not? Did they feel guilt or remorse?"

"I'm sensing an 'or' here," John said.

"Or . . . is this all just some sort of bizarre experiment?"

Lewis let that thought sit with them for a time before he removed his pipe from his teeth and examined it. "So what do you believe, Captain?"

"You pretty much know it at this point." John considered for a moment before answering. "Most of our people believe that the Orangemen, both good and bad, are angels, both pure and fallen. We believe this not only because of their physical appearance but because of all of their actions during and since the last days."

Prisha looked at John and Kendra. "And you have evidence that they are in fact immortal beings and not living, as we understand living?"

John and Kendra glanced at each other almost shamefaced. She spoke. "We know *some* of them can die."

"Then why do you think they can only possibly be angels and demons?" Lewis wondered without passion.

John found himself feeling defensive in a way he hadn't since he used to argue with Sofie in the old days. "Come on, Jack. You were there. What they did here and on Earth—they fulfilled the book of Revelation to the letter. You have Bibles, so you know that."

"Perhaps," Lewis answered in a carefree way. "But there are many inexplicable things in Revelation, as you know far better than I. Take the 'woman of the wilderness' in chapter twelve. Who is she? The Virgin Mary? It seems so, as she is crowned with twelve stars and clothed with the sun. But then a dragon stands before her, intending to devour her male child as she delivers him. And the dragon somehow doesn't and she gives birth to a child who will rule all nations. So why then does she flee into the woods after seemingly being delivered from this dragon? Frankly, the entire section, as supposed prophecy, mystifies me."

"As it does many people," Kendra muttered through clenched teeth.

He held up a hand in apology. "Forgive all my questioning. But are we to expect this all will literally happen, dragon included, just because another section of Revelation describes the saving of a hundred and forty-four thousand?"

"Our intention is not to offend," Prisha added. "But let me posit a different question, taking a middle ground of sorts. Isn't it possible that the Orangemen may have acted as God's agents and been mortal beings at the same time?"

"And in the end, does it matter what they are?" Lewis asked with a shrug. "It doesn't really. What if they're, I don't know, Nephilim, for example?"

John looked at him, glanced at Kendra, then asked, "How the hell do you know about them?"

Lewis took a worn family Bible from a leather pouch strapped to the arm of his rocking chair. "As you remind me, we read the same book. And as a matter of fact, I read about them just last night and got to thinking about them. The children of fallen angels and human women—it's an intriguing story."

Kendra turned to the older man. "What *are* you?"

"Excuse me, my dear?"

"What are you? You don't know anything. You both sit here and toss out a lot of crap and use it to tie us all into knots. Well, we're not buying it. We know what we know, and have faith in God and each other. And you won't do a thing to harm us, got it?"

"Kendra—"

"No, John." She yanked her arm out of his grip. "They keep beating around the bush about stuff, imply a lot, have no proof—and then accuse us of not having any proof! They're hiding something, and I'm going to come right out and say it."

"Are we demons?" Lewis asked with a beatific smile. "That's what you want to ask, correct?"

John clenched his jaw. "Are you?"

"If we were," the older man answered, "we likely wouldn't tell you."

"Fair enough," Kendra said. "So what are you, then?"

Lewis turned to his daughter as if he was trying to sift out the right words. Prisha answered. "If we all agree on one thing, I suppose you could say that we're against orthodoxy as a general rule."

"What's that mean?"

Lewis knocked out the spent ashes in his pipe against the side of his chair with three sharp taps. "Captain, I think I'm correct in assuming your leadership taught everyone in New Philadelphia to believe the events they witnessed are the only interpretation of those events, that they are, in effect, the truth. Therefore they teach orthodoxy. Yet, haven't you ever thought otherwise? That there might be another interpretation to what they witnessed—and what you continue to witness whenever you have an Orangeman 'checkup,' so to speak?"

John waved off that idea. "There is too much evidence there to suggest that mankind didn't in fact live through the last days, as predicted by Revelation. Too many coincidences."

Prisha nodded. "Agreed. There are far too many aspects of what happened to seem like coincidence. Many of our people also accept this. Or believe the Orangemen for some reason *want* us to believe that everything that is happening is prophecy fulfilled."

"But others," her father added, "point to our Eastern books to suggest that there are other interpretations of the divine. Then there are those strongly opposed to the idea of a God who would allow this to happen. And still others who don't know what to think. And yet—and yet, despite all these differences, all of us who live out here are united by this thought: never again. We're all going to make a better world here, a better humanity. We're in complete agreement with your people on that."

"To us, it doesn't matter what caused the near extinction of humanity," Prisha added. "We'll never go back to the way humanity was— self-absorbed, greedy, violent, arrogant, proud, spiteful. Never again."

John and Kendra sat in silence on the steps. After a long while, Kendra cleared her throat. "I guess we agreed to come on this mission because our beliefs were challenged by the Tylers. Four people were alive from the end times who shouldn't have been. One hundred and forty-four thousand, plus four. And they arrived here with the Orangemen more than a half century after all of the other Remnants."

"We volunteered," John added with hesitation, "because we had doubts."

Lewis looked up at the darkening skies, dense with purple and red swirls of clouds. After a while he slapped his thick knees with his rough palms and stood up. "It's getting rather late. I'm going to retire now. But once you're both well enough—which seems like it will be quite soon—we're going to take you to meet someone I think you'll be interested in seeing before you head home."

John pulled himself up by the banister instead of relying on his still-weak legs. "Your leaders?"

"We have no leaders," Lewis answered with a slight grin.

Prisha rubbed John's shoulder and smiled. "Someone even better."

CHAPTER 15

Kendra slid her hand across the bed she shared with John and found it empty. The sheets were cool. She rubbed her eyes and ran her other hand through her knotted hair, then sat up. Somewhere outside she could hear the easy undertones of voices chatting, a pair of them. The quieter one was clearly John's. She snatched her clothes from the floor, slid into her uniform pants, and pulled on an undershirt while still under the covers, not wanting the chilly morning air to come in contact with her bare skin. Then she splashed ice-cold water on her face from the baked-clay washbasin on the dresser and finger combed her hair in the bedroom's small mirror before heading in the direction of the voices on the porch. The men were drinking coffee from ceramic mugs.

"What would I have liked to have seen on Earth-of-old?" John said with a sigh. "A football game. You know, the roar of the crowds, all those people sitting there getting thrilled by a bunch of guys trying to keep a ball from landing in a certain spot. You?"

"Frank Sinatra," Jack Lewis answered. "He was a singer, supposedly one of the greatest. Pity we don't have any recorded music. The more often you read something or someone is once-in-a-lifetime, the more you want to—"

"Hey Kendra. Want some good and strong coffee?"

John's voice was bright and clear as he greeted her. It sounded just as it ever did, not a trace of illness clinging to it. Apart from the fact that his cheeks had hollowed out and his eyes were a bit deep set, it was hard to tell he had ever been sick. She surveyed him as he kissed her. Even the dark circles under his eyes that had been almost like bruises were fading. She smiled at him closemouthed as plans of hearty breakfasts and morning jogs ran through her brain. Just little bits of exercise at a time until he was back up to fighting strength.

"What's up?" she asked, tucking a stray lock of hair behind her right ear.

"We've got news," John said. "Jack here has agreed that we're both well enough to visit this mysterious 'someone' we're supposed to be interested in meeting."

Kendra looked at Lewis, who grinned as he stuffed his morning pipe with tobacco. "The someone wouldn't be so mysterious if he told us who it was."

"It'll be easier to explain once you see him," Lewis said evenly. "No need to stress your systems during your recoveries."

"Oh really?" Kendra eyed the older man. "You the doctor now too?"

"Kendra—"

She looked at John. "Prisha agree to this?"

He scratched at the now-ragged blond hairs on his neck. "We haven't, uh, talked to her yet."

Kendra looked at one, then the other, as she shook her head. "Where is she?"

"In the barn," Jack said, lighting his pipe. "Tending the horses. She is the animal doctor too, you know."

Kendra took the three front steps in a single shot. As she approached the barn, she could hear Prisha's soothing voice talking under the whinnying of the horses. The hay smelled fresh and clean.

"Prisha?"

"Over here."

At the back of the barn, Kendra stopped mid step. Prisha was atop a large covered wagon, the likes of which she had never seen outside history books in the Archives.

Prisha wiped her brow with her wrist as she paused from her work fastening a canvas across the wagon roof's skeletal frame. Then she stepped down from the wagon and gestured toward it. "My family built it when I was about four. Before that we had no idea if wheeled traffic would work on such uneven horse paths. But it's been good to use for distances or to carry a number of people. Just don't tell Father I was working on it. He'd be angry I was working on it in my condition."

"You're pregnant?"

"Yes. A little more than three months," she answered, her dark eyes wide with excitement. "Our first. My husband doesn't know. Neal's been on this, well, expedition since I found out. Some of our people thought it might be a good idea to scout a bit deeper into the valley to see if there might be more fertile land available beyond the woods we found you in."

Kendra took in the woman's serene face, awful in its beauty and possibility. Prisha's voice droned on about having gotten word from her husband last week through a messenger and how she didn't want him to find out through some third party, that she wanted to tell him in person. A blind and burning flash of hatred, as sudden as it was appalling, filled Kendra. She knew she wasn't being rational. This young woman had saved her life, saved her John. But still.

"You know, I was pregnant once. Dunno if your father told you that."

"Pregnant once—" Prisha's face held only blank confusion for several moments. "Oh. I'm sorry. Father didn't tell me, he didn't."

A shrug as Kendra's hands found her hip pockets. "I suppose your people don't believe in Confessors."

"Confessors?"

"People you—I dunno—people you tell your sins to, who help you to get yourself straight with . . . stuff."

"There's nothing for you to confess, Kendra. Not to me."

Kendra shook her head, laughing. "Oh you don't know the half of it."

"Would it make you feel better to talk? For me to be your . . . Confessor?"

She nodded.

"Then go ahead."

"I've never said this. Never, never. Not to anyone." She looked at the barn's roof. "Before I lost the baby, there was a moment I wanted to—it's a big, giant no-no where we come from. Whole human race wiped out and—"

"Kendra—"

"No one ever talks about it, because it's against the law, but girls do it in New Philadelphia for all kinds of reasons." She snorted and shook her head. "But none of them ever considered it for as screwed-up a reason as mine."

"Whatever your reasons," Prisha said, "you didn't go through with it."

Kendra shrugged. "Just didn't have time."

"How far along were you?"

"About seven weeks."

"There was time enough." Prisha took her hand. "If you claim to believe in mercy, have mercy on yourself."

"John," Kendra said after a time, "he doesn't know what I was planning to do."

"Was the baby his?"

Tears pooled in Kendra's eyes. "No."

"Then he never has to know," Prisha said as she stroked Kendra's quivering cheek. "Only the most reckless relationships are entirely truthful."

"Yeah." Kendra wiped her eye with the heel of her palm. "No shit."

The wagon was filled with supplies and hitched to the Lewises' two horses at first light. The air was dry and cool and warmer than it had been for the last week. In fact, it almost seemed as if they were headed for spring, not winter. The sun felt good on their faces, and those who sat in the back took turns on the wagon's front bench to get a feel of that sun for a time.

It was a great day, no doubt about it. John found himself feeling very glad to be alive. Part of him knew Kendra was right, that he should be more annoyed with the Lewises and their cryptic hints about their destination, especially since he understood all too well that they should get back home as soon as possible. But glorious days such as this one almost always forced him to push his worst thoughts aside. The bits of exercise he was getting—loading the wagons, occasionally taking the reins and steering the horses—also helped. As he sat on the bench next to Lewis, the sky was big and clear with only a few white clouds marring its blueness. The soft breeze brought only a hint of autumn with it into his nostrils. He wondered if any morning on Earth had ever been so fine.

He felt that life was damned sweet. Even at his worst times. Even when he was the most lost and directionless, he knew instinctively that there were glories in the world that were worth living for. Could be small things—Kendra throwing her arm around him as she slept. Or great ones—that time he had helped his grandfather deliver a little girl. He felt the sum of existence could be found in each act, just as surely as a sum of atoms made up each piece of matter. He might not understand it any better, but he could feel its significance just the same.

Almost always, Alex Raymond came to mind at times like these. It was hard not to think of Alex while being life affirming in any way. He had been, after all, the only suicide among all the people who had ever lived in New Philadelphia. The episode always seemed set apart from John's life, as if it happened in a story he had read in the Archives. But it wasn't. His patrol group had been the one who found him that morning hanging from a makeshift noose at the edge of the cliff, his eyes wide and bulging and staring right at them as he swayed in the breeze. None of them could understand it. What could possess anyone to do such a thing? Everyone had said he did it because he was the father of Kendra's unborn baby and didn't want to marry her. Even after everyone had, by general and ignorant consensus, decided that was the reason, John wasn't so sure. Taking such drastic measures—either good or bad—couldn't be based on any one thing, especially not something as simple as unexpected fatherhood. He must've had many tragic and maybe conflicting reasons that brought him to that cliff.

John was sure he would never know. And he would never ask Kendra about it.

"Will we be on the road much longer?"

"I know you're growing eager to go home, Captain," Lewis answered. "We'll make camp well before nightfall. We've a usual site we go to, and we're making quite good time. Then we'll break camp right after breakfast and be at our destination before the midday meal, I should think."

John thought to ask the old man about their ultimate destination but then saw the pointlessness in it. "Tell me something, Jack."

"Anything I'm able to answer."

"So you've really never seen any signs of Orangemen in all the time you've been out here?"

"Me? Direct contact, no," Lewis answered without glancing from the road. "But as I've said many of us think we've seen them about."

"Where exactly?"

He rolled his eyes skyward. "Up there. Bright things moving far up. You might not see them if the lights of your city are as bright as you say they are. But many of us out here in the darker corners have seen them, myself included. Of course, they could all just be tricks of the eye. Or the light."

"So you really don't know what they are?"

"I'm afraid not."

"Has anyone ever tried to investigate them? See if these 'bright things' land anywhere?"

"I don't believe so. It was discussed at one point, I believe."

John chuckled. "Your people ever do more than discuss stuff?"

"Sometimes. And many times I wish we had more of the definite answers your people believe they have. Sometimes I feel that might make our lives a bit easier."

"I'm not sure it makes things easier for us. Kendra and me—we ask too many questions."

"Of whom?"

"Of people who think they have all the answers. My mother, for one. An old girlfriend of mine. Funny, they've got the same mind-set. If only they were on the same side."

Lewis smiled at the younger man. "So your people do believe in questions, just not too many of them."

"Even the faithful believe in asking questions," John answered. "Augustine tried to refute inconsistencies he came across in Scripture, and he did that by questioning them. And he let his students question him."

"Augustine?" Lewis paused. "Can't say I know him."

John shook his head and laughed. "Then you, sir, are missing out."

The trip south was uneventful. Kendra was somewhat surprised by that. After their hellish trip here from New Philadelphia, she had been prepared for more excitement. Instead they came through a soft and still country. Leaves were still falling from trees that had not yet hardened into their bare-boned winter selves. The overgrown land around them had taken many long breaths in its time. It was undisturbed by the passage of animals, large or small, instinctive or intelligent. But still she wondered. Would saber-tooth tigers really be scared off by occasional human traffic? Kendra thought the people out here might have means other than walls to keep their adversaries at bay. And that could be a tactical advantage they might be very unwilling to share.

But there was just so much space, so much pristine land. Once out of the forest they found themselves in open grasslands, fields wide to the hilled horizon. Such land was all Kendra could think about. She well understood now how Prisha's husband might be enticed into going on an expedition out here to see if there were places for them to spread out to, to live, to build new communities on, to hand down to children, and to let those children have children.

They were living in a nearly empty world and had been put here to populate it.

It was the only thing that made sense. When Kendra thought of her own people back in the walled city, hemmed in on all sides by walls and hills and seas and a feared sky, her chest tightened. How could they have tolerated it all that time, all of them crowded together like that?

That night they camped out at the "usual spot" Lewis had described—a lean-to not dissimilar from the one they had dismantled to make their raft. It had been built near a stream they had been following most of the day. Lewis definitely knew the site well. After shuffling around for only a minute, he pulled a cord of burlap-wrapped firewood out of a hole that had been dug next to the lean-to's foundation and covered by a wooden lid sealed with some sort of tar. A few minutes after that, the old man had a fire blazing, while Prisha fed and watered the horses. John and Kendra were knee to knee in the lean-to, unpacking their bedding.

"Remember how we joked about just living out here? Not going back? I'm thinking we really should."

He gave her a sidelong grin. "I had a feeling you might."

"So . . . whaddya think?"

"I'm for staying out here." John sat on his bedroll, pulled out his canteen, and offered it to her. She shook her head, so he took a swallow instead. "I'm for it, Kendra. But we made a promise to the Weiss brothers, to Grace, even to Gordon—everybody we left back there wondering what the Tylers mean. Our word has to mean something."

"I know. You're right."

He paused with the canteen before his lips. "Of course, nobody's saying we've gotta *stay* in the city after we make our report."

The points of her smile brightened her eyes. "Clever boy. A separate peace."

"A separate peace. A real peace for both of us."

Their destination rose up in the distance: a sturdy log cabin of a far more modest size and somewhat newer appearance than the one that had been inhabited by generations of Lewises. The cabin was set apart in a clearing on the hill and commanded a panoramic view of the surrounding countryside. On a clear day the people who lived up there could likely see nearly all the way to the riverside campsite they had left that morning. Had these people also been the ones who'd built the lean-to they had slept in? It was a good strategic place to build a home and an even better one to retreat from, if the surrounding woodlands were as impenetrable as they appeared.

Lewis pulled on his horses' reins and brought them to a stop in the valley below. Kendra watched him contemplate their destination wordlessly, his lower lip caught between his teeth. No one asked why he had stopped. Kendra did, however, eventually poke her head out from inside the wagon to look at John when it seemed that the break had gone on for a little too long and without reason.

"I know you both think we've been behaving rather cryptically about all this. But we really didn't know what to say or even how much we should say."

Kendra blinked at him. "And now we're stopping here because . . . ?"

He glanced at her in a kindly way and then gave John the same easy gaze. "The man who lives up there has many of the answers to the questions you have."

"Can he tell us who the Tylers are?" John asked. "Or whether there are Orangemen out here who want to harm our people?"

"I'm not sure. What he can tell you is what he's learned out here over the past fifteen years. In that time he's discovered more about what happened to the human race than anyone else we know. And his discoveries have made my people—well, even less sure of our beliefs than we were before."

Kendra and John eyed each other. She spoke first. "And you think his discoveries will make us question our own beliefs? Question things we know to be true?"

"Undoubtedly."

Prisha looked out from her seat in the back of the wagon and addressed both of them. "You may have doubts about certain things— but not all of what you know is wrong. Father, make them understand that."

He nodded. "That much is true. What you learn may test your faith, but that doesn't necessarily mean you'll leave this place faithless."

John looked at him. "Okay. I'm officially done with this. Let's go."

The older man touched his arm. John eyed the hand clasping the crook of his elbow. "We're not being mysterious because we wish to be, Captain. It's simply not our place to say. And we don't believe in imposing our thoughts on anyone else."

"You heard him," Kendra said. "Either move or we get out and walk."

As they slowly rolled up a path that followed the contours of the hill, it seemed likely that whoever lived in the cabin had been watching them for some time. There was no outward suggestion—not a suddenly shut window or any quick motions outside the cabin—but the sheer absence of movement felt like watchfulness.

Lewis did not hide their approach, nor did he announce it in any way. The wagon drew up the path almost right to the front door. He tied the horses off at a nearby post. He did not move with the weariness of a man having endured a long journey or the excitement of a man visiting an old friend after a long absence. He climbed the porch steps one at a time with no deliberate speed. Prisha was at his side. Kendra and John followed a step behind. A knock and the door opened into a darkened interior that was illuminated only by a small fire and warmed with recently turned coals. A breakfast of some kind was cooking over the fire. It smelled like eggs and bacon, both probably taken from the animals in the yard.

"Come on in, Jack," a voice said. "You've brought company."

"Yes. You remember my Prisha, of course."

A man came into focus as their eyes adjusted to the dim light. He was well into his middle age, thin-framed but corded by wiry muscles. His strong forearms were emphasized by the rolled-up sleeves of his bright-red shirt. On his face he wore a neatly trimmed, reddish beard several shades darker than the graying and somewhat thinning dirty-blond hair on his head. The man reviewed them with a hard squint that hid the color of his eyes. John met the man's gaze and was about to extend a hand when he staggered back, almost tripping into Kendra.

"John?"

"Kendra McQueen," Lewis said with a somewhat exaggerated degree of formality, "allow me to introduce you to Samuel Giordano, John's father."

CHAPTER 16

"What're you talking about?" Kendra shook her head. "John's father was lost at sea—years ago."

The man who lived in the cabin fixed her with an enigmatic squint-eyed stare. He looked like he was doing nothing more than thinking about what to make for lunch. How could this man really be Sam Giordano?

She turned to John. He was still staring at the man Jack Lewis had just called his father. Lewis himself was looking down at his hands while Prisha seemed desperate to say something but unsure of what she could say to bring anyone any comfort.

John took a step toward the man and walked around him. The man took this intense observation without comment or action, apart from the fact that he turned to follow John sidelong out of the corner of his crowfoot-framed eyes. When John had gotten about halfway around him, the man grunted.

"You finished yet?"

John stepped back. "It's you. It's really you. My God."

"Of course it's me. Who in the hell else would it be? You think these people would lie to you?"

"Where's Christian? Where's my brother?"

"Dead." The man said this plainly. "Washed overboard during a storm at sea."

"You don't seem so cut up about it."

"I had to bury that grief a long time ago."

John clenched his right fist at his side. "My father loved Christian more than anything in the world."

The older man snorted. "You think I love him any less now?" He tossed his bearded chin in Kendra's direction. "Who's this? I don't like talking my business in front of strangers." He looked at Lewis. "What'd you say her name was?"

"My name's Kendra McQueen."

"McQueen," Samuel Giordano mused. "You Mitch and Jess McQueen's little girl?"

"Yes."

"How're they?"

"Dead. Of a fever plague, three and a half years ago."

"Hmm." He shook his head. "Must've been just a baby the last time I saw you."

"I was five when you went out on your expedition."

Sam snorted again, then looked at his son. "Sounds like our little research effort hasn't gotten more popular with age."

John shook his head. "You've been out here—all this time—and you never tried to—"

Lewis cleared his throat. "Perhaps Prisha and I should step out for a bit."

"Why?" Sam's question was a sharp bark. "You're not going to hear anything you don't already know, Jack. Besides, the bacon's fresh and there's plenty to go around."

"We'll stay, Sam." Prisha patted his shoulder and tried to smile. "Just let me get some of the preserves we brought along to go with that delicious bread I keep smelling."

Death always softened memories. It always tricked the senses. Even the worst relationships lost their harder edges once someone was no longer among the living. For those that still were, the hurt faded as the healing nature of everyday life asserted itself like creeping vines over raw and fertile mourning.

John had mourned his father and brother. A hard thing to do without bodies to cry over. Without a proper burial, there was always a remote expectation that someday they would come home, strolling along the beach, wild haired and bearded. He'd tried to take comfort in his mother's assurances that they died as they wanted to live and without regrets. He had always hoped she was right—that they would all meet again. But this?

Whenever he had thought of his dead father, the one of disappeared hopes, he recalled all the good things said of him during the ritual talk of mourning. Whenever he had thought of his living father, the one of etched memories, he recalled many small things—the shape of his knuckles and the wrinkles over them as he held John's boy-soft hand in his, the way he sat in a chair and crossed his legs right ankle over left knee as he talked or listened, the sometimes far-off look he'd get in his eye. All that was his father, the living one and the dead one, not this messy mass of hard contradictions that was sitting before him now.

Looking at *this* man, he began to recall the things he had suppressed about his father since his "death"—the skeptical eye, the remoteness, the rage or frustration just under his skin that had never found an outlet apart from a barked-out comment brought on by rough booze. This was his father without death to make him gentler, without time's passage to warm parts of him more than others. This was his father, alive again, here to contradict every memory. And he hated him for it—and for the fifteen years that separated them.

John said none of this as Sam Giordano told his story. He listened as they all did—even the Lewises, who had heard so much of it before.

The Council of Twelve had only grudgingly given its permission for Sam's venture to sail up the coast from the city, following the prevailing breeze and his instincts, and to report back two weeks later. In the years since the Arrival, few people had ventured more than a few miles up or down the coast—apart from, as John and Kendra now knew, those who had left in the days before New Philadelphia's foundation. Few Council members trusted Sam's motives or believed the effort to be a worthy one. But like many a politician before him, Sam had invoked the memory of a beloved dead leader in order to sway the weak-kneed and the unwilling. In his case, he had invoked the memory of his own father, the first John Giordano, who had served on the Council so many times. He told the Council's membership that his father's one great regret in life was that he had not been able to save more lives than he had. What if there were natural cures in the wild just waiting for them? What if the Orangemen wanted them to explore, to learn how to use nature without exploiting it, to grow as a race? Wouldn't such exploration be an important first step? And who knew what else they might learn in their journey through a world they hardly knew? Didn't that alone outweigh any risks?

Passion appealed to orthodoxy, reason to faithful hope. And somehow Sam won the day. It took him more effort to convince Petra to go along with the idea—and to let him take their older son with him. Against Sam's passion for exploration and Christian's youthful eagerness, however, she had relented.

Whatever books they had on sailing, navigation, and basic construction principles had been brought from the Archives, dissected, and analyzed. Whatever Sam's inventive, scientific mind could not deduce, he improvised with Christian's help. Within a few months they'd built a seaworthy sailing vessel and completed a test run in the city's harbor.

Sam tried to soften the blow to Petra by surprising her the night before they sailed with a hand-carved sign that he had mounted to the bow of the ship. *Petra* would be the name of the ship.

"She didn't want us to go," Sam continued as he stuffed his wide mouth with another forkful of eggs. "But Christian and I did lots of little things to make her more comfortable with the idea. Even so, she was a pain in the ass about the whole thing—kept finding quotes in Scripture about tempting fate." He sighed. "A lot from the book of Proverbs."

John glanced up from his plate. "Maybe she was right."

"How so, Johnny?"

"Well, you're here and Christian's not."

Father looked at son with something bordering on contempt. "Keep listening. Maybe you'll learn something instead of just acting on assumptions."

Kendra squeezed John's knee under the table.

Sam wiped his mouth with his fingers and continued. "We were three days out when the storm hit. We thought we were in waters far enough from the coast to be out in the deep but close enough that we felt we could make landfall if necessary. After the storm rolled in, visibility dropped to zero. The wind picked up and began tossing the ship around like it was nothing. Pitch-black sky with only the occasional flash of lightning to let you see your hand in front of your face. No sound except the storm raging, no way to talk. And we couldn't feel anything around us except the pelting, cold rain as we tried to steer in this overwhelming void."

Kendra watched the older man's eyes grow distant. This he had lived through. And no matter what John was thinking, his father was still living it each day. It was a way of living she well understood.

"I wouldn't have seen him go over if it hadn't been for the lightning right then. A flash and my boy's face was suspended in midair as he went flailing over the side. A flash again and just the empty deck before me and the black, roiling sea behind it." He shook his head and turned his attention to Prisha, then Kendra, who was sitting nearest him at the table. "I didn't even have time to look for him. Next thing I knew I felt something hit me hard in the back of the head—I don't know what—and then nothing."

"But how'd you wind up here?" Kendra asked. "This is as far from the coast as anyone has ever been."

"You might not believe me."

"Try us," John said.

"Better yet," Sam answered, "finish your breakfast and I'll show you."

The hike was short, only a mile or so, but was mostly uphill into a particularly tight thicket of woodlands southwest of the cabin. There were no major bodies of water in the area—and therefore no way for Sam to have been dumped here as they had been on their ride down the rapids.

The woods were dark, primordial. Despite being stripped by the season of their leaves, the branches overhead weaved a thick-enough canopy that little sunlight found its way to the forest floor. The ground was spongy with old leaves and the rotting husks of trees. No one had ever lived here apart from small animals, and no one ever would, at least not for a long time.

How old was this world? Kendra found it hard not to wonder. And stranger still that it seemed no animal life had ever developed on it, apart from the "menagerie" the Orangemen had decided—for whatever reason—to deposit here. How many planets like this one were out there? How many chances would God give humanity to begin again in a new Eden before he finally ended his experiments? She could hear Grace's voice, cragged with age and rich with experience, telling her that

God's love was infinite, his forgiveness unending, that it was in a very literal sense impossible for anyone to imagine. It was difficult to draw comfort from an idea beyond man's ken.

"We're here."

Sam pulled his hatchet from his belt and started to whack at an unruly thicket nearby. All of them stood back as Sam handed newly hacked branches to Lewis, who tossed them aside. After a few minutes they had cleared a space in the bushes about four feet wide. In another few minutes six feet. The widening opening revealed nothing significant, only a field as black as a moonless night. Yet something about it looked wrong to their eyes. The perspective was off—it seemed to have no depth at all.

In a few minutes a narrow band of orange a few inches thick began to reveal itself.

With the last of the overgrowth pulled away, Sam and Lewis stood back so the others could see what they had uncovered. In front of them an orange frame surrounded a void—literally a void in space. It was a place without substance, with only the metal frame to provide any proof of its existence. The frame was standing perpendicular to the ground without any braces of any kind.

"It's exactly one meter thick, two meters wide, and three meters tall," Sam said to no one in particular. "Just the right size to let a couple of Orangemen through comfortably."

Kendra and John circled the object. There was no back. The space inside the frame was equally black and formless on both sides.

"Here," Sam said as he picked up a discarded branch about two feet long. "Watch."

He tossed it directly into the center of the frame, where it disappeared from sight without much drama and in total silence. John looked at the back side in a half-expectant way, as if he imagined the branch would come through, just a bit late. He turned to Kendra.

"Okay. Where'd it go?" she asked Sam.

Sam continued to stare into the void. "If I'm not out of practice, it went back to the beach where I first fell through one of these things. But when it's black like that, I'm never really sure."

Kendra was flummoxed. "Out of practice?"

"And where's that beach?" John asked.

"About one hundred miles up the coast from your city," Lewis answered. "And about two hundred miles from here."

"You're kidding, right?" Kendra asked. "I mean, that's a joke."

"Step through if you don't believe me, kid," Sam said with some satisfaction.

"Our best guess," Lewis began, "is that this is some type of transportation portal that was used by the Orangemen at one time to ferry themselves around the planet. Obviously, this particular one has not been in use for some years. John, when your father was shipwrecked, he stumbled around blindly in the dark and must've fallen through one on that beach and somehow arrived on this hilltop. He wandered around half-starved for possibly as long as a week before my son-in-law's parents found him and brought him amongst us. He was the first contact we had had with your people since we left the beach."

"Get to the point, Jack," Sam said. He turned to face Kendra and John as he gestured at the portal. "This—this thing—is *technology*, not a miracle. This isn't the work of God. The Orangemen you stand in awe before and the ones you live in fear of are no agents of the Almighty; they're not angels and demons. They're intelligent beings like us, ones who wiped us out and are now studying us like damn lab rats."

"That's not true," Kendra objected. "You can't prove this—object— is technology."

"Maybe not," Sam answered, "but tell me: If it's a holy relic, why doesn't it appear and disappear as needed? Why is it set up like it's part of a transportation system?"

"Speculation, untested theories," John jumped in. "You should know better. Apart from having gone into one and come out another, you know nothing about them. You ever take one apart? See one built? Know what powers it? Besides, what makes you an expert on the divine? How could you possibly deduce the difference between something divine and something material? This thing could've been God's way of saving your life by bringing you here."

"I remember talk like that." Sam shook his head. "You sound a lot like the old Remnants, justifying everything to fit Scripture."

"I remember my father never took anything at face value," John answered. "And never tried to shoehorn a handful of facts into pet theories. That's not the scientific method at all. Frankly, I don't take *you* at face value because I know my father—and you are not him."

Lewis stepped between father and son, his rotund body acting as a subtle but likely ineffective barrier. He glanced at John and Kendra. "You've both had a lot to process today, and I admit that we may not have done our best to prepare you for it. For that, I sincerely apologize. I suggest we all return to the cabin for a while—"

"Before we do that," Sam said, "let me say this. I've learned how to *use* this thing. Jack knows all about it. It's controlled by will. It takes you where you want—or need—to go. And I can take you back to your city as soon as you want."

"What?" John asked. "There's one of these outside New Philadelphia?"

Kendra cocked her head to the side. "And the catch?"

Sam aimed his hard gaze at her. "No catch, McQueen. But I do want you to go back to your people prepared—which means I've got a couple more things to show you." At Prisha's surprised look, Sam turned to her and Lewis. "Things I've never even shown you. Things I hoped would die with me."

"With a build-up like that," Kendra said, "who can resist? Lead on."

Sam laughed, for the first time flashing clear brown eyes not unlike John's. "You're brave, McQueen. Good. You're going to need it."

CHAPTER 17

After they had returned to the cabin, Sam set out again in the early afternoon. He said nothing of what he wanted to show them, nor did he suggest that it needed to be seen right away. If Kendra had to guess, she would've said he was afraid. It didn't surprise her. People who talk about bravery were really cowards. She had known that since her Novice year in the Defense Forces. The biggest mouths with the cockiest walks were usually the ones who smelled like they had soiled themselves after being surprised in recon and ambush drills.

And then there was Alex. But she had thought of him too much recently and turned her thoughts away from his memory.

She worried about John. He had been unusually restless since his father had taken off. He couldn't stay in the cabin for more than a few minutes at a time. He stepped out for a third time after Prisha had tried to make some small talk with him. It was coming on dinnertime and Sam still wasn't back.

Kendra found John out on the front porch steps. He was whittling a three-inch-thick tree branch with his bowie knife. He didn't turn around when she opened the door.

"It's not him, Kendra."

She tucked her hair behind her ears as she sat on the porch steps next to him, elbows on her knees. "How?"

"He's too hard, too inflexible. He doesn't have any . . . compassion, I guess. At least not the way I remember he did. He was always skeptical, but the skepticism was bounded by rational thought. This . . ." He trailed off, turned from the late-afternoon breeze, and looked at her. "The Weiss brothers were worried the Tylers might be Hostiles in disguise. What if he's an Orangeman posing as my father?"

"Or," she began with some deliberation, "what if he is your father but changed? It's been fifteen years, John. People change, especially after—"

"It's hard to believe anyone can change that much."

"I know the Weiss brothers said they had this suspicion, that people might not be who they say they are. But have you seen any proof of it anywhere? I sure haven't, even when I've feared it myself. Not in the Tylers or the Lewises—or even your father. I think all of these people *are* who they say they are, like it or not."

"But he's just changed so much, Ken."

"But you've got to ask yourself if it's a logical change. From what you've told me, he was always skeptical about the fact that mankind really had lived through the events predicted in Revelation. Wouldn't an already-skeptical man who is made more bitter about life eventually become a hard cynic?"

John shrugged, hands in his jacket pockets. "But the bigger question is, would he still be an honest dealer? Despite his skepticism—heck, despite my mother's unquestioning faith too—I always trusted my parents. They always played it straight with Christian and me. That man—all this hinting and foreshadowing—I'm just not sure."

Kendra stood and shuffled around in the dirt at the bottom of the steps, hands in her back pockets. "Let's take a step back here. Your father's information about that . . . object he showed us is based only on his own limited experience with it, right?"

"So far as we know."

"So it's fragmentary." She grinned. "In that way it's really no different from the larger question we have about the Orangemen themselves. We're trying to understand things based on clues, hints, visits every couple of years, handed-down descriptions of what the Remnants saw and heard of the Orangemen on the day of the Arrival. Your father had drawn his conclusions based on those things plus his experience with that portal—but it's all colored by his experiences, just as our take is based on our experiences."

"You make it sound like we're all biased."

"Purposely biased, no. Human—yup." She sighed. "Seeing that portal reminded me that we're mortal and therefore we can only ever see the bits—never the whole truth of creation. We're too small to see the whole plan. We're too much a part of the plan to see the plan."

"You talk as if you still think there's a plan."

"You're kidding, right?" She shook her head. "Because your old man showed us some hole in space and claimed the Orangemen were mortal beings like us because *he fell through it*? That only proved to me how little we actually know and how fragmentary our understanding is. And you need to remind your father of that."

"Me?"

"Who else?"

John smirked. "I can think of better people to tell that arrogant ass that he doesn't know everything."

"Who, me? Sorry. It would come from no one better than you—especially since your arrogant ass thinks you know everything about what he's been through since he lost your brother."

John cocked his head at her. "Nice shot, Lieutenant."

"My aim is true."

He smiled at her, but the grin faded quickly. "Kendra, that thing *looked* like a mechanism, not something made by God."

They had been talking so intently they hadn't realized that the sun had almost set until a light brightened the immediate area. Prisha was standing in the doorway, little more than a silhouette against the fire-brightened interior. "He's back."

They found Sam inside, having slipped in his back door, standing before his table, drinking cupful after cupful of cold water from a lumpy clay mug that he kept refilling from a chipped clay pitcher. Lewis sat at the table before him, hands folded. Sam spied them entering the cabin over the rim of his cup, finished its contents, and set it carefully down on the table.

"It's all there still," he said to no one in particular. "Everything. I half expected them to have gotten rid of it, but it's all still there."

"You mean the Orangemen?" Prisha asked.

Sam nodded twice. "You'd be surprised how much they take just to screw with us. I've seen it. It's all about control with them."

A half-mad glee seemed to have overtaken his father. John approached him with caution. "I'm glad it's still there. When can we go see it?"

"Not now." He shook his head. "It's dark or getting there now. We'll go at first light. It'll all be truer then in that clear, cold light. That's how I first saw it. That's how you should see it, Johnny."

"Is it far?" Kendra asked. "Maybe we could get there before dark."

Sam took another long drink of water. "Took me most of the day to get there and back again. Besides, unlike where you're from, there are real beasts in these woods. Maybe you've seen a few of them."

Kendra and John glanced at each other.

Sam sniggered. "Thought so. Not fit to see them at night with an oncoming winter. Their hunger doesn't necessarily know about God's plan." He set the cup down. "Speaking of God's plan, you two aren't married, right?" He laughed again. "Then I better make sure I hang a blanket or something when you all sack out here tonight."

As promised, they were out at first light. It was a clear deep-autumn morning brightened by the kind of sunlight that sets everything in such sharp relief that even the most mundane rocks and tree branches appear more beautiful and ideally formed. It was the kind of day made for human eyes and one that would set even the most hardened hearts at ease.

Sam had changed again. Not hard, not mad, he seemed almost buoyant as he led them northwest and farther down into the valley beyond his hilltop home. They had set off on foot, as the path was too narrow and begrudging to let the wagon through. It seemed to Kendra that they were following the path of least resistance—a shallow gully that had been eroded by the rain's runoff down the nearest hills. It would be more difficult to hike back up, but she thought that even Prisha would be able to get back to the cabin with relative ease, despite her condition.

Father and son walked together but didn't walk close to each other. Kendra was a step behind them and the Lewises a step behind her. The two men didn't say much. Here and there one would point out something of interest on the horizon or underfoot. What that empty air they framed was filled by was anyone's guess—all the years between them or the loss they both shared or the things they wanted to say to each other but didn't know how. Yet there was something there, something permanent. When John and Kendra left this place—however they left this place—there would be no tender words between father and son. Their lives would separate again, and they would die a second death to each other. But this time, no mourning would be necessary.

Before midday the trek downhill came to a stop. Where the land leveled out, they were standing in a shallow riverbed seeded with tall clumps of wildflowers and weeds and grass now in their autumnal death throes. It ran in a smooth, flat line until it disappeared into the canopy of trees in either direction. How far past the greenery the river valley continued Kendra couldn't guess. Sam stood in rapt wonder for a while as each of them took turns providing one another with a quizzical glance.

"This is our destination?" Prisha finally asked. "A dry riverbed?"

"This isn't a dry riverbed, Prish."

"Sam," Lewis said as he pulled on his jowly face, "I'm afraid I just don't—"

John waved him off. "He's right, Jack. This is no riverbed. The contours are all wrong. We were walking down a dry gully—definitely something made by runoff. But this runs flat—and perpendicular to the gully. If this is where the runoff emptied into, it should've either pooled out here at the bottom or kept running downhill somewhere, not cut straight across like this."

"I don't understand," Prisha said. "Not enough water perhaps to keep going?"

"No." Kendra shook her head. "Look down it. This thing's straight. You can see it all the way down to where it's getting really overgrown. It's almost as if—" She glanced at John. "It's almost as if somebody deliberately built this as a canal."

"Or a road," John finished, then turned to Sam. "Okay. We've got a theory, Dad. Now prove it."

The older man slipped out of his knapsack, then extracted two collapsible shovels and handed one to his son. They began their work in a spot about ten yards from where they had been standing, nearest the hillside part of the bank. After a few minutes of digging up dusty clumps of clay, something few living human beings had ever seen was revealed.

Sam leaned on his shovel's handle. "It's called asphalt. I read about it in the Archives years ago. They paved and waterproofed roads with this stuff. It's a residue that comes from refining petroleum."

Kendra shook her head as she stared at the smooth black surface peeking through the brown clay. "How'd it get here?"

"The people who built this road put it here," Sam answered. "People who died a damn long time ago."

"You keep saying people, Dad," John said. "You mean intelligent beings like us?"

"No," he said, the hard edge back in his eyes. "I mean what I say. I mean *men* like us. Our ancestors built this road."

"Sam, that doesn't make any sense," Lewis piped up from where he was standing at the edge of the hole. For the past few minutes he had been running his fingers across the smooth black surface they had uncovered. "Be reasonable. This road or whatever it was has obviously been in disuse for quite a long time, maybe hundreds or even thousands of years—far longer than we've been on this planet. Considering the fact that none of us have the technology to do this, this road is simply a ruin of a long-dead race. It couldn't have been made by mankind."

Sam jammed his shovel into the pile of clay he had built up at his feet and walked along the center of the buried road, neither quickening nor slowing his pace through its weedy expanse after shooting a quick glance back to make sure they were following him. A quarter mile later he made a sudden dash into the woods and came out with a heavy object wrapped in thick burlap, which he held with some reverence before setting it at their feet and removing its weatherworn covering.

The object gave off a dull glint in the sunlight coming through the cross-stitched canopy of branches. It was clear that it was something metallic, maybe copper or bronze. But at that moment it mattered less what it was made of than what it appeared to be: the head and part of the shoulders of a man.

Kendra crouched nearest it. Pitted and dull, it was worn smooth in places like an old coin but not so much so as to have rubbed out every detail. The man's hair and beard had a flowing wildness to them that reminded her of photos she had seen of men who had lived during the

American Civil War. It was hard to make out his clothing, the neck and shoulders being too chipped and cracked, but it seemed that he was wearing a high collar reminiscent of what had been worn by many men in the nineteenth century.

"You asked for proof, son." Sam's voice was gentler than it had been. "So here it is. The long-dead race on this planet is us. The Orangemen never brought the Remnants to another planet. We've been on Earth all along."

Kendra looked up from in front of the bronze head. "We're only two generations removed from the Apocalypse. This place—everywhere we've been—it's all wilderness. There are no cities—"

"Except for this road and bronze bust," Lewis said quietly, "there's little proof that a civilization ever lived here—or that this is Earth."

"And a beat-up plastic bowl Kendra and I found on our way here," John added. "At least we thought it was plastic."

"But we would've seen *cities*," Kendra continued. "Ruins, something. Not just a damn bowl."

"Not if the Apocalypse happened a very long time ago," Prisha said, her gaze still fixed on the staring eyes of the bronze man. "A long-enough time and the Earth would've reclaimed almost everything we formed from it, just as if the world had always existed without us."

"How long?" John asked, calling Prisha's attention to him. "How much time would've needed to have passed for everything around us to return to this wilderness?"

She turned to him. "Hundreds upon hundreds of years. Looking at the thickness of the vegetation around us, I'd say it could've been a thousand years. We may never know."

"A thousand years," Lewis muttered in awe. "The Millennium."

John approached him quickly, his breath trailing from his lips. "You're a Remnant, Jack. How can this be? If you witnessed the last days as a child and that happened a thousand years ago, how in hell can you be here now?"

Lewis removed his cap, scratched at his bald head, and looked at John with empty eyes. "I don't know. I was a child, but I know what I saw. How could I forget the waters turning to blood, the scorching heat, the earthquakes—"

"Put that aside," John said to keep the older man's more maudlin thoughts at bay. "We're missing the obvious. The moon, the stars. I never heard of the Earth's moon being surrounded by a halo of dust or having a V-shaped gash in its yellow face like ours does. Was the moon even yellow? You're a Remnant, Jack. Can't you remember?"

"Yes," Lewis murmured, a hand on his chin. "Our moon didn't look like that at all. But the stars—it's hard to remember the stars."

A hand gripped Lewis's shoulder, and Kendra saw Sam standing beside them. "Here's my best guess. We're a long time in the future. A long, long time. The moon and stars could look an awful lot different in all that time."

"That doesn't explain my father or the others of his generation," Prisha protested. "How can they still be alive a thousand or more years in the future?"

"I've got that covered too. Maybe the Orangemen—whatever they are—took the survivors, all one hundred forty-four thousand of them—and put them to sleep somehow. Like flies caught in amber, only they weren't dead, just asleep. Then, for whatever reason, after enough time had passed, they brought them back to Earth." Sam shook his head and snorted. "Oh and left them a lot of Bibles and told them to be nice to one another for good measure."

"Shut up!" Kendra leapt from her crouch and began shoving Sam as hard as she could. The first shove was only a glancing blow, but the second nearly knocked him off his feet. John took hold of her and pinned her arms to her sides. "I am so sick of your self-righteous shit! You don't know anything. You're making all this up."

"I'm trying to find the truth, McQueen," he said. "What other explanation could there be for our bronze friend here? This is Earth, period."

"Earth? An Earth with freaking woolly mammoths?" This was met with silence. She laughed in his face. "Oh you know so fucking much, don't you?"

Sam looked at her with a degree of pity. "We had thousands of years of religious nonsense and then an all-too-brief window of scientific enlightenment, and then—just because some creatures came from space to suck our planet dry like an orange—we reverted to being primitives. If this is the best the species can do, we didn't deserve to survive."

Kendra shoved John away with an elbow to his gut and glared at Sam.

John turned to Lewis after a time. "You have any idea who he was?" he asked, lifting his chin toward the large bronze head at their feet.

Lewis looked down and studied the bust in a bewildered way for a moment before speaking. "I can't rightly say. But there is something familiar about the face, something perhaps literary—"

He had no chance to say more. A roar came from above them, followed by a blur as a lean, silken form pounced upon Lewis. Sam pulled his rifle from his shoulder as John drew his sidearm and Kendra the bowie knife. Prisha screamed as the saber-tooth fixed its powerful jaws around her father's shoulder.

Sam fired two shots in the air, hoping to scare off the enormous cat. But the beast, filled with either hunger or with bloodlust, ignored them. Kendra leapt forward and sunk the knife deep between the creature's ribs near the lungs. The tiger's jaws popped open, and Lewis's head hit the ground with a sickening, hollow thud as the tiger flailed, unable to dislodge the knife sticking out of its back. Kendra and Prisha pulled the wounded man out of the way as Sam and John opened up a volley of fire. The tiger surged forward, then quaked for several seconds before hitting the ground with a last, thick bubbling breath of air.

The two men raced to where Lewis lay near the tree line. His daughter was trying to stop the blood pouring from his neck and shoulder with the coat she had stripped off her back.

"It's okay, Father, no it's okay—"

"Forgive me." He raised a bloody hand and cupped her cheek with it. "I've loved you all the best I could without your mother."

He coughed and began to spasm as his eyes grew wide. Sam helped to hold him down as gently as he could. Lewis looked at his old friend and smiled in that bemused way of his as he gripped his hand. "Sam, I go to God. I believe that, if nothing else."

And with that, Jack Lewis died on what had once been a road.

CHAPTER 18

It had been easy to dig a few feet into the hard clay to find the roadbed. It took quite a bit longer to pull out enough of the hard and cold root-riddled earth to lay Jack Lewis to rest in a clearing in the woods. It was growing dark and overcast by the time they were finishing up, so they lit torches before they laid his body in the grave.

Prisha couldn't bear to speak. Sam refused to. John looked at Kendra, who nodded encouragement at him. After a moment he began reciting from the First Letter of Paul to the Corinthians:

> "Love is patient, love is kind. It is not jealous, is not pomp-ous, it is not inflated, it is not rude, it does not seek its own interests, it is not quick-tempered, it does not brood over injury, it does not rejoice over wrongdoing but rejoices with the truth. It bears all things, believes all things, hopes all things, endures all things.

> "Love never fails. If there are prophecies, they will be brought to nothing; if tongues, they will cease; if knowl-edge, it will be brought to nothing. For we know partially and we prophesy partially, but when the perfect comes, the partial will pass away.

"When I was a child, I used to talk as a child, think as a child, reason as a child; when I became a man, I put aside childish things. At present we see indistinctly, as in a mirror, but then face to face. At present I know partially; then I shall know fully, as I am fully known.

"So faith, hope, love remain, these three; but the greatest of these is love."

John picked up a clumpy handful of dirt and crumbled it over the grave. "I did not know Jack Lewis long or well. But he saved our lives. I know of no greater love than that. Good-bye, Jack."

Kendra sprinkled her own handful of earth. "Semper fidelis, Jack Lewis." Then she led Prisha away from the raw gully in the ground so John and Sam could fill it back in. Once it was a smooth rectangular mound, John fashioned a cross from two sturdy branches and set it at the top, then glanced up at his father. Sam shook his head as John finished the work, then took the remaining torch into the gloomy woods to meet the others back on the road.

The very first hints of morning were tracing reddish highlights onto the edge of the mountaintops in the east when they reached Sam's hilltop cabin. They were cold from the steady hike uphill in the dark, silent and numb. After lighting a large fire in Sam's hearth, Prisha and Kendra got into their bedrolls on the floor of the cabin and went to sleep. Sam went out to the porch with a blanket and a bottle. John followed him without knowing why.

Sam settled into a chair with the blanket around his shoulders and turned his lean leathery face to the morning light. He uncorked the bottle and handed it to his son without looking at it or him.

"One of Jack's in-laws made this. It's supposed to be whiskey. It tastes like shit, but it works with the full traditional effects."

John took a small swallow and found it not as bad as his father made it out to be. He straddled the bench across from where the older man sat so he could talk to Sam and still feel the morning sun on his face.

"I've never said this about anybody." Sam's eyes were on the reddening peaks in the distance. "But Jack Lewis was a good man. Fair. Honest. Without judgment."

"He seemed that way." John took another drink and passed the bottle back.

Sam took a swig. "He made me feel at home here. He didn't deserve to die like that—in front of his daughter."

"Would it have been better for him to die alone, with no one to bury him?"

A long pause. "Suppose not."

The sun had risen into the new morning by the time they spoke again. At least a half hour had passed. The bottle continued to meet outstretched hands.

"Dad," John began, "why'd you stay here?"

Sam blinked his creased eyes as if waking from a dream. "What?"

"Why didn't you come back?"

Another long silence. "I had reasons."

"Tell me."

Another minute passed. "Ah—what does it matter now?"

"Was it because of Christian?"

He took another drink and passed the bottle back to John again. The bottle was going on three-quarters empty. It had been nearly full when they started.

"Mom?" John took a drink. "Me?"

Sam kept his gaze on the blue-bright horizon, a sky as clear as the previous night had been overcast. "I was crazy at first. And I didn't know how the portals worked. I had only gotten here through them by accident. I wasn't sure how to get back to you overland. After a while I came to think it was better to die here with people who didn't have it in their nature to judge anyone."

"So you stayed."

"So I stayed." He gestured with flicking fingers for the bottle, and John handed it back to him heavily. "So I stayed among people who gave me peace and space. And then after a few years I found the road and the bronze statue and—"

"And what?"

Sam looked at him with dead eyes and a slack jaw. "And what? Are you kidding? And I discovered that what was left of human civilization had been built on the compost pile of the Earth. And then I had absolutely no reason to go back."

John ignored the edge in his father's voice. "Why, for God's sake?"

Sam scratched his bearded cheek. "Why, you whiny prick? You think I wanted to go back and tell those fools that this really was the Earth and further reinforce their misbegotten belief that they were living through Revelation on a 'new' Earth? Please."

"That's your reason?"

"You better believe it."

John leaned forward, elbows on his knees. "You know what I think? I think you're a coward. You couldn't go back among the living because you couldn't understand why a piece of shit like you had survived when so many others hadn't."

John stood and went into the cabin. He sat by the fire for a time, then stripped off his outer clothes and crawled into his bedroll next to Kendra. She was awake, an arm tucked under her ear.

"Hiya," she mouthed in the firelight.

"Hi." He smoothed her dark hair behind her pale ear, loving the simplicity of that contrast.

"You okay?"

"Yeah."

"So um," she began, "what do we do now?"

"Now we go home." He kissed her and rubbed his lips against hers. "Go home and make our report."

They slept nearly all of the next day and awoke again at dawn. Prisha had gotten up earlier to tend to the horses and repack the wagon. Kendra and John wouldn't be going back with her—not to her family's home, not through the miles of wilderness they had crossed since leaving New Philadelphia. They were instead going to take their chances with Sam through the portal. That being the plan, no one had expected Prisha to stay for breakfast. When they found her sitting there, they wanted to say something, anything. Yet nothing came to them, apart from telling her to help herself to some of the bread and the scrambled eggs. They ate in silence. John wanted to ask if either of them knew where his father had gone but thought better of it. If Prisha had sent him on some errand and was waiting for him to come back, it was none of his business.

Prisha ripped off and ate plump handfuls of bread while staring into the fire. Her face was still and quiet; under other circumstances someone would've called her serene. Kendra and John looked for things to do. Dishes were washed, fires were stoked, bedrolls were tied up, and bags were packed. John even stowed her father's gear. When Prisha finally saw it piled on a chair by the front door, she dropped the fat hunk of bread from her fingers, took possession of the items, and left the cabin through its front door. She passed Sam on his way in. He removed his wide-brimmed hat as she passed.

"Johnny. McQueen." He glanced at the grate over the fire. "Any coffee left?"

He lifted the pot from the grate, shook it, and tapped the side with his fingertips to see if it was still hot. Satisfied, he took a mug from his cupboard and poured out the bitter dregs. He slurped it with satisfaction for a time before looking at them.

"It's time for you two to go."

"What about Prisha?" Kendra asked. "She can't be alone."

"I hiked out to see our local tracker, told her what happened to Jack. The tracker's good. She'll find Prisha's husband and bring him home to her."

A small breeze picked up. The door had opened in silence. Prisha had come back from outside. "Are you going to the portal now?"

Sam looked at her over his mug. "I was planning on it, Prish."

"I'd like to come with you. I'll be with the horses until then."

She turned and walked out, leaving Sam's gaze on his now-closed front door.

The mile-long hike felt to Kendra like a short and brisk morning stroll. The clear sky made the day feel warmer than it usually was at this time of year. When they reached the site, they flung off their packs and drank deeply from their canteens. The portal looked as inert as when they had first seen it. Nothing seemed disturbed since they had last been there, apart from the digging they themselves had done freeing it from the tangled overgrowth. Sam ran his hand along its orange-tinged metallic edge almost as if he were feeling around for some kind of on switch.

The truth was not far from the first impression. Each touch was purposeful and specific. Each seemed as if Sam were turning on a device or mechanism—not asking the divine permission for passage. This was something far subtler than the parting of the Red Sea. The idea ran through Kendra's mind and disturbed her. She blocked it out and concentrated on getting through the next few minutes.

Sam stepped back from the portal. The void in the center of the orange frame changed from black to an almost-milky white. *Almost* was the only accurate way to describe it. Milk had substance, and that substance affected its color. This was still a place without substance, only now it was nearly white.

Sam turned to them, as if he sensed their questions. "It has some kind of memory, made through physical contact. If you touch it with the place you want to go in mind, it sort of 'routes' you there. It's ready for us now."

"So what was it before?" John wondered. "When it was black?"

He scratched his neck. "*Not* ready for us."

Kendra smirked. "Try again, chief."

"Still a portal. But a portal to no place in particular." Sam turned back to it. "I've always wondered if it was black when I fell through that first one. Did it somehow sense where I needed to go and sent me here? Other times I think the black just goes to another dimension entirely—someplace living men aren't allowed to go."

"Like heaven," Kendra suggested with a cockeyed grin.

"Or hell," Sam answered without one. "Me, I don't care to find out either way. You ready? Best way is for me to hold your hands and take you through."

"Sam."

"Prish?"

She stepped forward. "I'd like a word before you go."

"Prisha." Kendra saw her face and couldn't say anything more.

"You changed all of our lives by coming here," Prisha said, not really looking at either of them but at a point just over their shoulders. "I don't mean because your being here got my father killed. I blame you for that, and I don't blame you. I am sickened by the sight of you and understand it wasn't really your fault. I never want to see you again and yet hope there's an afterlife where we will meet and all of this pain will then make sense. It's as John said when we buried Father: we understand things only partially. Yet somehow knowing so little makes everything seem so clear to me. And that's why I know that I'm right in telling you that what you learned here will change your society irrevocably. So I must ask you this: Does truth trump peace? Think about that before you carelessly destroy your people's world."

And with that she walked down the hill, the tips of her long black hair flapping in the breeze. They watched her until she disappeared from view.

"Well," Sam said, head down, kicking at a loose stone. "Guess we should get going."

"You said you needed to guide us through." John jerked a thumb at the portal. "How can you know how to bring us through there?"

"It's hard to explain, so there's not much point in explaining it."

John started to speak, then let his father continue.

"Let's just say that this thing . . . recognizes me on account of my having traveled through it, so—"

"When you say you traveled through it," Kendra said, "where exactly have you been?"

Sam looked at her for a long while before answering. "All over this planet, looking for things. Why, I don't know. Maybe more proof that we're on Earth. Maybe just to find other people. I dunno."

John shook his head, eyebrows raised. "You've been all over this planet?"

"Yup. They've got these things everywhere."

"And the one you mentioned before?" Kendra demanded. "Is it very near the city?"

Sam gave her a grin. "There's *several* near your city, McQueen. All in the hills and mountains nearby."

"And you've been to them?" John asked. "You've *been* to the city?"

Sam opened his mouth and closed it, fishlike. "It's time to get you home."

John sent a right hook into his jaw, knocking him down before Kendra could react. She bent to help Sam to his feet, then stopped. She stepped back from both of them.

Father looked at son with a mocking stare. "We even now?"

John clenched and unclenched his fists at his sides. The adrenaline was shaking through him. "How can we be?"

Sam got on his knees and pulled himself upright without assistance. "Suppose you're right. Now both of you grab your gear and hold on to my wrists as we walk through."

They were blank. They were white. Their world was colorless and endless and without form, and each of them felt it had always been like this and at the same time somehow they knew and believed that they had lived lives somewhere else at some other point but couldn't remember them apart from an odd nagging feeling that this was not all that there was to existence. They weren't moving or floating or going anywhere. If time was passing, they didn't know it. If they had bodies, they didn't know them. If they were individuals, they did not care. For all they knew, they were in utero—but they were still human enough to realize in that animal part of themselves that no mother's womb had ever been white and bright, nor had it ever been cold and barren. Human love was felt, even in the womb.

But here there was no love, no warmth.

No womb.

And then—a moment later or a lifetime—they found themselves tumbling out onto a drenched field on a mountaintop in the pouring rain. The rain came down angled and hard from stone-gray skies. As thunder flashed around them, the freezing rain matted their hair and seeped through their clothes. The biting cold told them it was winter and that they were still alive.

John struggled to get off his knees but felt as if he was about to vomit. "Where?"

Kendra gagged and squinted about her. "There, John. Look there."

Before them was a glow coming through the trees downslope from them. It was the kind of warm glow that emanated from gaslight and civilization.

As they struggled to their feet, they found Sam already standing, at ease and surveying his surroundings. The rain had washed the blood from his split lip, but it highlighted the bluish bruise forming on his jaw. His hair was wet and wild, his beard dribbling water. He looked like a man of another era, raw and hard and unfinished and not part of the contemporary world.

John staggered toward him. Sam's fist flashed out, a quick left jab to John's nose. He felt the bone break and then hit the ground in a heap.

"How about now?" Sam leaned over him, hands clasped behind his back, the storm raging around him. "We even now, son?"

"Leave him alone, you son of a bitch!" Kendra tried with slippery hands to help John to his feet.

John pulled his arms from her grip and stood up. "We're going to tell them about you," he said over the wind and the rain. "All of them. Not just the Council—but Mom, everyone you ever knew."

Sam nodded. "I suppose you will."

"Jesus Christ, why won't you help me? Come back with us."

The older man turned toward the glow in the valley below. The hardness of his face faded for an instant, almost as if the curious young explorer who had disappeared from this world had suddenly returned again unchanged. But then the moment passed, the hardness returned, and Samuel Giordano shook his head.

"I killed her son." He began to walk back to the portal, still alive in its milky whiteness. At the threshold he turned. "Get out of the rain, Johnny."

An instant later he was gone.

John fell to his knees and vomited up his breakfast and much of the blood that he had been sucking into his fractured nose. Kendra was beside him in only slightly better condition. After a while they dragged each other to their feet and helped each other put on their packs. Kendra paused after taking a few steps toward the city.

"Do you know where we are, John?"

He looked around, realization dawning. "This is the field where we met when you were a girl."

"A portal. *Here*. Of all places. What—what does that mean?"

The rain hid her tears. Her voice couldn't.

"I don't know, Ken. I wish to God I did."

Kendra looked toward the now-exposed portal. Its orange-striped metallic edge shone in the rain, but its interior was again dark and inert. All around it were broken branches, bits of bark, chunks of evergreens—telltale signs of their dramatic entrance. "That felt like—well, it seemed like where the Remnants said they were before the Arrival. The White Place, remember?"

John took her hand and squeezed it. "Hey, hey you," he said. "Don't you dare. Not now."

"Yeah." She nodded, stiff lipped. "We have to get you and that nose of yours home."

Arms around each other, soaked and shivering, they made their way down the slippery slope to the world they had known for all of their lives. When they needed to steady themselves by holding on to a tree trunk or an outcropping of rock, they did so for as long as necessary to get a grip and help the other down.

They soon found themselves standing on the edge of a level plain that marked the outskirts of their civilization. Here before them were orchards, barren of fruit and foliage at this time of year, that had been planted during the baby-boom years before Kendra's birth. Someday the wall would need to be brought out here to protect their food supplies. An enormous project for another generation. For now, John and Kendra were only too glad to be able to march down the orchards' endless rows until they saw the top of the city's wall towering over the trees. They could see light—and with it, the promise of warmth and food—through cracks in the shuttered windows at the top of the nearest gate's guard tower.

The air was so choked with rain it felt difficult to breathe. They marched on despite this until they reached the huge city gate. John pounded his fist against it and saw above its massive wooden frame the number eight etched in the stonework. They were at Gate Eight and close to the center of town, not far from where General Weiss lived. What would he think when he saw them?

John pounded and pounded again. Kendra kicked at the door.

"Oi!"

They looked up, squinting through the falling rain, and saw a sentry with six of his fellows aiming carbines right at their heads.

"Oi! Who goes there?"

"For the love of God, man, open the door!" Kendra called.

"Who? Talk fast, friends."

"It's Giordano and McQueen of the Defense Forces, you half-wit!" John yelled up. "Now open the damned door!"

The man disappeared over the slick stone parapet. Kendra and John slumped to the ground and leaned against the smaller door that had been built into the enormous gate. As they heard the big bolts being pulled back behind them, Kendra gripped John's hand and smiled.

"Not very patient, are we?"

"Should we be?" John wiped the stinging rain from his face.

She shrugged, grinning. "Patience is as close to perfection that our human condition allows."

As the smaller door opened, John and Kendra flopped backward and fell inside the gate, where they found themselves faceup, staring at the same rifles that had been pointed at them earlier.

"In the name of City Protector Gordon Lee, I arrest you!"

CHAPTER 19

The darkness scurried with the movement of mice. Kendra felt their ghostly touch long after their thin paws and thick bodies had slid over her feet and hands, long after the flick of a fleshy tail touched her face as she slept. She had no need to see them or to know how many were out there in the room scratching, shitting, sniffing, slipping over one another. The invisible exists. She'd always known that. That was enough.

Kendra was in a wine cellar near the center of town. Before the first candle had sizzled out, she recognized it as belonging to the house where the Khan family lived. She had gone through school with Emily Khan. But there was no sign of the family. Where they were, she could only guess. Her guards had given her no answers. Her *guards*. Most of them were smooth-faced Novices barely able to hold a carbine. A few she had even helped train just last year. If they knew anything at all about what was going on, it was information so low-level as to be barely a step above rumor.

By meals served and chamber pots emptied, she guessed that she had been here for nearly three days. Three days ankle-shackled to a fieldstone wall with a long chain. Three days of trying to keep the mice patrolling for crumbs in this now-barren cellar from biting her face.

Three days of wondering if John—or anyone else she had known and loved—was still alive.

Whoever was now in charge *(Did they say Gordon Lee? Lee? What?)* had not been expecting their return. That much seemed true. The muttered conversations she had witnessed, their desire to split her and John up to maintain some control—it all seemed part of a very uncoordinated effort to figure out what the hell to do with the two of them. If somebody in charge had known they were coming, they would've been dragged before him ASAP.

So what were they doing? Questioning John right now? Why hadn't they asked her anything? Interrogating them at the same time was the best way to corroborate their stories. So why weren't they doing just that? She chuckled, then shook her head.

You could anticipate malice but not incompetence.

The squeaking and scratching in the dark—God in heaven. She found herself trying to wipe away tears and imagined her face was crisscrossed with blackened tear tracks. Oh why wouldn't they give her any light? Just a nub of a candle when they brought food that always burned out before she finished eating or peeing. And then and always the dark and fighting the dark—fighting to find that last scrap of bread or her cup of water, fighting to keep the stink of her chamber pot from overpowering her, fighting to find a place on the dirt floor to grab some moments of sleep free from rodents. Fighting to keep a beachhead of light within her as the dark sought to creep inside.

She rubbed her hand against the ichthys tattoo on the inside of her left wrist. She couldn't see it, but she knew it was there. Christ had returned from the dead on the third day. Why shouldn't she? Did she still believe that?

It isn't the first time you've been locked away, Kendra. And it isn't the first time that you couldn't be found for three days. But it wasn't dark then. And you weren't really alone then, were you? No, even if you had wanted to be, you couldn't have been alone.

You were fourteen, just a few months away from joining the Defense Forces. You were gangly, awkward. Your arms and legs were too thin and long to be of much use other than to trip over, but your body was changing too and you knew it and you started to like the curves that were coming in and you used them all you could in your overt stupid teenage way and on nobody more so than Alexander Raymond Jr.—Alex with his dark hair curling over his forehead and his artist's soul and his coward boy's heart. Alex. He feared you as much as he loved you. You controlled him and you ruined him. But that night you wanted more than anything for him to be wrapped around you.

How many times before that night had the two of you gone up to the hills through the secret trapdoor in the city's walls? Ten, a dozen times at best? It was midsummer then, and you had been curling around each other since your first flirtations in the spring. Sex no longer hurt as it first did. And the less it hurt the more you wanted it, and you both soon realized that there were just too many places in the city where you could get caught. Alex was terrified of getting caught. Was it Alex who had found the secret way out of the city? Had he found that tumbledown Remnant cabin in the hills? At this distance, six years, you don't remember exactly who found your retreat. It doesn't matter. All that you remember is the warm thrill you felt as you crawled through the secret tunnel in the city wall and waited for him outside that ruined cabin.

But Alex wasn't there when he was supposed to be. You waited and paced. The yellow cloud around the moon seemed as bright as midday. When you finally saw him silhouetted against the sky, you knew without doubt that it was not Alex Raymond. So you ran toward the woods, fearing you were about to be caught by one of the elders. Then you looked back and saw nearly translucent wings unfold, glint blue in the moonlight, and take flight. You suppressed a scream and ran harder.

Branches lashed your face and your desperate outstretched hands. The moonlight, so bright in the clearing, was now muted and dull, hardly penetrating the treetops. All around you was dark, dark, dark. The warm breeze slipping past the tree trunks swayed branches and bushes, but apart from it and your own breathing, the night was silent. And the silence terrified you. You knew even then that the woods throbbed at night with snapping branches and scurrying feet and mating calls. But it was all completely still.

You didn't know how the Remnants had evaded death at the hands of the Orangemen on Earth. They never explained it to anyone except tangentially—in Defense Forces drills. But you hadn't had any drills; you hadn't had any training at all. So you ran and prayed to God, but you had already reverted to the animal instincts of your ancestors and tried to escape through cunning and silence. You were nearly through the woods and could see moonlight in the next clearing just before you. With every step you heard the flap of monstrously large wings. With every beat of your heart you heard a sword being freed from its sheath.

You neared the clearing and your heart beat even faster.

He's gone. He must be gone.

You took deep breaths through your nose to calm yourself.

But what if he's out there, just past these trees? Maybe he flew out over these woods and is just waiting right there?

You took a step forward, your breath gripped in your chest.

A hand snatched you from behind, covered your mouth, pulled you close. When you turned, an oversized orange face contemplated you. He moved his hand from your mouth and studied you from the edge of your hairline to the tip of your chin. You could feel him exhale against your cheek. His breath was sweet and warm but not in a familiar or even rec-ognizable way. That warmth, that sweetness was not of anything remotely human.

He started to open his perfect line of a mouth, then stopped. Then he gathered your body into his arms and flew up and into the evening sky. And you were flying—flying, Kendra!—in a way no human being had ever done before. It was frightening but familiar—a primeval feeling. Did men once fly with angels? Was this one taking you back to God? You clutched his neck tighter, a child's grip, as his wings took you farther into the sky.

Kendra, you were flying.

Wherever you landed, you knew you were far from home. No stretch of these woods looked familiar. Not that you would have recognized something familiar at that moment. Your mind was too full of afterimages of what you had just seen—almost-unbearable moonlit vistas of distant mountain peaks rushing toward you, the lights of your city falling away, the deceptive calmness of the ocean as you whirled first toward it and then away from it, the rush of greenery exploding under and around you as your pilot cruised down to his landing. On the ground you shivered more from the thrill than the actual temperature on this mountaintop. Your heart thrilled. You understood what that meant now.

A hand gripped your wrist and led you toward a cave you hadn't seen upon arrival rising out of the rock face. Inside the cave was warm, glowing white. You had expected a campfire, but this glow neither flickered nor burned. It was simply light and warmth resting in what once may have been a true fire pit made by men. The walls and high ceiling of the great cave were alight in relief.

The hand did relax its grip but did not let you go once inside the cave. The beautifully formed face seemed even more perfect in this light despite its foreignness—the just-oversized eyes and head, the inhuman blankness of the slate-gray eyes. But then your curiosity buried your fear, and you began to regard the face as an individual and not as a representative of a race you were supposed to fear. This Orangeman wasn't quite as tall as you had been told they were. And he wasn't as strange. That look was curious, maybe even bemused, but not devoid of emotion. Your voice came to you without your realizing it.

"My name's Kendra." A pause. You touched your free hand to the top of your breastbone. "Kendra. Do you understand me, milord?"

He tilted his head but said nothing.

"I was told your people know human languages. Do you understand me?"

The head straightened. It almost seemed as if a smile was curling the edges of the mouth.

"This isn't the year of one of your visits," you rambled on. "Has something happened? Are my people still safe?"

He leaned forward, and the hand that gripped your right wrist brought you closer. It wasn't really painful, just compelling. Your eye caught sight of the sword attached to his belt.

"Please speak to me." Your voice quivered as you were reminded of a long-forgotten childhood memory. You were three, maybe four. You had done something wrong—broken something maybe—and were trying to apologize for it in your father's disappointed silence. "Please speak to me, great one."

A nod, very slight. "You are intelligent for one so young." The voice was deep and strange in its perfect pitch. "And brave. These are valuable traits."

"Who are you?"

An enigmatic look spread across his face. "Call me Samael. Why not?"

"To whom do you belong? To those who saved us? Or to those who destroyed us?"

He shrugged in an almost human way. "Depending on your perspective, to both or neither. I come from a third place."

"And why're you here?" You stuck your chin out when you asked. "What do you want with me?"

"To know you, girl." He smiled at you. You had never heard of an Orangeman smiling before. "As I have known others of your kind."

Samael took a step forward and pulled you closer at the same time, then sniffed your hair. Then he released your wrist and walked toward the mouth of the cave. As he did a wall of white light not unlike the ball of light that had been keeping you warm covered the entrance. A moment later and he *was gone and you were a fly still alive in a bubble of white amber. But that was only the beginning.*

All these years later you've convinced yourself that when he came back and took you that first time you didn't resist him because he had been gone for so long and you were afraid that he had forgotten about you. You were alone in a sealed cave with no idea when or if that light would go out, and you were terribly hungry and thirsty. The few people you told your story to backed up your thinking. Grace Davison had tried to explain it both as the psychologist she once was and as the preacher she had become. Traumatic bonding with a captor, she had said, perhaps influenced by powers beyond man's comprehension. You were barely more than a child. You couldn't have fought off such a powerful creature, not to mention an armed one.

But that isn't quite true, is it, Kendra?

Like the first night, he left you, again without food. You were sore and tried to sleep, but you weren't sure if he would return. You spent much of the time alone, touching the light he had left, all that light that warmed and illuminated but did not burn. You ran your fingertips, wet with snot and tears, loosely across the ball in the fire pit or the wall sealing the mouth of the cave, as if contact with it might make you understand him better. Lying alone in that light for hours, you found yourself thinking less of your parents and the people you knew who now must be desperately looking for you and more of Samael, the perfect slope of his shoulders, the taper of his wrists, the powerful way his thighs flexed as he walked, and you realized you were no longer crying about what had happened. You wanted him back.

Your heart had thrilled. You had been thrilled by the flight, by his power and control, by his absolute otherness. Could Alex have given you that? Could anyone in your city? This was something unknown and unknowable, something happening to you and you alone. Was there a purpose in this? After all, you had always wanted to know more than the people around you, the city, its rituals and routines. You wanted to know the rest of this world and the world beyond—his world. You wanted to be in this cave and on this mountaintop, and you wanted to see the next. He was beautiful, truly beautiful, and you wanted to pull his beauty inside you and have it light your every pore from the inside. The first night he raped you. Even though you didn't fight, of that you were sure. But in the most desperately hidden corners of your heart, you can't deny that you wanted more than his food that second night.

Samael brought more food with him upon his return, and for the first time, conversation. Later, as you lay against the curve of his side and hip, warm in the white light, he must've sensed some change in you and spoke to you as a man might. The things he said made little immediate impact, but you've never forgotten them.

"I'm not supposed to be here, little Kendra."

"You mean here with me?"

He turned to you and grinned in his nearly human way. "Not on this planet."

You said nothing for a long time, your heart beating hard in your chest. "Do you feel you're, um, meant to be here?"

His gray eyes looked almost confused. "It is my will."

You rose up on your elbow to face him. "That's not what I mean. I mean, is there a higher purpose to your being here now?"

"How does one so young ask so many profound questions?"

You tucked a lock of hair behind your ear. "We're considered adults by my age. We're supposed to think about bigger things."

He sat up, shaking his head. "No, little Kendra. You're something far more than a well-trained parrot. You are without fear."

"I ran from you when I first saw you."

"To survive, but not out of fear," he continued. "You ask questions of one that others would bow before. Your eyes are . . . old. Is that the right human word? It will have to do until I think of another."

You grinned, all pride and embarrassment, and bit your lower lip. "So if you're not supposed to be here, why are you?"

He lay back down. "Those among my people who saved your race from the Rebels believe they are wise. They believe in guarding over you rather than interfering with you. They believe that by keeping apart from you, you will be able to find the best parts of yourselves more easily. Some of us, however, feel that it is important not to entirely abandon the old policy of . . . occasional interaction."

"You said you knew others of my race. Who?"

"The mother of your race, for one. And many others."

"The mother—" You searched his face. "I don't understand. Many others?"

He sighed. "I am very old. And there have been many women." He traced a hand from your shoulder to your upper arm, goose-bumping the flesh. "But none like you. Never anyone like you." The lustful admiration in his face brightened into something greater. "You almost make me wish I were human."

"Why?"

"Why do you think religion runs so strongly among your people, despite the fact that your science was once great enough to disprove so many of your original concepts of the universe? Why does it persist now, despite the despair you must have felt knowing your race was all but destroyed? It's because greater beings have walked among you from time to time and you have stood by them almost as equals, despite your mortality, despite your lack of knowledge, despite your innate fears. And you did so because of faith. Your faith endures because human beings must strive to overcome their weaknesses—and their weaknesses help them believe that things can get better through will and faith. They either find a way to overcome or die. Your faith is your greatest gift, and it is something utterly lacking in beings like myself. For those of us who are less ignorant, faith is the most remarkable attribute a thinking being can demonstrate."

You said nothing. The silence washed over you comfortably. Finally: "How's that got anything to do with me?"

Now he laughed, and when he did it was good-natured and almost human sounding. He took your hands and kissed them. "Oh Kendra! Your faith is greater than any other being's I have ever encountered. It etches your whole being and lights you from inside. I see you and wish I could possess but a taste of it."

You looked at his large orange hands surrounding yours as they rested in your naked lap. Your cuticles were bloody where you'd picked at them, your nails ragged, your palms coarse from manual labor. And his hands were pristine, perfect.

"Samael?"

"Yes?"

"Is this—this between us—God's plan for me?"

He gave your knee a gentle squeeze. The movement sent a not-unpleasant shiver up your leg. "Of that I have no doubt."

Intimacy. You learned the true meaning of that word in those three days, didn't you? On the first day you learned how exposed and ashamed another could make you feel. And on the other two days—when Samael almost never left your side because you didn't want him to—you learned how willing you were to bare yourself completely.

And that's what he was to you, wasn't he? Samael was a man because he made you feel like the woman everyone in the city claimed you now were but hadn't let you be.

What made him a man to you? The way he ran a hand down your bare hip as you straddled him? His smell? His taste? Or was it his very inhumanness—the curve of those translucent wings draping you as if you were inside a blue tent—that made him seem like more of a man than any true man you had ever met?

Maybe it was none of the physical things at all. You left the cave and walked the hills with him in the morning light, pointing out trees and plants you had never seen, flowers in bloom, birds slicing in arching curves through the air. You bathed together in a mountain stream and told him about your secret childhood dreams of seeing other worlds as the Remnants had done in humanity's last days. He never once seemed bored by what you were saying. In fact, he hung on your every word. Then he tried to describe the way this world looked from high above, gave up on his description, and snatched you up in his arms to show you. Three massive sweeps of his wings and your chilled, wet skin was dry in the warm summer sun as you soared over vistas as beautiful as the ones you had seen on that first night, only now throbbing in brilliant daytime colors.

His wings were now your wings. You felt as if you were the woman described in Revelation who was given eagle's wings so she could be nourished for a time in the wilderness.

He turned you in midflight to face him. As you kissed you laughed in your throat—thrilled like a fool—unwilling to think about anything more than the next moment. He crushed you against him, and you felt his heat against you as he brought you down to a field springing with white wildflowers, where you thought of nothing but the grass beneath you, Samael above you, and the warmth of the sunlight as it shone in a bluish hue through his translucent wings.

"No more," you begged with a grin after a long while.

He kissed your neck. "Oh no, little Kendra. I'm not finished yet. Hours and hours," he said, and you grew suddenly fearful, "before I'm sated."

"Hey! Hey!"

You'd hardly heard the cry when Samael got off you and whirled around. Two rapid cracks echoed against the trees in quick succession. Samael slumped back on top of you. A warm liquid was pouring over you. You screamed and scratched and pushed and finally managed to slide yourself out from beneath him. You ran from the field, naked and bruised, your breath sharp in your chest until you stumbled face-first into the grass. You reached down and pulled a jagged branch from your heel and tried to stand. You winced and staggered forward and saw blood spattered on the white flowers by your feet. Out of the corner of your eye, a figure was running toward you, a carbine in hand.

"Kendra! Kendra McQueen!"

The sound of your name coming from a human voice dropped you back to the ground. As you tried to hide your nakedness with your arms, a leather jacket whipped across the air and covered you whole. Your gaze found a mustache, wire-frame glasses, short dark thick hair, a familiar face.

"Colonel Weiss?"

He squeezed your hand. "You're going to be okay now, kid." He held you tight against his barrel chest, but you could still see Samael immobile on the ground.

No.

It wasn't possible.

"He was an angel." Your voice was far away, flattened. "You killed an angel."

Weiss gripped your face between his two hands. His hands were slick with the thin, reddish liquid that had burst from Samael onto you but still didn't quite seem like blood. "No, not an angel. It was a Hostile. No true guardian would do this to you."

You tried to look away, at Samael, at the life you almost had.

"Kendra, listen to me. I swear to you," he said. "I swear it was not whatever it told you it was. You have to believe me. Those things lie about everything."

"He said I was special." Your mouth quivered, but you didn't cry. "He said I was unique."

Weiss stroked your matted hair as a father might. "You'll survive this," he growled. "You'll grow stronger. And someday you'll prove to the world that there is no one like Kendra McQueen."

Weiss. The thought of him brought Kendra back to herself, to the cellar, to the earth under her fingers. She had to get out, find him. A rodent ran across her bare forearm in the dark. She lashed out, grabbed it, then flung it toward where she thought the far wall was. A thud in the dark, nearer than she expected, then silence.

She had to get loose. She ran her manacled hands down her body and almost punched herself because of her stupidity. In a moment she had unbuckled and slipped off her belt.

Amateurs. Stupid. So stupid. Almost as stupid as I've been.

Ten minutes later, belt buckle in hand, the manacles were off her wrists. Two minutes after that she had popped the lock that had kept her feet chained to the wall.

She would be ready for them.

CHAPTER 20

That sound she knew.

A popping of thick wooden dead bolts being pulled back, then the heavy bar being lifted from its brackets on the door. Kendra snapped out of her combat nap and found the hiding place she had probed with her fingers just an hour or so before. With a heave, she pulled herself up and into it.

Ignore the light. Don't be blinded by it. Follow the sound.

The door creaked open. She could hear the undisciplined giggles of teenagers on the other side, one female, the other hoping to be male when his voice finally changed.

"Quiet. You know we're not supposed to talk in front of her."

God, grant me strength.

The sound of boots on the landing was dry and scratchy, tracked-in dirt on wood planking. She counted off the seconds in her head. The light from outside had probably reached the back corner of the cellar where she was supposed to be chained up.

"What the—"

Bingo.

She cleared her throat and they looked up. Kendra was braced between the ceiling beams above the top of the staircase near the door.

"Hiya."

Kendra leapt down, swinging the manacles in her right hand, and connected with the female Novice's forehead. With her left foot she kicked the male Novice down the flight of steps before him, his carbine sailing in a wide arc in the opposite direction to the dirt floor below. Her foot caught in his jacket, and she found herself being pulled along by his momentum down the steps. She knew falls like this and relaxed instinctively to shield herself from the worst of it.

Two seconds later her human surfboard was immobile on the dirt floor. She was up on her feet trying with squinted eyes to find his carbine in the semidarkness. A rustling sound above her told her she didn't have time. She pounced back up the wooden steps two at a time and grabbed the ankles of the female Novice, who was trying to crawl to an escape. After a quick look through the doorway suggested no one was waiting in the Khans' kitchen, she snatched the girl's sidearm from its holster, shoved it against her temple, then pulled her down the cellar steps by the back of her curly brownish-red hair, now generously streaked with blood.

Kendra ripped the nub of a candle out of the girl's pocket and tossed her face-first to the floor next to her comrade. She lit the candle with the girl's matches and set it on the ground, then scanned the area for the carbine. There it was—in the back corner she had been chained to, not far from the chamber pot. She slung the rifle over her shoulder by its leather strap, kept the sidearm in her right hand, and picked the chamber pot up with her left.

Kendra stood over them in the flickering candlelight. The girl's eyes were unfocused, maybe a concussion, but she was groaning and half-awake. Sure the boy was faking unconsciousness, she dumped the contents of the pot on his face.

"Jesus Christ!" he sputtered as he sprang into a sitting position. "Jesus Christ!"

"Lord's name." Kendra smirked and then gave his face a close examination. "I know you, you little fucker. You're Daniel Hernandez. You were in Captain Giordano's company two years ago."

"Look, please don't—"

"*And* you copped a feel off me when you dumped me down here."

"Please." He wiped piss from his eyes and groaned as he tried to sit up. "Please, please don't kill me."

"Anyone else upstairs, Danny boy?"

"No, no."

Kendra squatted and felt his leg. He had fractured his shinbone, but it didn't appear too serious. She leaned her knee on the broken bone, and he screamed. His voice was somehow more masculine just then.

She glanced up at the door, a serene look on her face. Nope, he wasn't lying.

"You know, little fucker, this break isn't too bad. I think it'll set just fine. Unless it gets worse. Then they'll have to amputate." She jerked her chin at him. "You ever see an amputation?"

He shook his head.

"They say they've got some kind of anesthetic now, but I dunno. Last one I saw, the guy bit *clean* through the block of wood they had set between his teeth. And most of his tongue."

"God, please—"

She leaned over him, her breath on his face, her breast against his chest. "Wanna cop a feel now?"

He looked away from her. "You're crazy, crazy."

"Yup. And I'm the one with the boots and the guns. So why don't you do you and your little girlfriend here a favor and tell me where I can find John Giordano?"

"I don't know." Tears were rising in his almost-black eyes. "I swear."

She stood up, pressed her toe into his shinbone, and he screamed.

"I swear I don't know!"

"Then tell me where I can find your master, little fucker. Where's Gordon Lee?"

She left them in the cellar manacled to each other and then chained to the wall by Hernandez's bad leg. She left the door to the cellar steps open. She wanted someone to find them when they didn't report in and didn't want their deaths on her conscience. There was enough guilt there already.

The streets were empty and lined by long shadows. It couldn't have been long after dawn. She decided to explore the city along the roofs of the row houses that formed the blocks near the Khans' home. As a kid she and her schoolmates had jumped with ease across the alleyways separating these blocks. If she was lucky and quiet, she could make it all the way to Lee's house three blocks over without ever coming down to street level.

Nothing out of the ordinary. Novices were being put through their early-morning paces by their drill instructors. This month's farm-shift teams were shuffling off to the barns to make repairs. A crew was working on one of Lee's newfangled gas lamps, another on replacing a fractured wooden sewer pipe. But something seemed wrong. After a moment she got it: no older people, not a single Remnant. And even a lot of Firsters were absent. Just people her own age and those a bit older and children.

What had he done with all of them?

Keeping low along the roofs, she made her way down to Lee's block. She jumped the alleyway and landed on the opposite roof almost noiselessly. One roof over from her destination. She crouched and scanned the immediate area. No guards.

Big head honcho now and no guards. Maybe that little Hernandez was lying. Maybe Lee lives somewhere else now.

Noises from below dropped Kendra to her belly. She crawled on elbows and knees to peer over the parapet. There were Gordon and Sofie Lee's three girls marching off to school, giggling and poking one another and playing as young girls do, careless and stupid. And then before and behind them—bingo—a quartet of guards.

She could hear Sofie's voice under her, sending reminders and farewells up the block while the girls yelled back promises of obedience and declarations of affection. Kendra couldn't see her, but it made sense that Sofie was probably standing at the front door. She couldn't hear anyone else after the girls left, not Lee, not any guards. Kendra waited for a few minutes on the roof flat on her back. A bright-blue sky was dawning almost completely devoid of clouds.

A good omen.

Kendra checked to see if the carbine was loaded and then the sidearm in her belt. She had been in the Lees' home a few times, not many. She closed her eyes and tried to visualize it. The layout was like all of the other row houses built in this vicinity. But the furniture and all that stuff that goes along with three young girls—those were serious variables. All she needed was to slip on a misplaced wooden duck on wheels. Even with those distractions, she was sure she could get the drop on at least three guards—if any were still inside—if she needed to. And maybe even on Sofie, good as she had been back in the day. Weiss hadn't lied when he said his niece had been one of the best soldiers he had ever trained.

A quick look into the yard and Kendra threw her feet over the side of the back wall. After securing finger- and toeholds in the mortar between the brickwork, she made her way down and dropped into the sunny back garden. Sheets and towels, white and crisp, were flapping on a clothesline in the chilly breeze. The back door was to her left and led into the kitchen. She glanced through an open window shutter and found the kitchen empty, the home quiet. She tried the door. Unlatched. All she needed to do was creep in.

As she was about to grasp the handle, the door sprang in and away from her. She flattened against the wall. Sofie was coming out with a laundry basket. Kendra leveled the rifle at the woman's head.

"Don't. Move."

Sofie jumped and dropped the basket, exposing her midsection. She was five or six months pregnant.

Kendra took a small step forward. "Anyone inside?"

Sofie shook her head. A slight pout edged the corners of her mouth. "You first."

Sofie grinned. Kendra pressed the weapon's barrel into the base of Sofie's skull as she reached for the door. The house was semidark inside. The morning light had yet to reach the back corners of the first floor. The air was close and dry from the warmth of the fire and seemed only recently devoid of its bustle and activity. It almost crackled with the recently extinguished energy of children.

"Kendra," Sofie said without turning around. "Kendra, please talk to me."

"Sit in this chair, both hands on the table, palms down."

Sofie did as she was told. A lock of her strawberry-blond hair fell out of its bun and into her eyes. She grinned thinly.

"How're you alive, Kendra?"

"How does the wife of the new head honcho *not* know that I'm alive?"

"Gordon doesn't tell me everything." Sofie shrugged but kept her hands on the table. "Is John okay?"

A pause, then through her teeth: "Yes."

"We gave you both up for dead when you didn't come back right—"

"I'm sure it broke your heart." Kendra shifted her gaze across the kitchen. The sink was still filled with breakfast dishes. The water pump on the edge of the sink dripped off rhythm onto the glazed blue and tan ceramic bowls. The dishware piled up like that prevented her from knowing how many people had been at breakfast. "Where's Lee?"

"He's probably in the Council chambers. That's where he usually is this time of day. Wanna go for a visit?"

"Where's Weiss?"

"My father or my uncle?"

"Really. Keep being cute, Sofie."

"Probably in the hills. With the others."

"What others?"

"The others who didn't . . . agree with us."

"Careful." Kendra took a step closer and raised her rifle again. "Let's not start again with the cuteness."

"Most of the Remnants are in the hills. A lot of the Firsters too."

Kendra shook her head. "Can't be all of them. Not Grace Davison. She's too old."

Sofie's inscrutable grin quivered and fell. Real emotion now appeared to seep through. "Kendra . . . Grace is dead."

An old woman's death should never feel like a sucker punch. But this one, sharp and sudden, did because the second Kendra heard it she knew it was true. If Grace were living, their city wouldn't be like this. No way.

"How?"

"She was almost a hundred years old, Kendra."

"I don't care who you are, Sofie. I don't care who you're related to. I will kill you if you lie to me."

"No. You won't." Confidence widened Sofie's smile. "I trained you. The last thing you could do is kill a pregnant woman. The *last* thing."

Kendra nodded once or twice, then flipped her carbine over and rammed its wooden stock into Sofie's forehead. Sofie's face went from smug satisfaction to wincing pain. Kendra slipped the sidearm into her hand and the rifle across her shoulders as Sofie sat holding her bruised forehead.

"Maybe I won't kill you. But I will pistol-whip you until you tell me what I need to know."

Sofie's eyes blazed through the pain. "Do you think God will forgive you for this, 'little' Kendra?"

Kendra readied the pistol, but she stopped in midmotion as she heard the pounding of racing footsteps behind her. Four guards were coming through the front door, carbines at the ready. She clucked her tongue as they snatched the weapons from her and shoved her facedown on the table. They were all from her squad.

Her hands were bound with rope behind her back, her eyes blindfolded. "*I once was lost but now am found, was blind, but now I see.*" Exploding gasps and muffled conversations rising and falling in uneven rhythms. She was being led down a busy street, maybe right down the main boulevard past Central Square. Had to be near the square. The winter sunlight was much stronger on her face here, unblocked by any buildings on the tightly packed streets. "*For Thou art my lamp, O Lord; and the Lord will lighten my darkness.*" How could such morons have gotten the drop? "*And be ye kind one to another, tenderhearted, forgiving one another—*"

No, dammit, no. No forgiveness. None.

Her feet tripped as they hit the first step, but the guards steadied her by her elbows. She shrugged them off and carried herself up the other five steps with ease. Definitely the Council chambers. It was the only building with front steps like these, raised up as it was because the land here had always been a bit marshy. She remembered her father telling her that the building stood on thick stilts set on drained land.

When they pulled the blindfold off, she was where she expected to be. The Council chambers hadn't changed much except for the addition of gas-lighting in sconces mounted along the walls.

Gordon Lee's sign of progress. Really just a dog pissing to mark his territory.

The back door that led into the Council's chambers opened on the left side of the dais. And there was John—her John—coming toward her, his hands bound in manacles before him. His grin broadened as he approached her, sure-footed and true. Her throat tightened. He was whole, safe. Rage was swapped out for confidence in her chest. The world would be set right again. Yes, it would. She would make sure of that no matter what. Even if she would never be forgiven by anyone for what she had to do.

"Hey," John said as his guards brought him to stand next to her before the dais.

"Hey yourself."

He looked her over. "You okay, Ken?"

"Yeah sure. The nose?"

He laughed and lifted his bound hands to give it a gentle touch. "Just a hairline fracture. My old man swings like a scientist."

"Good. Now how the hell do we get out of here?"

The door John and his two guards had come through opened again. This time Gordon Lee appeared with a quartet of guards flanking him. Eight guards total now, two for each of them and four for Lee.

Lee looked no different, other than the fact that he was wearing some variant of the ceremonial gray-and-blue robes worn by the Council while in session. His face still held its pinched look, like he was either suspicious or smelling something rotten. His narrow mouth was relaxed and almost bored, his black hair still longish and falling in styled waves over his ears and shoulders. He sat in what was now the only seat on the dais, a high-backed chair of heavy oak that neither of them had ever seen before. It looked outsized in its position at the center of the old rectangular Council table and somewhat ridiculously like a throne.

Lee didn't glance at them as he took his seat, seeming to be preoccupied with the papers on the table and his own efforts in looking magnificent and authoritative as he sat there. Kendra barely suppressed a giggle as she watched one of his baby-faced guards stare at him with something bordering on religious awe. She was a young girl, two years into the Defense Forces, and probably only a few years older than Lee's eldest child.

John grew annoyed by the show. "What the hell's going on, Gordon?"

"Quiet!" The baby guard on John's left belted him in the ribs with the butt of her carbine. John winced and doubled over.

"Hey you." Kendra leaned over to look at her. "You get yours first."

The male guard near Kendra raised his rifle, but Lee held up a hand. "Please. Wait. We're all friends here. They don't know what's happened. They need to understand what's at stake."

John's brow ridged. "What exactly is at stake?"

"The fate of the human race," Lee replied, as if it were the most obvious answer in the world. "Whether we will all live together as free and knowledgeable citizens or as adherents to an outdated, deceitful, and ignorant orthodoxy."

Kendra chuckled. "Well, since you put it like that—"

John shook his head at her, then turned to Lee. "It kind of feels like we're on trial here, Gordon. That doesn't seem too free to me."

The rifle-butt girl stood in his face. "You will address Protector Lee as 'sir' or 'Your Lordship.'"

"So you're what?" Kendra leaned over to look at her again. "One of his concubines?" The female guard raised the rifle to Kendra's face. John threw his body between the two women. "We're citizens of this city, you son of a bitch!" Kendra yelled at Lee as the guards sought to restore order. "What's happened to the Council?"

Lee held up a hand to restore calm, then told the guards to let the prisoners sit in a pair of chairs at a table on the left side of the dais. Lee came down the steps and approached the table as soon as the guards were in position.

He stood before them, face calm, hands clasped behind his back. "The Council of Twelve was dissolved more than two months ago, when it was conclusively proved that its members had lied to the people for decades. A transitional government, under my direction, is now in place until such time when free and fair elections can be peaceably held."

Kendra shifted in her seat as she tried to find a comfortable position for her bound arms against the back of her chair. She gave up trying and sat sidesaddle on the chair so she could lean against John. "You kids really believe he's going to have free elections? I mean, in your lifetimes?"

"Gordon," John said quietly, "what was the Council lying about?"

"Everything, John. Everything about our existence here, how the Remnants got here, who the Orangemen really are—everything. Our entire world has been a complete fabrication."

"Pretty big claim."

"I will tell you everything," Lee promised. "But you've got to answer some of our questions first. Where have you been all this time? What did you see in the wilderness?"

"You know we're under orders to report directly to General Weiss."

"General Weiss is no longer head of the Defense Forces, John."

"Who is, then?" Kendra asked.

"My wife, of course."

She whistled. "Of course."

John shook his head. "We don't recognize your authority."

Lee walked away from the table but kept nodding, as if the movement would prevent his guards' eyes from drilling boreholes into his suddenly fallible-seeming brain. "You asked what they had been lying about. Yet both of you have said you didn't entirely trust the Orangemen."

"Not to you, I didn't."

Lee held up a hand, the robe draping off his bare forearm. "No, but you did to my wife, a long time ago. Remember? Perhaps you suspected, as we now know, that the Orangemen—both our protectors and our destroyers—are aliens."

"That old chestnut? Man, I thought you had something for a second," Kendra answered, her jaw set. "And yet still no evidence, not before man's fall and still none now."

Lee provided her with a toothless smirk. "Would you believe me if I told you the evidence has been under our very noses all this time?"

Kendra scoffed. "Well, that sounds to me like the Remnants can't be the great liars you make them out to be."

"Or maybe the best place to keep such a secret would be right out in the open," Lee said with a shrug. "You might even have read that in a book once."

"Gordon," John said with a level gaze. "Talk to us. Don't play games."

Lee held up a finger to his lips and closed his eyes. "Just a few more questions. If you won't tell us about where you've been, remind us of what you know. First, in what year was the Earth destroyed?"

"Oh for the love of—" Kendra began.

"Please. Indulge me."

"It was 2491," she said through set teeth.

"And how many years have our people been here?"

"Fifty-two," John answered. "Almost fifty-three. Come on, Gordon."

"Last one, I promise. Just give us a brief description of human civilization before its end. Level of technology, all that."

John and Kendra looked at each other. He nodded at her, agreeing to go along. "You know as well as I do that it was pretty advanced. Gene therapy had cured a number of serious diseases. They had nuclear-powered spacecraft capable of getting them around the solar system fairly easily. They had built a domed city, probably as large as ours, on the moon. And they were in the process of terraforming Mars—something *confirmed* by the Tylers."

"Speaking of," Kendra added. "Where are they?"

Lee gave his guards a hooded look, then cleared his throat and went on. "Let's go to the Archives. We'll find your answers there."

The Archives, John thought, *everything went back there, didn't it?* Back to where the original volumes of mankind's previous civilization were housed. And now so did they, this time with their hands newly unbound so he and Kendra could descend the narrow staircase into the fortified bunker. The dry air was rich with the scent of yellowing paper as they drew downward. Memories flowed through John's mind of beloved days and nights he spent here reading, wandering, exploring, listening to his namesake grandfather—all in the hopes of capturing in full and complete detail a fragment of a civilization he had never known. And with those memories came the old familiar feelings of loss and isolation and dislocation. Everything all the same. Well, not everything. The scent of burning kerosene lamps was missing. Lee had replaced those lamps with sconces of piped-in gas, which he turned on by twisting a switch mounted in the wall at the top of the steps.

Before them stood the heavy wooden stacks that had been built so long ago by the Remnants, their weight being tested under the couple hundred or so additional volumes their people had written and added to the Archives since the Arrival.

Lee walked ahead of them, running a hand almost absentmindedly across the spines of a row of books to his left. They all knew classics of world literature were there, mostly translations into English. He pulled a very thick volume from the shelf and flipped it open. The expression on his face was somewhere between smug and bemused.

"You say the world as humanity knew it ended in 2491?"

"Gordon," John said. "Come on already."

Lee held out the book. It was a Samuel Putnam translation of *Don Quixote* by Cervantes, opened to a page none of them had ever had reason to look at—the copyright page.

"If the world ended in 2491," Lee continued, "then tell me: Why is there not a single original volume here that was printed any later than 1962?"

CHAPTER 21

Kendra tore through the literature section, a lifetime's worth of art in her arms. She snatched Ernest Hemingway's *The Old Man and the Sea*—a first edition from 1952. She pulled several volumes at random from the shelves nearest her and furiously flipped to the copyright pages of each. It wasn't possible. It couldn't be—1941, 1938, 1945, 1926—no no no. She grabbed *From Here to Eternity* by James Jones down from the shelf. His descriptions of army life had made it one of her favorite books during her Defense Forces training. She must've read it a half dozen times.

Copyright 1951. First printing.

John attacked the history books and stacked one upon another in a pile on a nearby table after scanning them for their printing dates—1920, 1931, 1906, 1936, 1950. He yanked Lewis Mumford's *The City in History* from the shelf. That book he knew. After all, it had served the city's founders well when they were planning out New Philadelphia. Copyright 1961. He moved to the biography section and found in his hand a book titled *Al Smith American*. Copyright 1945 by Frank Graham.

"They can't all be published before 1962," Kendra muttered. "Somebody—at some point—would've noticed."

Lee folded his arms across his slim chest. "I assure you that they are. I've made an exhaustive check. Not a single one published after 1962. It's really blindingly obvious when you start to think about it. Why would a civilization as advanced as ours had been still need paper books?" He tapped his chin with his forefinger. "I can say with the evidence before us that the world our parents and grandparents knew ended around 1962, *not* in 2491. Add to this other cursory facts—the kinds of weapons, tools, and supplies the Orangemen left the Remnants with. They also attest to this. So why lie to us, the two generations born here? It's quite simple. Because the Orangemen didn't destroy us. We destroyed ourselves. These Orangemen—who could be anything, but let's for a moment assume them to be aliens who were passing by our wrecked world—took some kind of cosmic pity on us and deposited the survivors here on this primitive planet, where we could do little harm to ourselves or one another. And they left us here with an admonition to 'be good' and plenty of Bibles to show us *how* to be good. Those little daily reminders in Revelation are a convenient way of controlling our behavior, keeping our technology primitive, and, not coincidently, ensuring the Remnants would stay in charge."

"You're making a lot of guesses there," Kendra said. "And you don't even have all the facts. You don't even know that this planet is—"

"*Kendra,*" John snapped, then turned to Lee. "Let's say you've got something, Gordon. What's the point of telling us the world ended in the twenty-fifth century?"

"That I'm not sure," Lee said with a shrug and a smirk. "Best guess? They must've thought it was better to contrast our brave new technologically inferior Christianopolis with an even more highly advanced, decadent past."

"A stretch," Kendra said.

"Really?" Lee said. "Almost every Remnant we've ever known deplores technology, even when it's clear that things like advanced medicine could save some of our people from infectious diseases—why, your own parents, Kendra! Even the fragmentary history gathered and preserved here tells us something of the technology of the mid-twentieth century. We know mankind had cures to many diseases at that time—as well as had the atomic bomb and germ warfare in 1962. Maybe it was one of those things that did us in—or maybe something else. But it's not much of a stretch to think that's why the Remnants talk down technology—to keep us from getting back to a point where we could destroy ourselves again. Why else would technological improvements be so taboo in the City of Brotherly Love, Part Two?"

"You must've confronted the Remnants with this . . . information," John said. "What did they say?"

"Denied it, of course, the arrogant bastards," Lee said. "Some of them were downright indignant. They said: How could *we* not remember what the world had been like? We were *there*, they said, and then somehow assumed we'd all still believe their poltergeist-soaked stories of angels and demons and seas turning to blood. The legendary geniality of Andrew Weiss dissolved when we brought our evidence before the Council. He even threatened to arrest me. My own father-in-law."

"But he didn't."

"I hadn't played my trump card yet, John."

"Let me guess. Something to do with the Tylers," Kendra scoffed. "The very people who came among us and *confirmed* the Remnants' descriptions of the world's end."

"Convenient, eh?" Lee said. "And also ridiculous. The Tylers show up being no older than I am yet claiming they were survivors of an Orangeman attack on the Mars base that happened, what, *more than fifty years ago*? You don't find that strange?"

Lee nodded at one of the guards, who then disappeared into the stacks. She returned a few moments later with two heavy volumes. She looked at the spine of one and handed it to her "protector" while holding the other in reserve. Lee thumbed through the book until he found the page he was looking for.

"You remember the Tylers well, then?"

John nodded. "Of course. We were their guards."

"This," Lee said, handing them the book, "is a photograph of the first lady of a country called Argentina. It was on the South American continent. She died at age thirty-three on July 26, 1952. Her name was Eva Perón, often called Evita."

Kendra and John stared at the picture. Apart from the fact that the smiling woman in this black-and-white photo seemed to have blond hair, she was the very twin of the woman they knew as Eva Tyler. Both women even liked to wear their hair upswept in buns.

Lee gestured for the other book, and the guard filled his out-stretched hand with it. "And this is a biographical dictionary of great Americans, which quite fortunately includes with each listing photos or paintings of important persons throughout that country's history. He's a bit older here, but I think you'll recognize this man as well."

They took the book and looked at the photo next to the entry for William Tyler Page, a public servant best known for penning something called "The American's Creed." Page died in 1942. Though an old man in this photo, neatly bald and wearing glasses, the heavy features and hard line of a mouth were the exact same as the man they knew as William Tyler.

"The Tylers were fakes, copies," Lee stated. "I don't know how, but that's clearly what they were."

"*Were?*" John asked, his voice edging up. "Jesus Christ, Gordon. What did you do to them?"

For the first time a look of genuine sorrow clouded Lee's face. A little boy lived in that look, one who was clearly in the wrong and felt suddenly shamed by those in the right. "They're dead. When some of my followers found out the truth—"

Kendra stiffened. "How could you—"

"I didn't." He shook his head emphatically. "It was in the early days. Sofie and I didn't know everything. People were angry the Council had withheld this information from them. Things spiraled out of control. There was fighting in the streets, lots and lots of injuries. Far worse than the few fistfights we had here before you left. Protesters were pulling down the government's authority piece by piece. And then someone got the idea to interrogate the Tylers—"

Kendra's mouth curled in disgust. "Not a single murder in a half century and a whole family slaughtered ten minutes into your watch. You son of a bitch."

"What do you think I am? The children are safe. We're taking care of them. They're innocents, obviously."

"How is that obvious?" A bitter catch in Kendra's throat made her choke out the words. "Aren't they 'copies' too?"

"But they're not copies."

John and Kendra eyed him with suspicion.

"I've found no record of the originals—Eva Perón and William Tyler Page—ever having children together. And Page died in 1942, an old man during Perón's childbearing years. Granted we have limited knowledge of the era, but it seems unlikely they even met."

John returned his gaze to the pictures and shook his head. "So the adult Tylers were, what? Copies of people who were dead but who had children together?"

"And these children *never* existed before?" Kendra added.

"Gordon, you have to understand how insane this sounds."

"I know." Lee gripped the back of a chair. "I'd agree, if that's all I knew. But I now know they're not the only ones."

Kendra's mouth popped open, then closed again, before she cleared her throat. "Who else?"

"Kendra, I—"

"Come on, Lee, who else?"

He took the biographical dictionary from her hands and flipped it open to the "R" entries. Once he found the page he sought, he handed it back to her. "You, of course, remember the late Alexander Raymond Sr."

Her blue eyes fixed on him hard. The open page beneath her wasn't even in her peripheral sight. "Alex's father?"

"He was one of the youngest Remnants, just a boy of six or seven on the day of the Arrival. John, you might recall I was apprenticed to him as a teenager. They had asked for volunteers to form the official Engineering Corps. I knew everything about him, every line on his face, every hair in his beard. I *loved* that man. I loved him as much as my own father." He tapped the book in Kendra's hands. "According to this, Alex Raymond was an influential cartoonist who most famously drew a newspaper comic strip called *Flash Gordon*—about a spaceman, ironically enough—in the early- to mid-twentieth century." He gave Kendra's shoulder the barest encouraging touch. "Kendra, look and tell me that's not the man we both knew."

Kendra looked, as did John over her shoulder. A middle-aged face stared back at them—broad forehead, slightly jowly, a clipped-thin mustache, slick dark wavy hair. It was without doubt Alexander Raymond Sr. Younger, yes, but him. It was hard to forget those features. Similar ones had played variations on a theme across her Alex's face.

She took a defiant step toward Lee. His guards snapped to attention and drew their weapons. She stopped but kept her gaze on their leader. "He grew up *here*, Lee. He looks the same as this man, sure, but he grew up here. He was a childhood friend of the Weiss brothers. How can a copy come of age?"

John had taken the book from her and was evaluating the cartoonist's face. He hadn't known the elder Raymond as well, but this man looked an awful lot like him. "Wait. Let's back up. All of these people you've named so far died *before* 1962, the year you claim the world actually ended. It says here this Alex Raymond died in 1956."

"That's right. So there's no way any of these people could have been snatched up by the Orangemen around 1962 and brought here. There's no way they can be the originals, say, with their memories somehow lost. And that is especially obvious in the case of Raymond Sr., who as Kendra keeps saying, grew up here."

"So how did these copies come about?"

"John, I don't know," Lee said with a surprising modesty. "I'm baffled by it. But I've found that to be the same with everyone I've located in the Archives. In each case, someone was copied from a person who had died before 1962."

"Everyone?" John's head jerked up from the photos in the book. "There's more?"

"How many?" Kendra asked.

Lee pursed his lips and paused for a moment. "Nearly three thousand and fifty of the Remnants. At least, those are the ones that people in my group can identify."

John stared in disbelief. "Three thousand—"

"What about us?" Kendra demanded. "Our families?"

"Not so lucky there," Lee said. "No Giordanos or McQueens or Lees who look like our grandparents. But there may be another reason why we haven't found them."

"And that is?" John asked.

He shrugged. "Maybe they simply aren't in any of the books the Orangemen snatched up. Of course, that said, books tend to identify famous people. What if the originals of our Remnant ancestors were not famous—or famous enough—to be written about? What if they were just ordinary people?"

John said nothing. It was all almost too much to bear. Even all that blood pounding in his ears couldn't drown out Gordon Lee.

"Okay, so let's extrapolate." Lee clapped his hands together. "What if *every one* of the original one hundred and forty-four thousand was a copy of someone who died on Earth *before* the end of the world?"

"That makes the rest of us—everyone born here—no different than the Tyler children," John said.

"Exactly," Lee agreed, nodding. "We're all creations after the fact. A new mixture taken from a sampling of humanity. In fact, I'm even starting to wonder if the livestock they gave us are copies of dead sheep, cows, oxen."

John and Kendra looked at each other again. Living creatures copied from dead ones—all of those "extinct" animals they saw in the wilderness . . .

"So I ask you," Lee continued, "as one intelligent being to two others, can any of this really be biblical prophecy come true? I know one's faith must be tested but—"

"So what are we?" Kendra said in a low voice to no one in particular.

Lee took it upon himself to answer. "Free, Kendra. We're free for the first time in our lives, free to live life however we want."

Kendra eyed him. "But what *are* we?"

Lee smiled. "Does it matter? Without rules, without a preening orthodoxy, we can do and be whatever we want."

"No, dammit, no," John said, rubbing the back of his neck, "it's not that simple. Even if all of the facts have been wrong, all of this," he said, gesturing at the books around him, "all of this proves one thing. Life isn't easy. All the rules you're dismissing out of hand are the very things that make it easier for us to coexist. Without them life goes from being not easy to unlivable. At least by human standards."

"But we may not be human." Lee shrugged. The gesture made him look small in his loose robe. "An issue for another day. As will be my questions for you. Remember, I still need to know where you've been all this time."

John smirked. "And maybe if we're 'real' and not just copies of the people who left the city months ago?"

"Yes," he said quietly, "there's that too. Guards."

Kendra hurled the heavy volume she was still holding at the tip of Lee's nose. The stinging blow made him recoil, just as John jumped between Kendra and the guards. She snatched the sleeve of Lee's ceremonial robe and pulled it free of his arm and wrapped it around his neck in a tight noose. Already his skin had begun to glow red.

"Anybody here thinking I'm not crazy enough to kill him?" She grinned at the guards. "Drop the guns."

"On the ground, facedown, now!" John barked. He snatched the two sidearms and two carbines from the guards as Kendra held the wriggling and red-faced Lee in her vise grip.

"You first, Lord Protector." She pushed him toward the steps as John covered their escape with one of the carbines.

"John," Kendra called as they ascended the stairs.

"Yeah," he said, walking backward up the steps.

"I have less than zero idea what to do once we're up these stairs."

He laughed. "I do."

"Hit me."

"We find Weiss and make our report."

"Sounds good to me," she said as she shoved Lee face-first out the bunker doors.

They ran. Once up the stairs and back into the bursting sunlight of their fortified city, they ran and ran hard. Lee was dispatched at the end of the block with a shove and a rifle butt to the kneecap. Kendra was glad to have that scream. She wanted to hurt someone, wanted to lash out. John was with her, a pace ahead, shoving aside the confused faces on the city streets. Here and there, on sidewalks and at intersections, they would scare someone off with a barked threat or a proffered weapon. No one inside New Philadelphia had leveled a gun at another human being in two generations; it was a terrifying thing to do and have done to you. Kendra felt sick and uneasy. How well it fit into Lee's theory that mankind's assertiveness and aggression had done them in. But she also knew it made her feel safe, and that made it feel almost right.

Crowds pulled away from them. Were they shocked by the threat of violence? Or because two old friends and colleagues long given up for dead were running through their streets? Whatever the reason, it kept resistance at the city's center nonexistent. They had to do less shoving once they were away from the Archives and near the manufacturing district, where the escape tunnel built into the city's walls remained hidden.

The run hurt more than it should. They were feeling their injuries and recent imprisonment and were slow to react to the people around them. But keeping each other safe pushed them forward despite their labored breathing, the stitches in their sides, their thirst and hunger. When they reached the corner nearest the tunnel, they found the area deserted. John stopped short, and Kendra nearly ran into him. They both leaned against the stone wall, hands on their knees, as they tried to catch their breath.

John peered around the corner. "Trouble."

Kendra peeked over his shoulder. "Four Novices are trouble?"

"Sitting on top of the tunnel they are. We've gotta wait."

"No, we don't."

She flicked off her carbine's safety and ran at the Novices while screaming at the top of her lungs and firing several shots in the air. When the kids dispersed in a panic, she smirked at John. He jogged toward her, his weapon's stock at his shoulder, circling for snipers as he did.

"Don't do that again."

"Why?"

"We're not here to kill our own people, Kendra. Got that?"

She felt the sting of his scolding. "I'll get the tunnel open. Cover me."

As Kendra crouched to work the pulley system that slid the stones away to reveal the tunnel, the Novices she had chased off were now pounding back toward them, this time led by several of the guards who had been in the Archives with them.

"Terrific," she muttered.

John sighed, then squeezed off a round that whizzed over the lead soldier's head. Kendra jumped involuntarily as the bullet hit masonry. The soldiers took up positions pressed against the walls.

"You're out in the open, Captain," one of them called back. "You don't have anywhere to go."

"I swear by God we're leaving this city. We're leaving whether or not I have to kill you. Make a choice." As they hesitated, John muttered to Kendra, "Get in now. I'm a step behind you."

"John—"

"Go!"

She ducked back down and popped the mechanism, then slipped in and slid headfirst on her belly into the tunnel. Keeping his rifle level aimed at the corner, he crouched before the hole. The lead soldier was the one Kendra had called Lee's concubine. She was out to prove something, and that made her careless. John could see more and more of her inching around the corner all the time. He waited a second, then two, and found his shot. He squeezed off a round and hit the fleshy outside part of her right thigh. As she dropped into the open and her team struggled to pull her back behind the wall, he dove into the hole. Kendra was already pushing a heavy stone toward the exit to block it.

Before them were the hills circling New Philadelphia, the past and future of their civilization. Their frozen breath hung around them in a cloud as they got their bearings. Then they raced through the heavy brush, carbines slung, hand in hand, not knowing who or what they were and out to discover if they had been raised by the most artful of liars.

CHAPTER 22

If history was always written by the victors, how could the losers know themselves?

All human knowledge was fragmentary. Nothing known was whole or complete. Every great civilization had been stitched together from inseams of information; each was only ever remembered by the torn bits of cloth that remained.

As John hiked with Kendra into the wintering hills, he thought of these and other things as they found themselves on the edge of a world not of their making. The tide was drawing away the sand from under their feet, but the urge to survive was still strong.

Near the top of the hills, not far from the tumbledown cabin where they had spent their first night together, John felt the ground rushing up toward him as Kendra shoved him down hard. She spread herself across his back to shield him. He lay still at her urging, but after a few minutes of cold grass tickling his nose, he ventured to speak.

"Kendra—"

"Wait."

"Ken, there's nothing out there."

She let him turn over to face her. "I thought I heard something."

"You're paranoid."

"Better paranoid than dead."

"What's the matter with you?"

She looked at him, her lips parted, the black waves of her hair roping around her ears in the wind. "I don't know what's wrong and what's right, John. What's real and what isn't. All I do know is that I have to keep you safe."

"We'll find Weiss and the others. We'll tell them what we saw out there, and we'll make sense of things. Believe me."

She wiped the standing tears from her eyes and said in a firm voice, "If Samael wasn't an angel, wasn't a Nephilim, if he was just some alien *thing*, then—"

He squeezed her hand. "Ken, I'm not saying I understand everything. But I do know one thing: Gordon Lee can't be right."

"But the baby—"

"Was loved and mourned and rightfully so." He kissed her cheek and rubbed her shoulder. "Up and at 'em, Lieutenant. Let's find the others."

The abandoned cabin wasn't more than a mile or so from their position, but it took an hour of crawling through frost-hardened thickets to reach it. It was already dusk by the time they glimpsed the cabin silhouetted against the sky. The coming night air fluttered with a dusting of snow, and the wind held no noises apart from the stirring of evergreen foliage and winter-bare tree branches. They hadn't been followed. John began to wonder if a serious attempt had even been mounted once they were through the city walls.

The cabin had changed little since their first night there, other than it being much colder. They needed to risk starting a fire in the fireplace if they were going to get through the night without gear. Warming themselves against each other and near a fire had a great appeal, even if they would be forced to sleep in shifts. They found the nubs of candles they had secreted in a crack in the stonework of the hearth, lit them with matches Kendra had swiped from the Novices, then began to scavenge for wood and kindling. A fire large enough to keep them warm was burning within an hour. They watched its smoke drifting into the night sky through the hole in the thatched roof. Someone would see this. Someone would come. They took to their expectant vigil.

About an hour and a half after the haloed hazy-yellow moon had reached its zenith, a dozen gray and wrinkled heads rose out of the dark woods beyond the tumbledown cabin's walls. The Remnants had come.

Their fleshy, balding, worn, and worldly features were still a happy and familiar sight, despite their coming out of the brush like that. So, John realized, this is what the Remnants had been like during those rough early years of exile, surviving by silence and cunning. It was hard to imagine that either of them—or anyone—could pry any truth from such mouths.

As the Remnants entered, John and Kendra came to attention. Neither raised a weapon. John spoke for both of them. "Captain Giordano and Lieutenant McQueen request permission to report to General Weiss."

A flash moved among the graceful, grizzled faces, a shock of faded red coming to life. Then they heard that voice. "John? Kendra? Dear God, is it really you?"

John saw his mother coming near. Her face was worn and flushed and tired. A hundred thoughts flashed through his mind, things he wanted to say to her but didn't know how. For the first time he realized she was beginning to take some of her last breaths in middle age. Yet at the same time, next to the wizened visages around them and with that unexpected joy in her eyes, she appeared almost as young as Kendra. Not today but soon, he would talk to her.

"We've come home. Will you have us?"

"Oh thank God," Petra said with her hands folded, her eyes lifted to the sky. "Thank you for bringing our children back to us."

Her face cracked open as she burst into tears. "None of that now, Mom." He gripped her by the neck and pulled her to him to kiss the top of her head. "I haven't always been the most understanding son," he whispered in her ear. "But you have always been a mother filled with love. And hope. You never did anything wrong by me, Mom, never ever."

They camped that night in the cabin, each taking a shift on guard duty. The Remnants—and Petra—shared their provisions with Kendra and John as they talked late into the night. From Petra they learned how Gordon Lee's faction had sown doubt among the city's population, how he and Sofie had led street protests against the Council, at first simply demanding to see the Tylers but later campaigning more vigorously for their handover. It was then that the talk of a new government began to surface in public. Some had even urged the Council's overthrow by violence if necessary. At the time these appeared to be a few radical voices—squeaky wheels attracting outsized attention. At least that's what the Council thought. Then Grace Davison intervened. If anyone could assuage the people's fears, this most respected woman could.

For two weeks she was as dynamic as she had been twenty or thirty years earlier. She addressed crowds of the angry and confused, speaking to them always in a strong voice with a message of reflection and prayer. She warned them that evil often came into the world through the best of intentions—that it often came disguised as a gentleman. She told them to assume nothing, to be open to any possibility. And to always be accepting of unity and of peace.

Few in the angry crowds—even many Seconds who had never been taught by her—came away from her talks without something new to consider. To those who were still angry, Petra was dispatched. She met with them in informal groups, over tea in common rooms or at lunches in family rooms, always cajoling, charming, convincing. If Petra couldn't go, she would send one of her lieutenants, a devout Firster or

Second, to talk members of their respective generations down from the battlements.

All of this was done outside the Council's privy. Petra, however, was certain that these actions had the members' blessing. Both Chairman Weiss and General Weiss had signaled their unwillingness to resort to harsh measures against the protesters. And though both men had clashed with Grace and Petra over the Tylers, each knew that the two women could serve as pressure valves on a pent-up populace overflowing with questions and depleted of patience. For the first month, the Weiss brothers waited on word from John and Kendra. Even as more and more time passed, they and the Council continued to hope that the findings from their recon mission would provide some answers to who the Tylers were and what they actually represented.

Everything broke open from the most unexpected of places: the Archives. Somehow, the Lees had discovered that the two adult Tylers bore an incredible resemblance to long-dead people. The revelation that no book in there had been published after 1962 only reinforced the growing belief that the Council was hiding a great deal from the people of New Philadelphia—and nothing seemed more representative of their secrets than the sequestering of the Tylers. One night, a group of two or three dozen men and women loyal to the Lees overpowered the guards around the Tylers' villa and somehow set fire to it. An hour later Petra walked over to Grace's house to tell the old woman that both parents were dead, the children taken by the protesters.

Grace didn't come to the door, hadn't even called out to tell Petra to enter. As close as the two women were, Petra had never entered Grace's home without being bidden. This time she did. Grace was sitting up in her chair in the dark, her fixed eyes reflecting the glow from the distant inferno beyond her open window.

With Grace gone, the Tylers dead, and the Council seemingly disgraced by what had been found in the Archives, the city's leaders knew that their administration had come to an end. Petra went to the Council to urge them to explain their side of things—to at the very least publicly theorize as to why the Tylers looked so much like people who'd died in an era supposedly five centuries removed from their own. A violent and anxious public could be heard in the streets through the barred shutters as she spoke. Their anger held the Council's attention far better than her finest oration ever could. Yet these restless citizens weren't the deciding factor. The idea of abandoning New Philadelphia came from an unlikely source. But it was from a voice that carried far more weight than anyone else's ever could.

"What would you have us do, Petra?" Andrew had asked. His dark eyes had been watery and tired but firmly fixed on her. "Go to war with our own children? Because that's what will happen if we stay."

Petra had shaken her head as if she had been slapped. "What do you intend to do?"

"Go back to the mountains." Andrew rose from his chair and pulled off his ceremonial robes. "Go up there and wait for a miracle."

Jake Weiss believed one of the mottled blessings of growing older was the fact that you needed far less sleep than you did when you were young. He often wondered why that was. Was it because you had less to exhaust yourself with—less labor, less sex, no young children to chase after? Or was it the Almighty's way of giving you more time toward the end of your life to reflect on your failings? Whatever the reason, he found himself glad of late to have these hours. Without them he wasn't sure he'd have been able to ensure his outcasts' survival in these mountains during these winter months.

These hours had also convinced him that he had made terrible mistakes in his efforts to protect humanity. He had lost the unity of his people. His paranoia about infiltration had kept the Tylers isolated and likely had gotten them killed. Killed. His mind reeled. The first murders in more than a half century. Murders committed on his watch, as much his fault as if he had done the lynching. And John and Kendra. He'd sent them out to die alone in that wilderness. He was relieved that most of their families were already dead. It was hard enough looking at Petra every day.

He indulged Petra more than he should. He let her go on wild-goose chases like this one up to the tumbledown cabin just outside the city. Every wisp of smoke on the wind these days was a clear sign that her surviving son was on his way home. He assumed this campfire had been set by a couple of kids, freed of all the morality the Remnants had sought to instill in them, needing a little light to screw by. It couldn't be anything more. It was certainly no sign that the dead were coming back home.

He emerged from the cave that had more or less been his residence and office since leaving the city and out into the morning light. From his slightly elevated position he could see all of the lanes in their tent-and-cabin makeshift town, located about a day's journey in good weather from New Philadelphia. The morning was already noisy with coughs and grunts and greetings and the shuffle and struggle of early-morning chores. He stretched and took a step toward the nearest latrine, hoping the line wasn't too long. Even a tepid shower would take some of the chill from his bones. Along his lane he nodded at people he had known his entire life—a ragtag collection of Remnants, Firsts, and Seconds—carting firewood and water and airing the blankets of the sick and the dying. He was about to round the corner when he heard an excited murmur rising up the lane before him, which faced east to the outskirts of camp. Everyone was now looking in that direction. Even with the sun in his eyes he

knew Petra's unmistakable tall frame. And after a moment he realized that flanking her on both sides were John Giordano and Kendra
McQueen.

He kept still and waited for them to approach. When they stopped
three paces before him and saluted, he was almost too overcome to
return it.

"General Weiss," John said. "We've come to make our report, sir."

A roar lifted out of everyone's throats, these haggard men and
women so beaten down by their recent plight and now so suddenly
bright with hope. He kept his composure until he looked at Petra,
beaming as she stood alongside her son. He broke through the crowd
pressing in around them to shake their hands. Only much later would
Weiss realize that this—the innate ability to believe even when all
reason told them not to—was what had kept humanity from the
abyss.

"You didn't make a liar out of your mother, Captain."

Cleaned up and rested and fed, John and Kendra were sitting in what
these wretched outcasts of the city called the Main Cabin. It was part
supply house, part informal meeting center, and the most solidly built
thing in the town. Here they learned that leadership among the outcasts
had devolved into little more than a vague civilian/military arrangement
between the Weiss brothers. The Council had resigned. Much of the
Defense Forces leadership remained in the city, now loyal to the Lees.
Messengers had been dispatched to the last serving members of the
Council in the hopes that they would come to hear the report. After an
hour of waiting for anyone else to arrive, John and Kendra told their
story to the Weiss brothers. Petra sat in on the meeting for reasons that
remained unexplained.

Andrew Weiss was ashen and gray but for a pinch of color in his cheeks. He had lost some weight off of his thickset frame. His features looked too big now, his eyes and mouth and nose all outsized. His skin seemed to hang off the bones underneath. A very sick man suddenly rekindled by a last burst of energy. Jake Weiss still very much looked like himself, strong and hard as granite. It was difficult for John not to think that this shared leadership wasn't in name only simply to avoid the appearance (if not the reality) of a military takeover.

Whatever their reservations they spoke at length. John felt oddly detached from their story. Petra gasped when she learned her husband was alive and had been outside the city gates only days earlier. The Weiss brothers listened in silence, even when John revealed Sam's belief that this had been Earth a long, long time ago and that they were now in the very distant future.

"So in conclusion," John said as he set his cooling mug of tea down on a nearby table, "I guess we need to know if we've been getting the truth all these years from you."

"From us?" Andrew asked, his thick salt-and-pepper eyebrows arching.

"Not from you specifically, sir. From the Remnants in general. Did you know anything about the things we've uncovered—or about the things Lee found in the Archives?"

"Captain, Lieutenant," the general began, leaning forward, elbows on his knees. "The world did *not* end in 1962, no matter what the hell Gordon Lee says. We were there—"

"We need to know what we are, sir," Kendra added.

"Lieutenant—Kendra—" He rubbed his clipped mustache. "Please don't get the wrong idea. We're as much at a loss as you are."

"Just tell us, please. Is this the Earth?" Kendra asked. "Are the Orangemen just . . . aliens? What—what has all this been for?"

"Kendra." Andrew's voice was just a shade harsher than his brother's. "We just don't know. But from the testimony you've given, it's not hard to believe that, contrary to our long-standing beliefs, this is Earth and that we're somehow on it a long time after humanity was all but wiped out."

"But you don't know for sure."

"Of course we don't, Lieutenant," he shot back. "How could we be certain? We didn't even know of these portals right outside the city."

Kendra shook her head. She stood up and stormed out, knocking over her chair in a fit of almost-adolescent rage. John was about to say something, but then his mother lifted a hand at him and followed Kendra out.

Kendra didn't slow down until she was on the outskirts of the settlement near a guard post. Her breath came out smoky and heavy in the frosty air. It was not yet midday and did not feel like it would get much warmer.

"I snatched your coat on the way out," Petra said from behind her. Kendra turned to find John's mother holding the jacket in her extended right hand. A look of something like sympathy played in the corners of her lined mouth.

Kendra took the jacket and put it on while shaking her head. "You don't understand. You think you do, but you don't."

"Try me. I just found out my husband is alive and has no interest in coming home to me."

Kendra tucked a lock of her hair behind her ear. "I was sorry to hear about Christian. My condolences, Petra."

"I stopped mourning his loss a long time ago. At least now I know for certain that he's at peace, awaiting resurrection to the new life."

"How can you still be so certain?" Kendra asked through her teeth. "How can you possibly believe that after everything that's happened? After everything we just told you?"

"Why is it so easy for you to think that the Orangemen are something other than what you know them to be?" A closemouthed smile lit Petra's face. "How can you be of such little faith?"

"I don't follow you."

Petra gestured in the direction of the path along the perimeter. Cold as it was, it was a bright winter day with little wind and a sunshine that glistened everything into a crystal radiance. A walk in that sunlight would be good if for no other reason than it would be warmer than standing still. Petra stepped down the path and Kendra followed, her arms folded and her hands warming in her armpits.

"So how am I of little faith?"

"You listened to the Scriptures; you heard people like Grace talk about what it meant to have faith. You have heard us talking about the dead rising to new life, the resurrection of the body—not the soul, Kendra, the *body*. And you know that the kingdom of God must be made here, in this world."

"Yeah, so?"

This stopped Petra in her tracks. "Kendra, don't be dense or juvenile. Maybe we didn't interpret Revelation correctly. Maybe we were being too literal. But it's coming true. All of it."

"How do you see that?"

"Those Remnants who came from people who had already lived on Earth years ago—people like the Tylers, like old Alexander Raymond, so many others—I believe those are the dead rising to new life. And if I'm right, that means the kingdom of God is at hand."

"If that's true, then why don't they have memories of their original lives?"

"Of that I'm not sure. But I'm sure they are the dead returning to life."

Kendra stopped to think about that but then felt the contrarian's pride grip her again. "Sounds too good to be true."

They began walking again side by side. As they did, one slow step after another, Petra slipped her arm in Kendra's. "My son loves you so very much. You can see it just coming off of him. Do you believe it?"

"Believe what?"

"That he loves you?"

"Of course. Why wouldn't I?"

"I don't know." Petra gave an almost indiscernible shrug. "You can't prove such things, after all."

CHAPTER 23

A month later the bony finger of winter had dug itself deeper into the outcasts' ribs. The wind blew hard and raw across their provisional town. The snow piled up thick on the north-facing parts and made the level site feel uneven and uphill. After a while, red-cheeked and exhausted, people stopped trying to keep lanes clear and stayed indoors to wait for some kind of thaw. Food stocks brought from the city during their exodus, already low, were now facing rationing. A fever plague had burst through the camp to baffle their doctors. Too many had been buried in their blankets under piles of stone on the unrelenting frozen ground. The survivors were weary with an exhaustion that was more than physical. Even the younger and more energetic outcasts felt as if everyone's lot was just beyond enduring, each load a pound or two too heavy, each ration of happiness lacking that particular ingredient that would make it true joy. A single thought held sway: enough, no more.

Still, a few joys were had among them. Four hale and hearty children were born to Seconds. Eight couples announced betrothals with marriages planned in the spring. Petra had expected a similar announcement to come from her son and Kendra, especially after it became clear that they were sleeping in the same bed each night. But no announcement came, and no explanation for their relationship was given.

Many Remnants were mortified. Petra tried to explain to them how it was like marriages of old. Theirs was a pledge made to each other in the sight of God in his wilderness. It wasn't carnal, but a commitment formed by the circumstances and challenges they faced together in primordial isolation. The elders, she felt, needed to understand that.

She also knew such talk was to be expected. How many idiotic words had passed among them in the last month? A hundred thousand? A million? And what percentage of them were joyful and without malice? What percentage perfunctory? And how many things were left unsaid? If the bean counters among the Remnants were really counting sins, none could say any of them had been very charitable in even the most general sense.

Petra spent the morning wandering along some mountain paths, deep in reflection. The day had come on sharp and clear and cold. The thin and frosty air at this altitude was purifying and had to be pulled in deep. It made her feel at ease, as did the wide-open landscapes of snow-capped mountaintop groves of evergreens. Her prayers and meditations since sunup were all focused on material concerns—food and water and medicines. But these problems were only a symptom of a greater illness. If they didn't find some relief soon, there would be an attack on the city. She was sure of it. The talk was there—and propped up by hunger and desperation. They had come so far in the last fifty years. To kill one another over scraps of bread . . .

Most of the talk was coming from the youngest generation. And while her voice had been influential, she knew it wasn't what it had been, especially among them. Too much of this life had gotten between her message and her audience. There was a lack there, not of faith but of trust. And if you wouldn't trust the messenger, how could the message, however pure and pacifistic, get through?

The bare trees around her swayed in the wind. A sprinkle of snow swept off the branches above before coming to rest on some rocks near her. She went toward them, her heels crunching the fresh pack of snow in the stillness of the forest. The snow had been warmed by its flight and had begun to melt on the rocks. She loved it so. It was all such endless beauty, right there. Even though she knew the snow, and the cold, was bringing death with it, she found it hard not to be overwhelmed by its purifying grace.

Grace. She looked to the sky and wondered what her mentor thought of her now. A married woman living without her husband. A preacher whose own son ignored the sanctity of marriage. A believer whose faith was battered by facts and weakened by doubt. She thought of paying a visit to Grace's son or daughter, who were both here among the outcasts. Through their eyes she might glimpse her old friend and perhaps know what she might have thought. She snorted at the idea of needing such a physical lifeline. So faithless. No wonder no one listened to her anymore. No one should. They needed someone far better than her. But there was no one.

And yet—and yet—some of the greatest figures in history only became saints after emerging from the midst of their own depravity.

"Thank you," Petra said to the sky and the wind and the trees, and watched her frozen breath join the rest of nature. And with that she walked back to their rough scrap of civilization.

Kendra was warm in her bed when she felt the first hint of the morning chill on her bare skin as John slipped as unobtrusively as he could from under their pile of blankets. She watched him through slitted eyes as the first snap of cold air hit his lungs and he slipped back into the clothes he had tossed on the floor the night before. He kept his slim back to her until he pulled on his thermal undershirt. He stepped toward their stone hearth and lifted the percolator coffeepot, shook last night's cold contents twice, decided there was enough there, and rekindled the coals.

Kendra kept her eyes half-closed and her breathing steady. She didn't want him to know she was awake. His mind was struggling with something, and she knew he didn't need an audience. Still, she did want him back in bed with her. Their morning routine these days never included shaking coffeepots or getting dressed. After a while she thought she had figured out what was troubling him and decided there wasn't any point in keeping up her pretense.

"So ask me," she said with a sleep-clogged voice. "Better hurry if you're gonna do it. Life doesn't last forever."

He turned and smiled, his face broad and showing he hadn't known she was awake. "Ask you what?"

"Ask what you've been wanting to ask me."

"You'll say no. You'll think it's a bad idea."

She found herself grinning wide. "You're not gonna know unless you ask, right?"

"Things have changed."

"Not between us."

"No, Ken. But things have changed. We're not sure of anything anymore."

"I'm sure of you." She sat up before she said this, knees up, blanket wrapped around her chest. He was sitting on the edge of the bed now. Goose bumps rose on her forearms, but she wasn't sure if the chill was causing them.

"And I'm sure of you. But is that enough? Do we go through a ritual without complete faith?"

"You don't think it's right what we're doing now, do you, Johnny?"

"No. I guess I don't. But is that just a reflex?"

"You've got a better understanding of right and wrong than anyone I know." She rolled her eyes. "You're kinda my moral compass."

He laughed, chin down, and squeezed her thigh. "I could say the same about you. So will you?"

She laughed too. "Do you even have to ask?"

266

"And here I was thinking that my needing to ask was what had started this conversation."

A clear knock at the cabin door interrupted them. Kendra let out a groan and lunged over the side of the bed to grab her clothes as John went to answer it. On the other side, Petra was waiting patiently.

"May I come in?"

"Sure, Mom." He held the door open. In a one-room cabin there wasn't much place to hide a half-dressed Kendra shimmying into her uniform pants.

"Kendra," Petra said as she moved toward a chair by the hearth, "good morning."

"Good morning, Petra." Kendra bit her lower lip while giving John a wide-eyed look behind his mother's back.

After an offer of coffee had been extended and accepted, Petra sat watching as the pot started to percolate on the grill. "I've come to discuss a matter with both of you." Petra turned to them, her green eyes catching the warm light from the hearth's fire, her face wan and weary. "I've given considerable thought to what we've been hearing around our camp. And I've come to believe that we need to do something to prevent such talk from getting out of hand."

"Petra," Kendra began.

"Look, Mom, we—"

Petra glanced from one to the other. "We will go to war with those left behind in the city if we don't do something to stop such talk."

A burst of laughter erupted from John. "That's what you came here to talk about?"

"What else could be more desperate?"

"What would you have us do?" Kendra asked with relief as she poured each of them a strong cup of coffee.

"Talk to your generation," she answered. "The ones here—they still have faith. Otherwise they wouldn't have chosen to come into exile with us. Have them listen to reason."

John scratched his earlobe. "To many of them, reason is going back to the city and fighting their way in if need be."

"That's not reason; that's their stomachs talking."

"Still justification enough, Mom."

"Justification?" Petra set her mug down on the table nearby. "What justice can be found in children fighting parents, in siblings warring over salted meat and blankets? There's nothing in that except the *old* thinking, acting like beasts. That's the thinking that led us down the path from where our race was meant to be."

"And you know that how, Petra?"

"Ken, please."

"No, John." She turned back to his mother. "How do you know that? Did God tell you? Did you get specific instructions from a burning bush or from a finger writing on your wall? How do you know that fighting our way back into the city isn't the right thing to do?"

Kendra watched Petra contemplate her for a time with a seemingly profound sadness.

"I know you've been troubled, Kendra. But your troubles cannot excuse the idea that murder is ever justified. And that's what we're talking about here—not fighting for survival against Hostiles or predators, but premeditated murder on a separated part of our own people, members of our own family."

"Mom," John said after a long time, "I agree with you that this kind of talk isn't the best answer. But more talk, more preaching and evangelizing to our disheartened people, isn't the solution either."

"So what should we do, then?"

John folded his arms across his chest and cocked his head. "Not sure. But I'm pretty sure that seeing the general might help."

Kendra shook her head, eyes wide. "You're both insane. Whether we uphold principles won't matter one bit if we all damn well die out here."

"You're wrong, Ken."

"Tell me how I'm wrong."

"Staying true to ourselves in a world that's always trying to make us less than what we are is everything. It's the only thing. What we really are or however we got here, how we live here and now is all that matters."

The Weiss brothers still walked together when they needed to talk. It felt good to do something familiar, despite their changed circumstances and the difficulty two aging men had walking in foot-deep snow. As they walked they often found themselves talking in hushed tones in the woods. An outside observer would never be able to tell why, but it was clear that a greater affection was emerging between them as they moved deeper into their mortality years. Their eyes lingered on each other's expressions longer; unsaid words rode across an invisible bridge between their eyes. But mostly, they also had less to argue about. The losers usually do. Politics, prophecy, the Tylers, even Sofie and her children—all in the past now. What was left was what had been there at the beginning: an older brother and a younger, two lifelong compatriots who knew each other better than anyone else would ever know them. However imperfect, it was the closest to unconditional love either man had ever known.

"A month more, two tops," Jake said as he snapped dead branches from a nearby pine tree. "After that we'll start to contemplate eating the dead."

"God forbid," Andrew said, unable to stifle a shudder.

Jake glanced sidelong at his brother's phrasing. "We have to do something, Andy."

"Go back to the city?" Andrew asked, his bushy gray eyebrows raised. "I guess we have to. But go back with our tails tucked between our legs, hoping they won't kill us? Or go back to lay siege?" He shook his head. "The first option is . . . risky. The second is blasphemy. We'd be going there to kill our own children, Jake." A pause. "My own child."

"Know what I've heard?"

"I'm sure you're gonna tell me."

"A lot of Seconds have been talking about finding those portals around the city. Figuring out how they might be able to use their systems to slip past the perimeter."

"How in God's name did they find out about them?"

"Dunno, Andy. I know it wasn't either of us. But secrets have a way of leaking out when so many conversations begin and end with what food you'd most like to eat if you could get hold of it."

Andy mused on that one. "Fair enough."

Jake continued their slow walk, gloved hands thrust hard and deep into his coat pockets, his brother a step behind. "Had a visit this morning from John Giordano."

The older Weiss brother sniffed, then rubbed his cold nose to mute his displeasure. "With his mother? Or his mistress?"

Jake let that pass. "Alone. He thinks attacking New Philadelphia would be a mistake."

"He got out of his warm bed and trudged through all this snow to tell you that?"

"He thinks there's another way, Andy. He wants to go back home and talk to them, make them see reason."

Andrew looked at the sky, now clearing in the east. A bright-blue dome was sliding out from under the gray overcast. "Talk to who? Sofie?"

"Possibly. His recent experience in the city makes him think Lee is willing to listen to reason. He also believes Lee doesn't have it in him to lead. So if he can exploit any doubts—"

"A big if. And the bigger if is *if* they let him in."

"Huge. But what other choice do we have? We can't let the people here starve—and we're not going to be able to stop the ones who want to attack for much longer."

"It's a hard road back in deep winter," Andrew mused as he glanced down the slope in the direction of the coast. "When does Giordano want to lead his party out?"

"No party. Just him."

The brothers walked downhill back toward their campsite. Andrew stopped at a fork in the clearing. By continuing south for a half mile they would arrive at camp. To the west and they would find themselves in another little clearing that had been serving as their cemetery. An obvious place to make a decision.

"I say let him go," the former chairman said with a sigh. "Men with empty hands have nothing to offer but hope."

Kendra didn't know John was gone until she came off guard duty the next morning. She entered their tiny cabin stamping snow off her boots. The cold tingled out of her as she bent closer to the hearth's warmth. At first nothing seemed out of place. The fire was low—but only because no one was at home. His coat was missing—but maybe he had gone out to help someone who was sick or someone else in need. Just this week he had twice raised roofs that had partially collapsed under the weight of all that snow. But his rifle was gone too. Out hunting? Possibly. Nothing seemed amiss as she stirred the coals and put another log on the fire before pulling off her hat, gloves, and greatcoat.

Then she saw it sitting on the crate that passed for their nightstand. She lifted the quill and inkwell off the parchment and knew what he had written before she read it. She read it twice through anyway before pulling her coat on again and heading down the lane to Petra's.

She didn't bother to knock. Petra was inside drinking tea with five of her disciples. They were men and women both, almost all Firsters.

"You no-good bitch."

Petra glanced up at her, nonplussed, then turned to the others. "Would you mind giving Kendra and me some time alone?"

Kendra waited until they had all filed out in silence. "This was your idea, his going."

"Ah, so that's what this is about. And no. It was his."

"Going back to the city? Without telling me?"

"He does a lot of things without telling you—or me. You know as well as I that John has always been his own man."

"And you know we barely escaped from there with our lives. Yet you allowed your only living son—"

Petra held up a hand. "I didn't 'allow' him to do anything, Kendra. He told me that he was going, and that's all. He felt he had to do this."

"He said nothing else?"

Petra allowed herself a small smile. "He did say something like, 'When Kendra storms in and asks why,' I should tell you, 'To keep you safe.' He said you'd understand that."

Kendra said nothing, just shook her head.

"He also said to say, 'Semper fidelis.' But he thinks you already know that."

CHAPTER 24

Kendra McQueen spent that night assembling her supplies and stuffing them into her pack for her excursion back to New Philadelphia. It was more than a day's journey overland in good weather. It seemed unlikely she'd get there that quickly. So she packed three days' worth of rations as well as snowshoes, a winter tent, some rope, plenty of dry matches, two sidearms, and the carbine she had taken from that Novice, along with a hundred rounds of ammunition split between the three. She broke down the weapons, cleaned and oiled them, then reassembled them and set them next to her pack. Then she took up John's bowie knife and held it in balance resting on the edge of her hand as she sat on their bed. It had been his grandfather's. It was a precious thing. Why would he leave it?

She did another survey of the weapons as she strapped the knife in its sheath to her belt. It was enough, more than enough to get there and fight her way in if need be.

Once on the road, she found it hard to sleep the first night, even though the day of slogging through foot-deep snow was strenuous and the winds had seemed to rise up that morning with the express purpose of flaying the skin off her face and pushing her back toward their refugee town. On the second night it took all of her last reserves of strength to get the tent up and the fire started. She crawled inside and fell into a heap. The chill never completely left her, even wrapped in her bedroll. And tired as she was, real sleep remained just past the tips of her fingers.

For a long while her mind just couldn't rest, never lighting on one thought long enough to work through it with any coherence. She thought of the Weiss brothers and Petra, wondering what they had thought when they realized she was gone. She thought of Grace and of the Tylers and of Alex Raymond, all the dearly departed who had never really departed from her but who still inhabited every room she ever slept in, always there, always just past her peripheral vision. And she thought of her parents too. She could hardly recall their faces as they had been during their last fever illness. She saw instead her father as she knew him when she was five or six, with his thick mustache and wavy bush of dark-brown hair, farmer tanned with red-brown neck and elbows, holding her hand as he taught her how to find her way home by following rivulets and remembering details from all along their hikes. She could see her mother, heaven-bright with her blue eyes and halo of black hair, glowing at Kendra aged three or four, feeding her bits of broken food from her well-worked, loving fingertips. The love she felt when thinking of all of them was *heartbreaking*. She had read that word a thousand times and had never really known what it meant in all its awful fullness until now. Heartbreaking: to know people once lived and no longer did, to know they were real and of this world and no longer were, to hope but never know if you'd see them again—this was heartbreak, pure and true.

And now—no, she wouldn't think of that. But thinking of her parents made her think of Alex and his death and how he had been found hanging there. She was thinking clearly enough in her dark and rustling tent to know that spending another hour with Alex's memory was unnecessary. She put him away and found herself back in the place where she didn't want to be—thinking of John and why he left and why he had found it necessary to keep her out of his plans.

He might leave her, do what he felt he needed to do and feel justified in the doing, but none of this meant that she would just sit back and take it. He was her John as she was his Kendra. She would find him and save him, even if it meant saving him from his nobler ideas. She needed his moral clarity, his black-and-white thinking. Why did he feel he had to go back? They had already tried with those fools in New Philadelphia and the broken and ignorant old-timers here. The Remnants. Were they all liars or just delusional? Didn't matter.

What had they called it in the wilderness? A separate peace. They would forge their path. Now. Right away. The minute she brought him back. They belonged to each other. That was all that mattered really. They owed this world—whatever it was, whenever it was supposed to be, whatever they actually were—nothing. They owed each other everything.

The thought made her peaceable. With it clutched to her chest she finally slept, though not for long. An hour, maybe two, later, she was awake. Or rather, she was awakened. She was unsure of the time. It was still before dawn. A voice that was not a voice called to her and told her to get up, get dressed, go outside. She slipped into her clothes and greatcoat, then untied the tent flaps. Though the wind had died down, the predawn chill flushing her cheeks told her she was not asleep, no longer dreaming. The voice that was not a voice kept guiding her. It was fully recognizable and completely unknown. It made her weep. She wiped the warm tears from her cold cheeks with the back of her gloved hands the way a child would. While walking she had a vague sense that she was again a child, stepping with a child's innocent confidence. All that had happened to her in the years that she had lived between the ages of fourteen and twenty was washed away as weedy topsoil to reveal the hard white stone of the real Kendra beneath. She felt clean and ready, if not exactly good.

After twenty minutes of hiking, she came to a clearing far inside the dense woods that surrounded the place where she had pitched her tent. This clearing was not only free of snow but also terribly bright and warm. She squinted into the bluish-white light, a hand shielding her eyes. Once inside the clearing, she was surprised that she had not seen the glow through the trees; in fact, she was sure on a night like this one such a brightness could be seen all the way back at their ramshackle town. Her outstretched hand warmed up as she entered the clearing. She had felt this sort of warmth before.

In the middle of the clearing was a glowing white rock, and on this rock sat an Orangeman—a male one. He hopped off the rock with an effortless, inhuman precision and grace and took a step toward her. She felt the fact that she was unarmed more than she knew it. She reminded herself that this Orangeman was not Samael. His corpse was buried somewhere in these mountains.

"Were you the one who called to me?"

His slightly too large head and iris-less eyes seemed to acknowledge her more than his expression did. "I was sent here for you, Kendra McQueen."

"You're not the first of your people to come to me. How do you know me? Through him?"

"We know all about you."

"If you've come to harm me, Orangeman, know this: I will fight you and kill you if I can. If you've come just to tell me something, tell it whole and true. I'm tired of your race's games."

The Orangeman's face was still passive. "Bold words for such a little thing."

"Maybe. But do what you will and let it be done."

"I come to ask a question."

"Then ask it."

"Why do you turn from what your ancestors learned so bitterly?"

"What do you mean?"

"Your ancestors were told by the Lamb and by generations of peace-makers to love one another. Why do you seek to wage war among yourselves, after so much destruction has been visited on your race?"

"We're starving. And if you are truly the servant of the Almighty, and if he truly exists, then you know that the God of Abraham and Isaac and Moses does not hear us."

"Ah." The sound was the closest to complete weariness that she had ever heard. "The God of Abraham and Isaac and Moses but not *your* God." When she said nothing, he continued. "And so you would do this—sin once more—after so many years of peace?"

"What are you, Orangeman? What is your name? Why are you here, and why are you using our Bible to keep us in your thrall?"

"Is that what you really think?"

"I don't know what to think. I'm tired of stories and interpretations. Just tell me what you are, what you want, or leave me in peace."

"Has your kind learned nothing in all these years? Have you no true understanding of this age of peace that you so carelessly wish to throw it away? Mark me. Your Revelation was written to teach you one thing: patience is everything. It is the key to your future."

"You still speak in riddles, Orangeman. Patience. *Your* people brought the Tylers among us. Some of *your* people destroyed most of the human race. Haven't you had time to reflect on your own actions and realize they have had consequences? You set us up to act like wooden soldiers—guided by nothing but blind obedience—and you expect us not to react as such?"

"Even soldiers have a choice."

"Not this one."

He shook his head without disapproval. "You are loved, Kendra McQueen. All of you. You are all loved so much as to be allowed to decide everything—even whether you love back. The choices are your own, as are the consequences."

"What choice have I had? What've I done to be left alone like this?"

He stepped toward her. "Child of man, you are not alone. You have never been alone."

"'Child of man,'" she scoffed. "Tell me, what are we, the people who lived and their children born here? What were the Tylers, Alex's father, all those people who existed before?"

"Your fallen race's eternal question. 'What are we?' And though it has been answered to the best of your understanding in a hundred disciplines and in a thousand tongues and in a million moments of personal decision, still you ask it."

"We ask because we see only pieces," Kendra said, "not the whole."

"Much of it is beyond your ken, yes. But enough exists here, on this plane of existence, for you to infer your place in the universe."

"Then explain it to me."

"Imagine, even when your science was far more advanced than it is now, the makeup of dark matter was unknown, though it was felt and inferred by its gravitational effects on all visible matter—your stars, galaxies. Such is the influence of the invisible on the visible since before time, as you understand it, began. I come from such a place, as did your remotest ancestors."

The hair rose on her arms. She felt as she had the first time she saw Samael. She was in the presence of something far beyond her and all-encompassing, yet part of her, all at the same time.

"What are we?" she asked in a whisper.

"Like matter or energy, nothing that can ever be destroyed. Like consciousness, nothing that can ever be completely known."

"But what you're saying is what is knowable is already known."

He looked as pleased as those placid outsized features would allow him to be. "To answer your question. You are what I called you: a child of man. How you came to be here does not matter. All of you are a new step out of the river of your history, cleansed and pure. Look to that part of yourself that feels the truest. It knows what I say. To backslide into what your ancestors were—that is a choice. And it begins with you."

"How?"

"You have been called to a purpose, Kendra McQueen. Have you not felt that all your life?" When she said nothing for several heartbeats, he went on. "You are to go unarmed into the city your people built and end this division."

With a flutter of his great translucent wings, he rose from the ground and alighted on the top of the rock. Behind him, now fully revealed, was an olive tree in full bloom at the very center of this warm place. It was dark green and massive, likely a thousand years old, its trunk a thick, hard cord—a living burst of life beyond possibility in the depths of winter.

"Take a branch from this tree and bring it toward the city's gates. There someone should recognize it and let you in. Once inside, if you follow your conscience, the fall of the last of the wicked will bring peace to all mankind."

Kendra glanced from the impossible tree to the Orangeman's face and back again. "If you know me as well as you say, you know why I'm going to the city and why I'll be armed."

"I know nothing of a time not come, of choices not yet made."

"I'm going to save John. Just my John."

"In your Talmud, it is written: 'Whoever destroys a soul, it is considered as if he destroyed an entire world. And whoever saves a life, it is considered as if he saved an entire world.'" He looked at her and seemed to smile. "You are free to choose as you will, beloved Kendra."

Kendra awoke warm in her bedroll with no idea of how she had gotten there or whether it was day or night outside. She sat up gingerly, still half in dream. She paid as little attention as she could to her bare legs sliding against the cool cotton. A little more movement, anything sudden, and she would drop out of her dream completely and forget everything she now remembered in it. Every sensation suggested her memories were just a dream. Nothing special had occurred. Would a visitation leave her with a pasty mouth and a painfully full bladder? She pulled on her boots over her bare feet and untied the tent flap to squat bare-assed in the bitter, frosty morning—yes, she could see now it was morning—and watched her urine first forge a stream in the snow, then run downhill between her booted feet. No, she was still confused Kendra McQueen. No visitation. No messenger. No role to play. No debate about God giving her a purpose. She was going to the city to bring her John home. She hitched up her panties and found a clean patch of snow to scoop up and chomp until her mouth felt more or less clean. Then she went inside.

Next to her bedroll, lying on its side, was her pack with a bright-green-leaved olive branch sticking out of it.

She took the branch in her hands, a precious thing. For a long while she sat with it in her lap. Then she wrapped it with care in a spare shirt and replaced it in the pack.

In less than an hour she was off—breakfast eaten, tent collapsed, pack and weapons shouldered. She glanced through the intense sunlight reflecting off the snow at the ring of evergreens around her and got a sense of where and when she was. If she kept a hard pace downhill, she could make it to New Philadelphia before long.

Then what, McQueen?

The wind had tapered down into a prevailing breeze that made her head feel clear and cold. Just the sort of weather for sharp thinking. By midday she had reached the valley just over the far side of the high hills that surrounded the city. She sat against some snow-free boulders in the lowest part of her surroundings. The huge stones blocked most of the wind. Being too close to the city now, she ruled against cooking a meal and instead ate fistfuls of dried fruit and some salted meat. She washed it all down with teeth-rattling, cold water she had captured in her canteen from a mountain stream.

The snow in the valley was deep and thick but packed down hard. Who had been out here? People fleeing the camp? Patrols out searching for the Remnants? For her and John? No matter. It was just another mystery that did nothing more than simply exist to perplex and bewilder. Okay. Fine. Maybe games were played to satisfactory conclusions, but no one ever said life had to be.

Kendra took up the pack again and the carbine and set out on her snowshoes. Ten paces later she stopped. She was not far from the city gates. She unhitched the pack and pulled the bedroll free from its straps and tossed it aside. The winter tent followed. She glanced back at them just once before continuing on.

When she reached the top of the hills, she could see the city almost shimmering against the setting sun. Even from the distance she felt its humming, a low, atonal sound less than mechanical and more than animal. Typically human. Here and there in shadowy places she could see lights sparking to life. Around the gatehouse towers and haloed by the purple sunset, guards stamped themselves warm. She glanced up at the darkening sky, nearly split in two between the ending day and the oncoming night. The place seemed strange to her, totally unknowable. Was this how the Orangemen from on high saw them? She began to hike over the ridge toward the city.

Halfway down the steep hillside she stopped again and looked at the great stone monster, this work of three generations, a fortress built to protect and keep them, the point from which they were to secure a new human civilization on this world.

And for what?

She felt her eyes watering. She blinked the tears away and cursed herself.

John's right. He's always right. He tries to see all of us at our best. Maybe we're descended from copies of the original humans, or maybe the Remnants had been plucked out of the time stream with their memories falsified just before they were placed here. Maybe we really are the survivors of God's wrath and are meant to repopulate the Earth. Maybe this all happened last week or a thousand years ago. It doesn't matter. John's right; the Orangeman's right. We're human in the way that counts most.

Kendra didn't turn back after she had dropped her carbine and sidearms and ammo boxes in the snow. If she had, they would've appeared to her as no more than small black pinpoints on an unmarred white surface. And before long they would be red with rust and ruin.

The sun had set behind the hills in the west before Kendra found herself skirting the walls of the city. After tossing her snowshoes away, she approached at a midpoint between two of the city's twelve gatehouses, with the idea that she wanted her arrival to come with as much surprise as possible. She didn't imagine that her old tunnel was still operational but approached it first and found it as she expected it—sealed with new mortar and bricks still undulled by their first winter. Then she began to tramp along the well-worn paths of snow around the walls—the endless retreads of a winter's worth of sentries—intending to stop at the first gatehouse she came across. They probably wouldn't shoot her on sight. She had no proof of this. But it was hard to believe the Orangeman would've sent her all this way just to have her die knocking at the door.

She didn't want to die and thought she was too young to do so but found herself accepting the possibility. This strange sense of peace held her as she moved toward the gatehouse. She couldn't remember when it had first begun to bloom, but she was sure now that she had felt it in fits and starts ever since that night John had carried her down from the mountain after Jake Weiss had killed Samael. That serenity had remained with her ever since, but she knew it only in the moments when she understood she had been living on borrowed time since her flight.

A rustle in the frozen brush dropped her to the ground. She tore off her gloves and reached for the bowie knife still attached to her hip.

Then she shook her head, wiped her suddenly sweaty palm against the knife's sheath, and stood up. She found herself almost nose to nose with a young girl no older than thirteen or fourteen. Her face was fresh and clean. A lock of pin-straight black hair hung out from under her fur-lined hood as her brown eyes went wide at the sight of Kendra.

"Er, um, hi."

Kendra squinted at her. "Hi yourself."

"Look, I totally know I'm not supposed to be out here," she stammered with nervous tears in her eyes. "Oh—please don't tell my mom and dad."

Kendra stepped toward her, her palms out. "It's all right. Who're your parents?"

"Don't you know?" The girl's face flushed with bright fear as she looked Kendra over—her face, her clothes, her pack with the olive branch sticking out. "Oh my God!"

She turned and ran stumbling to the gatehouse, kicking snow up from her boot heels. Kendra flung off her pack and darted along after her, overtaking her in four long paces. As she tackled the girl into the hard-packed snow, she kept her grip lighter than she normally would. Kendra held a hand over her mouth as she sat on the girl's sparrow-wide chest.

"I'm not here to hurt you, kid. *Shhh*. Don't yell."

The girl's eyes were wide and panicked. Kendra could feel her breath coming heavy and moist against her palm. She slipped her hand away and patted the girl's thin shoulder.

"My name's Kendra. What's yours?"

"Kendra?" The girl's eyes showed recognition. "The one who—my mom—"

"Your name, kid. Just tell me your name."

"Irene. Irene Lee."

"Irene. Gordon and Sofie's eldest, right?"

She nodded, just once.

"I know your grandfather—Andrew Weiss. And your great-uncle Jake. I've just come from them, in fact. What're you doing out here? You're not on guard duty?"

"No, I, um—"

"A boy, right?" Kendra grinned.

"If I say yes, will that get you off my chest?"

Kendra shifted her weight but only slightly. "How'd you get out here?"

"Through the tunnel."

"The tunnel's closed."

"It's not. I just came through it ten or fifteen minutes ago."

Kendra stood up. "Show me." She gripped Irene by her upper arm and made her wince, then eased up a bit as she led her back toward the place where she had dropped her pack.

"So," Irene asked, head down but tossing her chin in the pack's direction, "is that an olive branch?"

"Yeah," Kendra said, hefting the pack on her shoulders.

"Do you really come in peace?"

"Why do you say that?"

"That's what olive branches mean, right?"

"How do you know that?"

A sharp intake of breath slid through Irene's small white teeth. "You're hurting me."

Kendra eased up. "Just tell me."

"I dunno. I was looking stuff up in the Archives about my name, Irene. She was a Greek goddess. Olive branches had something to do with her."

A nearby sound brought Kendra's gaze up to the gatehouse above her, its guards invisible. "Show me how you got out here."

"If you come in peace, why sneak in?"

"I'm not in the mood for anyone to kill me before I get inside to say what I came to say. Get me?"

"Yeah, okay. Sure."

The girl kept her head down, her eyes averted. She looked small and frail and wanting to look smaller. Kendra thought if Irene could pull her head inside her own body, she would. She smiled to herself as she followed in the girl's tracks.

"You must have a good memory. I read all about the Greek gods when I was your age, but I sure don't remember anything about olive branches."

"How come you got one in your pack, then?"

Kendra smirked and watched her frozen breath rise and scatter. "Long story."

They didn't speak for a while. Kendra kept her guard up but found nothing to disturb the sound of their steady crunching of snow.

"I kinda want to be a botanist," Irene said. "I'm really into plants, growing stuff."

"Good job. Better than any one I've ever had."

"What've you been?"

"A soldier. An idiot. And now a messenger. Not sure if I've ever been good at any except the middle one." Kendra stopped the girl by the elbow again. "You know John Giordano, right? Has he come to the city in the last few days?"

"Dunno. A lot of people have been showing up lately." She pointed at the wall in front of her. "It's here."

This was definitely not her escape hatch. She knew her spot and had just seen it cemented up. This was another, at least half a klick from where hers had been.

"Show me how it opens, kid."

Irene reached her gloved hand up to head level and with an expert touch pushed three stones into hidden housings in rapid succession. A moment later the stonework slid back in silence to reveal a passage about six feet high by three feet wide. Another hidden passage, but full-sized and not at all like the crawl space she had shimmied herself through so many times.

"Son of a bitch," she muttered. "What were these guys playing at?"

As Kendra peered into the passageway, the girl leaned against the edge to get her attention. "You're really not going to hurt anybody, are you?"

Kendra turned to her. "Irene, I could've killed you before you ever saw me. That's what I've been trained to do. But I'm not here to hurt anyone. I'm here to try and talk sense to your father."

"Good luck with that."

"What?"

"You'll see." She took a resigned step into the passage. "Come on. I'll show you."

CHAPTER 25

Kendra was impressed. Irene was smart and stealthy and proved the old adage Novices told one another while in training: to get from one place to another without being noticed, follow a teenager. They're the only ones sneaky enough to have already mapped out all the routes, the variations in sentry duties, where guards would be at given points in their rounds, everything. Irene moved through the streets and checkpoints with smooth deliberation but without speed or fear, each step predetermined. Kendra wondered what Irene's boyfriend would think once he realized he'd been stood up.

"So where are you taking me, kid?" Kendra asked when they paused at one dark corner a few blocks from the point at which they had pierced the city wall.

"Stop calling me that. You're, like, only a few years older than I am."

"A few more than you might imagine. Same question."

A heaving sigh was followed by a rolling of her eyes. "To the Archives."

"The Archives. Why there?"

"He's always there these days."

"In the middle of the night?"

"Trust me."

The route to the Archives—Kendra could do it in her sleep. From any direction, she knew how to get to that fortified bunker that housed the greatest of human treasures—knowledge—safe from the world. Thousands of spines, millions of words. All her life she had tried to absorb each bit of light from the long-lost polestar of Earth-of-old. Could she ever have imagined how contradictory and divisive all those words would someday be? Even their dates now mocked their ignorance.

At the stone steps that led to the bunker below, Irene lifted the first oaken cellar door with strength that seemed impossible coming from such reedlike arms. Kendra lifted its partner from the frame and felt the rushing scent of musty old paper filling her nostrils. She glanced over at the girl.

"No guards, Irene?" Kendra peered inside at the flickering gaslights below. "Not even a lonesome sentry?"

"He doesn't really need them anymore."

"Why's that?"

"My m—" Irene shook her head. "Forget it. Lights are on. He's there. Nobody else would be."

Kendra looked again at the stone steps, then back to the girl. "No need for you to stay."

"You said you wouldn't hurt him."

"And I won't. I promised you. All I want is for him to help me bring our people back together."

Irene snorted. "Good luck with that."

"Again, kid, meaning?"

"Again, 'kid'?"

"And you? You gonna be okay?"

She nodded at the branch in Kendra's pack. "I will be if you really do come in peace."

The stone steps still held their perfume of earth and old paper and sweat. The gaslight seemed brighter than it had the last time she had been here. She could hear indistinct muttering—more than Lee here?—as she approached the stacks. Rounding the first corner she couldn't help but trace the book spines with her fingertips. She found him standing amid a pile of books, some about waist high. To his left and right two tall desks had been pulled near each other. A high-backed stool stood between them. She knew the style of this seat well—a swivel. It was one of Lee's first inventions as a teenager. Lee himself was hunched over one desk, his back to her, his face obscured by long locks of his black hair.

"Well, of course it doesn't make any sense," he was muttering. "Why should it make any more sense than anything else? Others can talk all they want—got to have a basis in fact—"

"Gordon?" Kendra called, resisting her urge to pull out the knife.

He flinched and turned. He squinted his eyes to focus them better and recognized her only slowly. How long had he been sitting down here absorbed in his close reading?

"Kendra? Kendra McQueen?"

His face seemed more lined than when she had last seen him, just before the start of winter. His hair was matted, and a scraggly beard that came in thickest at his upper lip and chin covered his face. She knew he was only in his early thirties, but he looked older.

"Come to wreck my other leg, have you?" He hopped off the stool with the aid of a lacquered wooden cane. She hadn't noticed it as she came in, obscured as it was by a pile of books. "Go ahead, take it. I can finish what I need to do as a complete cripple."

Kendra had forgotten how she had smacked his knee with a carbine while escaping. She drew the olive branch from the backpack.

"I come in peace, Gordon."

He cocked his head. "Is that why you're brandishing a tree branch at me?"

"It's not a tree branch," she began, then shook her head. "I mean, it *is* a tree branch. An olive branch. It's an ancient symbol of peace. You know, from the Greeks."

"The Greeks—" His gaze suddenly pulled back and seemed lost in the distance. "They had their gods and myths too. No more use to them than the One True has been for us, eh?"

The casual blasphemy raised her hackles. "You don't know that for sure."

"Which part, my dear? The mythical nature of a bunch of capricious gods lording over the ancient world, or the absolute obsolescence of ours?"

"Gordon, please. The Remnants and everyone who followed them into exile—they're all dying out there in the wilderness. They're sick; they're starving, desperate. I've come home to ask—"

"Desperate? You call a little less than three squares desperate? You know how many weeks I've been down here trying to make sense of things on far less food than that? There's always a reason, a good and logical and, I might add, *scientifically provable* reason for every piece of superstitious malarkey meant to oppress and paralyze thinking men."

"Gordon, listen to me. They're desperate and dying, and there's a lot of people coming here—"

"Coming?" He laughed with his arms folded against his chest. "Let them come. It's not like they're the first to show up unannounced to cause trouble. First the Tylers—though I am sort of glad they did come—and now these others—"

"Others?" Kendra stepped closer to him. "What others? Do you mean John?"

Lee gave her a quizzical look. "Giordano? Is he here too?"

"Don't *you* know?"

He sighed and began to putter among his open books. "Nobody tells me anything these days. But with him I'd expect her to at least—"

Kendra swept around the desk and slammed the book he had been thumbing through shut. "What're you saying? That the big boss man doesn't know that John's here?"

Annoyance fled from his face, replaced by mocking laughter. "You really have missed a great deal, haven't you?" He seemed to savor her flashing anger. "Testing that pacifist stance of yours, now aren't I?"

"Keep testing. See how far you wanna take this."

"But that's what I do best, Kendra. Test, analyze, come to conclusions. Here's my working theory on you right now. I think you'd like to beat me to a bloody pulp or cut pieces off me with that knife you keep fingering. But you won't, because you believe you're on some sort of 'divine' mission."

Kendra said nothing.

"Perhaps Petra sent you? To get her son back? Am I right?"

"And what do you believe in, other than the great Gordon Lee? Aren't you on a mission to save us all from our unenlightened selves? How's that working out for you?"

He held up a hand to emphasize a thought that died stillborn in his throat. The same hand then beat an unsure path to his mouth. The smug confidence went out of his dark eyes and took a little light with it. For a moment he almost looked humble.

"I admit, much of my research doesn't have a provable formula as yet." He shuffled through some of his notes. Kendra glanced over his shoulder at the ink-blotted pages filled with deletions and revisions written above and around previous lines. "But what the others have said simply doesn't make any sense."

"What others?"

"The people from the wilderness," he muttered. "Some of them said they knew you—or heard of you, anyway."

"Was one of them a woman named Prisha Lewis?"

"Dunno. There's a number of them here now mucking up the works. Anyway, the point is that they claim—get this—that we're *actually on Earth* and that they have evidence strongly suggesting that it wasn't destroyed a generation or two ago, but a thousand or more years ago."

Her society and upbringing had trained her to hate no man, but she found it hard not to hate Gordon Lee. And yet even with that hate eating at her, she told him the truth as gently as she could.

"We *are* on Earth, Gordon. And it was destroyed long ago. I've seen the evidence. In the wilderness there are ancient roads in an advanced state of decay, a bronze statue of—"

"Now how can that be, my dear? Our ancestors were *brought* here right at the end."

"And you claim the world ended around 1962, not in 2491. Is that any stranger?"

"But that—that's just Remnant misinformation, not a gap in the historical record of a millennium or so. And it's not as radical an error as being on Earth this whole—" He mused on the idea for a few moments. His eyes pleaded with her even if his voice had regained its smugness. "But how? Where were the survivors all that time? Thousands of years—where?—and then here, *on Earth*, for a half century?"

"None of that matters now, don't you see? That was all another life. We've got a new life here and now, but we won't have it unless you help me bring the exiles home. Otherwise there's going to be a war and people are going to die, killed at the hands of their own families. Can't you see that?"

"Pointless bloodshed," he mumbled through the fingers curled around his lips. "I've always been against it. Told Sofie that myself right after they killed the Tylers—"

"Forget the past. Won't you—please—help me now?"

"Forget?" Lee looked at her with worn-out eyes. "How can we forget anything? The past—it's all around us. If these others from the wilderness are right, we live *on top of it*. How can we go forward if we don't know where we've been and why we're here?"

"By helping each other. I came to make peace. That's what I can offer."

He snorted. "I can offer nothing."

"Gordon, where's John? Please tell me where I can find him."

"The others from outside the city," he continued as if she hadn't spoken. "Did you know they're the ones who had the books of Eastern culture that have been missing since the days after the Arrival? At least that's one longtime mystery solved."

Kendra gripped his arm to keep him focused. He met the gesture with wide-eyed alarm and confusion, as an animal caged. When he finally spoke, he looked only at the hand on his arm.

"There's life all around us, Kendra. It's out there growing over so much death."

"I know, Gordon."

"And it doesn't make any sense. Why is it here? What does it all mean?"

She slid her hand down his wrist to grip his hand in hers. "Stay with me, Gordon. Where's John?"

A throat cleared behind them as casually as a bird might flap its wings. Kendra turned to find the only person who had ever gotten a drop on her: Sofie Weiss Lee. In one hand she held a carbine. In the other was a whistle used by drill instructors, which she blew once to bring a half dozen guards down into the Archives. Kendra, once relieved of her olive branch and pack and knife, was led upstairs with her wrists bound by strong cords. Irene stood at the top of the steps shivering in the snow and looked at Kendra with wide and unsure eyes.

They had built a prison. A prison in New Philadelphia. In the now-depopulated west wing of the barracks, where Kendra had spent her third year in the Defense Forces, a prison now stood subdivided by bars and complete with narrow bunks and chamber pots. The air—which had previously smelled of rubbing alcohol and soap—was now tinged with damp and dirt and a hint of defecation.

She was alone in her cell, though its bunk beds suggested it was meant for two. About eight feet by eight feet, if she had to guess. The floor in here had been swept. And fresh linens were folded on a feather-stuffed pillow on the top bunk.

She scratched her ragged nails through her scalp to clear her head.

Knowledge is power, right? What has been learned here? Lee's a broken man, not in charge. Sofie definitely is—and no longer pregnant. What happened? Don't think about that. Other people are here in the city from the wilderness—Jack and Prisha's people? Were some of them in the cells I walked past? Young men and women, my age, a bit older, all asleep at this hour of the early morning. Who were they? If they came from the wilderness, why had they come? Curiosity? They must've heard about the city all their lives from their parents and grandparents. Why show up now? John. Where is he? Lee didn't seem to know anything about him. Did he never make it to the city? Don't think about that.

She could hear the outer door to the wing opening at the far end of the hall. She remembered that door led to some supply closets and a weapons locker. In the semidarkness no one stirred as the light footsteps drew closer. She held her breath and waited for someone to appear before the dimmed gaslight sconce outside her cell.

It was Grace Davison.

At least it was someone who looked like Grace Davison. This was a woman in her sixties, with short-cropped salt-and-pepper hair, caramel skin, and dancing dark eyes that were clear of cataracts. This was Grace Davison, not as Kendra had known her recently, but as her mind's eye had always known her. Seeing her alive—and younger—Kendra felt no fear, but only the same feeling of love she had always had for her.

But it couldn't be her. It just couldn't.

"Hello Kendra." The voice was even, warm, known. A pair of loving hands gripped Kendra's own between the bars. Real hands. Alive.

"Grace." She swallowed after calling this woman by her old friend's name. "How are you here?"

The familiar smile emerged. "Because you need me. I'm always here when you need me. I promised you that the night you came home from the mountains, remember?"

"Petra—she told me you were dead."

An unfathomable smile creased her face. "Is that what your heart believes?"

"No." She shook her head. "But this can't be. It just can't."

"What has been written is coming to pass."

Kendra stiffened. "Oh no. I don't want to hear it. Don't speak to me about Scripture and prophecy. I don't know what to think or what to do. I came here because I was told to come, that's all."

"Do you still trust me?"

"I trust Grace Davison. She never did any wrong by me."

"You're on a mission of peace. Don't stray from it, child. No matter what happens."

"What will happen?"

Grace's shoulders shrugged in their familiar way. "I don't know. Those decisions have not yet been made."

Kendra shook her head in anger. "More decisions and vague suggestions. Come on. How many countless generations of human beings have been told that they have the ability to choose the right path and, having done so, still suffered? Haven't all the lives cut short or the lives dragged out in endless suffering set things right between us yet? If God's really there, why can't he just for once come right out and tell us what he wants?"

The woman outside the prison cell pursed her lips in the way Grace had done. This simple expression—more than anything else she had said or done so far—convinced Kendra that this was, for all intents and purposes, Grace Davison alive again.

"You want me to tell you that your standing here is proof enough, that I should just see and believe and obey. And I do, Grace, and I will. But will you just please tell me what the truth is?"

Grace looked into her eyes. "No one knows the whole truth. We all know a piece and that only partly. Don't you see that? Here's what I do know. A loving family is what the human race is supposed to be. And only through love, like its twin, heartache, comes understanding."

"No, Grace. We're all too different. Too hateful and greedy and sinful and plain old fucked up. That's the problem with mankind's fall. As much as we'd all like to be what God or whatever intended us to be, part of us wants to be this way because like this we're human. There's no decision that we can make that can change our nature."

"Then we're lost," she answered. "The lowest state of man is when he feels he has no choice in life. At that time he is most like the animal he was never intended to be and least like the image in which he was created. Yet from these struggles here and now, a new kind of human may come of age, fully formed from the animal shell in which his species had been encased."

Kendra listened to this not without sympathy and almost entirely because this was Grace Davison doing the talking. But it was all too much, and she was too tired to go on. Had she been free, she would have run away. Had she had the courage of a saint or a hero, she would've leapt at the opportunity being given. But she was just Kendra, no more or less. She would do what was needed no matter what and in spite of everything.

"I'm in agony. Don't make me do this."

"I can't make you do anything." Grace removed a key from inside her rough woolen coat and held it up. "Now what will you do?"

Kendra reached between the bars and took the key, pausing only a moment to squeeze the old woman's warm fingers again in her own before unlocking the cell door.

CHAPTER 26

A deep, mournful horn blew out long in the distance in repeating two-tone beats. Kendra knew the sound: the general alarm calling everyone in the city to their emergency posts, to arms, to battle stations. And she knew from its particular repeating pattern that it was not a drill. New Philadelphia was under attack. It was the attack they had long been preparing for, and it was happening with the city at only half strength.

After remembering the master key Grace had slipped into her hand, she began fitting it into the locks of the half dozen occupied cells in this wing. She rattled bars and yelled at the occupants to get up, get moving, that the city was being attacked. Her actions were met by around a dozen pairs of sleep-heavy eyes that stared at her with marvelous wonder. She recognized no one but imagined she had looked at Grace in a similar way moments before.

"All of you, get up and go back home," she said. "Whoever is about to attack isn't going to sort us out by citizens and visitors."

"Who are you?" a ruddy, red-haired young man asked with some bewilderment. "How did you get out of your cell?"

"My friend Grace here—" Kendra turned to discover that Grace was no longer there. Not even a farewell. "Never mind," she said to the man. "All that matters is that you and your people get the hell out of here."

"Why?" The young man asked the question as if the very idea was crazy. For the first time, she noticed they were all wearing very rudimentary garments, cloaks and cassocks of rough cloths, the kind worn by the poor or the clergy on Earth-of-old. It seemed a bizarre joke.

"Why? Why? What's the matter with all of you? Because someone carrying a bumper crop of crazy will *kill you* if you don't leave here. Either whoever's outside the gates or the batshit-nuts woman who's taken over the city."

"Why would anyone harm us?" another baffled young man protested. "We've come in peace."

"And we will leave in peace, even if we die here," a confident young woman said, stepping forward. "Of that you can rest assured."

Her dark and attractive face was familiar. Something about the jaw and the long nose Kendra recognized, even though she knew they had never met.

"You're Kendra McQueen, aren't you? I'm Nishtha Lewis, Prisha's older sister. You're just as she's sketched you."

"Prisha's sister? Is she okay? Her baby?"

"She's fine. And the baby's doing well, going to be born sometime in the early spring."

Kendra took a step toward this young woman. She was maybe thirty but carried herself with the kind of confidence Grace had. "If you know me, then you know I can't let you stay here. We couldn't save your father and—"

"No one blames you. Not even Prisha. Not anymore. But our generation is tired of the wilderness, of . . . dislocation. We come in peace to be with our brothers and sisters here in the city. And we fear no man—or any creature. Your coming was foretold. No one told you this then, but when my father found you, he knew that our long isolation was ending."

"What the hell're you—"

The horns blew again and again. Panicked voices could now be heard outside. They each looked out toward the barred windows, as if they could somehow see the threat outside the city walls from where they stood. When Kendra turned back to the outsiders surrounding her, she was surprised to find their faces beatific, at ease.

"I have to leave you."

Nishtha nodded and smiled. "I know. You're meant to stop this."

"How do you—"

"Go. We'll see each other again, Kendra McQueen, in this life or the next."

Kendra paused for only a moment to watch them serenely wait for their futures before she took off in a full run. By design, the barracks were far from the city walls and were well protected in that way. Being a low building, however, it was not an ideal place to see what was happening along the city walls. It did offer one good vantage point: its main watchtower in the center of the quad. From there she could see for blocks, maybe even up to the market area.

Every part of the barracks was deserted—everywhere she ran, every hall, every room. Even the armory had been left unguarded, its heavy oaken doors unbolted and ajar. As she stopped in front of them, the doors seemed to breathe her in. She had come in peace. Would it be wrong to defend herself in order to secure that peace?

She went in and found little left in stock, just a few boxes of ammunition, six or so sidearms. She slipped a .38 Super Automatic from its rack after finding a box of matching bullets. It all felt wrong, even as she loaded the magazine and snapped it in place. It was a sin. A pox upon her. But she left with the weapon anyway.

All around her in the distance she could hear yelling, scrambling of feet, rushing, barked orders, counterorders, cries of small children—all moving away from her. She took the nearest exit to the quad and found the expanse dusty and deserted. She raced to the high tower and climbed the ladder rung by rung with the pistol in her waistband until she reached the booth four stories above the ground. From this height the center of New Philadelphia spilled open before her. Everywhere people were running—some to the gatehouses but most to points deeper into the city, places believed to be better protected from outside attack. As best as Kendra could tell, the city's few remaining defenders were headed toward the northwest section of the wall. The city center was quieting. The blood had left the heart and was flowing toward the extremities. But what to do with all that life? The defenders were disorganized and chaotic. She could see a few commanders attempting to take these unseemly mobs and make soldiers of them again. But it didn't matter. Even if every single one of them was brought under control, they just didn't have the numbers. If the attackers wanted to breach the walls in another section, they could do so without resistance. Whatever forces the city had were getting too concentrated. New Philadelphia—a half century of a new human civilization—would be destroyed from within.

Then the impossible—or something close to it—happened. She saw him. Just outside the front gates of the barracks. It was him. She was sure of it even though she had seen only a glimpse of the back of a dirty-blond head. John was bolting away from the barracks toward a retreating column of soldiers. Had he been held prisoner here the whole time? He was grabbing them by their elbows and arms as if to urge them to stand fast.

Kendra jumped out of the guard booth and sped down the ladder by keeping her feet on the outside of the vertical posts and letting gravity do the rest. She darted across the empty quad and was moments away from the main gate—her John, outside, right now, right there— when she was stopped by a frightened and completely alone Irene Lee. She had been hiding in a shadow-blanketed corner behind a stone support pillar.

"Irene?"

The girl winced when she saw her. "I'm sorry. I'm so absolutely sorry—"

Kendra seized her by the shoulders and held her tight. "Forget it. Why are you here alone?"

Loneliness was the only thing that made a human being wail like Irene did, the feeling of supreme abandonment that seems to only ever find relief with death. "My mom *left* me. She just—"

"Look, I can't stay. I can't hold your hand. Now go. Hide someplace until it's safe."

The girl looked at her with still eyes. "But please, won't you just—"

"Go, dammit!"

Irene fled in an awkward clopping run, spurred on by equal parts terror and embarrassment. Kendra hoped to see the girl again on the other side of this to let her know . . . something. Something that still wouldn't make this moment right.

Kendra yanked open the gate and looked into a swirling mass of human chaos. Instinct told her that John had been to the right of the gate. A dozen yards distant was a group of Novices and other soldiers looking like they were trying to organize themselves.

"Who's the unit commander here?" Kendra barked as she marched forward with practiced, recognizable authority.

"I am, ma'am," a half-finished voice snapped back. It belonged to a boy, maybe sixteen, still straddling the fence between youth and manhood. His pockmarked brown face was clearing and already growing dense with black stubble.

"Did a captain just come and talk to you?"

"He did, ma'am. Told us to stand down, that the threat wasn't real." He shook his head in involuntary disbelief. "He ordered us to protect civilians at all costs."

"So why aren't you at it?"

"Well, ma'am, we're waiting for another officer to confirm it."

"I'm an officer, mister, and I'm confirming the captain's orders. Stand down and help the civilians. And spread the word."

"Yes, ma'am."

"Now where'd the captain go to?"

"In that direction," the boy said, pointing down a westerly street. "He was in a hurry, but I think you can catch him if you double-time it."

Kendra took off but struggled to make her way through the crowds that were pushing her in the opposite direction. Clawing her way forward by inches, grappling for each step, she snatched at pillars or doorframes to hold her ground whenever she felt the overwhelming press of humanity drawing her back. In those seconds of rest, she looked back to see the Novices and their pockmarked commander doing their best to control the incoming hordes and direct them to safety.

But John was gone. She was sure he was headed to the part of the wall where the hostile forces were massing, so she moved with deliberate steps against the tide. Realizing her futility, she forced a locked door open with her shoulder and ran past frightened children and some huddled men and women crouched within to the roof. Deserted. With luck she could race along the row house roofs for blocks until she was closer to the wall.

She paused at an intersection to get her bearings. Judging from the crowds three stories below her, she was still due west of the main action. But to keep going in a straight line, she would have to go back downstairs, force her way through the crowds in the intersection, and then make her way along the next block of roofs. No good. She looked at the gatehouse nearest her, which was about six blocks perpendicular to her position. She hooked a left and raced along the rooftops until she reached the next corner. From there she climbed down the stairs and found herself on a mostly deserted block running near the wall.

She pulled out the pistol with reluctance. She had little interest in killing anyone but less in getting shot by a twitchy Novice or some advance scout of whoever was outside the walls. This part of the city reminded her of a party after the guests had gone. Papers, dishes, and bits of food and clothing littered the ground. A wooden toy cart was tipped on its side, its right wheel spinning in the breeze. The streets were empty apart from a few dogs likely just entering their new lives as strays. The wall was a block away, the gatehouse another two blocks south.

When she scaled to the top of the gatehouse, she found it empty. Whether the guards had fled in a panic or left the gate to defend the part of the city that was under attack, she didn't know. The path along the wall's battlements to the next gatehouse—maybe even to the one after that—looked clear. She could see flashes, brighter than anything generated by gaslight, popping in the distance. It wasn't something that looked stoppable.

Each gatehouse stood about a mile from its mates, not counting the width of the gatehouses themselves. Always a fast runner, Kendra knew she could cover the distance easier than most, but it was exhausting nonetheless. The flashes kept popping off; a roar, low in tone, increased as she drew near. She kept waiting for the heat on her face as she drew closer to the flashes, but the air stayed damp and cold. Light without heat.

At the second gatehouse she stopped to rest and drink some water from one of its stores. It was warm in the gatehouse and almost silent, despite its proximity to the action. If not for the flashes she saw out the window, it might have been any night she had been up there on guard duty. She watched the lights beam and fade over the rim of the clay cup she kept refilling from the water keg. Then—inconceivably—she again saw John in the distance. He was nearer the lights than she was and moving toward the edge of the crowd of defenders. She would lose sight of him the moment she went through the gatehouse door, but she started running toward him anyway.

The cold, bracing after those few minutes of warmth inside, didn't sting her for long. She felt neither cold nor fatigue as she ran. When she finally reached the massing surge of defenders, she felt the air pop with the sudden force of explosions but felt no heat and heard no sound apart from the panicky cries of those around her. She made her way to the parapet's edge with her elbows and shoulders. From there she saw the enemy forces threatening the city for the first time.

Portals. There were portals everywhere. They had been amassed at the edge of the foothills surrounding the city's northwest quadrant. They appeared to vary in size and shape—some allowing no more than a single fighter to come through at a time, others able to accommodate many more—but even at this distance it was clear that each was surrounded by a distinctive orange band. And out of these portals poured hundreds of ragged but armed men and women to join thousands of others in the fields around the city. They were the hungry and angry outcasts she and John had lived among these winter months, all those who had come to believe themselves foolish for having followed the Remnants into exile. Her heart sank. The Weiss brothers had failed to stop the attack. But how had the exiles found so many portals? How did they discover how to work them?

Then she looked to the sky. As much as the sight of a civil war frightened her, she was even more terrified by what literally hung in the air above them—dozens of Orangemen, hovering in a protective wing above the fray, their silvery swords drawn and at their sides.

Kendra watched the scene in transfixed wonder. Now and again another concussive flash would herald the arrival of another band of reinforcements. She strained to make out their faces but recognized no one at this distance. As the defenders jostled against her, she was pulled away from the parapet and her own observations. She searched the immediate crowd for faces she knew and saw no one. A moment later she found herself nearly nose to nose with Sofie Lee, whose flanking guards were pushing through the mass of defenders.

Sofie's recognition was immediate and outraged. Kendra spoke before she could get a word out.

"Sofie, you need to stand these people down. This isn't what we're supposed to be doing. Do you realize who's out there?"

Her statement was met with an explosion of pain on the side of her head. Only after she fell against some surprised Novices did she realize that she had just been pistol-whipped. She looked for Sofie and her men. They were all gone by the time her vision cleared.

The swelling from a growing bruise stretched the skin on her temple and cheekbone. She stumbled through the crowd, looking for John, looking for Grace, looking for anyone who would help her. She tripped and fell against thrusting bodies again and again; each time she was shoved off, tossed aside, kicked away. She stopped and held up her hands and called out to them. Few heard her. And those who did ignored her plea, too trapped by the idea of taunting their attackers below.

They had reached the end of the play. Kendra whirled in a circle and watched the frightened faces around her, teeth bared, eyes wild. The men and women she knew and loved were gone. Primal fears had taken over; the animal had taken the reins. War had come, and all they had struggled for and won would be lost. The tide had pulled it all away. Love and hope, solidarity and peace—all these illusory dreams were now ready to take their place in the dirt with a plastic bowl and an asphalt road and the bronze likeness of a once-great man and the body of a very good one.

No.

She wouldn't allow it.

Kendra drew her pistol from her waistband and flicked off the safety, firing two shots in the air. The shots silenced and pushed back the crowd around her. Their silence hushed those farther back.

"Listen to me!" she yelled in a raw voice. "Listen to me! The people outside are not your enemies. They're our starving brothers and sisters. Do you really think they want to kill you? They're desperate. Look at them! Take a good look! Lay down your arms!"

Somewhere a voice behind her yelled: "But the Hostiles—they're back! They've come to finish us off!"

"How do you know that?" Kendra shouted. "How do you know who they really are?"

"Those mirror-gate things—the flashes—they're coming out of the air—"

"You don't know. None of you! But we do know those are our people out there. *Our* people. This is the war no one wins. And you know that—you goddamn know that!"

A burp of jostling erupted among the faces turned toward her. She saw a hand jut into the air and heard a voice call her name. "Kendra! Over here!"

A moment later John was standing in the circle that had been cleared around her since she had fired those shots. His arms looked gangly and long. He held them loose, as if he had just run a marathon. His hair was mussed and stuck out in odd waves, and his face was careworn and tired but pierced with joy as he looked at her. Only her.

"Always good at making a scene, eh, Ken?"

"Better than you are at telling me where you're going."

She stepped toward him and he to her when the report of shots rang out from somewhere beyond the circle. She didn't connect the shots to why John was suddenly falling into her arms, why he was resting his whole weight on her, why she was holding his head at an awkward angle above a pool of blood spreading in the snow on the stone walkway beneath him.

But then she saw his face and, somehow, understood. The care and the exhaustion long etched there were gone as he looked up at her with his head cradled in her lap. It was gone now, all of it, except the love and joy he had in him, all for her, all of it always for her.

"Hey," she said through her teeth as tears fled into her mouth. "Hey now. It's okay, Johnny. Shush. It's okay."

She looked at his eyes, nothing else. The love stayed there through the wincing pain, even as the light faded from them. His lips moved in thick motions, but nothing came out. He found her hand on his face with his own and gripped it once, hard.

"I know, I know. I love you too, John."

Only after the light fled his eyes did she close them and kiss them and scream her anguish to God.

She didn't know how long she remained there, how long the eyes of those who had surrounded them and done nothing continued to watch her in cold silence. The world was very far away now. Death had moved out from the background and was close to her shoulder and ready. Everything felt slow and still. The blinding lights that had drawn them to these ramparts in the first place were no longer seen.

Then at once she looked up and saw Sofie at the circle's edge with a pistol hanging loosely in her right hand.

Kendra kissed John's face once again and let his head come to a gentle rest on the snow-covered stonework. Her sidearm was still in her hand.

Kendra never let her gaze move from Sofie. Ten paces at best separated them. Kendra had firsthand knowledge of Sofie's marksmanship. The gun she dangled at her side could be raised and aimed and fired faster than Kendra could do it, even in peak condition. But it didn't matter. None of it mattered. Kendra felt her own gun drop from her hand. So many other things fell away with it, far more than she could ever put words to. She stepped toward the woman who had been John Giordano's first love. There was no indifference in Sofie's darkening features as she aimed her gun at Kendra's forehead.

Kendra opened her arms wide and continued to step toward Sofie. Kendra's arms reached around Sofie even as she brought the pistol in contact with Kendra's forehead. The barrel was only slowly losing its recent warmth. Kendra thought the side of her swollen face must be a tempting target. The bullet would splatter the blood pooling under her skin all over them and the crowd and the snow and maybe John too.

Kendra brought her lips to Sofie's cheek and kissed her. "I forgive you, Sofie. I forgive you; I forgive you."

Sofie's face contorted with rage into a tear-streaked grimace as she shoved Kendra away and fled into the crowd. Kendra stood as she had before, with her arms outstretched, as she watched her disappear. Then, with concentrated effort, she lowered her arms.

Silence. How long it went on no one knew. Then breaking it was a voice, clear and loud: "Open the gates! Let them in!"

And another: "Lay down your arms!"

And another: "For God's sake, let them in!"

And still another: "Kiss our brothers and sisters! Welcome them home!"

Kendra retraced her steps and sat down in the snow next to John and waited for what would be the rest of her life to come to her. It was snowing again. Against the flashes of light from the portals, the falling flakes shimmered in brief sparks and faded. She pulled John's head back into her lap. People began to approach her, caution mincing their steps and love filling their eyes.

A moment later there was a tremendous roar unlike anything anyone living had heard. The ground beneath them shook and ruptured and split as if the sky had crashed into it. And then Kendra McQueen accepted the blackness and silence she had always feared came with the true death.

CHAPTER 27

Seventeen years later many things were different. But in a lot of the everyday ways many things were just the same. The sea air still sweetened the old city. Harvests, good or bad, were still an endless preoccupation. People still worked the fields and hunted in the hills. When they weren't busy, each of them could be found at one time or another relaxing on the grass in the old Central Square, eating picnic lunches, laughing, listening, talking, flirting. And preachers still stood on the raised stone platform at the square's center, hoping to keep the spirits of the old up and those of the young in line.

Today was no different. An old woman with long white hair cinched in a bun and topped by a rusty-colored patch in her bangs took to the platform to reflect on what had passed since the siege of the city, the last night the Orangemen had been seen. Some of the young people there listened out of politeness for a respected Firster or hoped to learn a little more about beings who'd disappeared years before they were born, others because it was just too fine an autumn day to be anywhere but in that sun on that broad field of bright grass. But no matter how young or old they were, everyone in the audience knew the story. Petra Giordano had told her version of it often enough.

"Only a fallen man can rise again. Only a civilization utterly destroyed can be remade. So it is with mankind today," she intoned.

Petra moved around the platform with quick and dramatic steps, trying to draw the eyes and attentions of as many of her listeners as she could. Some even met her gaze.

"Beloved brothers and sisters, what I've told you is not a fantasy written to satisfy whims or to fulfill prophecy. It is not a product of malicious deceit, is not legend to entertain or propaganda to convert, but is rather the cumulative truth that comes from the corroborated questioning of eyewitnesses. *I* was one of those eyewitnesses. It was seen, and it was lived. It is now as much a part of the makeup of the human race as the thousands of years of destruction that came before it."

A slim sixteen-year-old boy with dirty-blond hair stirred uneasily in his spot on the grass. He had been restless ever since joining his friends in the square and discovering that Petra would be one of the day's speakers. His grandmother's assurances had often done more to stir J. J. Giordano's doubts than to ease them.

"The wall *fell*. The dead *rose*. *Peace* poured forth." Petra's lined face was aglow with affirmation and looked almost youthful. "Brothers and sisters, we are loved. We know it now, just as we now know how love has changed the fate of mankind. It permeates the universe. It is as quantifiable and as tangible as water and just as needed for the body. And it always has been—we've just been too angry or envious or selfish to see it. Whatever you believe, however you interpret these events, know this: you are loved without condition."

J. J. stood and slipped between picnic blankets and away from his friends. He didn't turn back to see if his grandmother watched him leave. He hoped she had, just as he hoped his friends would think he was gutsy to do so. Loved without condition? What did that even mean? What could possibly have changed all that much?

J. J. had no destination in mind, only a place to leave behind. He had nothing to study, no chores to do, but he didn't want to go home. Instead he walked toward the fields and orchards near what had once been Gate Eight. As he approached it, a solitary stone portal standing like a watchman against the hard-blue sky, he found it difficult to imagine that an enormous wall had once curved all the way around the city. It was easy to see where it had been—lots of its stonework still lay in neatened piles circling New Philadelphia—but it was impossible for him to picture everyone cowering behind it, afraid of everything and everyone. On that last night with the Orangemen, the earthquake had taken that ridiculous wall down clean but had left the old city more or less intact.

He was glad it had. The idea of living cooped up behind it seemed just crazy. He climbed over some of the fallen stonework instead of going straight through the gates into the fields. He liked wild growing things. And there, among these tumbledown slabs, he had found all sorts of wildflowers and crabgrass and even the young shoots of trees. Life came up through almost anything, given a chance. In a hundred years or a thousand, all this debris would be the bed of a new little wilderness, if only everyone would let it alone and stop trying to figure out what to do with it.

He often wished his grandmother would let things alone. How many nights had he listened to her interrogate his mother about what had happened that night? He knew she wanted to know how her son, his father, had died. She needed to make sense of his death. But try as he might, he couldn't understand his mother's patience with that old lady.

The world was at peace . . . and maybe that was a big thing. He didn't know. He hadn't known it any other way. They had opened the gates and let the exiles back in. Before long those living in the wilderness came to meet them. Many of them had stayed, and many of New Philadelphia's citizens had gone to live with the Lewis family and their people out there. He had no idea what it was like to starve, but he figured it might make people do some pretty crazy things—even make peace with their worst enemies to make sure *no one* starved. But brotherly love and a new humanity on a new Earth? He didn't see it.

People still held grudges. People still tried to get the better end of a deal. They still got stomach bugs and broken bones and suffered in childbirth—although many old-timers claimed all of this happened a lot less than it used to. And nobody seemed to be thinking of brotherly love as they hushed up around him whenever they had just been whispering about his mother.

J. J. hiked out just past the orchards by following the main river that ran through the outskirts of New Philadelphia. The dwellings there, built mostly by those who had come in from the wilderness, weren't part of the city proper but weren't a suburb either. He liked these homes a lot. They were more a part of the natural world than any dwelling yet devised by human beings. Their roofs were covered with vegetation, their walls with flowering vines and ivy. They made the old stone city with its geometric lines and curves look odd, almost abnormal, to the human eye. For J. J., these outlying homes suggested that the world of man wasn't meant to be built.

A silhouette of a man emerged from the direction of the old cemetery. He came from behind a tree about a hundred yards off and began to approach. J. J. found it strange that he didn't even raise his hand in greeting. His heart leapt, not knowing who he was or what he wanted.

Yet he had the odd sensation that he knew him. As the man stepped out of the sun's glare, J. J. saw that he definitely wasn't any man he knew; in fact, he wasn't a man at all, just a boy about his own age. His face was soft, his hair dark and long and wavy and hanging over his eyes. Even after seeing and not recognizing his face, J. J. still felt as if he knew him, so much so that he thought his merry eyes seemed somehow wrong, not meant for his face. It was an irrational thought but there just the same.

"Hello."

"Hi," J. J. answered. "Do I know you?"

"I'm afraid you don't. I haven't lived near here in a long time."

"Are you one of the others?"

His lips curled into a playful smile. "There are no others anymore."

J. J. laughed. "Come on. You know what I mean. The people from the wilderness."

"No, I'm not. As I said, I'm of the city."

"Why're you wandering out here?"

His smile never left his face. "I could ask you the same thing."

"Well," J. J. said, tensing now, "I asked you first."

"I've only just arrived. I was out here in the groves thinking about someone I'd very much like to visit."

"So why don't you go see them?"

"It's been a while. A long time."

"Maybe I know who you're looking for. What's the name?"

"Kendra McQueen."

"Kendra—" A surprised laugh popped out of J. J. "That's my mother! You know her?"

He nodded, hands in his pants pockets. "I did. A long time ago."

J. J. was about to ask him how but stopped. "Sir," he said, not knowing why he was addressing someone his age like that, "what's your name?"

He looked at J. J. with those mirthful eyes. "Alex Raymond."

"Alex Raymond." J. J. shook his head. "No, really. Who are you?"

"Why are you getting upset?"

"You goddamn know why," J. J. said, grabbing him by the front of his sky-blue shirt. "Somebody put you up to this. Who was it, you son of a bitch?"

"No one," he answered without anger. "I assure you. I mean you no harm, nor your mother. Though I would appreciate it if you could direct me to her."

J. J. looked all along the boy's face without letting go. A gentle hand took hold of his right wrist.

"What's your name, friend?"

He felt his grip slacken. "Jacob John Giordano. Everyone just calls me J. J."

"J. J. it is, then. Would you please take me to see your mother? I've got a message for her."

"What message?"

"I'm afraid I have to tell *her* first."

"She's not big on surprises."

He grinned again, then laughed. "Believe me, I know."

An hour later they found his mother inside the quad of what had been the old barracks. It was near the harvesting season, and she was giving a lecture to some of the older children about various techniques. They stood toward the back under some poplar trees that lined the edge of the yard and listened to her for a bit.

J. J. studied his mother. She was just past her thirty-seventh birthday. Her hair was still almost all black. Her body was strong and thin from her farmwork. Her blue eyes had around them the creases that come from spending a lot of time squinting in the sun, but they were bright and playful, even as she talked about mundane topics like crop rotations. After a few minutes J. J. saw that she had spotted him from the corner of her eye as she was speaking. Her gaze then rested on the young man standing next to him. Her eyes widened for just a second; then she smiled back, almost mischievously.

"Class dismissed. We'll pick up again after midday meal tomorrow."

She didn't leave the raised platform as the students raced past. The boy claiming to be Alex Raymond didn't move forward, nor did she, until after the three of them had been left alone in the yard.

"Hey you."

"Hi there, Kendra."

She clapped chalk dust from her hands as she descended the platform's three steps. "I'd like to say I'm surprised to see you, Alex. Grace, all those years ago—she wasn't my imagination, then?"

"No. I'm afraid not."

"I'm—" Her voice quavered right there. In dreams and in very still waking moments, J. J. would remember that catch sounding down through the years that followed. "I'm so happy you're among them."

"You sound as if you had doubts about me."

"Fewer than about my own chances."

"You've always thought too little of yourself."

She began to open her mouth, said nothing, then looked at him sidelong. "Have you come to judge me, Alex?"

"No. Not to judge."

"Why are you here, then?"

"I'm supposed to give you a message." He glanced around. "Is there someplace we can talk privately? Maybe have something to eat?"

"Mom." J. J. grabbed her arm. "You're not gonna go off with this— whoever he is."

Kendra took her son's hand and kissed it. "I've dealt with a lot worse."

J. J. wandered the streets for hours, not wanting to talk to anyone or stay anywhere for too long. After a time he found himself on the beach and sat there looking out at the waves, then up and down the long, curving shoreline. What had it been like that first day? Had he been there, what would he have believed? He stayed on the beach long after it got too dark and too cold to be there, thinking.

Toward dawn he gave up. Tired and hungry, he wandered back to his house. He didn't want to see Alex Raymond's face again. In fact, he felt like punching it. He found his mother alone, sitting at their table, sipping coffee from a clay mug he had made as a little boy. The fire in the hearth was low. She was wearing his father's leather jacket from the old Defense Forces.

It was hard to describe the look on her face at that moment. Words came to his mind, but none was a perfect fit. Relief. Satisfaction. Expectation. Her face seemed complete in a way that no human face had ever looked. Every human expression had something waiting in it. The human race had always been waiting for something: a response, a piece of knowledge, a shred of hope. Kendra's face was absent these things.

"Is he gone?" J. J. asked as he took a chair at the kitchen table. She squeezed his forearm as he sat at her elbow.

"Alex? Yes. He's gone."

J. J. glanced around. "Did he, um, disappear?"

"No." She laughed one of her good, true laughs, deep and throaty. "Front door. About ten minutes before you came. Oh, he was very real. Had dinner, two cups of coffee, and quite a few tea cakes." She indicated the place setting before him with her chin. "That's his plate."

"How was your, uh, visit?"

"Good." She nodded, not looking at her son. "I got to say some things I had been wanting to tell him for a really long time."

"Mom, you don't think he's really—"

"J. J."

Her son shook his head and sighed. "Will he be back?"

"Here? I'm not sure. He's got a lot of people left to see. But yes, he's coming back."

She paused. Dust motes drifted along the slanting morning sunlight coming through the east-facing windows. J. J. watched them for a while in silence. Where do they come from, and where do they go to when the light fades?

"They're all coming back."

"What're you talking about, Mom?"

"Alex isn't the only one who came back."

"Who, Mom? Who's coming back?"

Her eyes were pooling with tears. Her son had never seen her cry before. "Everyone who ever lived or died loving someone more than himself."

"Everyone? I don't understand."

"Alex is just the beginning. Grace Davison, Jack Lewis, my parents, my grandparents—everyone. Even"—she reached out to squeeze her son's hand—"even someone—a child—I've never met in person but always wanted to, even when I was afraid to." She shook her head. "God in heaven, I don't know how that's possible."

"Because it's *not* possible, Mom."

"You're wrong," she said through her teeth.

They sat in silence for a few moments, one foot and one generation apart. "And Dad?" He squeezed the hand she had given him between both of his. "Is *Dad* coming too?"

"That's what Alex came to tell me. I'm waiting for him now."

"Mom, look at me. Look at me. How can it be him? It *can't* be. You of all people know that. It's a copy, a fake."

"I don't believe that." The tears that had been pooling in her eyes were now streaming freely down her cheeks. "If it's him in all the ways that matter, how can that be a lie? If he comes back to me . . . the how doesn't matter at all."

J. J. trembled for the first time in his life. He looked at the front door, expecting a knock. His knees shook, and he felt light-headed. His mother stroked his face and smoothed his hair from his forehead the way she had when he was a little boy. He kissed her cheek and then cried in her arms like a baby and without shame. Then he wiped his face with the heel of his palm and stood up.

"I'm going to go out now, Mom. I shouldn't be here."

"Why, J. J.? You just got home."

"You need to see him first. I'll see—I'll see him soon enough."

She moved to argue, then stopped. "And always," she said after a moment. "From now on."

J. J. began to wander the city streets. At such an early hour, it was odd to find them filling up with people. Step after step, block after block, people he knew well—and some he didn't—kept coming up to him to tell him of a long-dead brother they had just seen, a father or mother buried decades past, a son who disappeared in the early days after the Arrival, a famous face from a book in the Archives. One man claimed to have seen Abraham Lincoln; a woman, Mahatma Gandhi.

He wandered from neighborhood to neighborhood in a befuddled daze, sometimes being introduced to someone's long-dead loved one, other times being hugged or kissed by someone for no reason at all. Pawed and clawed by this confused mass of humanity, he felt stifled and alone. In desperation he sought out his grandmother but got to the corner of her block only to learn from a neighbor that she had gone out as soon as the first news broke. Where had she gone *now*? To preach? To witness? To find her Christian? Perhaps even her husband? He spent the next two hours looking for her white mane on frenzied streets in vain.

So J. J. walked alone and tried to take it all in. Without wanting to, without believing it was even possible, he did so hoping to see his own father. Others may have wanted to see another kind of father. Yet that day J. J. wanted to see not God, but John Giordano, the man he had only ever glimpsed in charcoal sketches made by family friends and in hearthside stories told by his mother and grandmother. He wanted to hug him and memorize the waves in his blond hair and kiss his cheek. He wanted to brighten the way his mother had when she saw that boy and believed he was Alex Raymond. He wanted to have the kind of faith in reunion she possessed be rewarded with the knowledge of fact. He looked and looked and found no one but the smiling faces of those who had already seen and believed. How could they know for sure? And who was he to say his father would be among the pieces of this game that he was unequipped to comprehend?

For hours he walked among the living and the returned, the known and the unknown, the most famous people in human history and the most personal intimates of their lives since the Arrival. And as he walked a hush began falling over the old city and the winding countryside interwoven with those earthen dwellings that were as much a part of nature as they were an extension of it. And everywhere he went all the faces were looking up; all the faces were aglow as they bore witness to the clear and coming end of the human race as they knew it and the beginning of the next step in human evolution.

What were they all marveling at? Above them a massive white object topped with bright spires and resting on a shallow, silvery bowl was tearing through the upper atmosphere—a city alight and descending from the sky. J. J. thought it beautiful. And believed.

Wherever it had come from, whatever it would be, they were growing certain of one thing: for the first time ever, they just might be ready to meet it.

ACKNOWLEDGMENTS

Books might be written in isolation, but they're never published without considerable help. This novel would never have made it out of my drawer without the following people.

First and foremost my undefeatable agent, Jennifer Lyons, who believed in this novel from the very beginning and never gave up—never, ever—and Jason Kirk, my terrific editor at 47North, who worked like anything to make sure it was published and took on *Ocean of Storms* as a bonus. A special thank-you also has to go out to Caitlin Alexander for her generous editorial suggestions.

My late father, Anthony Mari, taught me by example what a man should and should not be. Without him, I would not be who I am.

My in-laws, José, Rose Marie, and Joseph Estela, have always treated me as a member of the family. There's really no way to ever thank them enough for that.

The definition of friendship is having someone who sticks by you through the years no matter what and who always tells you the truth. These names have always defined friendship to me: Kevin Mari; Mike Mongillo; Andrew, Chris, Gary, Jess, and Judy Dieckman; Meg Mullin; and Dann Russo. And to Jeremy Brown, my buddy and coauthor of *Ocean of Storms*, all I can say is: I don't deserve to be this happy.

In the end, though, this book is owed to the women who have most influenced my life: my phenomenal wife, Ana Maria Estela, who has always given me the three things a writer needs—time, space, and honest opinions; my late grandmother, Frances Benevisto, who taught me the best way to learn how to tell stories was to listen to good ones; and finally, my mother, Regina Mari, who didn't live to see this novel's publication but who believed in her great heart that this book was "the one."

We did it, Ma.

ABOUT THE AUTHOR

Photo © 2016 Ana Maria Estela

Christopher Mari was born and raised in Brooklyn, New York, and educated at Fordham University. His writing has been published in *America*, *Citizen Culture*, *Current Biography*, and *U.S. Catholic*, among other magazines. His previous novel, *Ocean of Storms*, was written with Jeremy K. Brown.

Co-2
L-2017